Unto them will he come, son of Verdaine.
By the blood and the blade
of the one who is and who is not,
will the sacrifice be made.
Through Nadra's tears will the debt be paid.
Their majesty will once more be gained.
When the Prince of Dragons be named.
~ Second scroll, article nine of Verdaine's Prophecy

BOOKS BY TAMERI ETHERTON

*Song of the Swords**

The Prince of Dragons

The Stones of Resurrection

The Temple of Sacrifice

The Ruins of Betrayal

The Veils of Deception

The Keeper of Stars

*The Fatal Fae**

Fatal Illusion

Fatal Assassin

Fatal Legacy

Fatal Forever

Fatal Destiny

*Court of Stars**

Sunset in Shadow

*Chronicles of Eidyn**

Child of Fire

Dragon Mage

*Daring Ever Afters**

Enchant

*Books that are part of the Aetherverse: The fantastical realms of Tameri Etherton. Characters and storylines intersect within the books with magical consequences.

To Lynn and all who believe in the magic of dragons.

TEACUP
DRAGON
PUBLISHING

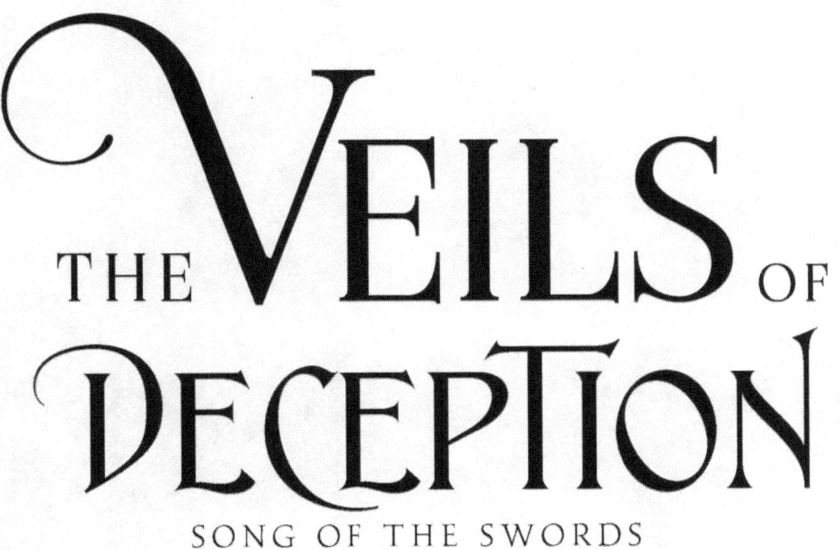

THE VEILS OF DECEPTION

SONG OF THE SWORDS

TAMERI ETHERTON

Aelinae
World Map

N
THE WALL
THE NARTHVIER
LAN GYLLARELLE
MIDVALE
PADERAU
THE TELMARAN ISLANDS
SILDEN R.
THE ULLAN DESERT
SEA OF JADEN
JADEN FLATS
L ROAD
LANT OSTER
HIDDEN VALLEY
GREAT BARREN GORGE
ELDERS PASS
JANSEN STRAIT
NES OF DAAR
JANSEN PLAIN
WASTES OF SLOE
THE EASTERN SEAS

Pendrian Wastes
Western Seas
Denk Scarbos
Caer Idris
Spine of Ohlin
Isle of Ardyn
Caer Danuri
Mount Nadrene
Danuri Provence
Gaarendahl
Celyn Eryri
Talaith
Lake Oster
Ahkae
Summerlands
Stones of Kaldaar
Sitari
Summer Seas

The Narthvier
The Weirren
Lan Gyllarelle
The Ullan Desert
Telmaran Islands
Sea of Jaden
Paderau
Jansen Strait
Wastes of Sloe
Eastern Seas

THE TWO KINGDOMS
The Wall
The Narthvier
The Ullan Desert
Sea of Jaden
The Telmaran Islands
Great Barren Gorge
Jaden Flats
Hidden Valley
Jansen Strait
Elders Pass
Jansen Plain
Eastern Seas
Wastes of Sloe

THE SUMMER SEAS
MEKIAE
SRINIVAS
THATIRAKA
MNABAIE
SCIABARRA
AHKAR
DETARRE
SUMMERLANDS
ANTHOS
NYLS
SALDANNA
MENURRA
WINE FIELDS
PIRATES COVE
SITARI
The Sea Kingdom

We shall see.

Taryn's words echoed after them as the vortex closed. She resisted the urge to blast their way back to Aelinae and confront that smug fuck Kaldaar and all his godliness. Despite her rash desire to confront him, she wouldn't. Mostly because she couldn't be certain doing so wouldn't kill all of them. Also, because she knew they had to leave Aelinae, at least temporarily. They had to give Kaldaar time to fully flesh out his body, as well as his plans for the world if they were to save it.

If pressed, she couldn't say how she knew, she just did. It was like a dream that continued to taunt the back of her thoughts: flimsy in shape, but vast in scope. Kaldaar had claimed she wasn't strong enough yet to defeat him, but what if the opposite were true? What if it was the god who wasn't ready? That he couldn't be defeated while he was little more than mist and parlor tricks? The form he now wore was ephemeral, but would soon take on solidity.

She hoped.

She feared.

A shudder wormed its way along her spine and she tightened

her grip on Rhoane and Kaida. She couldn't see them, but she felt them. They were tethered together, a ragtag team of misfits exiled from Aelinae. Their lives were literally in her hands, and she silently vowed not to let anything happen to them in the vast emptiness of space.

Kaldaar was behind every horrible thing that had happened to them on Aelinae since the very beginning. But what was Ryko-to's role in it all? Ever since she cleansed the Temple of Ardyn, he'd been quiet. Too quiet. Did he know Kaldaar was close to returning? They'd both burrowed into her mind—was their mental torturing simply a distraction? If so, it had worked. She'd been focused on Zakael and Marissa to the point of not seeing outside of her self-imposed blinders. Well, no more. Everyone and everything had meaning. Every detail could be significant in their battle for Aelinae. Even Myrddin. Was he to be trusted? Or was he as duplicitous as the others? After all, it was his papers that led them to the ruins. Were they being played like puppets?

The fight with Zakael at Mallaqai's ruins had a purpose—she had to figure out what. If Zakael had sacrificed Adesh to open the vortex for the sole purpose of returning the dragons to Aelinae, why? Why did he need the dragons? And why sacrifice Adesh when opening the vortex didn't take blood or the blade? There had to be another reason behind Zakael's actions, and not knowing what her half-brother hoped to accomplish filled her with dread.

She'd left him crumpled on the cold floor of the ruins, alive but not by much. Panic wrapped around her heart and she winced at her stupidity. She should've killed Zakael as brutally as Rhoane had attacked Cashiel, but she couldn't. Not yet. A tiny part of her hoped Zakael could be reformed. She held fast the belief that in the end, he would fight beside her, not against her. It was a risk to leave him alive, one that might've given Kaldaar a fine gift. He needed a new Shadow Assassin and Zakael would make a formidable weapon.

Was Zakael more valuable to Kaldaar alive or dead? As Kaldaar's Shadow Assassin, Zakael's power was limited to whatever he could steal from others, or glean from the god. Alive, he was Overlord of the West, with a vast amount of ShantiMari under his control. Would Kaldaar risk allowing Zakael so much power? Another option she had to consider was that he could choose Cashiel to be his new assassin and spare Zakael's life. If Kaldaar brought Zakael from the edge of death, he'd be in the god's debt.

If only she knew what they both wanted. Zakael longed to be a god, but Kaldaar already was a god.

Her thoughts spun into oblivion as they traversed the silent void. What did Kaldaar want? What was his end goal? He claimed Aelinae was his kingdom, but it wasn't. Not really. Aelinae belonged to Nadra and Ohlin. Unless Kaldaar meant to finish where the Great War left off and destroy the elder gods. Yes, that must be it. Kaldaar had been exiled after the war. He'd spent over four thousand seasons plotting his revenge and wouldn't stop until all of Aelinae's gods were decimated.

That would leave him unchecked to destroy other worlds.

Not if Taryn could help it.

Now that they had the papers—the maps that showed where portals opened in Aelinae, leading to other worlds where she suspected the rest of the seals were hidden—they could search for the seals while Kaldaar thought them lost to the void.

He didn't know who she was, but Taryn remembered. Over her short time on Aelinae, she'd been given many names and titles, but only one served her now—walker between worlds.

Kaldaar must not have known she could control the void or he would never have shattered the mirror that closed off the vortex. Or perhaps he did know and she'd walked right into a trap. Either way, it was up to her to see the three of them to safety. Despite the moniker, she was woefully inexperienced. She'd never learned how to make portals or manipulate the void.

It didn't matter. She'd never run from a challenge before, and right or wrong, she'd figure it out.

The inky darkness suffocated in its entirety. A momentary terror seized her thoughts—of when she'd first stepped into the vast expanse of nothingness and it had tried to consume her.

That first time she'd been with Brandt and hadn't heard or smelled or felt anything except the disgusting darkness creeping into her soul. Of course, it had been Kaldaar trying to seduce her. She'd fought him off then and would continue fighting him until her last dying breath.

She cleared her mind of the awful memory and focused on her senses. The seductiveness wasn't there. Perhaps because Kaldaar was no longer in the void itself, but on the other side of the portal. At least, she hoped he wasn't there. A faint panting came from her left, surprising her. As for sight and smell, nothing.

Rhoane. She sent the thought to her beloved, hoping for, but not expecting a reply.

I do not like this, mi carae.

Emotions flooded her: relief, joy, fear, elation—they all cascaded through her mind to every cell in her body. She'd been slightly afraid Kaldaar had ripped Rhoane and Kaida from her at the last minute, leaving her alone and stranded in the emptiness.

Nor do I, but this is how we travel from one place to another. At least for now.

With the vortex closed, I can no longer see our path to the darathi. Can you?

No, but I can get us to safety.

Where are we going?

Taryn debated only a moment before she replied. *Home. Or at least, what was my home before Aelinae.*

His sharp intake of breath didn't come from inside her mind, and she pulled his hand up to her lips. The warmth of his skin was reassurance that even though she couldn't see him, he was there, by her side.

We need a secure place to stay until we decide our next move. Kaldaar will not look for us there?

Dammit. She hadn't thought of that. *He might. We need to be vigilant, but right now, that's the only place I know for sure how to get to.*

Truth be told, she didn't know anything for certain. Not a damn thing. The best she could do was provide them with shelter and a place to catch their breath. It might be for a minute; it might be forever. She wouldn't know until they stepped into the pub. And even then, she wasn't entirely sure she knew how to control the void enough to get them there all in one piece. It was nothing more than a gut instinct, and Brandt had always taught her to trust her intuition.

She closed her eyes even though she couldn't see anything and pictured the pub. She put the door in the cellar into her mind and shut out everything else. *Please,* she begged whatever gods might be watching, *please let me guide us to safety.*

Earth. London. Home.

Despite her desperate longing, she never thought she'd return. It had been little over a season on Aelinae, nine months on Earth, since Brandt took them through the portal—and his death only minutes later. During those early days on Aelinae, she'd mourned her life on Earth and believed she'd left her memories in the cavern with her destroyed belongings. Now, her heart did a little flip at the possibility of returning to London, where she'd once had what she believed was a normal life. She and Brandt had worked as archaeologists, but their lives were far from adventurous or exciting.

Nothing would be the same. Everything she knew before Aelinae was tinged with the knowledge of who she was and who she'd become. Aelinae had shaped and molded her. Given her a new normal. She didn't miss her old life, not really.

But, a tiny voice said in the back of her mind, *Earth has whisky and T-shirts and jeans and cheeseburgers.* And dammit, despite herself, giddiness bubbled in her belly.

It would be nice to see Donyatella, too. To give her landlady a proper goodbye this time. Her excitement evaporated as apprehension snaked its way to her heart. What if Dony had rented their flat? It had been a long time since they'd disappeared. Even when their jobs took them away from home for long stretches of time, they'd always let Dony know where they were. When they'd left that morning, they hadn't had time for goodbyes or explanations. As far as Dony knew, they'd simply vanished. What landlord would keep a flat empty when they could make money with new renters?

They'd find out soon enough. A light glow emanating from the edges of a door signaled the end of their journey. A moment later, the door swung open of its own volition. Taryn swallowed her anxiety and stepped into the dank cellar where nine Earth months earlier Brandt had blown her boring world apart.

She breathed deeply of the must and ale and dirt—scents that were the same now as they'd been her last morning on Earth. It was a relief in a way that not everything had changed as dramatically as her life had. At the moment, she needed the normalcy of her former life. Kaida sniffed the air, a low growl coming from deep in her throat.

Rhoane stepped into the cellar, his eyes wide, face pale. "I agree, Kaida. Traveling the darkness is not enjoyable at all." He dusted himself off and shook out his hair.

Her fingers itched to smooth the braids that swung loose. The only time she'd seen his braids wild and himself unkempt was when he'd been broken. To see him less than calm did nothing to settle her nerves.

"Follow me." She didn't have to imagine what they were feeling at the moment. She'd lived it in reverse when she stepped into the cavern in Mount Nadrene. Awe, apprehension, and an excitement to discover more, all bundled into a mass of what-ifs and what-the-hells.

At the top of the stairs, Taryn paused, listening. Soft sounds came from the kitchen. It was impossible to determine time based on the kitchen's activity. They could stay there until it was quiet, or they could prance right through the melee and hope no one freaked out at seeing two strangely dressed people and a huge wolf-like beast.

What was she thinking, bringing them here? She'd put them all in danger and not just from Kaldaar. She wasn't human, nor was Rhoane—and the last time she looked, Earth didn't have magic. Or, not much, as Nadra had once told her. Magic was dying on Earth, which was a natural progression of things, according to the goddess.

Magic. ShantiMari. Two halves of the same whole. Taryn flexed her fingers and wondered whether there were differences between the two. Wasn't all power some form of magic? And not magic like parlor tricks or Vegas shows. True power that came from the elements. What about spells? Where did they fit into the scheme of things? She hadn't learned any spells, but her evil half-sister Marissa had been quite proficient at them.

How far she'd come from her first encounter with her family. Those terrifying, heady days when she thought she was Brandt's granddaughter and nobody special.

We are all uniquely special, mi carae.

Taryn gave Rhoane a grateful smile. She hadn't meant to leave her thoughts open. "Thank you." She brushed his lips with hers. "This will all appear strange to you. If there's such a thing as reverse déjà vu, this is probably what it feels like."

Warmth seeped from her cynfar and she smiled to herself. Whether together or apart, their pendants connected them. She opened the cellar door and idly wondered what would've happened if Cashiel had tried to remove the talisman. Every chance he'd had, he avoided touching the silver charm. Once in their flat, she'd ask Rhoane about it.

She led them through the short hall to the kitchen, where she tried to sneak past without being seen.

"Miss Taryn?" A familiar voice called out and she paused, half-turning toward the speaker, and smiling broadly at the round, cherub-like face of the head chef.

"Guillermo!" She rushed to greet him, happy for the normalcy of seeing someone she knew.

"You were gone a long time this trip. Where is Mr. Brandt?" His gaze went to Rhoane and Kaida. "You can't have a dog in here, Miss Taryn. Dony would have a fit."

"We're just passing through. Do you know where Dony is?"

He shook his head, but a quick glance up the stairs gave him away. "Soup today is French onion, your favorite. You let me know when you're hungry." Again, he looked at Rhoane. "Your friends, too. I think I have a nice lamb bone for your, erm, pet."

"Thank you." She hugged him again, a little too hard, before turning to the stairs that led to her flat.

By the time they reached the landing on her floor, the emotion of the fight at the ruins, followed by the trip through the void, left her shaking with exhaustion. All she wanted was to strip off her filthy clothes, take a long shower, and have a proper cup of tea. Then she would see about saving Aelinae.

Thuds followed by a weird scratching came from the roof and Taryn stopped to listen. It sounded like a heavy tree branch swiping across the slate tiles, but there weren't any trees close enough their branches would hit the roof. Strange, but not the worst thing to happen today. With a shrug, she continued to her door, remembering a moment too late that she didn't have the flat keys with her. They were with her other Earthly belongings Rhoane had burned. Bollocks. She'd have to use ShantiMari, not altogether certain it was a good idea.

Brandt had heavily warded her when they were on Earth—

perhaps one of his reasons had to do with not using her power there because of random backlashes. Or maybe he'd warded their flat and if she used foreign ShantiMari, she'd get a nasty surprise. Would Brandt's power recognize hers? Surely, it would. Otherwise, how else would he know what to ward? Her thoughts tumbled and spun, delaying the inevitable.

Inside the flat was her past. A past she never thought she'd have to confront.

With trembling fingers, she reached for the doorknob. The door swung open and Taryn glanced at Rhoane. "Did you do that?" He shook his head, his hand hovering above the hilt of his sword. She gripped her sword as well. "Something's not right." More scratching came from the roof.

"I do not like this, mi carae." His snarl matched Kaida's growl.

"Nor do I, but we've precious few options." She pushed the door open and stepped into the small foyer where hers and Brandt's umbrellas and wellies sat, as if welcoming her home. That tiny bit of familiarity lodged a sob in her throat.

The sound of voices coming from the lounge stopped abruptly and Taryn tightened her grip, but left the sword sheathed. A deeper growl came from Kaida and she stroked the grierbas's head. They were all on edge, and for good reason. She stepped into the living room, wary.

Taryn's landlady Donyatella stood stock-still near the bookcase, her eyes wide. For a split second, she appeared as solid as stone. A heartbeat later, her face softened. Taryn blinked, unsure what she thought she just saw. For the briefest moment, her old friend could've been mistaken for a statue—like a marble gargoyle—which was too bizarre not to discount. With the way her life had been going, anything was possible. Dony's gaze flicked to her left.

She wasn't alone. But that wasn't what stole the air from Taryn's lungs.

CHAPTER TWO

Aquick glance around the room opened a flood of emotions Taryn wasn't yet ready to deal with. All of their personal belongings had been removed from the walls and bookshelves, with only a few scattered novels resting on their backs. Their furniture was there—including Brandt's favorite chair in front of the fireplace. In the window alcove, above the cushions where Taryn had spent many hours reading, fluttered a scrap of fabric. That small detail, unnoticed by everyone else, threatened to loosen the flood of tears she barely held back.

That fateful morning when her life was irrevocably changed, she'd heard Nadra telling her it was time to return to Aelinae. Startled, she'd torn her T-shirt on the window frame. It was the last time she saw her home in London. It was the first day of her new life on Aelinae.

She breathed deep and inhaled Brandt's scent of cigars and cologne. Faded and stale, but still present. How she wished he was there with them. Her gaze went to the woman who stood beside Brandt's chair, her hand tucked into her leather jacket. It wasn't menacing, the way the pretty blonde held herself, but it wasn't friendly either. The tension in her jaw and narrowing of her eyes made Taryn cautious. The woman reminded her of herself. Tough, streetwise, and not to be fucked with.

Why were Donyatella and the blonde in her flat? And why were they both giving off waves of apprehension? She almost chuckled at the image she and Rhoane must present. Dressed in Aelinaen garb, they were better suited for the Dark Ages than for modern London. Hair wild, clothes torn and dirty, swords tucked at their sides, they probably gave the poor women a shock. And Rhoane still wore the Crown of Awakening. What a sight they made. Even she'd be intimidated by their appearance. Kaida padded to her side and sat, her focus on the woman, but otherwise unflustered. That, at least, helped settle her riotous emotions.

Taryn smiled at Dony, hoping the landlady recognized her through all the leather clothes and grit. A mischievous glint entered the publican's eye and a wide smile broke across her face. She held out her hands for Taryn, and she reached for them, grateful she'd not been forgotten.

"Is that a lycan?" the woman asked, her face ashen. She took a step backward and waves of fear cascaded from her.

A lycan? The fuck? "Kaida is a grierbas. Sort of like a great wolf, but vastly different."

Taryn scratched Kaida's head, wondering when, exactly, lycans became a thing in London. What the hell had happened in her absence? Or had they always been there and she'd never noticed? Had her warding hidden certain aspects of life that were now visible? She wasn't sure what to think or how to respond to this new, unfamiliar London. Nothing would ever be the same. The sooner she accepted that, the better. Especially in London with Brandt gone.

The woman flicked glances from Taryn to Kaida, and then to Dony, but said nothing.

Taryn pulled her attention from the pretty blonde to ask her landlady if she'd rented out the flat. The last thing she needed was to find accommodation elsewhere. Did she have money stashed away? Did Brandt? She couldn't remember. They'd had a bank account, but would there be money left? What happened when people simply disappeared? Did the government take everything? Mad imaginings of vast fortunes scooped up by greedy politicians suffocated her thoughts.

In answer, Donyatella enfolded Taryn in a rib-crushing embrace. She breathed in the unusual scent of her friend. Earthy, like dust from a sand pit, but also warm like fresh cinnamon rolls. Her stomach growled with anticipation. Dinner—or breakfast, she really wasn't sure—had been too long ago to remember.

"Welcome home, child," Dony whispered, for her hearing alone. "You were missed."

It was the same greeting she always gave, but this time felt a little more important, more real if that were possible. She pulled away and indicated the blonde woman who watched them, her features and stance apprehensive. Something about her wasn't right, but Taryn couldn't pinpoint what.

Dony's wan smile and sorrow-filled eyes were directed to the woman. "This is Nikala St. James. She works nearby and has recently lost her father. This room brings her comfort. I did not break my vow to Brandt, it must be known. I protected your identities as I always have. Nikala was called to the flat on her own, and it would seem, the doorway opened for her."

Protected their identities? Did that mean Donyatella knew who they were all along? And what the hell did she mean that the flat called to Nikala? The gnawing of her empty belly increased, but not for food. More odd scratching came from the roof and Taryn cocked her head, studying Nikala, but also listening. Rhoane shifted, his head mimicking hers. A frown pulled his lips low and his hand hovered above the hilt of his sword. They shared a questioning glance.

Do you know what makes that sound?

No idea. This…isn't how I remember London. Things have changed, and I don't think it's just me. Be wary.

Always, mi carae.

She extended her hand to Nikala. "I'm sorry for your loss, truly. I'm Taryn."

The woman had lost her father and Taryn knew only too well how it felt to be adrift after such an important death. A tiny tremor buzzed up her arm as she shook Nikala's hand. The woman had ShantiMari, but it was cloaked, perhaps warded. Just like Taryn had been before going to Aelinae. Perhaps her flat had called to that part of Nikala. Her mind raced with questions upon questions that she had no way of answering unless she confronted the woman and they didn't have time to spare. Nikala's presence was a distraction Taryn didn't need. She had to focus on the reasons she and Rhoane were in London.

"Are you a faerie?" Nikala withdrew her hand and very nearly wiped it on her jeans.

From touching Taryn or the ShantiMari, she wasn't sure.

"Not faeries, no." Seriously? Lycans and faeries in London? At her side, Rhoane stiffened and she pierced Dony with a questioning gaze. "It would seem quite a lot has happened since I've been gone. I'd love to catch up after we've freshened up. There's something we're looking for that maybe you can help with."

And by "catch up," she meant her old friend had better explain exactly what was happening and why her flat was letting complete strangers squat there. And where the hell was her stuff? Dony glanced from Taryn to Rhoane, her lips tight. Each time she looked at Rhoane, the soft crinkles near her eyes deepened. As if she were either afraid of Rhoane, or didn't like him, or something else. But Taryn couldn't understand why. They hadn't met until that moment. Unless Dony could tell he was Eleri and didn't approve, but how would she know such a thing?

It was as if she'd entered an alternate reality and was woefully unprepared. Just like when she'd entered the cavern on Aelinae with one difference—this was London, her home for most of her life. Aelinae had been foreign and terrifying and yet she'd learned to navigate her homeworld with the help of Rhoane and the others. She'd have to do the same now on Earth. A world she thought she knew, but was proving to be as equally as foreign as Aelinae had been.

A flash of light caught Taryn's attention, and she stared at a beautifully carved pendant dangling between Nikala's breasts. It wasn't the amulet itself that held her interest, but what was hidden inside the tiny glass vial. They were weak, but vibrations of ShantiMari came from the bauble.

Rhoane, her pendant. Do you sense it as well?

I do, Darennsai. Distant murmuring transferred from Rhoane's thoughts to hers. *A female faerie is trapped within.* His worry-laced words brushed her mind.

Now Nikala's question made sense, even if Taryn didn't entirely understand how faeries were a thing in London.

Is she alive?

For now. She aches, though—for home, for freedom.

"Your amulet, where did you get it?" Taryn's fingers twitched, anxious to free the trapped woman. Was Nikala the one who trapped her? If so, why? And how? Why would someone put a faerie in a glass prison, and why did Nikala wear it so brazenly?

Nikala wrapped her fist around the charm and a wave of anger broke against Taryn's awareness. The woman had power, yet it felt wild, uncontrolled. She mumbled something about leaving and moved to step around them, but Rhoane blocked her with a wall of ShantiMari. If he hadn't stopped Nikala, Taryn would have. She added her power to Rhoane's, but kept herself in check.

Nikala grimaced and pushed against their invisible wall, but it was useless against their combined strength.

"You cannot fight me." Taryn infused her power with compassion to quell the anger that flooded Nikala's features. "I don't want to hurt you."

"Just.Let.Me.Leave." Nikala ground out the words, each one a verbal punch.

"I can't do that. Not until you tell me about the amulet. Do you know what it is?" Taryn kept her tone calm, soothing.

Rage wafted from the woman in ever increasing pulses. Irrational fury that alarmed Taryn as much as it confused her. By the look on Nikala's face, she struggled to control not just her Shanti-Mari, but her emotions as well. The radical notion that something or someone manipulated her brushed Taryn's thoughts. She'd been compelled by the phantom and knew only too well how awful it was to fight against an invisible foe.

The phantom—holy cats, what if whatever manipulated Nikala was the same phantom from Aelinae? Was it possible? Of course it was. The worlds were linked by more than a portal and perhaps Taryn's presence on Earth gave the phantom power there. But then why would it be controlling Nikala? And, if not the phantom from Aelinae, then what? Or who? More questions. More riddles. And not a single answer. Bollocks.

Their swords harmonized a song Taryn didn't recognize. The tune was for them alone and not shared with the others in the room. As she always did with her sword's songs, she looked for the meaning in the words, but this particular song was sung in a language she didn't recognize. More like a chant than words, the melody vacillated between piercing and delicate.

Rhoane reached out as if to take the pendant.

Careful, my love. Something's not right here. Taryn didn't need to warn Rhoane, but his grimace had her worried.

I agree. The woman in the vial, she shrieks in my mind. There is a bond between these two, but it is unclear exactly what or how strong.

Nikala stepped back, her fist balled in preparation for a swing. Sweat beaded on her forehead and her eyes took on a crazed, fanatic glossiness—cementing Taryn's beliefs that Nikala's thoughts were no longer her own and a battle waged in her mind.

Who was this woman? Why was she so keen to fight over the amulet? Was she fighting to keep control of the pendant, or to protect what was inside?

Taryn tried to ease her mind to the faerie inside the amulet and was forced out by Rhoane's ShantiMari.

Darennsai, she means to attack.

He meant Nikala. The brief emotion Taryn sensed from the trapped faerie was worry and not for herself. What the bloody hell was going on here? She'd walked away from one chaotic event straight into another. It couldn't be coincidence. What if it was? What if it was just random chance that Nikala chose to be in her flat on the exact same day, at the exact same hour that Taryn returned? Yeah, so totally not a coincidence. So then, why? Why them? Why now? Unease trickled over her skin like molasses and she flinched against it.

Do not hurt her. I don't think she means us harm. But something dark does. Whether it's part of her or not, I can't tell. Taryn didn't dare try to enter Nikala's thoughts, not until she knew what was going on.

Rhoane's grunt echoed in her mind. She hoped she was right about Nikala and the woman in the amulet. The song of their swords became a gentle hum with dark undertones. What were they trying to say? Blasted swords and their confounding songs.

Can you understand the words? Maybe he could unravel the mystery.

Only a fraction. I think we are to use our swords to halt the dark force commanding Nikala.

They crossed their blades at Nikala's throat. Taryn hoped Rhoane was right and their swords would block whatever it was that haunted the woman. Nikala's eyes widened and she swallowed hard, nearly cutting herself on the sharp edges. Nikala blinked once, then again, staring at the dragons that fluttered around Taryn's fist. She tightened her grip on the hilt and steadied herself.

"Nikala, please stop." The care and concern in Dony's voice slammed into the three of them. Taryn had almost forgotten she was there, she was so silent and still.

Tears made Nikala's eyes glassy lakes of cool blue. She shook her head—against Dony's pleading, their ShantiMari, or something else, Taryn couldn't be sure. But the agony she saw on the pretty woman's face was clear enough. Whatever was inside Nikala meant to fight. A ball of malevolence gathered behind her —amorphous and dark just like the phantom had been at the Stones of Kaldaar when Taryn saved Sabina from becoming its vessel. What did this phantom want?

A flash of Rhoane's ShantiMari came from her right, surprising her and clearing the dark thoughts that distracted her mind. A moment later, Nikala was thrown backward and pinned against the wall. The full force of Rhoane's ShantiMari whooshed through Taryn's veins and she sucked in a breath. He was being gentle, but Nikala had pissed him off royally. In one smooth movement, he sheathed his sword and strode toward the woman. The shadow receded as if it had never been. Whether Nikala knew it was there or not, she couldn't be sure, but Taryn would've guessed she hadn't known.

"We are not the enemy here." Rhoane's intent gaze didn't leave Nikala's face.

She couldn't possibly know the effort it took Rhoane to keep his voice low, calming and friendly, but Taryn felt it with every syllable.

"We wish you no harm." He dipped his chin to indicate the pendant. "But the woman in your amulet is in pain."

"Pain? How?" Nikala fought against his power, but her words were steeped in concern, her eyes full of confusion.

"Rhoane, be gentle." She sheathed her own sword and put her hand on his shoulder. "I don't think she knows what's in there."

"I promise you. I would never hurt her." Tears rolled over Nikala's cheeks.

A nice promise to make, but by wearing the pendant, she was already breaking it.

"I don't know where the amulet came from. Faerie, maybe."

Faerie was a place as well as a people? Taryn recognized the name, but from where? An image of a young woman with cobalt-blue hair stung her mind and she winced against the pain the vision brought. Where had she seen the woman before? In a dream? A vision? In person? She tried to grasp the image, but it slipped away.

Rhoane gently unfolded Nikala's fingers from the pendant and spoke calming words in Eleri. They buzzed along Taryn's skin, and she leaned into his soothing tones. She could listen to him speak Eleri every moment of the day to eternity and never tire of hearing his lovely voice. Something about the way the words flowed from one to another, it was more a melody than a sentence. Sort of like the chant their swords sang, but even prettier.

He glanced at her, his eyes full of sorrow. "She hails from a faerie kingdom on Cilachaem. Time is short, but this is not our fight, *Darennsai.*" He spoke English, with anger cloaking his clipped words.

Will she die?

If she does not return to her home soon, yes.

We can't just leave her here. We have to do something.

And we will. But we must think about our own situation, first.

What if they're somehow related? Myrddin's papers mentioned a world called Cilachaem. This can't be coincidence.

We shall see. Rhoane's words brushed her mind and her stomach pinched at his use of the same phrase she'd said to Kaldaar.

Either they'd been led to this moment, or the stars had

aligned with alarming coincidence, but either way, she couldn't turn her back on Nikala or the woman in the pendant.

"What will become of her?" Taryn spoke aloud, asking Rhoane more than Nikala, but curious about answers from both.

"She is frightened, but this one brings her serenity." He cocked his head toward Nikala. "She will survive for now, but needs her home." He pierced the woman with one of his glares that made hardened knights waver.

Nikala didn't even blink.

"What can I do to help?" All malice disappeared from her features and her words struck an honest chord.

She would fight Taryn and Rhoane to protect the woman in the amulet, but she wouldn't intentionally put her in harm's way. Interesting.

Taryn and Rhoane released their ShantiMari, and Nikala dropped to the floor. She landed like a cat, fingers splayed, shoulders hunched. They reached to help her stand and when Taryn's fingers touched her skin, a spark flared. The woman was definitely being suppressed. Whoever warded her had gone to great lengths to keep her ShantiMari from flowing freely. For better or worse, Taryn sent a small sliver of her power into Nikala's bloodstream. It wasn't enough to undo the wards—that could be dangerous and lead to catastrophic consequences—but it was enough to allow the woman to explore her power safely.

Rhoane's ShantiMari joined Taryn's, and she shared a quick grin with her beloved.

"What are you doing to me?" Nikala rubbed her arms and shuddered.

"Nothing, Nikala. It is your own ShantiMari responding to ours." Rhoane stepped back to show he was no longer a threat. "You have been heavily warded."

"What's shawnted marri? Is that a fae thing?"

Again with the fae. Hopefully Dony would know what the bloody hell Nikala was talking about. She and Rhoane chuckled at Nikala's pronunciation of ShantiMari. Taryn still had trouble pronouncing a few Elennish words, and was positively awful at getting inflections correct in Eleri. She could give the woman a break for not understanding.

"ShantiMari is power derived from the elements. Some people call it magic, but it's so much more." Taryn turned to face Donyatella. "Do you trust this woman?"

Donyatella regarded Nikala, her gaze cool and calculating. Taryn desperately wanted to trust her, but if Dony didn't give a glowing recommendation, she would tuck that desire aside.

Several long seconds later, Dony nodded. "I do. She is not herself today, but I would trust Nikala with my life. She's good people."

That would have to do. Nikala clasped the amulet between her fingers, and Taryn placed her hand cautiously around the woman's.

"Protect this amulet. I don't know where Faerie is, but she needs to return home as soon as possible."

Taryn closed her eyes and searched the glass prison for the woman lying semi-conscious within. Nothing blocked her this time and she found the faerie curled tightly in a ball, surrounded by a ring of tiny white flowers.

Sleep well, darling. You will soon be with those you love. Be strong, for a short while more. A flood of information burrowed into Taryn's mind, and she shuddered at what the faerie told her.

Nikala's gaze bore into hers. "Why is the amulet so important to you?"

How much should she tell the woman? What she discovered in those few moments was enough to worry her immensely, but she had the sense Nikala wouldn't understand most of it.

"She was betrayed by someone she trusted. I know how that feels." She didn't elaborate, but saw Rhoane stiffen in her peripheral. He didn't know she'd meant Marissa, not him, and she wished she could forget his part in the scheme. Bringing her focus back to the woman, she said, "I know who she is to you, Nikala, but you don't yet know who she truly is."

Nikala sucked in a breath and her eyes went wide with apprehension. "I'll protect her with my life." She hesitated, then asked, "But please, who is she?"

"I am not the one to tell you." It did not fill her with pleasure to say the following words. "That is your path."

"Taryn, we have work to do." Rhoane touched her sleeve and she nodded.

Yes, they had work to do. Another world, another crisis. At least this one didn't involve any deranged gods trying to kill her. At least, she hoped so.

Nikala gave Dony a quick hug and whispered an apology before she headed for the door. Kaida watched her with a curious glint in her golden eyes.

She is in great pain, Darennsai. Not only from the woman in the amulet, but someone she loves is hurt and she feels helpless. There is much confusion, rage, and darkness in this one.

Taryn buried her fingers in Kaida's soft fur. "I know, Kaida. Something has twisted her mind."

Or someone.

Yes.

"Where is Brandt?" Donyatella pulled Taryn from her dark musings to another, harder truth to accept.

Brandt and Dony had been great friends, often talking long into the night about things that hadn't interested her. Adult things like politics and the state of the world. She'd always thought they talked about Earth, but in retrospect, it could've been Aelinae or any number of worlds. She saw now that in Donyatella, Brandt had a true friend and confidant.

Saying the words was difficult, but Dony needed to know. "I'm sorry, Nona Dony. He is with the gods now."

She was once again the little girl who lived above the pub and needed all the love and soothing Dony could provide, except now, she also needed to give in return. She leaned in, absorbing Dony's comforting embrace and filling her friend with love.

How her life had changed in so short a time.

Being there, in the flat, brought all the heartache and sorrow to the forefront of her mind and heart. It was almost too much to bear. Rhoane took her hand and she gripped it as if it were the last tether she had on reality. Quite possibly, it was.

CHAPTER THREE

Taryn shut the door behind Donyatella and rested her forehead against the wood. Flakes of paint scratched her skin, but she didn't care. She was home. Even if it was empty of her belongings, this was the only place she'd ever really felt safe. Now that Brandt was gone, it was her space to protect. Hers and Rhoane's.

Kaida nudged her hand and she stroked the soft fur on her muzzle. What did Brandt say every time they returned home from one of their trips? She cycled through her memories, searching for the words. It was important to keep up the tradition. Especially now that Brandt wasn't there to say the greeting.

"Ahn ominay desidera, tonscalaly desola."

Lights flickered on and warmth rippled across her body. She lifted her head from the door and glanced over her shoulder to where Rhoane stood, eyes wide, a smile on his grimy face. Kaida yipped and padded to the lounge, with Taryn following.

A fire roared in the ancient fireplace and pictures adorned the walls. All of her beloved books were stacked neatly on the shelves, exactly how she'd left them. A crocheted blanket draped over the back of their small sofa, and on the window seat where Taryn had torn her shirt, a novel lay abandoned. It was the one she'd been reading the morning Nadra called them to Aelinae.

All of their possessions were there. Vases and trinkets from their travels. Masks from Venice hung on the wall beside photos of Brandt at a dig on Murano. Taryn smiled at the memory. She'd been five at the time. Too little to be of much notice, but old enough she understood what the grownups discussed.

She traced a finger across Brandt's smiling face. "I miss you, Baba."

Rhoane snuggled against her back and wrapped his arms around her waist. His chin rested on her shoulder, and she felt his breath against her skin. "He is here, in all of these precious memories, but he is also with you through his ShantiMari." His lips brushed her cheek and she leaned into him, into his strength.

"I never thought I'd return and now that I'm here, it's like he died all over again." Tears slipped down her face to drip from her chin. "At least on Aelinae he could visit."

"And why do you think he cannot do that here? Is his spirit limited to just Aelinae?"

"I…well, to be honest, I never thought about it. I assumed I'd never return." Ghosts, or whatever Brandt was now, had only recently become something real. She still wasn't sure what to make of it. She turned to face Rhoane. Their lips were mere inches apart, tempting. "Speaking of which, we need to shower and change clothes. We smell like burnt onions and boiled eggs. Then we'll see about dinner. After that, we can look at the scrolls and figure out our next move."

She led him through the rooms in part to reacquaint herself with the flat, but also in the hope that he would feel more comfortable. He didn't say anything, but she sensed his anxiety and understood all too well what he was thinking. His world, the one where he grew from a child to a man, where all of his family were, was gone. Now, there was only Earth and Taryn, with no promise he'd ever see his home again.

A reversal of when she'd first arrived on Aelinae and only had Rhoane.

Instead of how it was for her—to go from an ultra-modern civilization to one more medieval, he had to contend with electric lights and fast-moving automobiles, not to mention the constant barrage of noise from the big city. She slipped her hand in his and gave a little squeeze. In that touch, she wrapped her ShantiMari with his, making a mini buffer to protect him from too much too soon. At least he wouldn't have thousands of strands of power to shut out here on Earth. Small blessings, indeed. Although, the thought that Earth's magic was dying filled her with sorrow.

She couldn't save them all. But damned if she wouldn't try.

In the kitchen, she used her power to stock the small refrigerator with milk, fruit, veggies, cheese, and yogurt. They would only be there a few days, if that, but hunger knew no time restraints. A bottle of Bordeaux appeared on the counter, along with fresh tea and sugar. Rhoane picked up the bottle and raised an eyebrow.

"Wine. Although not as good as the Summerlands', I think you'll approve. They have Guinness in the pub. You'll definitely like that. No grhom here, though. Sorry. We'll see what else tickles your taste buds later. Shower first." Taryn sniffed herself and made a face. "When was the last time we bathed?" Gods, it had to have been a week at least. Did they bathe during their stay with the Sitari? "Honestly, Rhoane, I don't know what day it is, where I am, or what's happened to us. The past moonturn, it's been—well, a lot has happened. I don't even know where to begin."

"With a shower. Then food. Then sleep. Then we can decide what comes next. Is that not what you said? It sounds like a good place to start." He kissed the tip of her nose.

Shower, yes; food, absolutely. But sleep could wait. She needed to take a peek at the scrolls. If for no other reason than to quiet her mind.

Her cramped little cubicle of a shower was too small for the both of them, so they showered one at a time. She tried not to think of the glorious shower Anje had made for her at Paderau. It was spacious enough for four, but only she and Rhoane used it. As she dried her hair, she heard Rhoane humming a song in the bathroom. Vaguely familiar, she sang along, the words coming naturally to her.

With a start, she recognized the tune as the one her sword sang to her on the ship between Cashiel's beatings.

She peered into the foggy room and unabashedly admired Rhoane's fine body for a moment before asking, "That song, how do you know it?"

Shampoo flung from his head with his shake. "I am not sure. Does it displease you?" He rinsed his face and blinked through soapy water.

"I heard it on the ship. I could've sworn Ynyd Eirathnacht sang it to me. It's lovely, but sad."

"I did not think it sad, but I see it vexes you. I shall hum a different tune, mi carae." His hair flowed over his shoulder in one solid chestnut wave. No longer sheanna, he wore his hair long, as was his right.

Her fingers flexed with a desire to curl in the silky locks, but she kept them pinned to her side. That didn't stop her from assessing his nakedness from head to toe. A low growl came from deep within and she closed her eyes. The dragon inside her—the one Cashiel had hoped to steal, but failed in his attempt—snarled at Taryn's restraint.

How she understood her dragon's need. She would love nothing more than to take Rhoane to her bed and never leave, but there were other concerns that needed them both first.

"Darennsai?" Rhoane stepped out of the shower and reached for her. "You look pained. Have I said something that upset you?"

"Not at all, it's just...you are so fucking sexy and we have to save the world, but really all I want to do is make love to you over and over and over until both worlds end. Is that horrible of me?"

He took her in his arms, not caring that he was getting water all over her and the floor.

"Mi carae, you carry too much weight on your conscience. I am here. Allow me to take some of your burden." He nuzzled her ear with a rumble of desire that broke her.

She ground against him, her want building. "I need you, Rhoane. Here, now." She yanked open her jeans and wriggled out of them with frenzied movements.

She needed this. Needed to feel Rhoane inside her to reset her balance. The events at Mallaqai's ruins haunted her and she needed to know something was the same—that she was the same. She remembered who she was, but that reality was too much to bear. Too overwhelming and daunting. For five minutes, she wished to be nothing more than a woman loving her man.

Rhoane stripped off her shirt and fumbled with her bra. He'd never seen one before and the tiny clasps befuddled him in the most charming way. She shimmied out of the contraption and tossed it to the floor. Her knickers followed.

He could've slammed her against the wall and she would've been perfectly happy, but instead he carried her to the bed, where he lay her down a little too gently. She wanted it hard and fast, but he hesitated.

"What's wrong?"

"This world, it is not for us to save. Nor is that burden ours for Aelinae. You cannot be everything to everyone all the time, Taryn. For this moment, I wish you to be a woman, nothing more." His words echoed her thoughts, as if he'd plucked the sentiment from her mind, but her thoughts weren't open. He simply knew the right words to say.

His future was as complicated as her own. Neither of them knew for certain what would happen, or whether they would survive each day, which made moments like this bittersweet.

He placed his hands alongside her face and lowered himself until his lips brushed hers. "Let me share your suffering. Together, we are stronger." His mouth claimed hers, and she melted beneath his touch. In one swift movement, he entered her and she was lost.

If he said anything else, she didn't hear it. Firecrackers popped in her mind and every nerve ending was a whizbang of delight. She'd feared he would be gentle, but his frenzied pace matched her own and within minutes they were sweating, gasping messes. It was precisely what she needed. By the look of sheer bliss on his face, he needed it, too.

They clung to each other until their bodies no longer convulsed, their want met for the moment. Taryn traced the lines of the tattoo that crossed over his shoulder to his chest. It matched the one on her wrist, the one she'd had applied in the Summerlands before Sabina's wedding—the Eleri symbol for the three strands of ShantiMari.

"Let's get married." She grinned up at him, and he cocked his head to the side.

"Now? Without our families?"

"Not here, but back home. I want a huge wedding, with all of our friends surrounding us. You do still want to marry me, right? When you asked before, in the Summerlands, it wasn't just to make me feel better?"

"It would give me the greatest honor to be your husband." A wicked grin gave him a mischievous look that made her belly tighten. "If I recall, you never told me what a love sword is." He shifted his weight, his erection thick against her thigh.

"Oooh, I think you already know." She tilted her hips to accommodate him better and gasped when he entered her. "Yes," she panted into their movements. "That."

Their powers combined and flexed in much the same way they had in Ulla when Rhoane had healed her. The odd scratching sounded above them, but she shut it out. Tiny glints of Brandt's ShantiMari floated like motes of dust and she knew in here, nothing could harm them. Brandt's wards protected them, but so did their love. She flung her arms to the side and arched into her orgasm. Rhoane cried out his release and she saw him as the god he would one day become. Son of the terrarae, he would plant seeds for future generations on worlds not yet born.

It was their fate. Hopefully, it would be enough to save them all.

An image of water pierced her mind and she winced against it. The rift was there—in the depths. Only they could heal it. Where? How?

Rhoane kissed her forehead and the image subsided. "Shall we be married in Talaith, or the Narthvier?"

She forced her thoughts back to the moment, back to Rhoane. "Why not both? We can have two celebrations. Hell, we could get married at Caer Idris if we feel like it."

"Now that would be something." A dark shadow passed over his features, quickly replaced with a bright smile. "I do not think your half-brother would approve."

"You think he's still alive, too?" She rolled out from under him, and padded to the bathroom to reclaim her clothing.

"I do not believe Kaldaar would allow him to die. Not yet. He needs Zakael, and as long as there is that need, your half-brother shall live." Rhoane stood in the middle of her bedroom, looking lost. "What shall I wear?"

Bugger. She hadn't thought that far ahead. Brandt's clothes wouldn't fit him and they didn't have time for shopping. Shanti-Mari would have to suffice.

"Come here." She stood him in the center of the room and studied him like a sculptor would a piece of marble. "I'm not exactly sure if this will work, but you can tweak it to be more comfortable. Ready?"

Standing naked, arms out, an expression of acceptance on his face, Rhoane nodded. Gods, she loved this man. Flaws and all, he was truly her soulmate. She couldn't imagine going through their ordeals without him by her side. For him, she would fight through the most heinous trials. She just hoped she wouldn't have to.

Imagining suitable clothing wasn't as hard as she thought it would be—she dressed him in the male version of what she preferred to wear. Within moments, dark jeans hugged his ass and a black T-shirt clung to his torso. Instead of sneakers like she wore, comfortable ankle boots slid onto his feet.

He whistled and patted the foreign clothing. "I had hoped you were not dressing me in a gown." His wink tickled the memory of her first days on Aelinae when she'd stubbornly refused to wear a dress.

"You'd look fetching in one, to be sure." She took his hand and rubbed the back with her thumb. "I wish this was a pleasure visit and we had the luxury of time, but we don't. Let's get to work."

While Rhoane gathered the scrolls and papers they'd pilfered from the cave above the Sitari island, as well as those they took from Zakael, Taryn searched Brandt's records for where he obtained the seal. Knowing how he came to have one on Earth might help in their search of other worlds.

His office looked as though he'd been there just that morning. A stack of papers sat neatly on his desk. A pipe rested in an ornate shell they'd found on one of their digs. Cigar and dust and Brandt's cologne clung to the still air. She breathed deeply and let the emotions wash over her. A pang of grief hit her harder than any blow Cashiel had dealt.

She doubled over and curled into a ball while nearly a year's worth of mourning flooded her senses. The musty carpet filled her nostrils and she coughed between silent, dry sobs. More than enough tears had already been shed—enough to fill an ocean. Crying into the floor wouldn't bring Brandt back, nor would it help in their search, but she'd spent too long burying her feelings.

Sorrow roiled over her in waves, lessening in intensity until a strange sort of peaceful acceptance settled in her heart. She would never be the same woman who'd grown up in this flat, but everything she had learned there—especially love—shaped the woman she was now. And that was the kindest blessing Brandt had given her.

From where she lay, she could see through the legs of Brandt's desk to an overstuffed bookcase. A chuckle threatened to turn into a coughing fit and she pushed herself to all fours. Brandt was possibly the most unorganized person she'd ever met, which meant she usually ended up filing his receipts and papers. Somewhere in her past, she must've seen something about the seal, but passed it off as a benign relic from a job.

Excited, she crawled to the file cabinet and prowled through the A files first, for Ardyn, and then searched S for seal. Within five minutes, she not only had a name for the seller—not the British Museum, which she was quite relieved to know Brandt hadn't stolen an artifact—but a business with offices in Edinburgh and London. According to Brandt's records, the seal was purchased from the London branch ten years previously. No other items were bought or sold through them. Not altogether unheard of, but it made the hairs on her arms raise. The name of the company itched against her skull—SIRE.

It was a place to start. Albeit one that didn't fill her with confidence.

CHAPTER FOUR

Delicious aromas wafted from the kitchens up through the flat, beckoning, and Taryn's stomach rumbled in answer. She would've preferred to stay inside all night, but Guillermo had promised soup and she couldn't let him down. She added Brandt's receipt to their pile of pages and scrolls and headed to the front door. In her pocket was a spare flat key, cash, and her passport. Out of habit, she'd grabbed it, and that one little piece of her past life gave her the normalcy she sought.

Kaida and Rhoane flanked her as they made their way to dinner. At the base of the stairs that led to the dining area, Taryn heard voices and paused. Dony's, she recognized. The other was unknown, yet tickled her memory.

"Guardian. I am honored by your presence." The woman's voice vibrated with reverence.

Dony chuckled and for a ridiculous second, Taryn was jealous.

"Child, it is I who am honored. Please give your queens our regard. We, as always, will uphold our oath." Dony spoke to the stranger, but her words eerily echoed what she'd said to Taryn a short while before. Who were the queens she mentioned? Dony's voice lowered and she half-whispered, "And tell that willful brother of yours, he'd do well to remember his manners, as you have."

Even without her enhanced hearing, Taryn clearly made out the reprimand. Who was the willful brother? More importantly, why was she eavesdropping?

"He can be a brat sometimes." This from the woman.

"Indeed." Dony chuckled.

Taryn continued down the last few steps, making sure her presence was known, and ducked beneath the doorway to enter the pub. Dony stood with two women, one with brilliant blue hair and a hauntingly familiar face, and the other Taryn had met in her flat—Nikala.

Their expressions couldn't have been more different. Dony regarded her with open affection; Nikala not so much. The blue-haired woman's eyes widened and her lips trembled.

"Is it really you?" She bent to pet Kaida, her gaze never leaving Taryn.

She cocked her head and a vision of the woman played out in her mind. One she'd thought was a dream, nothing more, but she knew this woman. Knew what caused her pain. Knew it hadn't been a dream, or an illusion as the woman had thought. Her name was Aurora MacNair—Rori—and they'd met on Cilachaem, in a place called Faerie.

Rhoane, she is the woman from the strange dream I had on the ship just before we landed at the Sitari islands. Remember?

I do. Is she a threat?

I'm not sure.

A pull of ShantiMari drew her attention to the woman's jeans pocket, where Taryn sensed the presence of more pendants, similar to Nikala's. In the dream-vision, a tiny faerie had been sleeping in Rori's pocket. Taryn winced against the memory. She'd told Rori the faerie was her daughter, but why? How could a faerie she'd never met be her offspring? Yet even then, standing in the pub in London with bizarre realities unfolding all around her, the words rang true. The girl was her daughter, but not her flesh and blood. More riddles. Fabulous.

One thing she knew for certain was that the fae in the amulets were part of her path. Rhoane would be overjoyed with the news. The sarcastic thought didn't improve her mood. The truth was, living beings were trapped in glass prisons and these two women flagrantly carried them like trinkets.

Yet in her dream-vision, Rori had protected the sleeping faerie, and Taryn didn't sense she wanted to harm the trapped fae, but to help them. The same with Nikala.

"You're Rori," Taryn said at last, when she realized they were waiting for some kind of response from her.

She looked at Nikala, a question in her eyes. What the ever-loving hell was going on here? More imprisoned faeries? Why? Who would do such a horrendous thing?

And, more importantly, were these women enemies? Kaida seemed to approve of them both, which only slightly mollified her suspicion. Rhoane stood to her side, quietly lethal as always.

As if to answer her unspoken question, Nikala lowered her head in acknowledgement. "Rori will return the amulets to where they belong."

Relief rolled in chilled waves down her back. The altercation in her flat was too recent to forget. Fighting either of the women for the amulets wasn't something she wished for, but she would if it meant the trapped faeries would be safe.

"We shall be visiting Cilachaem soon. I hope to see you there."

"Cilachaem?" Nikala looked to Rori for an explanation.

"It's the ancient name of my world." Rori shrugged as if Nikala should've known and conversations about mythical lands were commonplace.

Once again, Taryn wondered how much she'd been shielded

from by Brandt's warding. Or had London changed in her absence? She suspected the former and feared the latter.

"We've sort of fallen out of calling it that. Now we refer to either Faerie or Elvenwood." Rori straightened, taking her hand from Kaida, who nudged her to continue with the petting.

For Kaida to give her that much attention meant something, and Taryn kept alert to both the grierbas and the strange woman. Rhoane, however, was not at all pleased with Rori's explanation.

His disapproval didn't end with a grunt. He crossed his arms and glared at Rori. "To the disservice of everyone living there. By referring to only those kingdoms, you cancel all the other races that call Cilachaem home." Rhoane held himself in check, but she heard the anger that laced his words. "I was led to believe ogres and giants also called your world home. What of them? Or the brownies? The dragons? Do you not respect other cultures?"

When did he learn so much about Cilachaem? Perhaps he'd read it in the notes while she was searching for information on the seal. Or he knew of it from the Eleri people, with their prescient knowledge. Either way, she felt woefully unprepared.

Taryn placed a hand on his arm. *This is not our fight, remember? We'll sort out the dissention on Cilachaem when we go there. How do you know so much about the races there?*

The papers hold clues to each world. Not locations of the seals, but customs and habits of the people—who was helpful, who was not. A bit gossipy, but there were gems to be gleaned from the writings.

Taryn nodded and turned her attention to Rori. "When we met before, you said you were at the palace of your queen, Eirlys. Is that where we would go to get information about your world? Do you have a library there?"

"We do, but the best library is at Elvenwood." Rori cast a nervous glance to Rhoane. "As the name implies, it's the elven kingdom." The sweetest blush stained her cheeks.

If she had to guess, she would say Rori had a beau at the

elven palace. Taryn almost snorted. A beau? She'd been on Aelinae too long—it was starting to affect her speech. Next thing she knew, she'd be talking with a proper Talathian accent and using convoluted language to impress the nobles. The day she did was the day she needed to be slapped.

"Then that is where we shall meet. I have many questions for you, Aurora MacNair." Taryn bent to kiss Rori on both cheeks. "Kaida here says thank you for the scratches."

"You're welcome, Kaida. Great name. Speaking of which, Faerie—I mean, Cilachaem doesn't have dragons. We haven't for millennia, as far as I know."

"Then perhaps it is time." Rhoane's expression softened and a little half smile quirked his lips.

What was he up to? She knew that sly look in his eyes. He knew more than he was sharing, but she'd get it out of him. Her own lips lifted at the thought. Interrogating Rhoane might be fun.

Taryn shuttled her naughty thoughts and asked Dony, "Can you tell me where to find a place called SIRE? They deal in antiques, I believe."

A flash of alarm crossed Nikala's pretty features. "That's, erm, my company."

Another coincidence. This was feeling more like a set-up every second. She opened a thread of her power and breathed deep to keep from losing her shit. Who or what was manipulating them? And what did Nikala, Rori, and trapped faeries have to do with Aelinae?

Rhoane's jaw tensed and eyes narrowed. "We are in need of information about something Brandt bought from you within the past," he looked to Taryn, "twenty-three seasons."

"Years. In the past ten years." Her empty stomach let the world know its grumpy state, and she put a hand over her abdomen with an apologetic smile.

Nikala chewed a cuticle, her discomfort palpable, and not

because of Taryn's grumbling belly. She sensed the anger Nikala had displayed earlier, but thankfully, she kept it in check. It must've been exhausting to be constantly battling that much rage. A pit of guilt was quickly smothered by familiar warmth. Taryn understood far too well how awful living each day on the brink of madness was. Whatever ailed Nikala wasn't welcome, of that Taryn was certain.

Nikala offered to take them to the offices right away, but Rori reminded her they had an errand to run and they agreed to meet later. Taryn sensed Nikala's desire to be gone from the pub, but Rori—despite having somewhere to be—gave off the opposite vibes. She had questions for Taryn, but they would have to wait.

After a brief farewell, the women turned to go and Dony led them to a table. As they were taking their seats, despite the din of customers in the pub, and several meters' distance, Taryn heard Rori tell Nikala she couldn't believe Taryn was real. Taryn nodded to herself, having had the same reaction to meeting Rori.

"What do you mean?" Nikala asked, and Taryn squinted, as if that would help her Eleri hearing to better capture what came next.

"I met her inside an illusion. I thought I was losing my mind, to be honest. But then, I had just broken free of the amulet and chased the witch responsible for kidnapping me."

"You were in one of those amulets? And you broke free? Fuck Rori." Nikala's astonished words matched Taryn's thoughts.

She sensed genuine emotion in Nikala's tone, which also surprised her. Nikala cared a great deal for Rori, and was also afraid for her. These women weren't her enemies; they were victims of something much greater than imprisoned faeries. Rhoane was right—this wasn't their fight, and they had Aelinae to protect. But if she combined their objectives, perhaps she could help Rori and Nikala in the process of finding what she needed. Taryn turned her attention from the women to the menu. Suddenly, she had no appetite for food.

Rhoane believed Cilachaem had dragons, but Rori claimed he was wrong. Did that mean at one time the world had dragons and they left? Or did something happen to them? Could Mallaqai have been to Cilachaem and exiled their dragons as well? If so, where? Where were the dragons?

CHAPTER FIVE

Hayden awoke with a start, the vision playing out in his mind like an inescapable nightmare. He glared at the sheer draperies, confused by his surroundings. This was not his room in Paderau, nor was it the Crystal Palace. Panic shoved the horrific images to the front of his thoughts, and he swayed against the fear that nipped his heart.

Taryn. She was in danger, but too far for him to reach her. Where was she?

He held his head and breathed like she'd taught him. Deep inhales were followed by slow exhales. Morning light drifted through the curtains and cheerful birdsong greeted the day. He lifted his face and breathed in the sweetly spicy scent of the Summerlands. He was in the palace at Menurra. He was safe.

Beside him, Sabina stirred and he curled into her body, his hand cupping her belly protectively. Their heir. A child born of Light and Dark to a Summerlands princess and an Aelan lord. Their child would want for nothing and would be loved beyond measure. He whispered the promise into his bride's onyx tresses and tightened his grip on his family.

Whatever threatened Taryn sought to destroy not just his

cousin, but all of Aelinae. He saw it clearly in his nightmare and knew its truth in his heart. What had she said in his dream?

There's something we need to take care of. We'll be back soon. Give everyone my love.

Where was she going? What did soon mean? She'd already been gone more than a week. He kissed his wife's cheek and rolled from the bed to gather his clothes as quietly as possible so as not to disturb her, and not call attention to the servants who always seemed to be hovering nearby.

He dressed with purpose, his mind flinging out ideas and possibilities faster than he could process them.

Taryn. He cast the thought like a net, hoping their connection was strong enough to reach her. When she didn't reply, he wasn't so much disappointed as saddened. She and Rhoane had left the morning after his wedding and he'd not had time to thank her for ridding him of Kaldaar's presence.

Hayden's steps slowed on the marble tiles that made up most of the palace's walkways. He'd not allowed himself to think of Kaldaar or the repulsive presence since his wedding night. How was it the god had so completely insinuated himself into Hayden's being? He flexed his fingers, eager to work out his frustrations in the training arena. At this early hour, he doubted anyone else would be there and he would be free to annihilate stuffed dummies with abandon.

Another thought chilled his veins—the image of Myrddin watching him right after Taryn and Rhoane banished Kaldaar from Hayden. In those wonder-filled moments when snow fell softly on the wedding party, Myrddin had worn a look of sorrowful exhaustion. And behind him, Hayden could've sworn he saw the faceless, formless shadow of Kaldaar.

But Myrddin was a friend. He had no reason to doubt the man's loyalty to Lliandra and the Light Throne. Hayden had known Myrddin since birth. If Myrddin appeared distressed, perhaps it was due to the god's manipulation of the joyous event.

In any case, it was too late to worry about it now. Myrddin had sailed with Lliandra and the others to Talaith four days past. If they weren't already, they would soon be at the Crystal Palace and life would return to somewhat normal.

If only Taryn and Rhoane would return.

Hayden sped through the corridors to Flik's private training area and let himself in through the unlocked gate. Flik had given him permission to use the smaller area as a favor to King Faisal. Usually reserved for Flik's assassins-in-training, Hayden preferred it to the noisier, clumsier crowd in the general arena where Faisal's soldiers went through their daily sessions.

The sound of swords clanging brought him up short and he listened a moment before continuing. So much for a private workout.

Flik's stern voice reprimanded the pair in the arena and as Hayden crept closer, he recognized them as Taryn's guards, Darius and Timor. To the side, her other guard Carina sat with Taryn's maids. To his surprise, the blacksmith Iselt stood with the group. They hadn't noticed him, nor had Flik. For a moment, he debated leaving, but he needed to train and they were available.

Flik glanced his way and motioned him to the others. "Put your sword away, young lord. We're working with daggers today."

Hayden was neither surprised nor affronted that Flik spoke to him so casually. In this arena, Flik was the master and everyone who entered obeyed his rules. Noblemen, commoner—it mattered not. Flik trained only those deserving of his time. It was an honor to step into the dusty ring—one that Hayden wouldn't squander because of protocol.

They trained hard for nearly three bells, rotating partners and weapons. As Flik promised, they started with daggers, but quickly moved on to flying stars and hand-to-hand combat. It reminded Hayden of Taryn's first days on Aelinae when she would train with his father's soldiers. No one knew who she was back then, but he had known she was special. Never before and not since had he met a woman who attacked training with as much enthusiasm as her.

It made him miss her all the more. Back then, before he knew she was his relation and the Eirielle, he'd been wary of sparring with a woman, especially one more talented with a sword than he. But now…now he could hold his own against his cousin. If not for her, he might still be happy to let someone else run the kingdom while he spent his days dithering in the castle.

By the time Flik called a halt to their session, Hayden dripped in sweat. Taryn's maids were also drenched, being unused to the heat and physical exertion. At least they dressed sensibly in loose-fitting trousers and lightweight blouses. If they'd had to wear the cumbersome velvet gowns Lliandra had made her ladies wear, they'd faint. Taryn's guards and Iselt showed only slight discomfort, having trained with their employer longer than the maids.

The blacksmith patted him on the back with a cheeky grin. "You're not as soft as you'd like us to believe. I reckon you'll make a decent spy."

"Is that what you're doing here? Training to become one of Faisal's assassins?"

"Nah, I'm only here to pass the time." His gaze flicked to Darius and back so quickly Hayden might've missed it. "I got a smithy in Talaith, but didn't fancy sailing back with the empress. On accounta me sailing in with Adesh and all, she still don't trust me." He scratched his bald head, his gaze unreadable. "Can't say that I blame her, really. If the king were to offer me a position here, I might be inclined to accept."

"I could put in a good word, if you'd like." In the few weeks they'd been in Menurra, not only had Iselt proved himself trustworthy, Taryn had vouched for him, and that was good enough for Hayden.

"'Preciate it. But if I'm going to work for the king, it needs to be on my own merit. Thanks all the same."

"I'm sure Taryn wouldn't mind another sword in her guard. Have you asked her?" The thought of Iselt going back to Talaith didn't sit right with him, although he couldn't say why.

"She's offered me a place many times. I don't think soldiering's in my blood." He glanced at Flik with a shrug. "I do like swinging those spiky balls at dummies, though."

"You mean the mace?" That was the one weapon Hayden didn't care for at all. The throwing stars, however, were in his top three.

"I know what it's called. I make enough of them for the empress, don't I?"

The guards approached cautiously and Hayden excused himself. Although Flik had no problem treating him like an equal, to Taryn's staff, he was still Lord Valen. It was too easy to become complacent around Taryn. She despised titles and all the protocol involved with nobility, but Hayden was born to it. For him, it was like drinking wine—a pleasant ritual that left him a little light-headed at the end of the night.

He'd hoped the training would wash away the anxiety his nightmares had brought, but it didn't. Not completely. An uncomfortable nagging at the back of his skull tugged at his thoughts, as if he were supposed to remember something that he'd forgotten. As he strolled through the courtyard garden nearest his rooms, he rifled through the events of the past few moonturns, but nothing came to him.

The empress had signed new treaties, satisfying the Danurians and merchants who had been affected most by the illegal taxes. Eliahnna promised to keep him updated on her mother's health considering it was obvious to everyone that she was fading, even though the empress herself denied the fact. The best they could hope for was to prepare Eliahnna to take the throne. The sooner, the better.

A fade could last anywhere from one season to several dozen, but Hayden didn't think they had that much time. Something disturbed his aunt's mind, and his fear was that it had nothing to do with her fade.

He slipped into his rooms and was pleasantly surprised to see his bride up and about, a smile on her face. The fact she hadn't stopped grinning since the wedding didn't matter. It filled his spirit to see her happy. That she was almost taken from him twice was enough to keep him vigilant to her safety.

"My love, you look ravishing this morning. I see that pregnancy agrees with you."

Sabina put a hand on her belly and rolled her eyes. "Yes, but so does every type of pastry our cooks make. I can't stop eating." Her gaze went to a table overladen with plates piled high with delicious treats.

He snatched a chocolate-and-pear stuffed delight and popped it into his mouth before heading to their bedchamber to undress. Sabina scolded him for stealing from their child, but her laughter followed him down the short hallway. It was good to hear her laugh. It helped offset the horrors they'd lived through over the past moonturn.

A shudder wracked him and he shoved the vile memory of what Kaldaar had sought to do to his bride from his mind. When he hadn't succeeded in raping Sabina through Herbret, Kaldaar had overtaken Hayden. Whether Kaldaar knew Sabina was already pregnant with Hayden's child or not, he couldn't be certain, but Hayden knew for sure that Kaldaar was desperate for Sabina to be his vessel. The seventeenth of her kind. *Sabinth Aarendhi.* She would never not be the seventeenth vessel, but at least the danger of Kaldaar claiming her had passed.

Or would be once she gave birth to their child. A fissure of dread passed through him, and he sloughed it off. Both Sabina and the child would be fine. Taryn would be there for the birth, same with Rhoane and Faelara, just as they had been when Queen Prateeni gave birth to her heir.

Everything would be fine. His bride and his baby would

survive and they'd be free from Kaldaar forever. Everything would work out fine. It had to.

A bath waited for him in the large room they used for their toiletries and Hayden gratefully stripped out of his soiled training clothes. Three servants rushed to take his belongings and he shook his head at the surplus of bodies in the bathing room. Really, one would suffice. His beloved Oliver had stayed in Talaith, citing his age and health wouldn't do well on such a long voyage. Hayden suspected he stayed to play cards with Rhoane's valet, Alasdair.

The pair had grown close over the past season, and Hayden wouldn't put it past the men to be planning something. Hopefully nothing devious or debauched. But seeing as Alasdair was a faerie from the Narthvier and Oliver an Aelan from Paderau, he couldn't for the life of him figure out what their scheme might be. It intrigued him that the pair were friends. Perhaps it was nothing more than two servants bonding over their errant charges.

Gods, but he was getting to be more like his cousin every day. Was everyone suspect now? Would this servant try to slash his throat in his sleep? Or would that one kidnap his wife? Or was he like her in another way—perhaps Alasdair and Oliver were more than friends. If so, he hoped they were as happy as he and his bride. Everyone deserved love and yes, if that made him similar to Taryn, he welcomed the comparison.

He submerged himself in the tepid water and held his breath while he stared at the gorgeous ceiling. Sirens and mermaids frolicked in the colorful tiles. Through the hazy vision, he thought he saw a water dragon swimming across the painted sea.

He sat upright with a sputter and wiped his eyes, but there was no dragon in the tiles.

A servant rushed to wash his hair and Hayden reluctantly let them bathe him, all the while sneaking glances upward to catch a glimpse of something he believed didn't exist. Yet his own cousin was a *darathi vorsi*—an air dragon. What else did he tell himself wasn't true?

What else would he discover before this was all over?

Taryn. He sent the thought into the wild once more, desperate to hear her voice.

Are you bathing?

His hands immediately covered himself, a blush staining his cheeks. *You can see me? Where are you?*

I can't see you, but I…smell soap. The kind used at the palace in Menurra.

His heart leapt and he had to remind himself that he was a lord in his bathing chamber and that he wasn't alone. Shrieking or cheering or any other outlandish behavior would be regarded as unlordly at best, a sign of madness at the worst.

I had a terrible dream. Are you and Rhoane safe?

We are. Please don't ask where. How's the baby?

Loving warmth infused him and a smile stretched his lips. *Strong. Healthy.*

Tell Sabina she better not have that baby without me. Worry edged her words, but he chose to hear the joy in them.

What's so important you'll be gone so long?

The same threat that almost destroyed you. Hayden, her whisper brushed his mind, *we're not on Aelinae. Kaldaar has returned and he controls Caer Idris.*

A jug of hot water poured over his head and he frantically wiped it from his eyes as if being able to see could help him better hear his cousin's thoughts.

How? What are we to do?

Prepare Eliahnna to rule. Prepare for war.

Her presence faded until he was left staring at the ceiling, shivering in the Summerlands heat.

Prepare Eliahnna to rule. *Prepare for war.* Taryn sent the thought to her cousin with deep regret. It would come to war in the end. There wasn't a doubt in her mind. If they could avoid it, that would be fantastic, but she believed Kaldaar wouldn't settle for anything other than an all-encompassing war that saw him victorious. It was his comeback tour—the one that would see him vindicated for supposed wrongs. It didn't matter that he was the one who brought about the Great War—that it was his betrayal and treachery that caused him to be exiled. Kaldaar would retaliate until all of Aelinae suffered for his misdeeds.

Hayden's presence dissipated and Taryn stared out over the Thames, her eyes darting between the strands of ShantiMari she caught glimmering across open sky. Some were strong and bright, others little more than tattered wisps. Nadra was right: magic was dying on Earth, but there was still enough to give her a headache. Tuning out all the threads was difficult enough for her—Rhoane must've been miserable, even with her subtle diffusion.

She glanced at his handsome features, at the strong jaw, the straight nose, and dark brows. Locks of brown hair spun with the breeze and she captured the moment to imprint on her memory. He looked calm, peaceful. No worry clung to his gorgeous moss-green eyes. No stress made crinkles at the edges of his lips. His smile was soft and content.

"Don't the lights bother you?"

"They are beautiful. I still do not understand the concept of electricity or what a billion people means, but you were right when you told me your hometown was crowded. Yet I see hope. I see love." He cocked his chin toward buildings across the river. "There is a family over there visiting for the first time. They are full of wonder, as am I." He turned to her and delight sparkled in his eyes. "I thought I would be overwhelmed by the sounds and sights, but I am not. I feel at home here." He stroked the sides of her face, his gaze full of the joy and hope he mentioned, and more. Fierce protectiveness cloaked his movements, his words, and his gaze. "I have lived with your memories of this world for a full season. Your love is my love. Your fear is my fear. Now tell me, what causes you distress? I see it in the pinch of your lips, the clenching of your fists."

Like a guilty child, she hid her hands behind her, but then released the fists she'd unconsciously made and buried her fingers in Kaida's fur. A movement to her left distracted her momentarily, but she forced herself to be present with him.

"Those women, Nikala and Rori. Their path is part of our journey. If we can help them, I think we should. But that's not what has me most concerned." She gazed over the river at the boats traveling up and down the water as if they could provide answers. "Hayden spoke to me in my mind just now." She tapped her temple for emphasis. "From across time and space. How? And does that mean Kaldaar can track us?"

"We should assume he can, but hope that he is far too busy to bother with us at the moment." His lips brushed her forehead and she sucked in his warmth. "Do they have gods on this world?"

"Yes, but it's…complicated. There have been, and probably still are, many wars fought over religion."

He nodded as if he heard her words, but his face scrunched as if he tried to process the meaning. "Aelinae has no formal religion. People are free to worship whom they choose. My goddess is Verdaine, but I also revere and respect the other gods. Perhaps that should be a teaching here as well."

"I wish it was that simple. Nadra once told me she sent me to Earth because there were lessons here I needed to learn for Aelinae's future. Perhaps that's one area where Aelinae got it right. The one war Aelinae had was due to the gods' behavior, not the practitioners' differing beliefs. And now, I think Kaldaar is planning a second war, even greater than the first." She sighed and wrapped her arms around his waist. "I told Hayden to prepare Eliahnna to rule. I hope it's not too late."

"It is never too late. I am concerned about the timing, though. Amdi ailing in Ulla, Lliandra afflicted as well, Zakael is newly crowned, Eliahnna has been named heir to the Light Throne for less than a moonturn: does Kaldaar hope to take advantage of new, untested rulers?"

"It would fit with his theory of chaos." She gazed at the lights that illuminated the London skyline and searched for threads of ShantiMari. "Nadra once told me ShantiMari on Earth will be completely wiped out within a few hundred years. Now that I know what it is to have this power, I couldn't imagine living without it."

"Your being raised without ShantiMari might've helped save you on the ship with Cashiel."

At the mention of her half-brother, her stomach pinched and a flash of his brutal beatings clouded her thoughts. She blinked to rid herself of the memories. The wounds Cashiel caused were still too new. Her body might've healed, but her heart had yet to fully recover. The amount of hatred he had put into his assault was overwhelming.

Again, a movement in the shadows drew her attention. Someone loitered there, but tried very hard not to be seen.

"It's hard to believe it's only been a few days since you were nearly dead and a few weeks since I was. I mean, we both sustained horrific injuries. How is it we're alive?" Truly, neither of them should've survived—she the beating, he the poisoning—yet here they were, hearty and hale. She held her hand between them and turned it to better see all the runes. They glittered and shimmered against her skin and there, just below the flesh, a field of stars drifted in a nebula of pinkish purple. Keeper of Stars.

"We are meant for far greater things than the machinations of your family. I once believed it was only you who would ascend to Dal Tara, but now we know our destinies are bound beyond these mortal bodies." He placed his hand over hers and roots grew from his flesh. "I am Surtentse, and you Darennsai. Together, we are the worlds we will create."

"Worlds we'll create… That's kind of mind-blowing." She rose on tiptoe and kissed his nose.

A couple walked past arm-in-arm, the woman's head tilted toward the man. To the world, they appeared very much in love, but Taryn sensed his apprehension. A waft of anxiety-riddled perspiration made her wrinkle her nose. Kaida growled, low enough only Taryn and Rhoane heard, and not at the couple. A second figure skulked several paces behind them, but didn't appear to be following the couple.

We are being watched. Rhoane's thought brushed hers.

I know.

Taryn caressed Rhoane's hand between hers, striving to appear as happy and normal as the couple who passed. "When I first met Rori in that vision, I thought it was another of my confusing dreams. She had a sleeping faerie in her pocket—the both of them had been imprisoned in one of the glass vials, but Rori broke free. Anyway, that little fae princess, I knew her."

A tear tracked its way down her cheek, and Rhoane wiped it away with his thumb. Kaida wedged herself between them as if to hug her. These were her greatest loves, her most stalwart companions, and best friends.

"In the dream-vision, I told Rori the princess was my daughter. Do you think…I mean, this is madness, right? But do you think you and I created Cilachaem?" She dipped her head, embarrassed at such an outlandish idea.

Rhoane lifted her chin to look at him. The love swirling in his eyes mirrored what she was feeling in her soul.

"I do not discount anything when it comes to you. To us. We walked between worlds. Anything is possible."

"With *you*, anything is possible. But seriously, twisting my mind around the time-space-conundrum-shenanigans does my brain in. How could we create a world before we are gods? Is there a God Academy or anything? I feel like we need lessons."

Rhoane chuckled and that little half smile that made her knees weak lifted his lips. "I think if we asked Nadra, she would tell us it is part of our path to learn. Gods can be rather vexing, can they not?"

"Quite." She frowned at the skulker and turned them toward the pub. "We should see if Nikala has returned."

And see whether our followers are friend or foe.

As luck would have it, SIRE's offices were within walking distance from the pub, just up a short lane, but first they had to cross a busy street. Rhoane swore at several cars and threatened to obliterate them with his sword. As much as he enjoyed the lights of the city, cars he did not like. At all. They were loud and fast, and Taryn felt his terror every time one approached. Cyclists riled his agitation as well. Kaida, on the other hand, loped across the traffic as if she hadn't a care in the world. Of the few foolhardy cars that honked, they received a loud bark in reply. Taryn was certain the family across the Thames could hear Kaida's angry snarls.

Once safely across the street and halfway up the lane, Taryn chanced a glance over her shoulder to see that not one, but two shadowy figures had followed them, one lagging behind the other. Whoever they were, they'd be dealt with after seeing to Nikala.

Neither of the two security guards manning a huge desk in the lobby of SIRE's building even blinked when the three of them strolled into the brightly lit space. Despite it being past nine o'clock at night, several of the offices upstairs had lights in their windows and Taryn hoped one was SIRE's. She approached the men with an easy smile and asked if Ms. St. James had returned. One of the men checked a computer and told Taryn Nikala hadn't been in since earlier that evening and to try again in the morning.

Disappointed at the news and physically exhausted, she knew they should head back to the flat, but her mind was too awake for sleep. "Want to see the city?"

Rhoane slipped his hand into hers. "I would love to."

What the hell. Saving the world could wait a few hours while they played tourist and walked the streets of London. The fresh air would do her good. Despite the hour, couples and groups out for a bit of fun crowded the street outside of SIRE's building. A quick scan of the area didn't show the two stalkers they'd picked up, but she sensed they were there, lurking.

As they strolled, several people gasped at the sight of Kaida, with a few slinging insults at Taryn for not following proper leash laws. She'd become so accustomed to Kaida's presence, she hadn't thought about how others might view her. To them, she was probably an oddity, and slightly terrifying.

"Can you not look so scary?" Taryn asked the grierbas half in jest.

Within moments, Kaida slimmed to a sleek white dog, no bigger than a border collie. Taryn and Rhoane shared a "What the fuck?" look. Never in all her days did she imagine Kaida had ShantiMari. It opened a whole new area of surprise in her mind. Did other creatures have power? Was Kaida special? Was it due to her being close to Taryn and Rhoane? She sent silent questions to the wily beast, but Kaida simply grinned and shook out her fur. Typical. *What did grierbas know of ShantiMari* would probably have been her reply, anyway. Taryn chuckled at herself and at Kaida for always surprising her.

She fashioned a collar and leash, earning a snarl from Kaida, and turned them toward Tower Bridge. It was a clear, crisp evening with spring lingering while summer waited. It used to be her favorite time of year in the city: early May before it got too hot, but the bone-chilling cold of winter had passed. As they ambled along, she recounted adventures she and Brandt used to have in the city, most of them centered around the Tower and museum. They would have to stop in tomorrow, of course, and see their associates, but it was not a social visit she looked forward to. For over two decades, Brandt had been a consultant to the museum. He had many friends who would mourn his death.

It struck her how many invisible ties their lives had made. People she barely thought about might be wondering what had happened to her. Were they mourned? Or had people moved on and Taryn had it all wrong? Memories were transient squatters to some, vital to others. How would history remember them? Certainly, in Earth's history, she wouldn't even be a footnote, but in Aelinae's, she and Rhoane would feature prominently. It was their choice whether they were remembered for good or ill.

Although, she was beginning to think it didn't matter what they did—some would revile them and some would revere. It all came down to the individual. Did she want to be revered? The idea of someone worshipping her didn't sit well in her belly. Hell, the entire notion of becoming a goddess didn't seem real. She wanted to believe Nadra and Ohlin knew what they were doing, but what if they were making it up as they went along and hoping for the best? That idea horrified her. She shunted it to the far reaches of her brain, where it couldn't pick at her confidence. She had enough trouble believing in herself as it was.

As they passed an old sandstone building, she glanced up at the lovely edifice. Hunched over the peak of an arched doorway, a gargoyle stared impassively as they strolled down the street. Taryn had the distinct feeling it was actually watching her. With the way her day was going, it didn't even surprise her that a stone sculpture might be real. Rori's greeting to Dony came to mind, followed closely by a story Brandt had once told her about Stone Guardians—immortal gargoyles that served to protect.

Dony's promise that she kept her oath dangled in Taryn's thoughts. She'd said she'd protected their identities. What did that mean? Dony hadn't been able to join them for dinner and now Taryn suspected her landlady had wanted to avoid answering uncomfortable questions. Or was forbidden from it. Who would Donyatella make a vow to? Who had the power to compel someone on Earth to protect the identities of people from Aelinae?

One possible answer buzzed in her gut, upsetting the calm her walking had achieved. A god had that kind of power. But which one? Nadra? Kaldaar? Ohlin? Or was there a newcomer to the game? The pantheon in her brain was already overflowing. All she needed was someone else trying to kill her.

We are still being followed, Darennsai. Kaida's wet nose tickled her fingertips.

Taryn sensed them, too. They'd fallen into step outside SIRE's offices. As of yet, they were simply observing, but she kept aware in case they caused trouble. When she casually glanced at their surroundings, she couldn't tell who among the crowd were their stalkers. They continued walking past the Tower of London and a powerful wave of ShantiMari buttressed against her.

Rhoane angled toward her as if he, too, felt it.

"There is much death here. Spirits linger when they should not. So much anger." Rhoane rubbed his temples and Taryn sent a thread of her power into him for comfort.

"It's oppressive. Strange, though. I never felt it before. Brandt and I often had assignments that brought us to the Tower. As a little girl, I loved coming here. They keep ravens on the premises and I would chase them for hours. Brandt had special access where the public couldn't go, but I always wanted to stay on the grass near the ravens. Tonight is the first time I've felt ShantiMari here. I guess Brandt's wards were pretty thick to keep me from sensing, let alone feeling, power." It wasn't so much a wave as a tsunami. A deluge of power that was equal parts claustrophobic and freeing.

They quickened their pace, leaving behind the remnants of death that lingered at the Tower, and headed toward the bridge. A group of students, arms linked and singing, blocked their way. Rhoane's eyes narrowed and lips thinned, but he didn't voice what bothered him. Once the group passed, he gazed up at the soaring Tower Bridge as they continued on. Lights illuminated the suspension rods and continued across the upper walkways, giving it the distinctive, fairytale appearance known all across Earth.

"These structures are quite formidable." He swept his hand to indicate the buildings on either side of the river. "How old is this city?"

She paused at the center of the bridge and leaned her forearms on the thick balustrade. "Thousands of years, but most of what you see here is new." Taryn pointed to the Tower of London. "That was once the highest building in the entire city. Queens and kings called it home. We're very fortunate it wasn't destroyed in any of the wars." She jutted her chin toward the skyscrapers beyond. "That's SIRE's office building there. The funny-looking one that angles at the top."

"I would like to fly overhead to see the lights, but I have a feeling that would cause a spectacle."

"Dragons in London? Yeah, it might. Although, the city's changed so much from what I remember it's possible they're already here. I don't know anymore what I was warded from and what was real." She petted Kaida, missing the deep coating of fur. "From the looks Kaida received, I doubt there are dragons, though. If they can't handle a grierbas, just think what flying beasts would do to their poor hearts."

Her gaze wandered to a muscular man she recognized from the embankment in front of the Tower. The way he casually leaned against the bridge railing, his legs slightly crossed, face in profile, he didn't look menacing. In fact, he appeared perfectly human.

"We should head back and get some sleep." They turned in unison, and for the briefest moment, the man's features gleamed in the bridge lights, giving him a mask of marble.

Like a damned gargoyle.

A second man, face gaunt, eyes vacant, rushed toward Rhoane. His lopsided grin transformed his face to an eerie kind of fanaticism that struck fear in her heart. What fresh hell was this?

"You reek of it. Give it to me." The man reached for Rhoane, fingers extended like claws.

Everything happened at once, yet in slow motion. The gargoyleish man eased away from the railing and started toward them while Rhoane sidestepped the fanatical man and reached for a sword that was not there.

Kaida growled and snapped at the man, placing her body between Taryn and him. She, too, reached for her sword and swore at the emptiness she found.

"Such sweetness. I must have it." The man's lips curled to

reveal blackened teeth. His clawed fingers scratched the air between them. "Please, give it to me, I beg of you."

"We do not know what you need, friend." Rhoane held his hands out to calm the man. "How can we help you?"

"Your magic. So pure." He lifted his face in rapture.

In the same instant Taryn saw his pointed ears, the stone-like man swept the fanatic into his arms and leapt over the railing of the bridge. Too fast for Taryn to react. Too fast for anyone else to notice.

A moment later, she heard a strangled cry. In a blink, the man, dressed entirely in black with muscles on top of muscles, stood in front of a startled Taryn and Rhoane as if he'd been there the whole time. Kaida yipped in surprise and Taryn gripped her leash as if her life depended on it.

"What the fuck was that?" A faint splash came from below and she glared harder at the man. "You killed him?" She hissed the words, fury igniting her blood.

"Scyver scum." The man spat on the ground for emphasis that wasn't needed.

Those two words conveyed exactly what he thought of scyvers. Whatever those were.

"He would've killed you without a thought. Have you finished your sight-seeing or did you want to attract more scyvers? There's fewer of them roaming the streets tonight, which is odd enough to warrant concern, but believe me, there are still a fair few who wouldn't mind taking a bite out of either of you." His thick Scottish accent was full of reproach.

Rhoane had at least six inches of height on the man, but not the bulk. The two men stood a foot apart, sizing each other up like two stags about to butt heads.

"What is a scyver? Why do they wish to eat us?" Rhoane's ShantiMari swirled around him in hazy circles, wary and ready, but not overly concerned.

"I'll tell ya on the way. You might want to tuck that power

away, though. They ain't got much sense left, but they can smell magic miles away."

Taryn gazed out over the river and swept to the Tower with dread in her heart. Magic hunters? This wasn't a London she knew. It wasn't a London she wanted to know. But it was one more hard truth she'd have to face.

CHAPTER SEVEN

The small group walked at a brisk pace, with the man, who called himself Silar, explaining something Taryn found quite unexplainable. Scyvers were new to London—to the whole of the United Kingdom, actually—and thus far, relegated to only the island. Their presence was not yet known on the continent, but Silar assumed it was a matter of time. How they came to be was a hotly debated topic among the magical folk.

The magical folk. Faeries like Rori traveled regularly from Cilachaem to Earth to keep the peace between the realms. Smatterings of memories flicked through her mind, of times she thought she saw a winged female, or of when she was very young, she often spoke to a handsome blond elf named Therron. She'd thought they were dreams or an overactive imagination. To hear Silar speak of magical folk as if they were a natural part of this world upset the fragile balance of sanity she struggled to maintain.

Brandt's wards had not only kept her from her power, but also from seeing other magical creatures. Now she understood why he had to protect her, but still didn't grasp Donyatella's part in the deception—and Silar was adept at steering the conversation away from who or what he and Dony were. At the pub's entrance, Silar bid them goodnight and disappeared into the shadows, leaving Taryn and Rhoane with more questions than answers.

Answers that would have to wait until morning, because Dony wasn't anywhere to be found. Taryn stormed up the back stairs, furious with her old friend. Was Dony spying on her? Or protecting her? She tossed her coat on the couch and flexed her hands before scraping them through her hair. Kaida shook out her fur and returned to her normal size with a muffled howl. She removed the collar and stroked her muzzle. In thanks, Kaida nuzzled her hand and put a paw on Taryn's knee.

"I don't know what's going on, and that scares me." She took a long, calming breath that did nothing to ease her frazzled thoughts and flopped onto the sofa. "I couldn't read Silar's thoughts. Could you?"

Rhoane hung their coats on the rack and shook his head. "He is a puzzle to me, and I, like you, do not understand what is happening here or if it requires our involvement. I am tempted to say it does not, but that man on the bridge—he was in great pain."

Taryn hadn't sensed anything from the man aside from rabid obsession. "Have you ever heard of Stone Guardians? Rori called Dony Guardian, and I don't know, Silar makes me think of a gargoyle every time I look at him. I'm not nuts, am I? I mean, we have dragon souls…maybe there are stone people?"

He sat beside her and looked into the distance. Murmurings brushed her mind, but she wasn't invited into the discussion with his Eleri ancestors. It shouldn't have bothered her, but it did. Wasn't she Eleri now? A little ping to her heart burst that lie. No, she wasn't Eleri. No matter that her ears were tipped and she had a dragon soul: she was born an Aelan, raised on Earth as a human, and would someday be a god. If she lived that long. Not only was she not Eleri—she was everything Rhoane's family hated and feared.

She groaned and rested her head in her hands. Kaida clambered onto the sofa and wedged herself between Taryn and Rhoane, even though there was barely enough room for just the two of them.

"The ancestors tell me there are stories about Stone Guardians —a race of people who served gods of old on this world, but not ours. Your friend Donyatella can shed more light on their history." Rhoane curled around Kaida, exhaustion clear on his features.

He didn't complain, but she could only imagine the energy he expended shutting out all the voices and sounds. Things she took for granted were new to him. She took his hand in hers and their runes flared to life. Kaida adjusted herself until her head rested below their entwined fingers. This was the first time in a long while she could remember them being completely alone. No servants, no family, no one else but the three of them.

For a long time, they stayed in their content little cocoon until Rhoane's eyes drooped and Taryn caught herself yawning for the hundredth time. The morning would bring even more questions, a fact she assumed neither of them were too anxious to confront. Hopefully—finally—they'd get answers.

On the way to her bedroom, she brushed the scrolls with her fingertips. "If it's Myrddin who hid the seals, where do you think he'd go?"

"Somewhere with power, wine, and women."

"Then maybe the library at Elvenwood isn't such a good idea." Her first instinct was to always search archives for written records.

"It is as good a place to start as any. We should include in our search bard's tales and folklore. Nobles are often too busy satisfying their desires to bother noting odd occurrences."

"Brandt used to say something similar. But with the caveat

that what's recorded as fact might well have been paid for by the one with the most to lose." She thought of Shakespeare and the tragic tale of Richard III. What was fact? What was fiction?

Rhoane took her in his arms and held her close. "That is why we must not rely solely on what has been written down. The Eleri have a rich oral tradition that you will not find anywhere, even at Verdaine's Temple, where they have extensive records that go back to the first seeds planted on Aelinae. Words, whether written or spoken, come with untruths. We must not be enamored of one at the expense of being deceived by the other."

His kiss silenced any further discussion. Myrddin and the other mysteries could wait until she had a full night's sleep. Perhaps after languidly making love. She deepened the kiss and Rhoane tangled his fingers in her hair. His thoughts opened to hers and she felt his apprehension at their quest, knew his confusion of what he'd seen in London, and understood his fear that if they failed, more than one world would suffer. They were thoughts and emotions she shared. Whatever was happening on Earth involved not just Aelinae, but Cilachaem. How many other worlds were tangled in Kaldaar's web of chaos?

They made love slowly, Taryn methodically using her Shanti-Mari to ease his worries while he did the same for her. They worked in tandem similar to how the Ullans healed, but much more intimate, far more intense. Their breathing and heartbeats became one until there was no Taryn or Rhoane, only a single consciousness.

No matter how many times she experienced the sensation, she was startled by the sheer vastness of their powers and their love. Taryn straddled Rhoane, and she arched into his movements, until he filled her completely. His hands held her hips and he rocked up to meet her thrusts, a look of contented bliss on his features.

The physical space of her room vanished until they floated in a field of stars. Roots and leaves etched into Rhoane's skin with tiny filaments trailing into the vast nothingness. One day they would be gods and create worlds.

But first they needed to mend the tear in Aelinae. Through it, evil seeped from world to world.

Rhoane's eyes widened and he cocked his head, as if listening for something, but there was only the two of them. He shifted until she was beneath him and his hair fell like a curtain on either side of her shoulders. A savage, sexy growl came from deep in his throat. Strands of her silver hair floated around them like mist and a vision buttressed her thoughts—a body of water surrounded by desert.

When she nudged the vision aside and gazed at the man she loved, she saw not the face she knew as well as her own, but a great mountain. A flicker of a heartbeat later it was gone, and Rhoane wore a half smile that made her pulse skip. Son of the terrarae. He was mountains and fields, meadows and forests; he was the land and the land was vast.

Their lovemaking opened her mind to possibilities she'd never imagined. It was frightening to the mortal Taryn, but the goddess she'd one day become embraced the challenges presented to her. Rhoane's pace increased and Taryn met him beat for beat. Did gods have sex? She hoped so, because this was *ahhhhhh, yessss, just there and oh my fucking hell, don't stop.* So good. Too good to ever imagine life without. They came undone together, in a crash of stars and waves, of moons and suns, of lakes and oceans, and of mountains and meadows. Everything that made them who and what they were, and what they'd become.

When she woke in the morning, stardust glittered on their skin and dusted every corner of her room. Kaida padded in to greet them, and even she had a sprinkling on her fur. Taryn lay back and stared at the ceiling, trying to recall all that had gone through her mind, but it was elusive. The amazing orgasm, that she remembered with clarity. Everything else? Not exactly gone, just…not solid.

Rhoane's lips curled with a sleepy smile, and she traced her fingers along his brow to his temple, thanking the gods for him. They'd been through the storm and had survived. She shuddered to think what else was waiting for them, but was confident that together, they could defeat any foe, visible or not. He snuffled and shifted to his side, his eyelids fluttering with his dreaming. Her heart swelled to see him so peaceful. He'd stood by her since before she was born, his loyalty never wavering, even when Marissa cruelly abused him.

Taryn didn't blame him for being broken after Marissa raped him. How could she? Her half-sister knew exactly what she was doing when she drugged Rhoane and took advantage of him. Taryn wrapped a lock of his hair around her finger and cupped his cheek in her palm. Her family had tried to coerce, manipulate, and destroy them at every possible turn. And each time, Taryn and Rhoane had overcome their trials. When would it be enough? When would her mother and half-brothers stop their incessant war with them? And for what? What did Lliandra gain by fighting against Taryn? What did Zakael get out of being Kaldaar's pet? What wasn't she seeing?

Surely, they believed there was a prize worth selling their souls for, but what was it? They had power—both ShantiMari and political. They had wealth. Adoration? Immortality? If she could understand their motives, then they had a chance of beating them at their own game. She shivered against an imaginary chill and rolled out of bed. *Beating them at their own game* —she sounded like Marissa. She didn't want to beat anyone, or hurt anyone, or even go to war. She loathed the fighting. If there was a way to bring peace to Aelinae without war, she'd find it.

An image of a stunningly beautiful woman with long dark hair and sorrow-filled brown eyes slammed into her mind. Behind the woman, hundreds of dragons looked on. Unlike the woman, their scale-rimmed eyes were filled with hope. The missing darathi vorsi. The woman was hauntingly familiar, but like her memories of their night in the stars, nothing more than a fleeting awareness. Who was the woman? And were the dragons the answer she sought? Would returning the dragons to Aelinae bring the balance she was supposed to restore? Were they harbingers of peace? What did the dragons have to do with them becoming gods, if anything?

Her hands fisted and she swore under her breath, frustrated she couldn't snap her fingers and have all the answers. With each step they took, a dozen new complications popped up. Which did they solve first? And would tackling this one lead to more trouble with that one? Some goddess she'd make. She couldn't get through a single day without courting disaster.

While Rhoane slept, she showered and dressed, trying—and failing—to not think about the gods they would become. It was too surreal. Rhoane had known since her birth that she'd become a goddess, a secret he'd kept quite well, but he hadn't known he would become a god. Why them? What was so special about an Aelan girl raised on Earth and an Eleri boy? She was the Eirielle, but none of the Aelan prophecies mentioned godhood. Nor did the Eleri scrolls. She'd never thought about how gods came about, because really, why would she? But now the idea obliterated all rational thought. Could she and Rhoane make demigods? What were the limits, if any? And how the hell did they create a world where Myrddin might've hidden a seal before they were gods? If she kept trying to answer that particular riddle, it would do her head in. Best to focus on the moment. On the innocuous.

In the cabinet, she found fresh toothbrushes and a new tube of toothpaste, albeit both almost a year old. She'd made a decent toothbrush in Aelinae with materials she could find there—a sturdy wood handle with three rows of soft bristles made from a horse's mane. How her maids had giggled at that one. That is, until they tried one for themselves. As she scrubbed her teeth, she decided she preferred the one she'd made on Aelinae. The plastic scratched her gums and left her feeling slightly abused. Perhaps she needed something gentler, like a toothbrush made for babies.

She chuckled on her way to the kitchen. In some ways, she was softer than when she left Earth, but in far more ways she was tougher. Her sword leaned against the wall in the lounge and she picked it up out of habit. They couldn't run around London with swords swinging at their waists, but she didn't like the idea of being without it, especially after last night. She could wrap them in shadow to make them appear invisible. Her gaze went to Kaida, and she scrunched her nose.

How did you make yourself less intimidating? Do grierbas have ShantiMari?

What does a grierbas know of these things? I am grierbas, that is all I know.

Taryn rolled her eyes at the ridiculous beast. *When we go out again, I would appreciate you looking as you did last night.* She scratched under Kaida's chin as thanks. "How about some eggs and bacon?"

Kaida's tail thumped the floor and she gazed at Taryn with bright golden eyes.

"I'll take that as a yes."

Swords and grierbas, as far as she remembered, weren't commonplace in London, but with all the changes she saw so far, she really didn't know what to expect. If she was afraid they'd stick out, she put those fears to rest while she got to work cooking up a feast. Their pitifully stocked fridge soon filled with everything she'd need to make sure they had a full belly to start the day.

Rhoane shuffled into the kitchen wearing loose-fitting Summerlands trousers and nothing else. The dark tattoo was still new enough to surprise her every time she saw it, but definitely not in a bad way. His long hair hung over his shoulder to his pecs and she might've growled at the sight of his chiseled abs. Damn. Unaware how hot he was, or what his half-naked state was doing to Taryn's body, Rhoane rubbed his eyes with the palms of his hands and yawned with a long stretch. She would never, ever tire of drinking in the beauty that was his body.

"I'd ask if you slept well, but I'm assuming not." She handed him a cup of tea and motioned to a chair. "Breakfast will be ready in a minute."

"I had bizarre dreams of creatures I did not recognize and worlds I do not know." He pulled a sheaf of papers toward him and scanned the first few pages between sips of tea. "There are fifteen worlds listed here, but only thirteen seals in the temple, and how many missing?"

"Five, but I know the location of one. So, four that we need to find." She buttered their toast and slid eggs onto his over-flowing plate before handing it to him. "Jam's on the table and more tea's in the kettle."

How easy it was to slip into the role of ordinary life. On Aelinae, she didn't have a kitchen of her own, nor had she ever made Rhoane breakfast, but this simple task was one she'd performed hundreds of times on Earth. A momentary jag of wistfulness settled in her belly. These moments were to be cherished, for once they left Earth, they wouldn't happen again.

Rhoane made notes while she thumbed through the scrolls she'd taken from Zakael at Mallaqai's ruins. Unlike Myrddin's pages, these were written in Elennish by the same hand that penned the papers she'd found in the tiny library at Caer Idris. A thrum of excitement coursed through her as she rapidly skimmed each page. As she'd hoped, they provided the third piece of the puzzle that had vexed her for six moonturns.

To keep Rykoto imprisoned, she'd need the blood and the blade of the one who is and who is not. Easy enough—that referred to her and Ynyd Eirathnacht, although, the "who is and who is not" was confusing. The next part wasn't quite as easy—she'd also need the tear of Nadra.

She tapped her lip, cycling through Elennish and English.

Tear in both languages could mean a rip or it could mean water droplets from the eyes. She tapped the page with her fingertip, mentally noting similarities between Elennish and English she'd not thought of before. Probably because it wasn't modern-day, but rather old English. For the scrolls, which tear did the scribe mean? She read further and her excitement turned to horror.

There, written in neatly formed words, was the recipe for how she and Rhoane would become gods. They weren't mentioned by name, but by the Eirielle and the Atharrach. In each instance of Atharrach, the word was scratched out and Zakael's name was written in a different hand than the rest of the page. Penned in the margins, in yet another elaborate scrawl, was an addendum to the original recipe. To supersede Aelinae's original gods, one additional item was required: the sacrifice of a still-beating heart. It was quite specific as to whose heart it should be—the Eirielle's.

Her fingers trembled as she handed the sheet to Rhoane.

"Remember those scrolls I brought back from Caer Idris? This is the missing part." The papers she'd stolen from her father's castle recounted the Great War, heavily favoring Rykoto and Kaldaar. One page also mentioned the blood and the blade, but ended before the reference to the tear of Nadra, and certainly had no mention of her sacrifice. A worm of despair wriggled into her thoughts—had her father written these words? Did he care so little for her that he would've sacrificed her to elevate himself? The answer, of course, was yes. And now her brother had taken up the mantle.

Rhoane read in silence, his brows furrowing and jaw tensing. "What does this mean?"

"If I had to guess, I'd say Zakael wants to use me to kill the other gods—including Nadra and Ohlin. Adesh was a practice run." She winced at the memory of his broken chest and the red lump of his heart growing cold on the altar. "Or what if he wasn't? What if Zakael was trying to bring Kaldaar forth to kill him while he's still weak?"

"You cannot be serious. Zakael is not powerful enough to strike down a god, even one who is not yet fully recovered."

"He's a narcissist, Rhoane. He had three victims to offer, all of them vile. That's like catnip to Kaldaar, but Zakael didn't count on our arrival. We interrupted him." She tapped the pages. "Otherwise, I don't think he would've had these with him."

"We must find the seals and return to Aelinae with haste. Whatever Zakael planned at the ruins, he is now aligned with Kaldaar. We cannot risk them releasing Rykoto as well. One despot god roaming Aelinae unchecked is enough to cause chaos and ruin. Two will destroy our world."

She leaned back and blew out a long breath. He was right, but how the hell were they to find the seals? "Where to first?"

"Cilachaem." He rolled the scrolls into a tight cylinder and tied a leather strap to hold them closed. "You made a promise to Rori."

Yes, she had. Seeing the world they may or may not have created filled her with anxious excitement. A thrum of discord rumbled beneath her emotions. Their arrival at Mallaqai's ruins was too perfectly timed to disrupt Zakael's ceremony. Who on Aelinae would've known he was there? And were she and Rhoane being manipulated? She swallowed the dregs of her cold tea with a cringe. The answer to both questions didn't sit well in her heart. Myrddin very well could have known what Zakael was doing, which meant she and Rhoane had walked into a trap. But did Myrddin get the outcome he wished for? He was cloaked in layers upon layers of deception, thin as gossamer, yet strong as wool. If he was involved with Kaldaar, she would see through his veils soon enough.

CHAPTER EIGHT

Myrddin bent over Lliandra's fevered brow and whispered words of endearment to comfort the ailing empress. Ever since their trip to the Summerlands, she had not been well. Myrddin suspected it had something to do with the night she disappeared, but she would not speak of it, even though at the time, he smelled Zakael's lust on her. On the two occasions Myrddin brought it up, Lliandra had shouted and stormed through her rooms, destroying precious objects that were not hers, abusing servants who she did not pay.

The objects and subjects belonged to the Summerlands queen and king, but Lliandra didn't care about them or anything except her own schemes. How foolish he'd been. How clearly he saw it all now.

For near on four hundred seasons, he'd loved Lliandra. Ever since the first time he saw her as a young woman, ripe with promise of being a benevolent leader. She had been as merry and charming as her sister Gwyneira, but it was Lliandra who he'd been ordered to seduce. Although, truth be told, he gladly would've ruined them both. Possibly even at the same time. But no, he'd been denied the one and foolhardy enough to fall in love with the other. Against his Master's wishes.

A change in the air alerted him to a familiar presence and he withdrew from his love with a gentle kiss to her brow. When he turned, the spectral form of his greatest foe and fiercest friend stood before him.

"It is done, then?" Myrddin motioned them to the balcony where he ensconced them in a cocoon of silence not even Kaldaar could penetrate. Five millennia of living had given him certain strengths his god was better off not knowing about—and Myrddin rather enjoyed keeping secrets.

They walked along the perimeter of Lliandra's vast suite of rooms physically present, but unseen by the passing servants. It had been too long since he'd been afforded a visit with Brandt and he hoped not to squander it.

"It is done. She has the papers and is at this moment offworld." Brandt studied his features, his ghostly lips tight. "Why, Myrddin? I trusted you. We all trusted you."

It was a question he'd been waiting a lifetime to answer.

"And now I hope to repay that trust. I know you have little reason to believe me, but hear an old man out, please." How many times had Brandt said the same to him when they'd argued over both significant and insignificant things? Brandt's death was a blow Myrddin never quite recovered from. In truth, he missed his oldest, dearest friend.

They entered the palace proper, still cloaked in shadow. Servants and courtiers milled about, but Myrddin's ShantiMari was too powerful for their eyes to comprehend. Eliahnna glanced up as if she sensed them, but her attention was riveted to something beyond Myrddin and Brandt. Despite his machinations, Eliahnna thrived and would one day become the ruler Aelinae needed. Not just Talaith, but the entire world would benefit from her calming influence. Taryn saw it in her before Myrddin ever had, a fact that continued to sting his pride.

Taryn was his greatest failure. And now, he believed she could be his savior.

Myrddin passed a serving maid he'd bedded two nights hence. She was once the favorite of Marissa, but did not mourn the crown princess's death. None of them did. She'd been gone less than a moonturn and the court behaved as if she'd never existed. Perhaps that was partly his fault. As the phantom, he easily overpowered their better judgement and was able to compel them to believe Marissa's lies. Those who fought strongest against his compulsion suffered greatly, but now he had no need to hurt the courtiers. Marissa's death had freed him in more ways than one.

He searched for young Hayden, forgetting the lord was still in the Summerlands with his bride. The wedding had been a triumph, no thanks to Kaldaar's meddling influence. After Taryn's success at the Stones, Myrddin had tried to keep Sabina safe from Kaldaar, but the god had found a way to circumvent his efforts. It was genius, really. Inhabit Sabina's true love, but instead of Hayden's seed infusing her womb, it would've been Kaldaar's.

The strength Taryn and Rhoane showed that night as they fought to free Hayden from Kaldaar's control was impressive. It was then Myrddin fully understood and believed in not just Taryn, but her betrothed as well. Kaldaar had punished him that night, more violently than ever before and in ways that didn't leave a mark on the mage's body. Myrddin hated and loved his god in equal measure. How many times had he envisioned the god's death? But he wasn't the one to fell Kaldaar. The god had seen to that. That's why he needed Taryn.

They floated into the gardens and Brandt lifted his face to the sunshine. Harvest would soon be upon them, but the sweetness of summer lingered. Brandt never faltered in his belief that Taryn would bring balance to Aelinae. But then, he never knew it was Myrddin who conspired against her.

"I have never told you the story of my childhood and if you'll indulge me now, I think you might find it an intriguing tale." Myrddin had never told anyone how he came to be—because no one knew who he truly was. He wasn't even sure himself, anymore.

"If you think to garner sympathy from me, put that idea to rest. I only helped you with Taryn to speed up her task. I have no doubt she would've discovered the portals on her own. But now that Kaldaar has returned, we have neither the luxury of time, nor the benefit of faith."

"Oh, but you are wrong, my friend. We have nothing but time. Soon, Taryn will discover this, I've no doubt. Now, about my tale. Listen without questions, if you can." Myrddin grinned at the offended expression on Brandt's face. "Oh come now, you know you can't sit through a speech without interrupting at least once. Remember how you would vex Lliandra to no end?"

"Which is why I was chosen to take Taryn away instead of you. The fool woman said she needed peace." Despite his words, humor laced his tone.

"You were the obvious choice, my friend. What did I know about raising a young lady? You'd already brought up Faelara— who better to raise the Eirielle? We can argue this all day, or I can tell you about my past."

In truth, Lliandra had begged Myrddin to raise Taryn, but Kaldaar forbade it. With Myrddin offworld, it would've upset the god's plans too much. Thus, Brandt was chosen. His death upon returning was unexpected and unfortunate, but in the end had served Myrddin's schemes.

The scenery changed from the palace gardens to an alley in a city that no longer existed. Rotting food and excrement littered the narrow passage. The smell slammed into his senses and Myrddin covered his nose with the cuff of his sleeve. Even though it was only a memory, the filth and horrors of that alley were as fresh as the day he last saw his childhood home.

"I was perhaps seven seasons old when Kaldaar found me. An

orphan, beggar, thief, sometime pimp, and part-time whore. When you're hungry enough, you'd fuck a vorlock for food. I suppose if he hadn't found me, I wouldn't have lived much beyond fifteen seasons. Winters were cold in this miserable place, much colder than in Talaith." Myrddin scratched his chin, trying to recall exactly where the city had been. It was lost in the Great War, as were so many other small towns and villages. North near Helben and close to the frozen wastelands. Yes, that's where the city had been. Farther north than even Caer Idris.

"Are you saying Kaldaar made a living child into a Shadow Assassin?" Brandt surveyed the alley, disgust clear on his face.

"I wish he'd only made me an assassin. Then I wouldn't have felt or cared or remembered. But I did. I have. I do." The scene changed to Gaarehdahl, Kaldaar's dark castle that rested on crags overlooking the Summer Seas. "Kaldaar took me on as an apprentice of sorts. He taught me how to read and write, how to murder and maim, and most importantly, how to manipulate those around me. I am not ashamed to admit, I was an excellent pupil."

In those heady days of discovery, he'd lapped up Kaldaar's teachings like the starved dog he was. Nothing was too savage for young Myrddin. No one penetrated the cold in his heart. He was an excellent weapon—the god had chosen well.

"I spent a thousand seasons with Kaldaar at Gaarendahl. In that time, I perfected the persona you see now. The humble mage, available to give counsel when asked. As the seasons passed, Kaldaar bestowed upon me greater responsibilities and with them, increased ShantiMari." He tugged on his beard. "Only once did I almost reveal how vast my powers are, and I was severely reprimanded by Kaldaar. Mind you, I lived in awe and fear of the god. To me, he was a father figure—a tyrant to be sure, but he cared for me in his own way and I never knew hunger."

"Were you there when he betrayed Daknys?" Fury sparked in

Brandt's eyes. "Did you turn your back on Rykoto when he assaulted his own daughter? Were you in part responsible for the Great War and the breaking of Aelinae?"

How could he explain to Brandt that it wasn't as easy as all of that? "Yes, I was there for all of it. Kaldaar made me watch as he and Rykoto raped Julieta. He even suggested I have a go, that my seed mixed with theirs would create an even more powerful child, but Rykoto wouldn't have it. Apparently, only the two gods were allowed to abuse his daughter, but not some quasi-mortal play-thing of Kaldaar's."

Myrddin saw it all as if it were happening right in front of them, and he winced against his own naivete. How foolish he'd been to think Julieta wanted what the gods had done to her. But that's what Kaldaar had told him. She wanted it, deserved it… craved it, even. Wasn't it an honor to bear the two gods' seed? What woman, human or immortal, would deny them?

It was depravity of the highest order and he'd believed his god because the truth would've been too much to bear. Julieta was innocent, but at the time, Myrddin's heart was too dark to believe anyone could be truly virtuous.

Brandt's ghost flitted outside the castle walls to hover over the sea. He could leave at any time, but he stayed. Curiosity was always Brandt's weakness.

"To what end? What did your complacency get you? Are you better off today than you were five thousand seasons ago? Have you fulfilled Kaldaar's wishes? Or are you still his agent? Is every-thing you speak a lie?" His agitation riled the waves, causing them to break upon the rocks with such force the foundations of Gaarendahl Castle shook. Even dead, Brandt was powerful, perhaps even more so than when he'd been alive.

Myrddin dropped the illusion to reveal the gardens at the Crystal Palace and calm settled around them. "Not everything I speak is a lie. Our friendship was—is—one of the few good things I've had in my life. Do I still do as Kaldaar commands?

That isn't as easy to answer. Have you ever tried to deny a god? I've done many things in my life that I'm not proud of, but just over a season ago, I finally had reason to hope." He twisted a treplar from a branch and bit into it. Juices dribbled down his chin and he wiped them with his sleeve. "Even taste is sweeter now. I lived five thousand seasons believing I was satiated, that my belly was full, but I wasn't living. Not truly. I wasn't hungry for food, but for power. I consumed more than my fill, but still I wasn't satisfied. Until now."

"Are you implying Taryn's return somehow made your life better? Because now you had a rabbit to snare?"

Myrddin chuckled at the idea. "You and I both know Taryn's not so easily caught. You raised her well, old friend. No, I'm saying when the pair of you returned, Lliandra sent me to kill Taryn. Of course, by the time we caught up to her, you were already dead and she was bound to Rhoane. To break their bonds, I would've had to kill them both. Normally, that wouldn't be a problem, but something in me shifted the moment I met her. I saw purity in her. Goodness. Kindness you instilled in her spilled out to touch those around her. She wasn't aware of it, nor do I think she is even now, but she's much more than the Eirielle."

Telling his truth, despite the ugliness of it, was freeing. Brandt might hate him forever more, but Myrddin felt lighter having removed the burden of his secret. He could never tell Taryn who and what he was, but Brandt could. Although, he doubted his friend would have the courage to confess they'd all been deceived by someone they trusted implicitly. Kaldaar had taught him well. Chaos was in his blood. Creating deception and disorder came as easily to him as pissing. The Telraicht Arts hadn't been formed by Kaldaar as most of the Brotherhood believed, but by Myrddin himself, with Kaldaar's blessing.

It was Myrddin who founded the first sects of believers. He taught them the ways of Telraicht-Noir ShantiMari. And it was

Myrddin who fed them his blood as sustenance when their powers threatened to incinerate them from the inside out.

It was also Myrddin who encouraged the Brotherhood to keep their practices secret. By staying in the shadows, others not of the Brotherhood formed opinions and spread rumors about the group, most of which were untrue, but served the purpose of creating discord and fear. The Brotherhood thrived on its reputation. Only recently, starting in the century before Taryn's return, but certainly even stronger since, the Brotherhood had shifted its priorities away from disarray toward a more organized sect, albeit, still twisted. Having seen what religion did on other worlds, Myrddin had encouraged the change. What better way to sow hatred in the hearts of millions than through fanatic belief?

Then Taryn had arrived and his own beliefs shifted.

"What now, Myrddin? She has the papers. She'll find the portals and other worlds. She'll return the seals to the temple, but all that will do is keep Rykoto imprisoned. That won't stop Kaldaar, or you, from destroying Aelinae."

And this was his final admission. His final truth.

"But it will. After the Great War, when the gods banished Kaldaar, he was weakened, and as such, his control over me lessened. I was able to form opinions without fear of reprisal. I could love another without being whipped to the bone. I wasn't free, not by any measure, but I was able to live just a little of my own life, albeit still tethered to Kaldaar by the smallest of threads." Myrddin lifted his face to the sun and listened to the sweet chirp of birdsong. He'd done many horrific things in his long life. It was time to rest.

Taryn would soon discover exactly how far his schemes reached. Just as she'd put wards on the remaining seals in the temple, he'd placed similar wards on the seals he'd hidden offworld. She'd know when she was close to finding one, but she'd suffer for it. A point he now wished he could undo, but he had to let the future unfold as it would. No more manipulating.

No more mayhem. When she found all the seals and returned them to the temple, she would unlock the key to everything: Aelinae's balance, her own immortality, how to defeat the gods—it was all there, in the seals. She and Rhoane only needed to decipher the code.

"It's time, my friend, for a new Aelinae. Kaldaar is going to fight me at every turn, but Taryn is my salvation. Through her, I can finally be at peace."

Brandt stared at him, a mixture of fury and concern in his aged features. Wisps of white hair tangled with the breeze and Myrddin half expected him to pull a pipe from his robes.

"You wish to die? And you're going to use Taryn to do it? No. I won't have it. You go too far, Myrddin." He crossed his arms with a huff.

It was just like old times. How he'd missed his friend.

"I have spent millennia disrupting peaceful kingdoms. I'm tired. I don't have regret for my deeds, not much at least, but I can at last see that what I've done can't continue. Despite it all, Taryn thrives. You saw what she did to the Shadow Assassin, how she turned a heartless, lifeless killing machine into something almost human. I raised him to slaughter her and, in the end, he couldn't do it. I see now why he resisted. She's better than us. Well, better than me, and certainly Lliandra, but you—you are just as pure as she. And now you hate me, I'm sure."

Brandt's ghost vibrated with suppressed rage that Myrddin felt as if it were the lash of Kaldaar's whip.

"You stole Gavyn to raise as your Shadow Assassin? A stillborn baby and Taryn's twin, you took to use as a weapon against her? And Cashiel? Was he also your idea?"

Myrddin nodded, shame washing over him in a deluge he deserved, but was surprised by all the same. It was the first time in as long as he could remember that he felt anything close to contempt for his own actions. But hearing the words from his closest friend, hearing the pain in the dead man's voice, the full force of what he'd done crashed around him.

"They were all my doing. I told you, Kaldaar chose an excellent pupil. I became myopic in my quest. I don't crave immortality like Valterys and his son, nor do I claim to desire sitting at the side of gods like Marissa, but I became addicted to my own power. Kings who believed themselves above me soon learned how wrong they were. I fed them to the runyon tree at Caer Idris, and was rewarded with even greater abilities. I was untouchable."

"Until Taryn."

"I was never able to gain her full trust, although I could see the desire was there, but she hesitated. Please let her know she wasn't wrong to question my motives."

"Tell her yourself. You've used me for the last time." Brandt turned his back to him and drifted to the low wall that kept people from falling down the steep cliff. "Is she in danger?"

Myrddin stood beside his friend and gazed out over the tranquil sea. Salt air stung his senses. "No more so than usual. She has to do this on her own, Brandt. No interference from you, or me." He studied the ghost's face, noting the very living-like emotions that shone from his eyes. "This is her final test, my friend. Hers and Rhoane's. You know what they are to become, and before you get cranky with me more than you already are, this was not my doing. True," he held a hand to stop Brandt's questions, "I asked you to show them the papers, but it was Nadra who bade me to coax the pair offworld sooner rather than later. I don't know what your goddess has planned, but I'm glad they aren't here at the moment."

"Is there anyone she can trust? Nadra? Why?" A movement above their heads drew their attention and Brandt chuckled. "Hello, my friends." He waved to two faces peering at them from between thick leaves. "I have business elsewhere, it would seem." Brandt faced him and said, "You have neither my forgiveness, my friendship, nor my trust, Alswyth Myrddin, but should you do right by Taryn, you can reclaim all three."

A pop of air and he was gone. Myrddin let his bubble disintegrate and glared at the trees. "What are you two miscreants doing up there?"

"Spying, what else?" Ebus slipped from the branch to land at Myrddin's feet with Gian joining him a moment later. "Heated discussion you were having."

A tremor of dread raced down his spine. "You saw us? Could you also hear what we said?"

"Hear you? No." Ebus's grin didn't set Myrddin at ease.

They shouldn't have been able to see past his ShantiMari shield.

A servant rushed toward them and in a heartbeat, both Gian and Ebus disappeared. Probably back to the branches where they could eavesdrop on unsuspecting courtiers. Taryn had chosen her spies well.

"Your Excellence." The servant bowed and wheezed to catch his breath. "There's an Ullan at the front gate. Claims to be a prince and is seeking shelter."

Another Ullan prince? Wasn't Loghan enough of a bother?

"Very well, I'm on my way." Myrddin strode from the gardens, his conversation with Brandt already drifting to memory.

He keenly felt the stares of the two spies on his retreating back and an unwelcome shiver of panic tangled his thoughts. Gian, the woodland faerie whose tongue had been cut out by Valterys, and who had a life debt with Taryn, could read lips.

CHAPTER NINE

Even though she'd been in the little office near the reception desk at the museum many times before, Taryn had never been there without Brandt and the sting of grief pierced her heart. A young girl of perhaps six or seven sat on a chair, with her legs swinging beneath her. She didn't look bothered, but Taryn sensed something inside the girl—curiosity and also confusion.

She tilted her head and pulled on a long black curl that bounced into a tight ringlet when released. Her deep-brown eyes tracked Taryn's movements as she paced the gorgeously appointed office.

Why were they taking so long? The museum staff knew who she was, and she had her ID card, so why the delay? She'd even dressed in chic black slacks and a button-down blouse beneath a smart trench coat. Instead of sneakers, she wore leather ankle boots that pinched her toes. Maybe she'd gone too far with the outfit and they didn't recognize her. She picked at a cuticle before flexing her fingers to stop the bad habit.

"Are you a princess?" The little girl scrunched her face.

Taryn stopped her pacing. The question and the little girl's curiosity intrigued her.

"I'm much more than a princess, but you don't have a name for it here on Earth." In the small space, she could smell the girl's fruity bath wash. A bright-pink bow nestled in her curls and a matching sweater covered her slender brown arms. Intelligence shone from her eyes, as well as awe.

"My mum says I can't be a princess because I'm a queen."

"And that you are." Taryn knelt and held out her hand. "I'm Taryn."

Her little hand slipped into Taryn's, and she felt a spark of ShantiMari. Tiny, untested, but there.

"My name's Samantha, but my friends call me Sam."

"It's nice to meet you, Samantha." Before they let go of their hands, Taryn sent a thread of her power to Sam's with a gentle request that it stay concealed until the girl was old enough to protect herself. The altercation on the bridge was too fresh in her mind and the idea that someone would hunt Samantha for her ShantiMari filled Taryn with horror.

She settled herself on the seat opposite Sam, mentally preparing for the questions she saw in the girl's intent gaze.

"My mum got lost in the museum, so they're making me wait here until they find her."

"Does your mum often get lost?"

"Sometimes." Samantha looked at her sneaker-clad feet.

The door opened and a Black woman who was the older version of Sam burst into the room. A museum security guard held the door open as he hovered in the hall.

"Darling. There you are. I was so worried." She enfolded her daughter in a hug, and Taryn smiled at the pair.

The woman's fear, anxiety, worry, and relief swept over Taryn like a steam train at full speed. She gripped the chair to steady her own rapidly beating heart. Superseding all other emotions, Taryn felt the woman's love. Fierce, ferocious, and infinite.

Samantha rolled her eyes behind her mother's back and grinned at Taryn. They stood to go, with the woman thanking

Taryn for watching after her daughter. At the door, Samantha waved goodbye and Taryn raised a hand in farewell. She rested her hand on her abdomen and breathed deep for several moments to regain her equilibrium.

That brief moment shared between Samantha and her mum was what a mother's love should be. What Taryn would never know. She swallowed the lump of self-pity and reminded herself that she had people who loved her just as deeply, and who she loved equally so. Yet the scar was there, and always would be—Lliandra had never, and would never, love her.

"Ms. Endion?"

An attractive woman about Taryn's age called from the opposite side of the office and it took her a moment to realize she meant her. For all of her life on Earth, she'd been Taryn Endion, using Brandt's surname as her own because she believed he was her grandfather. Now, the name chafed like sandpaper against her brain. Not out of disrespect to Brandt, never that. Even though he wasn't her blood relative, he was closer to family than any of her actual blood relatives. He'd raised her as his own and she would always love him.

The surname belonged to another Taryn. The girl who grew up on Earth without knowing who she was or the power she could wield. That innocent creature who'd always believed she was a little different, but loved her simple life. On Aelinae, she had numerous names bestowed upon her, and now, she didn't know which was her true self.

She stood and greeted the woman with a warm smile. "Thank you for seeing me."

"When I heard about Brandt, I..." She wiped her eyes and Taryn felt the sting of tears. "I'm so sorry for your loss. He was well respected in our community."

"Thank you." She'd known the condolences would be part of her visit, but nothing could prepare her for heartache.

Darennsai? Rhoane's thought brushed hers.

I'm fine. They miss Brandt. Nothing more needed to be said.

I am here if you need me.

They'd decided Rhoane would accompany Taryn to the museum and wander the vast space while she searched for the seal. Kaida remained at the flat—most likely sprawled on the sofa and having a well-deserved rest day.

The woman held open a door and ushered Taryn inside. "What is it we're searching for?"

She'd been dreading the question and had yet to form a coherent request. "A seal. Metal unknown, origins unknown, about this size." Taryn made a circle on her palm.

She took a seat at one of the workstations and pulled a pencil and pad of paper toward her. On it, she drew what she could remember of the seal, aware that what might've been revealed to whomever found it could be different from what she saw. After all, Rhoane hadn't seen the words that scrolled around the outside of the disc, but he did see other inscriptions.

The woman, who had yet to introduce herself, sat beside her and peered over her shoulder at the drawing. When Taryn finished, she scanned it and clicked several keys on her keyboard. Brandt had eschewed anything too modern, including phones and computers, but Taryn had insisted they at least have phones on them to communicate. As for computers, she knew just enough to be dangerous.

Her helper sighed and leaned back, giving Taryn a chance to sneak a look at her name badge. A spiral of guilt spun through her veins. Lois Tranton. She'd met the woman on numerous occasions and should've recognized her. An image of Lois with long ginger hair and laughing with Brandt whipped through her brain.

"You cut your hair. I like it."

Lois beamed. "Thank you." Her gaze flicked to a young man two desks over and her cheeks flushed.

The man, however, was clueless. Poor Lois. She'd have to be persistent to get noticed.

"Let's try another search. Can you give me any keywords at all?"

They tested several iterations of keywords, coming up empty each time. Taryn leaned back and gazed at the glass cabinets where bits of pottery and statuary were stored. When Rhoane found the seal in her backpack, it had been in a velvet pouch. She searched her memory for what else she could remember. It had been almost a year since she'd hidden it at Paderau.

"Limit the search parameters to the fifth or sixth century."

When Lois finished typing, a window popped up with a picture of the pale-blue pouch and a silver disk. No inscriptions could be seen, nor did it look particularly interesting, but Taryn's heart hammered beneath her ribs.

"It was found near Glastonbury Abbey." Lois tracked a finger beneath the words as she read them quietly. "It says the velvet bag and metal disk were discovered by an amateur metal detectorist. It's now privately owned."

Taryn picked at a nail. The pouch hadn't looked as though it had been buried for fifteen hundred years. "When was it found?"

She returned to the screen and scrunched her nose as she clicked through a few more screens. "Twenty years ago. The hobbyist sold the piece to a relics dealer called SIRE. Carbon dating was done here, although no offer was made to purchase for our collection. That's not unheard of. A blank silver piece without provenance isn't much of a draw. Maybe if it had been part of a hoard, but this was found on its own, sealed in a metal casket. That, too was sold to SIRE." Lois turned to her. "I'm sorry. That's all I can find."

"You've been a tremendous help. Thank you." Taryn flicked a glance to the young man who was absorbed in his work. "Good luck with that."

Lois laughed as she rose from her chair. "Girl, I've been trying for two years. You know what they say—never give up, never surrender."

As they passed his desk, Taryn used her ShantiMari to upset a stack of papers. Both Lois and the man bent to pick them up and when their hands met, Taryn snapped her power across his skin—not a vicious sting, just a little jolt to grab his attention. His eyes widened and he fumbled the pages, then laughed, which made Lois laugh.

"I'll show myself out." Taryn left the office, grinning like a fool. It was a simple thing, but she was a sappy romantic at heart.

What little information Lois could provide wasn't much help, but it was a place to start. At least she had a time frame to give Nikala, if she ever returned to the office. They'd checked again on the way to the museum, but she hadn't been in yet that morning.

Taryn found Rhoane standing at the end of a long gallery, staring at a tiled mosaic. He turned at her approach, brows furrowed and lips tight. She knew that face—knew it meant something had upset him.

"Look at this." He indicated the mosaic, and she peered at the colorful tiles.

Parts were missing, but not so much it distracted from the playfulness of the design. Water creatures frolicked in cerulean seas while mermaids sunned themselves on nearby rocks. Something about the symmetry, or perhaps the colors, nagged at her memory.

"This looks familiar." She tilted her head and squinted to better focus. "But at the same time, disturbingly different. Weird."

Rhoane pointed to a pair of serpent-looking creatures and a chill went through her veins.

"Xianqin." She barely breathed the word. "It looks just like her, but who is the other?"

"Taryn, there is a remarkably similar mural in the Summerlands palace."

She peered harder at the mosaic. "I don't remember seeing it.

Or this one, actually, even though I walked every inch of this museum several times when I lived here."

He scratched his chin and shook his head. "Perhaps there is a clue in the design. Do you have a recording device?"

"A what?"

He pointed to a group of schoolgirls taking pictures with their phones.

"No, I don't have one of those. I mean, I do, it's at the flat, but it's probably dead." Not to mention it couldn't take photos, but that was beyond Rhoane's understanding.

He glanced up and down the corridor twice before twisting his wrist in a circular movement she'd never seen him do before. His ShantiMari curled along her skin, warming in its embrace. A moment later, he clasped his fist closed and spoke several words in ancient Eleri.

"What are you doing?"

His half smile was full of mischief. "Your modern contraptions are interesting, but the Eleri have their own way of capturing images and moments."

A flash of memory—of when she'd first arrived at the Weirren and King Stephan had challenged her right to claim the title of Darennsai, Myrddin had used a large crystal marble to display the vorlock fight for everyone in the room to see.

"Do you need a looking glass to display the image? Remember how Myrddin showed the Eleri the vorlock battle with one?"

"I do recall that, yes. But no, Eleri do not need such simple tools." Rhoane took her elbow and led them from the gallery. "Myrddin gave you one such looking glass, did he not?"

"For my birthing day, just after I'd arrived in Aelinae. And before you ask, I figured out pretty quickly that he might be spying on me with it."

Rhoane chuckled, low and sultry. "You must vex him endlessly." His hand slipped down her arm and clasped her hand. "I still do not know what to make of him. I have known Myrddin all of my life, but can no longer deny he might at best, be playing both sides, and at worst, is an agent of Kaldaar's. It behooves us to behave as if he is the latter."

"I was thinking the same thing." She told him of the search and where the seal was discovered. "Glastonbury isn't that far from here if you think we should investigate, but I'd really like to get to the other worlds. Every day we're away is one closer to Rykoto's release."

"Agreed. Considering what he and Kaldaar did to break Aelinae the first time around, I shudder to imagine what they are planning for Aelinae now." Rhoane held the door for her, looking every inch a gentleman in his long tweed coat. Except for his slightly tipped ears and long hair, he might've fit in well in the modern era. Instead, he was a man out of time.

She skidded to a stop on the wet pavement. A man out of time. Or a man who could *manipulate* time.

"How many Eleri know how to manipulate time?"

Rhoane quickly glanced at those around them as if they might overhear. He held her elbow and led her down the steps. "Not many. I only know of myself and Kaleigh—she is the one who taught me—but I am sure there are more. I would guess less than a handful. Knowledge like that is powerful."

"Where did Kaleigh learn this secret power?"

"I would assume at the temple. Why?"

A dangerous idea formed in her thoughts—one she hoped wasn't true.

"What if Myrddin knows not only how to travel between worlds, but through time?" Her voice trembled with the immensity of what she asked. "Myrddin is the Welsh name for Merlin. Over fifteen hundred years ago, there was a glorious kingdom called Camelot. Merlin was a wise and powerful wizard who had the ear of the king. Sound familiar?"

"What happened to the kingdom?"

"It devolved into chaos. I would be willing to bet Merlin had a lot to do with that. Squabbling over the throne, affairs between the queen and her knight…it can't be a coincidence the seal was found close to where Camelot is believed to have been."

"I am not overly fond of coincidences. What do you think this means?"

She stopped beneath a tree and held his face between her hands. "It means you need to teach me how to manipulate time. If Myrddin can do it, we can too. But first, we need to address the gentleman in black who's been following us the entire morning."

Rhoane wrapped his arms around her back and pulled her close, his gaze just over her right shoulder. "He was sent by your friend Donyatella. I do not believe he wishes us harm, but I have been watching him all the same. There is also a woman across the street who has the same wild look as the man on the bridge."

She tilted her head to kiss him and caught a brief glimpse of the woman he meant. Standing apart from the crowd, she did indeed have the look of fanaticism about her.

Their kiss was gentle and sweet and filled with resignation. If her London, the one place she thought they'd be safe, was filled with constant threats, what the bloody hell could they expect on other worlds?

CHAPTER TEN

Gentle rain made for an uncomfortable walk to the station where they caught what Taryn called a Tube, but Rhoane thought looked more like a mechanical nightmare. It was a horseless carriage that sped through tunnels at dizzying speeds. His first experience of the abomination hadn't been pleasant, and now that they had two people following them, it would be even less so.

He sensed Taryn's apprehension and held her hand if only to let her know he was near, that she was not alone. This London, as she called it, was not of her memories. Her confusion and anger roiled over him in sporadic waves, each time surprising him in their intensity. She hid it well, but his betrothed was afraid of this London. Creatures roamed the streets she didn't recognize and that made her doubt her entire childhood.

If only he could ease her mind—tell her that Brandt had warded her for good reason. If these creatures had been a part of her life growing up, she would've known about ShantiMari and perhaps even Aelinae. Brandt had done well to keep her ignorant of both, even if she couldn't see the wisdom of her grandfather's choices.

As they approached the station, he glanced over his shoulder and met the steely gaze of the man dressed all in black, like Silar had been the night before. Perhaps it was a uniform these modern Stone Guardians wore. Unlike Silar, this chap had dark hair and a beard. What little his ancestors could share about the guardians wasn't enough to determine whether they were friend or foe.

He patted his side where his sword should've been and swore beneath his breath. Taryn had wanted to wear them, but cloaked in shadows. He'd argued that even cloaked, they were still physically present and would be more of a hindrance on the crowded streets. Now, he wished he'd listened to his beloved.

The stench of body odor, burnt onions, and grease—scents he associated with the large city—seared his nostrils and he gagged against it. The lights and sound didn't bother him so much as the smells. With such a huge crush of people it was inevitable, and even Talaith had areas where filth was taken for granted, but not on this scale. His delicate Eleri senses were on constant alert, which left him ragged.

Taryn glanced over her shoulder and Rhoane followed suit. The guardian kept a respectable distance, his attention drawn to the woman, and then sweeping back to Taryn and Rhoane. The pair entered the station seconds apart, yet the woman didn't seem to realize the black-clad gent was following them as well. Her attention was rooted to Rhoane. A little too intensely for his comfort. The fellow on the bridge the previous evening had unnerved him and left Taryn shaken. He'd rather avoid any further interactions with the fanatical magic hunters. Silar had called them scyvers, not a term Rhoane had ever heard, but one that sent rivulets of dread circling down his spine.

Noise from hundreds of people clamoring in their rush to make their trains made him wince. He didn't have the problem of blocking out vast quantities of ShantiMari here like he did on Aelinae, but the sheer volume of chatter was enough to drive him mad. At the little turnstile, they waited their turn and Rhoane caught the woman creeping closer to his right. He nudged Taryn to an empty entryway and she flicked a glance at the woman.

"Fuck." She tugged his coat and pulled him through the turnstile with her.

They hurried through the cacophonous passageways and jogged down the stairs, surreptitiously covering their ears. The train screeched as it slowed, piercing more than just his sensitive hearing. It scrambled his thoughts and made him dizzy. If he never had to be near one of the beasts again, it would be too soon.

Taryn scanned the crowd as they entered the carriage, her lips pinched, eyes narrowed. Rhoane saw them, too. The woman entered the carriage at one end and the guardian at the opposite end, with Taryn and Rhoane in the middle of the pair.

"What shall we do?" He flexed his hands and cracked his neck.

"Don't use your ShantiMari. Keep it locked tight." Taryn's head swiveled left to right, her eyes wide and full of caution.

The woman advanced, slow and lethal. Rhoane pulled Taryn tighter against him and turned her until the carriage door was at her back. She needed no protecting, and often claimed she wasn't a damsel in distress, but she was his love and he'd make damn sure no harm came to her.

With his back to the others, he couldn't see how close they were, but he felt them. Felt the crazed need of the woman and the fierce strength of the man. A waft of masculine scent and, oddly, rock stung his nose. A moment later, the black-clad chap brushed against his shoulder.

"Do not engage. Let me handle this." His rough voice was barely audible, but Rhoane heard and nodded his understanding.

Taryn's gaze bounced from the woman to the man, and Rhoane positioned himself to better see. The woman slithered from one pole to another, her too-wide smile showing her teeth.

Unnatural light shone from her eyes and people moved out of the way to let her pass.

The guardian blocked her path several paces from where Taryn and Rhoane stood. He felt the anxiety and rage she directed at the guardian as if it were meant for him. Taryn winced as well. She motioned for them to move to the far end of the carriage, away from the crazed woman. The train shook as they sped around a curve, jostling the guardian. The woman took advantage of the moment and slipped past him, nudging him to the side as she did. He righted himself and reached out, but she was too quick. In a heartbeat, she was face-to-face with Rhoane.

Despite the rapid beating of his heart, he kept his face placid, eyes narrowed, nostrils flared. The amount of effort it took to not react was almost as great as a physical altercation. The woman bent toward his chest and inhaled deeply as her face traveled from his torso to his chin.

The guardian hovered behind her, a menacing presence she either ignored or didn't see.

"What do you want?" Taryn broke the do not engage rule.

"I want 'im." The woman cocked her head and shuddered. Her accent was different than Taryn's. Harsher, more guttural.

"Well, you can't have him."

The woman turned to Taryn and hissed. "An' you'll stop me?"

Lights flickered with Taryn's rage, and she shifted as if to position herself between the woman and Rhoane, but he tugged her behind him. They were on a speeding demon; none of them could afford an accident in the dark tunnels. The woman sneered and the guardian reached for her, but she moved with lightning speed, gripping Rhoane's hand in hers and clamping her teeth into his skin.

Roaring pain shot from the torn skin to his mind and he saw her desperation, her need, her hunger in that split second. He snatched his hand from her grip at the same time the guardian grabbed the woman by her shoulders and jerked her away from Rhoane.

The pain intensified, a throbbing that started at her bite and wound its way up his arm toward his chest. Breathing came in labored gasps, but he couldn't tear his gaze away from the woman's tormented face. The agony of being separated from him—from his ShantiMari—seeped from her crumpled expression.

Taryn wrapped her arms around him and in a blink, they no longer rocked in the carriage, but stood on the platform of a station. He gulped in the putrid stench of the station, happy he could breathe normally once again, but disgusted by the taste that lingered in his mouth. Humans, with all of their technology and forward thinking, were a dirty lot.

Taryn wavered, and Rhoane gripped her as tightly as she'd held him before she transported them off the train. Her eyes rolled up, leaving only the whites visible.

"Mi carae, what happened?"

Her head lolled forward and she shook her head slowly. "I don't know. I'm just…drained. Like, using that much ShantiMari wiped me out, but why? I've never felt this before." She slumped into his arms and he half carried, half dragged her to the floating steps she called an escalator.

As they walked, heads turned in their direction—men and women suddenly took an interest in them—and Rhoane's belly filled with dread. If these were scyvers, he couldn't fight them all, not with Taryn weakened as she was.

This had never happened to her before—at least, not on Aelinae. She'd once jumped from Sitari to Ulla and back, on the return trip bringing Loghan with her. This quick transport shouldn't have even winded her, but she struggled to keep her legs beneath her.

They reached the bottom of the floating stairs and half a dozen people trailed them, all of their faces morphing into the manic expressions of the woman on the train and the man on the bridge. These had to be scyvers.

Rhoane lifted Taryn into his arms and climbed the stairs, using the escalator's forward motion to help propel him faster. He dared not use his ShantiMari for fear that would bring more scyvers. The city appeared to be overrun with them, or perhaps they only congregated near the Tower. Either way, he had to get Taryn to her flat. There weren't any black-clad Stone Guardians to help this time. It was up to Rhoane.

At the top of the escalator, Taryn roused enough to walk beside him, her pace achingly slow.

"There are scyvers behind us. We must hurry." Rhoane tugged her forward and she quickened her pace, but it still wouldn't be fast enough to escape.

They reached the turnstiles and he lifted Taryn as he leapt over it with ease, ignoring the shouts that followed. She wrapped her hands around his neck and he pulled her close. With scyvers and security guards chasing him, Rhoane sprinted for the exit.

His heart beat in time to his churning legs. No one stood in his way or tried to stop him when he crossed the threshold of the station. A beggar to his left rose from where he sat and another across the street turned to glare at Rhoane. Taryn moaned against his chest, and he tightened his grip on her. Not being able to use his power was a liability, but Rhoane had other skills to draw from.

He could slow time, but would that draw even more scyvers to them? He could become a dragon and fly them to safety. Or he could keep running and hope his Eleri strength was greater than his pursuers.

Neither of the first two were viable options, which left him one choice—to run full-out. His lungs burned with each inhale of cold, wet air. The boots he wore slipped on the cobblestones and he skidded several paces, one hand outstretched to brace for a fall.

"I think I can run now," Taryn murmured, but her voice lacked vitality.

The sound of footsteps not far behind him drove him to dig deep and push harder. They couldn't have his Taryn. They couldn't have him, either.

Whatever those creatures were, they craved only one thing—ShantiMari. In the seconds the woman's teeth bore into his flesh, he saw the pain she'd endured, knew what she'd been before she was turned into the pitiful shell that she was now. And he saw the man who'd done the atrocities.

Why? How could someone be so heartless as to twist a living being into the cruel mockery of life that they were now? What purpose did it serve? Several names popped through his mind—Marissa, Kaldaar, Valterys, Zakael, and to some degree Lliandra. They'd all done horrific things to elevate their stations.

A whip of guilt slashed at his heart. Even he had done terrible things in the name of progress. As much as he'd like to pardon himself of his crimes, they were still heinous, no matter the degree to which he thought the man responsible for the scyvers was even worse. He probably believed what he'd done was righteous, just as Rhoane had thought his missions were. Soon, he'd have to tell Taryn about his past. But first he had to survive.

He splashed through a puddle and swerved to miss one of the two-wheeled cycling contraptions that seemed to aim for him every time he stepped off the footpath into the street. They paid no heed to those walking and yelled profanities at the drivers of automobiles. Rhoane did not like the cyclers, not one bit. The one he avoided crashing into called after him, but Rhoane would not be deterred. He had the pub in his sights and he ran faster to reach what he hoped was safety.

Though, he couldn't be sure anywhere in the city would provide relief from the scyvers that hunted them.

When he rounded the corner to the pub, he was met with a

line of a dozen men, all dressed in black, wearing identical, fierce yet stony expressions.

"Get inside, hurry." Donyatella ushered him into the pub and directed him to the back, where she pointed to the booth. "Put her there."

Rhoane veered toward the stairs, knowing Taryn would be more comfortable in their flat, but the bald gentleman who'd killed the scyver on the bridge the night before blocked his path.

"Silar, get the grierbas," Dony told him, and he turned to storm up the stairs.

"I need to get Taryn upstairs."

"She will be safer here. Come, let me see to her." Dony beckoned Rhoane to the table, but he wavered.

He didn't know Donyatella, and wasn't sure she was to be trusted. Taryn's life was too precious to him to take risks.

"*Surtentse*, please. I know what ails her." Dony met his even gaze. "She used a great amount of ShantiMari, didn't she?"

He nodded and angled them toward the pub owner. "It was the only way to get us off the train where one of those scyvers attacked us." His hand dripped blood and Dony sucked in a breath.

"Get my kit." She motioned to a black-clad man he didn't recognize.

He disappeared behind a door, only to reemerge a few moments later with a metal box. Dony took it from him and opened it on the table. Inside, crystals of every shape and color sat beside tools he recognized from Flik's training yard. Small knives, awls, wicked-looking hooks, and tiny drills all rested on a bed of obsidian velvet.

"Come."

He shuffled to the table and made sure Taryn was comfortable. She roused herself and blinked at their surroundings. Her lovely skin, usually a tawny shade, was the color of ash and her eyes were veiled in a cloud of grey.

"Anje once told me there were repercussions for using Shanti-Mari, but I've never suffered ill effects using it on Aelinae." Taryn slurred. "Guess Earth doesn't like me as much. Heh." Her lips cricked up in a grin and her head lolled backward.

"It's not about liking you, *Darennsai*. It's the amount of ShantiMari you used. On Aelinae, it would've been a blip, but here, it was like setting off an atom bomb." Donyatella placed her hand on Taryn's forehead.

"Damn. I'm sorry, Dony."

She stroked Taryn's cheek, her face softened with affection. "Darling, you have nothing to apologize for. Wrap your wound." She handed him a strip of fabric, and he wound it around his bite.

She hummed softly while she mixed powder from several small pouches into a glass and added several drops of oil that reminded Rhoane of a plant that only grew in the Narthvier.

"What is in this? It smells like larell from the banks of Lan Gyllarelle." He picked up the vial and inspected the contents.

"You are not the only ones who walk between worlds. There is a robust trade from many worlds, if you know who to ask." A sly smile lifted her aged lips. "I know you don't trust me, First Son, but I love Taryn and will not see her harmed. By you, or my boys, or one of the poor souls out there."

Rhoane peered out the door to where Dony's boys blocked a small crowd from entering the pub. "What will become of them?"

"With any grace, they will die quickly. They are not so much alive anymore as subsisting. They hunger for your power. But their fate is not your concern." She stirred the contents of the glass and handed it to him. "Drink this. It will camouflage your ShantiMari and give you peace while you're here."

"What about Taryn?"

Dony pressed her thumbs over Taryn's closed lids and whispered an Eleri blessing before tipping a glass to her lips. Taryn moaned and tossed her head, but Dony shushed her and coaxed his love to swallow the mixture.

"With the help of the potion, she will recover now on her own. I will have Guillermo bring you food. Drink first, then sit, yes?"

He downed the concoction with a grimace. The sweetness of the Narthvier plant wasn't enough to hide the acrid burn of whatever else she'd put in it. His skin tingled and for a moment, his Glamour flared, then subsided. Almost immediately, the scyvers at the door settled and drifted off, some blinking as if they didn't know how they'd gotten there.

Dony slid from the booth and Rhoane took her place, cradling Taryn against him as he sang an Eleri lullaby his mother used to sing when he and his siblings were young. He pressed his lips to Taryn's forehead and hummed against her skin. He hadn't thought of his mother in a long time, but sitting there, on a foreign world far from Aelinae, he felt her presence.

Kaida bounded down the stairs and into the dining area, with Silar following close behind. He took up his position near the door and stood with arms crossed.

Rhoane's gaze went to the grierbas and he at once went cold and hot as he saw the image of his mother standing beside the great beast. He blinked and she was gone, but would swear she'd been real enough that if he reached out, he would've touched her creamy skin.

What did it mean? The last time he saw his mother's image had been when Queen Prateeni gave birth to her first son. He rested his cheek on Taryn's head and buried his free hand in Kaida's fur. It might've been his imagination. The past few days were fraught with dangers; it might've been nothing more than him missing his mother. Wishful thinking, perhaps. More likely, it meant trouble on Aelinae. And that meant Kaldaar.

CHAPTER ELEVEN

Naked bodies lined the wide hallway that led to the overlord's rooms. Kaldaar refused to call Zakael king and it humored him to see the petty tyrant sulk. Zakael was lucky he wasn't among Kaldaar's victims. Courtiers, nobles, servants, and thieves from the dungeons all jumbled together in a heap of death. Class and rank meant nothing to Kaldaar—their pain, their suffering, their ShantiMari: that's what he craved. He stole all of that and more from them before emptying their bodies of life.

Surveying the destruction left him wanting. It was not enough. It would never be enough. He needed the strength of a god to reclaim his full power. His wretched hand stuck out from his robe and he grimaced against the skin stretched thin over the bones. It was better now, but still not fleshed out enough to keep him from hiding. He jerked his sleeve over the disgusting thing and sighed.

Had he gotten it wrong by letting young Taryn and her paramour leave? Knowing he'd banished them to the same fate he suffered for millennia gave him no small amount of comfort, yet her parting message vexed him.

"You cannot defeat me. I know you," Taryn had told him in the ruins of Mallaqai, taunting him with her innocence. "I know your weakness. I also know you'll try to prevent me from returning, but I'll be back. Of that be assured." She'd sounded confident, powerful.

Kaldaar shook his head to rid himself of the image that sprang to his mind—of Taryn walking through the vortex, one hand clasping her paramour's, the other on that great beast. He should've killed them all. He should've left her sobbing for their deaths and begging him for her life. Yet he'd let her leave.

No, he'd banished her. Just as he'd been banished. She was just a stupid Aelan girl with a pretty sword. She was no god. She could not defeat him, Kaldaar, a god and father of the Telraicht Arts. He knew the deepest, most foul darkness—molded it, nurtured it, and embedded it into the hearts of his followers. He understood cruelty and how it could soothe a fractured mind and mend a broken heart. Hadn't he spent century upon century honing his ability to compel others to do his bidding? No other god was as adept as he at treachery. Hadn't he woven veils upon veils of deception?

Not even his brother Rykoto was as gifted at betrayal. Though he did try. What a clever boy to use Valterys as his puppet. Kaldaar quite admired his brother for turning the man from a loving husband to a brutal tyrant within the space of a few seasons. Through it all, Valterys had never known who set his ascension in motion, nor who advanced the coming of the Eirielle.

That honor belonged to Rhoane al Glennwoods ap Narthvier, lauded son of the Eleri King Stephan and Queen Aislinn: lover, betrayer, and bonded paramour of Taryn ap Galendrin. Kaldaar breathed in the stench of death and ran a grizzled fingertip over a bare bottom. He couldn't have predicted Rhoane would become an accomplished assassin, but when the lad killed Zakael's mother, that had been a moment worth celebrating.

Kaldaar had several scenarios planned for how he could rid Valterys of his bride, but they became unnecessary. Rhoane was so adept at his art, no one ever suspected foul play. Nor did anyone know that after her death ceremony, Valterys took Troyanna's body to Rykoto, where he fed the god the lifeless heart of his beloved.

His slippers made soft shushing sounds as he tread over the bodies to Zakael's rooms. His new servant had not yet recovered from the ordeal at the ruins, but it was time he and Cashiel awoke to their new lives. A living soldier and a new Shadow Assassin. It was too delicious. Kaldaar licked his lips in anticipation of what was to come.

A servant rushed out of Kaldaar's way, and he beckoned the boy forward. His furtive glances at the naked bodies and jangly knees were evidence of his nervousness, but the smell of piss almost made Kaldaar chuckle. Almost. He hated weakness of any kind. The lad trembled and his pants darkened with his defilement. It wasn't the first time someone had pissed themselves in his presence, nor would it be the last. Fear was a great motivator. He just wished it didn't stink so much.

"See that these are burned where the runyon tree once stood. Have food and drink brought to the lord's rooms immediately."

"Do you mean the king's rooms, sir? Or another lord?"

"Yes, the king, you stupid whoreson. Be off." He waved him away with a snort.

Insolent twit. Zakael was no more a king than he was a carlix. Oh, he might play at being king, but he knew nothing of ruling. At least his father had been a decent overlord. But Valterys was dead, killed at the hand of his own daughter.

How sweet that night had been—Kaldaar had watched it all through the eyes of his chosen son, Myrddin. He'd taken the form of a snowy owl and ghosted into the temple where Kaldaar was able to witness the near sacrifice of Princess Eliahnna and the fights that ensued to save her. Oh, how he'd reveled in watching

Taryn slaughter her father, but truly, when she murdered her half-sister, Kaldaar saw the opportunity he'd been waiting for.

Taryn pretended goodness, but Kaldaar knew her darkness, had sucked on it to sustain himself while he was banished to the edge of nothingness. He licked his lips and stared at the ceiling. What he would give to taste her once again. He'd had a sample the first time she passed through the void, but had been denied ever since. She'd grown stronger in her time on Aelinae, but was still vulnerable. When he regained all of his strength, then he'd bring her back and consume not just her heart, but her soul as well.

Taryn ap Galendrin would be his banquet and his alone. After he devoured her, he'd destroy the other gods. He needed nothing more than her blood and her blade. She was a means to an end. Once he alone stood on Dal Tara, then he would see about conquering other worlds. Aelinae was the beginning of his reign.

Several men came to take the bodies and Kaldaar sniffed at their stench. Everyday rustics knew nothing of the finer points of life. But they did give him an idea. His gaze swept the hallway. How many virgins would it take to make Rykoto strong enough to physically materialize? If he murdered his brother and stole his godliness, that might save him time.

He flexed his skeletal hand, excitement building. Yes, kill Rykoto—it was the only way. He'd planned to release his brother so they might fight side-by-side, but what would he need of his brother's physical presence if he possessed Rykoto's strength in addition to his own?

If the virgins didn't work, he could always sacrifice Zakael. Thus far, the wannabe king had shown himself to be more a liability than an asset. Too full of himself and his own plans, Zakael still believed he could outmaneuver the god. Kaldaar would give him one chance to prove himself worthy and if he failed, so be it.

He hurried through Zakael's suite to his bedchamber, where the young overlord dozed. Kaldaar gazed lovingly at him for only a moment before he became an amorphous mass. How sweet this young man's body was. It would be a pity to destroy it. Hopefully Zakael would not fail him. His essence wrapped around Zakael until he was moaning and whimpering. Such delightful sounds gave him almost as much pleasure as the actual fucking. Close, but not quite.

Kaldaar invaded Zakael's orifices and the wannabe king bucked against the assault. A moment later, he arched and writhed, his body twisting uncomfortably to suck in more of Kaldaar's essence. The god sighed and slipped even deeper into Zakael's body until there was little differentiation between one and the other.

He knew all of Zakael's wants, needs, desires, and was only too happy to fulfill every last one. Zakael's depravity fed Kaldaar. His anger slaked the god's thirst. And his body gave Kaldaar the solidity he was denied.

Zakael cried out and spilled his seed into the bed linens before slumping into the soft cushions and moaning like a wounded sheep.

The fucking had been too quick to give him any real pleasure and Kaldaar withdrew from his lover to became as solid as he could. With forced gentleness, he whispered, "You will serve me well, my son."

"Yes, Master." Zakael turned his face away from Kaldaar and curled into himself.

The last thing he needed was a sulky brat, but he sat on the bed and calmly guided Zakael to look at him. "Why does this upset you? Do I not show you the kind of love you crave? Do I not fuck you spectacularly? Shall we invite others into our play?" Just the idea of it made Kaldaar's body energized.

"You have been most excellent to me, my lord." Zakael's gaze went to the corner where Cashiel's wounded body lay slumped in a chair. "I miss my lover, is all."

It was a lie. They all lied. Eventually they all died, too.

"I am in your thoughts, young king. I know your sorrow has nothing to do with Cashiel, but rather with your half-sister. You are conflicted because she left you alive when she had a chance to kill you. After all the abuse you caused her, she showed mercy and you are unsure how to process that."

Zakael nodded miserably. "And now that she is gone, I will never have my chance."

"Your chance to what, my son?" He already knew the answer, but wanted to hear it from Zakael's lips.

"To possess her. To own her so completely she submits to me willingly."

"Yes, you wish to have with her what I have with you. I understand that desire. But I cannot allow it. Taryn ap Galendrin is banished from Aelinae and will never return. You are best to forget her and show only me the love you would've given her."

Zakael sat up and leaned against the headboard with several cushions supporting him. The bedsheets pooled at his waist, leaving his chest exposed. Kaldaar reached a bony finger to his breastbone and Zakael flinched from his touch. Kaldaar's predatory smile stretched his lips as he snaked his fingertip down Zakael's torso to beneath the sheets. The king pressed backward, but there was no escape from the god. He stroked the metal ring Zakael wore around his cock, running his finger along the smooth curves before he cruelly gripped his cock and chuckled. Despite his protests, Zakael's shaft stiffened admirably.

"This is for your pleasure, yes?" Kaldaar tapped the cock ring and Zakael nodded. "Take it off. You only have pleasure when I allow it."

"But, I can't. Not when I'm enlarged—it'll cause intense pain and possibly damage."

"So?" Kaldaar lifted an eyebrow. "I thought you liked pain.

Or is it you only like inflicting pain upon others and have no tolerance for it yourself?"

Zakael swallowed hard and ground his teeth together. "Very well, my lord." He sucked on two fingers before slipping them beneath the metal ring.

Agony crossed his features and deep blue veins protruded on his forehead standing out against his reddened face. It only made him more beautiful, this suffering.

His grunts were music to Kaldaar's ears. Watching him bravely endure the pain was too delightful. The petty tyrant deserved the torment he inflicted upon himself, but Zakael didn't see it that way. Pity for him. His muttered curses only fueled Kaldaar's desire to punish the brat. By the time he finally slipped the ring off his cock, tears streamed down Zakael's face. Kaldaar leaned forward to lick them off, grinning when Zakael whimpered against his touch.

Breaking him would be lovely. Too much pride had caused Valterys's fall, and Kaldaar would be damned—literally—if he'd allow the same shallowness to run amok in his pet.

"Shall we play with our Shadow Assassin? We'll heal him just as the Ullans would." He pinched the tip of Zakael's grotesquely purplish cock. "We will revive him and then you will go to the far lands and secure me warriors. The same as you procured for Amdi's arenas will now be mine. Oh, don't look at me with those doe eyes. I know all about your secret army and the tests you devised by selling certain creatures to the Ullan laird. You will continue your expeditions while I train the animals you've so cleverly hidden in the frozen north and swamps of the south."

He stroked Zakael's cock and gave it a vicious twist before dissolving into an inky blot of nothingness. Zakael gasped as Kaldaar entered him for the second time that morning. He sensed the man's reluctance, but also his excitement. His thoughts, the god noted, were now closed. How cute. That the wannabe king thought himself more powerful than Kaldaar was amusing, but would cost him dearly.

Zakael rose from the bed with Kaldaar's urging and went to where Cashiel lay slumped. He picked him up with ease and lay him on the soiled sheets. Methodically, and with as much care as a gifted Ullan healer, Kaldaar mended broken tissues and bones while Zakael fucked Cashiel. He knew nothing about the nuances of Ullan healing, but he understood how the body reacted to certain stimuli and though Cashiel existed somewhere between the living and the dead, his body responded admirably. With Zakael's brutal possession, Kaldaar was able to heal Cashiel so thoroughly there wasn't a mark on his body.

Now the fun could begin. His two playmates would soon learn who was their true Master.

Several bells later, the pair lay atop the mattress, spent, yet satiated. Cashiel stared at the ceiling while Zakael splayed naked on his belly. Thin slashes of crimson marred his back where Cashiel had whipped him a little too enthusiastically, yet Zakael's groans had been like a melody to Kaldaar's ears.

Cashiel had reveled in his role, transforming his anger gracefully into his punishments. He'd been the perfect specimen of dominance and submission. As he lay naked with an arm behind his head, Kaldaar drank in his beauty. Both of them were the epitome of manhood. And they were his. He hovered above his two most treasured chattels, confident they would serve him well. Cashiel would make an excellent Shadow Assassin. Zakael, too, had shown he could obey and be useful. He would live—for now. If he failed to bring his god an army, then his life was forfeit.

He drifted to the balcony and raised his face to the warmth of the sun. Now that he had his devoted vassals, he could turn his attention to Aelinae's other rulers. A quiet thrill vibrated through his bones. Amdi Agnar and the Lady of Light were easy enough to corrupt, but the Summerlands king and queen were proving more difficult. For a full moonturn, he'd tried to compel them, but they were protected by that bitch Julieta.

His essence vibrated with rage. Julieta, the fucking perfect daughter to Daknys and Rykoto. He'd ruined her, and yet she thrived. Even after he had convinced her own father to rape her, she didn't cower. Instead, she blocked herself from his endless searching, only to reemerge several seasons later, stronger, more confident, and more loving.

His wasted efforts to corrupt her burned eternally in his rage. No worry. That bitch could have the Summerlands. Kaldaar had control of the east and the west. The backwater island kingdom was nothing to him.

If only he believed his own lies.

CHAPTER TWELVE

Faelara stood with Baehlon at the back of the great hall, wincing with every flirtatious giggle that came from Lliandra's lips. Prince Gwainne didn't seem to mind and in fact appeared to encourage the lusty behavior with flirtations of his own. She caught his brother Loghan's eye and the two of them shared a small shrug. What could they do? The prince was old enough to choose his partners and it was widely known the empress had a bountiful appetite for pleasures of the flesh.

With the empress distracted by Prince Gwainne, Faelara snatched her opportunity to escape the palace. She tugged Baehlon's hand and slipped out a side door. She kept walking until they reached the far end of the palace and burst through a door into the sunshine. It was the first time in weeks she'd been out of Lliandra's immediate presence and she gulped in fresh air as if she were starved for oxygen.

In a way, she was. Ever since that day at the beach in Menurra when she'd nearly drowned, it was hard to breathe and she craved the taste of sea water. Something had happened to her that day, but she refused to confront the possibility of what it might've been. If she accepted the truth of what happened, then she had to accept that she'd died and been reborn. The question was, as what?

Without thought of where they went, she led them down the winding steps to the palace's private beach. When her slippered feet touched the sand, she glanced around in surprise. This was the last place she should've taken them. The orchards were far safer, but also had more courtiers hovering about. Here, they were completely alone. Not even Lliandra's guards came down here—well, not unless the princesses were present.

Baehlon walked beside her, his face twisted with worry. She'd tried to explain to him what had happened that morning in Menurra, but each time, it sounded too outlandish to be true. In the end, she'd simply said she was overheated from the heavy gown Lliandra had insisted all her ladies wear in the hot Summerlands. She doubted he believed her, but respected her enough not to insist she confess everything.

One day, though, they needed to find out the truth. Just, not today, or anytime too soon. She feared what their search might reveal.

They stood beneath a tree in the little cove where only a season past she'd spent many enjoyable days watching Taryn and the princesses frolic in the waves. Taryn had been newly returned to Aelinae, Kaldaar wasn't yet a threat, and Marissa still lived. So much had changed in just a few moonturns. How she wished she could turn back the clock to those happier, simpler days.

Sappy reminiscences would do no good. Taryn was off somewhere with Rhoane, Marissa and Valterys were dead, and now the empress had a new playmate to taunt. Lliandra had near exhausted herself trying to seduce Loghan into her bed, but the boy had shown great restraint in denying her. It didn't matter how many times he explained that Ullan healers did not fornicate for pleasure; the empress ignored his protests and upped her seductive behavior. It would've been comical if it weren't so sad to witness.

By the time they docked in Talaith, Lliandra was so vexed with the healer, she demanded they travel to Ulla at once. Baehlon had stepped in and explained to the empress that such an undertaking would take a fortnight to plan. He stood his ground and wouldn't let Lliandra badger or belittle him, which did not gain him favor with the empress.

Faelara glanced up at the man she'd loved for over six decades. How much time had they lost to pride? It took her almost dying for them both to realize their time with the living was precious and to not squander it any longer.

Sunlight glinted off his mahogany forehead and several grey hairs wove their way through his black braids. Bells attached to the ends chimed with each movement, a sound that had by turns irritated and soothed over the seasons, but lately had become the melody of her days. His dark eyes regarded her, fear lingering in them.

"Did you wish for a swim?" His silky baritone spiraled to her heart. "The last time you went in the ocean almost killed you and," he glanced over the tranquil water, "you haven't been the same since."

"Poppycock. The only thing that's changed is I'm no longer afraid to profess my love to you." She stretched on tiptoe to press her lips against his.

He lifted her into his arms and curled one hand behind her head, the other supported her bum. Despite her declaration, they hadn't made their relationship public and stolen moments like these were far too seldom.

Baehlon's hot mouth covered hers, and she swooned into the kiss, deepening her longing. His groan rumbled across her tongue and continued down, straight to her nethers. His hips rocked upward and she felt the stiffening of his cock through her skirts. In another time and another place, they wouldn't have to sneak behind the empress's back. Who was she kidding? Lliandra had never wanted them together and had actively sought to keep them apart. It was one of those mysteries Faelara might never know the reason for, or understand, but had accepted out of loyalty to her empress.

While technically, she needed Lliandra's permission to enter into a courtship with Baehlon, and he required Taryn's approval, they were old enough to make their own decisions, rulers and chosen ones be damned. If only Lliandra could be as supportive as Taryn, who actively encouraged the relationship, even going so far as to create situations where Fae and Baehlon would be alone. Taryn and Lliandra couldn't have been more different, in almost everything, including how they interacted with others. Sometimes Faelara felt as if Lliandra were punishing her for some unknown mishap she didn't know she'd made. It was difficult to ask forgiveness for something she didn't know she did.

Thank the gods for Lliandra's heir, Eliahnna. She, at least, heartily approved of the courtship, but Eliahnna did not sit on the Light Throne. Not yet.

Faelara pulled her angst-filled thoughts away from the petty empress and held Baehlon's face between her hands. She loved the juxtaposition of his dark skin against her pale flesh. The way his gaze always found its way back to her, no matter if he stood before kings and queens, or if they were walking the streets of Talaith. He was as much her orbit as she his.

"Why didn't we do this sooner?"

"Because the empress kept you practically chained to her side."

"No, silly." She nuzzled her nose to his. "This. Being together." She knew why, as did he, but the tragedy with his wife was ancient history. "It's time we let go of the past and make our own future."

"Says the woman who wishes to study with the Ullans." Baehlon's strong arms held her close. "Would it help if I begged you to stay here, with me?" He grinned and it was like the sunrise warming her heart. "Because I will. I am not too proud to beg, woman."

"I don't wish to practice Ullan healing, as you well know. I am simply curious how it is they use their bodies to heal."

"And all that Loghan has shared isn't enough knowledge? You wish to see it in practice?" He pulled her tighter against him. "I will show you how to heal with the body."

A shudder wracked her and heat flushed up her cheeks. Loghan had, indeed, given her all the information she needed, but her trip to Ulla wasn't just to learn their secrets for healing— it was to escape Lliandra and have time alone with Baehlon.

Faelara pretended to be aghast. "Why Sir Baehlon, here? In the open?"

His grin slipped from his luscious lips and his gaze became serious. "With only the sound of the sea to disturb us, yes, I would make love to you here, Lady Faelara. If you will have me, I would love you for the rest of my days on a beach, in a palace, or in some godforsaken desert beneath the stars. My heart has always been yours."

She covered his mouth with hers and devoured his taste. For too long she'd dreamt of this moment and if it were to be on the beach beneath the wide leaves of a horiscus tree, all the better. After all, the tree was said to have healing properties and legend told of an ailing princess who found herself stranded beneath a horiscus tree. For seven days and nights, the tree fed her with water collected on its leaves. Faelara glanced up to the thick foliage and nodded. This was perfect. The moment, the tree, her love, it was as it should be. No more hiding. No more waiting.

"I will have you, Baehlon. Forever and always, wherever we find ourselves."

She twirled her finger and a blanket appeared on the sand. Baehlon chuckled and set her down as if she were made of the finest hildgelt and could shatter at any moment. His nervousness washed over her, and she touched his brow with her fingertips.

"I love you, Baehlon de Monteferron. With all of my heart and mind and spirit, I have always loved you."

"Why do I feel like a lad still in short pants? Gods, woman, do you know how long I've hoped for this moment? Dreamt of it?"

"Yes, as a matter of fact, I do. I need your help undressing, please." At his cheeky grin, she held up yards of fabric with a huff. "I do hope when Eliahnna is the Lady of Light, she understands the plight of us poor souls who sweat half our weight during the summer. Lliandra is ridiculous to continue demanding we wear full gowns. She claims to be chilled constantly, but we suffer for her irregular body temperature."

"Did you wish me to help you undress? Or would you rather continue harping about your empress?"

She indicated he unbutton the many tiny little beads that held her dress closed. His breath tickled her neck and she dug her nails into her palms to keep from turning to him and continuing where their kiss left off. She could use her ShantiMari to strip them both, but this was their first time and she'd be damned if she rushed anything, including the delicious torment of undressing each other.

His lips seared the newly freed flesh on her back and she moaned into his touch. "We've wasted so much time already, let's not waste another moment." As if reading her thoughts, and wishing to sway her opinion, his tongue lashed over her tender skin, causing a cascade of shivers to slide down her spine.

He pushed her gown over her shoulders and she wriggled free of the blasted thing. Getting out of the many layers was one thing—poor Baehlon would have a time of it trying to get her back *in* the gown. Lliandra really was cruel. And not just for making them wear the velvet gowns at the height of summer.

She forced thoughts of her empress aside and stepped out of

the pool of fabric at her feet. She reached for the garters that held her stockings, but Baehlon stopped her.

"This is my pleasure, my lady." His lips caressed her neck at the little divot above her breastbone and she swayed into the lusciousness of his kisses.

A melody came to her, and she cocked her head to better hear. "What is that music?" Her words were husky and slightly slurred even though she hadn't had any wine.

"I hear nothing but the beating of my own heart."

Fae arched into his caresses, the music a distraction like a gnat that refused to fly away. When Baehlon's fingers hooked the tops of her smallclothes and gently lowered them over her hips, she had a moment of uncertainty. What if one of Lliandra's guards approached? Or someone from the palace? Or, stars forbid, the empress?

Searing heat came from her nethers and she gasped when Baehlon put his lips over her mound. His hot tongue lashed her little nub and she didn't care who might disturb them. She was lost to the pleasure of his touch. She moaned when he lay her on the blanket and hovered above her, lust on his lips and desire in his eyes.

His head bent for a kiss and she greedily sucked at the juices on his lips—hers mixed with his. It was intoxicating and enticing and oh stars, he parted her legs with a low growl that rumbled through her veins.

The music started again, but it wasn't instruments she heard. Voices harmonized in a tune she recognized. Her heartbeat quickened and she stilled a moment. It was the same tune she'd heard that morning in Menurra. Stars, no. Not again.

"Am I hurting you?" Baehlon held himself aloft, his cock resting against her sensitive nub, teasing, tormenting, tantalizing.

"You are magnificent. Make love to me, darling. Now."

His cock slid into her warmth, and she arched to take him deeper. The blasted singing drowned out the sound of his rapid breaths. She focused on his face, memorizing every sigh, each wicked grin. *This.* This was what she'd waited all those seasons for —to be with the man she loved wholly. She'd been a fool for far too long, denying her affection for him. Never again would she hide from her emotions. Never again would she lie to protect someone who cared little for her. If the empress didn't approve, she and Baehlon would move away, far from Lliandra's greedy neediness.

The singing tunneled into her brain, but she couldn't make out the words. If she stopped to concentrate on the song, she'd lose the connection she had with Baehlon. A spiral of doubt twisted her belly. Unless that's what they were hoping for— whoever they were.

Baehlon. Her love.

The sea is your love, Lady Faelara. We are waiting.

Baehlon arched and ground his hips against hers, his cock pumping in and out, in and…*ooooooh, yes, just there was lovely.* She bucked her hips to meet his, her passion mounting.

A breeze cooled their sweat-slick skin and she bit her bottom lip to keep from crying out. Baehlon's grunts were equally stifled and that tiny similarity tugged at her heart.

Faelara, return to us. Raise your voice in song. We have waited too long for you.

No. She shook her head and thrust harder against Baehlon's eager cock. She clawed his back as their pace became a fevered comingling of arms, legs, bodies. His mouth claimed hers, and she was lost to his scent, his taste, his touch.

Images of the sea tormented her. The dark beneath the waves beckoned, but Faelara shook her head. No, she could never go into the water. The song crescendoed in her mind, deafening her to all other sound.

Their pace matched the tempo of the song and she writhed beneath Baehlon, her release building. His gorgeous body covered hers and she felt safe, protected, in his embrace. She'd waited sixty seasons for this moment.

The sea had waited longer.

They came undone together, neither able to contain their cries any longer. Her breath came in pants and every nerve felt alive, connected to the sand, the sky, the tree, and the sea. She flopped her arms to the side and clawed at the sand, suddenly ravenous for the life-giving nutrients in sea water.

Baehlon heaved above her and she rose to lick his torso, taking his nipple between her lips as she did. A wild abandon filled her senses and she giggled at her brazenness.

A slow and steady groan came from Baehlon's sternum and he grinned with inner wickedness. "Do that again and I might have to reciprocate in kind."

Faelara.

Another giggle and she nipped him playfully.

She is here, Faelara.

Who? She tried to ignore the voices, but her gaze was drawn to a gorgeous creature with skin like sand and hair the color of a tranquil sea. What should have frightened her, didn't. This was right. This moment, their making love, the woman. It was as it should be. But why?

"Darling, you might want to cover yourself. There's a woman standing a few paces from us."

Baehlon rolled off Faelara and grabbed his sword where it lay with his discarded clothing. Naked, gleaming like a glorious marble statue in the afternoon sun, he stood before the woman with his sword raised. He looked every inch the knight protector he was. It was all Faelara could do not to burst out laughing.

"How dare you sneak up on us like this. I demand to know your name."

The woman inclined her head to Baehlon before turning to address Faelara, who had the good sense to pull her gown over her nakedness.

"Lady Faelara, it is time you return to the sea. They tell me you are ignoring their calls."

Baehlon advanced on the woman. "Fae's not going anywhere near that water. It damned near killed her last time."

The woman placed her hand on his sword and lowered it with a long gaze at his flaccid cock. A shiver of jealousy ran through Faelara.

"Sir Baehlon, they do not wish her death, but the opposite. The sea king has need of her intellect and compassion."

"And why should we believe you? King Baldev is a myth."

Bless Baehlon's heart. Faelara rose and stood beside him equally as naked, surprisingly unafraid.

"Last I heard, the Eirielle is a myth. Water dragons as well, but Faelara knows this isn't true."

"Fae?" He turned to face her, his bells chiming softly with the movement.

"I saw her. That morning in Menurra, and one other time when Rhoane and I were in the Summerlands for Prince Jayved's birth. I never knew if it was real or not. But in my heart, I suppose I knew it was." She peered closer at the strange woman. Her sand-like skin was dotted with seashells and tangled in her hair were threads of kelp. "You're Julieta, aren't you?"

Baehlon gasp-grunted and held his sword over his manhood.

"I am. I have been watching over you your whole life."

"Why?"

"You know why, darling. But that is not the reason I've come. It is imperative you see King Baldev, but not in these waters." She glanced toward the palace and grimaced. "I do not trust your empress. I fear Kaldaar has poisoned her...Amdi Agnar of the Ullans as well."

That would explain Lliandra's lingering illness and chaotic moods.

"I don't know what I can do. Why aren't you asking Taryn to help?"

"Taryn and her betrothed are…unavailable. But this is not her path. It is yours alone."

"I won't allow it." Baehlon moved half a step in front of Faelara and her heart swelled with pride.

Julieta stroked his cheek with her thumb and chuckled. "She does not need your permission, Sir Baehlon. But if it will make you more at ease, I can allow you passage through the dark waters."

His gaze went to the surf and he shuddered against Faelara. "That's up to Fae. If she wishes me to accompany her, I will."

"You said not this water. Then where?" Faelara put a hand on Baehlon's arm to let him know she was not in danger. His body absolutely vibrated with apprehension.

"Go to the Jansen Strait. It is in the Ullan desert, south of the Great Barren Gorge. There, you will find Xianqin waiting for you." She leaned forward and pressed her lips to Baehlon's.

He stepped back, but Faelara blocked him. Even though she knew what the goddess was doing, a little ping of jealousy pinched her heart. If left unchecked, her envy could be a huge problem. But she'd only just had Baehlon all to herself—she wasn't ready to share him with anyone. Especially not a gorgeous goddess with sea-colored eyes full of sadness.

Julieta pulled away with a sly smile on her lips. "Now you both will be safe beneath the waves. You have my grace, and my blessing." She flicked a glance to Faelara's abdomen. "Congratulations."

Faelara and Baehlon stared at the goddess as she turned, took two steps, and vanished. Her laughter floated on the empty air.

Faelara put a hand over her pelvis and looked up at Baehlon with a nervous smile. He grinned at her like a strutting peacock and enfolded her in his arms.

A baby. At her age? Why now? In that moment, Fae totally understood Taryn's resentment of the gods and their puzzles.

The singing drifted to her from beyond the waves and she

looked out across the sea. There, just beyond the surf, she saw a woman with auburn hair bobbing in the water. It was the woman from the Summerlands who'd tried to take Faelara to the depths of the sea and Rhoane had rescued her. The woman raised a hand to her lips and blew Faelara a kiss.

Then she was gone.

CHAPTER THIRTEEN

Taryn put a hand over her heart and gasped at the piercing jolt of—not pain, but something else. Something pleasant. She closed her eyes and let her mind wander until she found the source of the intense emotion.

Julieta stood on a beach with a very naked Faelara and Baehlon. What the bloody hell? Taryn gripped Rhoane's hand and pulled him into the vision.

What is this, mi carae?

I think this is happening on Aelinae. It's…good.

The love she felt coming from her friends swirled around her and Rhoane.

I feel it as well. They have finally consummated their love for each other. This is quite good. And about time. His chuckle tickled her mind.

Is Julieta allowing us to see this? Or are we doing this? And why are we seeing our friends naked?

It must be important.

They watched Julieta leave and Faelara put a hand over her abdomen. Tears filled Taryn's eyes and she sensed Rhoane's elation as well.

Muted singing, celebratory and welcoming, came from the sea and they saw a woman blow Faelara a kiss, then a slip of tail as she disappeared beneath the surface.

Warmth lingered in her heart, but the vision dissipated. "What does it mean?"

"I should have known." Rhoane shook his head. "That woman, she tried to take Fae from me that morning in Menurra when we snuck away to the beach."

"You mean when Fae almost died? Then she's no friend of ours."

"At the time, I would have agreed, but it is quite the opposite, I believe. She said we had Fae long enough and it was her turn." His intense gaze bore into her. "I believe she is Faelara's mother."

"Mother?" Taryn choked on her Guinness. "Fae's a mermaid?"

"Half. Think about it. No one knows who her mother is. Brandt never told anyone. Even Myrddin doesn't know. Why? Why would he hide something as important as a mother?"

"I guess I just assumed she was dead and didn't want to bring it up in case it hurt Fae."

"Exactly. That is what everyone did. Manners prevented us from asking. It was simple and brilliant."

"And cruel. I mean, Faelara grew up without a mother."

Rhoane took her hand in his and rubbed his thumb over her knuckles. "Not everyone longs for a mother who is not there. Faelara had Brandt, and that was enough for her. I never, not once in all the seasons I have known her, ever heard her wish for her life to be different."

They'd been raised by the same man, but Taryn didn't grow up satisfied. Maybe because Brandt was Faelara's real father and only Taryn's guardian—not truly her grandfather, even though she loved him like family. It was messy and complicated and a topic she didn't wish to belabor. Yet Rhoane was right. Faelara had once told Taryn they could choose their family and that if she truly saw those around her, she would see the love and acceptance she craved. Maybe that was Fae's way of telling her that yes, she missed having a mother growing up, but that she didn't need her mother's love to be complete. Her friends were her family and that was enough. She was enough.

Donyatella brought them their meal and sat in a chair opposite. "Gage tells me the scyver was only interested in Rhoane. Silar said the same about the gent on the bridge. How is this possible? You both have ShantiMari." Dony squinted at Taryn and pursed her lips. "Yet, I do not sense your power. Interesting."

Kaida lay sprawled in front of the fire, her tail thumping with the arrival of Dony's men. The dark-haired one—Gage—bent to scratch her between her ears, and Taryn caught him sneaking a piece of raw meat to the grierbas. The men sat in chairs flanking Dony and she looked like a child seated between them. But there was no mistaking who was in charge.

"You have questions about what is happening in London, and about us, yes?"

"So many questions. What are scyvers? Where did they come from? Is Rhoane poisoned from that woman's bite? Since when have faeries walked the streets of London? Are there trolls, brownies? Ogres? Elves? Do you have dragons, too?" Taryn raised her hands in exasperation. "What happened in the time I was gone?"

"You eat and I'll explain. I cooked this myself. Enjoy."

Taryn looked at the cheeseburger and chips. "It's perfect. How'd you know I was craving a really good burger?"

Dony cocked her chin at Rhoane. "This one asked what a cheeseburger was, so I made one for him."

Taryn laughed out loud at that. She'd forgotten about their time in Paderau when she'd made everyone pizza and Rhoane had been privy to her thoughts. She'd been terribly homesick and craved comfort foods. Now, she'd give anything for a steaming mug of Carga's grhom.

"Thank you, Nona Dony. It's perfect."

"Eat and listen." Dony gazed into the distance a moment before she began her tale with a brief history of how the Stone Guardians came to be.

They were created by the gods more than ten thousand years ago, to protect holy places, but also to keep mortals from the heavenly realm. Over time, they served new gods—both Roman and Greek—and made alliances with various rulers, but soon learned the folly of taking sides. At least, Donyatella and her boys learned this valuable lesson. There were Stone Guardians all over Earth who served kings and prime ministers, and there were others who served no one but their own selfish desires.

Stone Guardians were immortal beings, neither human nor god, without ShantiMari, but powerful in their own way. On this, Dony wouldn't elaborate, and Taryn remembered Silar's inhuman speed and strength on the bridge.

"Can Guardians be killed? Not that I want to, but it might be good to know what we're up against if we encounter some of the not-so-friendly stone guys."

"They can, but not easily. It's complicated in much the same way killing a god is possible, but difficult." Dony patted the arms of her boys. "It's a sensitive subject, as I'm sure you can imagine."

"Sorry." She swallowed a gulp of Guinness. "I didn't mean to upset anyone. Just curious. Why did you say you kept your oath? Who did you make a promise to?" Taryn mopped up the last of her ketchup with a chip and popped it into her mouth. Whether Dony added magic or not, it was the best damn cheeseburger she'd ever had.

"My boys and I, we stay neutral, but there are times when we choose to assist if we feel the balance is weighing too heavily in one direction or another. When Nadra asked me to keep watch over you and Brandt, I agreed on the condition that should we deem you unworthy, the agreement is broken."

"Harsh." She grinned and patted Dony's hand. "I'm glad you found me worthy."

Dony sighed and squeezed her fingers. "Unfortunately, so have these two." She tilted her head left and right to indicate Gage and Silar. "They wish to pledge themselves to your cause. You should know, I advised against it."

Rhoane straightened and leaned forward. "You would revoke your vow of neutrality for us? But there are no Stone Guardians on Aelinae."

Silar chuckled. "That you've seen, *Surtentse*. It is our job to be unseen, but always watching."

"Shut the front door. You have people on Aelinae?" Taryn shook her head in awe.

"We have people everywhere. I'm sure you will find Guardians on each of the worlds you must visit. Be warned, though. Not all of them are as nice as my boys."

Dony's boys nice? A shudder worked its way down her spine. "Duly noted."

"There are many pubs spread across the worlds like this one. Some names have changed, again, like this one, but they are known to us as *Darathi Ostgur*."

"Shoogly Dragon?" Rhoane cocked his head. "Why?"

"Because someone in the past thought it was funny?" Dony held her hands up with a shrug. "I don't name the portals, I just guard them."

Taryn cycled through the papers they had and the places that were marked on them. They might all be pubs. Knowing Myrddin, that made sense—the man loved his ale. But he'd also want to be near power. Her gaze flicked to the river. This pub was close enough to the Tower of London they could walk there. The Thames wound its way passed by several other palaces, but it was nowhere near Glastonbury. Why had Myrddin chosen the middle of the country? Fifteen hundred years of history crammed through her thoughts and she sighed.

That particular puzzle was for another day. "What can you tell us about the scyvers?"

Kaida padded over and nudged Rhoane's hand with her nose. He petted her muzzle, but she moved so that she could lick the wound on his hand. In a few strokes, the bite marks faded. She continued until his skin was unmarked.

"You have a remarkable companion, *Darennsai*." Gage scratched Kaida's ruff, and she closed her eyes in contentment.

"We're blessed to call her friend. She's constantly surprising us." That was an understatement. Outside of Aelinae, the grierbas practically became a new creature. What else was she hiding?

Rhoane flexed his hand before shaking it several times. "I do not feel the woman's pain. Her presence is gone completely. Thank you, Kaida. It is a kindness I will not forget."

"The scyvers are not your concern, *Darennsai*. The potion you both drank will hide your ShantiMari from them and you can go about the city peacefully. You have bigger concerns to focus on."

Taryn stretched and patted her full belly. "I guess it's time we begin our world tour." She chuckled. "Literally. We're off to Elvenwood, where hopefully we'll find Rori. First, one last check at SIRE. Nikala didn't show up to work today. Is that strange for her?"

Dony's brows dipped and lips pursed, too quickly to be interpreted one way or another. "She keeps her own hours. Until her father's death, she was hardly ever in London." Dony rose and her boys followed. "You will have to wait for Elvenwood, however. They are twelve hours behind us. If you go there now, it will be two in the morning and I don't think King Thane would appreciate being disturbed at such an hour."

"We'll find something to entertain us."

"We could play football." Rhoane indicated a telly propped in the corner. "The picture box is most intriguing. When you taught us your game, I did not realize it was not just for children."

"You taught them soccer?" Dony laughed and shook her head. "What I wouldn't give to have seen their faces when you first arrived. I'm sure they didn't know what to make of you."

"Like Kaida, Taryn is always surprising us." Rhoane practically beamed as he looked at her.

"I am happy for you. For you both." Dony held out her arms for a hug. "I might be made of stone, but I am a romantic at heart."

Taryn slid out of the booth and shook out her limbs. The power surge, or whatever it had been that knocked her unconscious, did a number on her muscles. They were sore as if she'd been practicing her *kata* for hours.

"Thank you for everything, Dony." She hugged her friend tight. "I don't know when or if we'll be back this way. Please look after the flat."

"I will. You be safe in your journey. I fear you will be tested many times before you complete your quest."

"Isn't that what the hero's journey is all about?" The light-heartedness she tried for didn't quite make it to her words. "We have each other."

Taryn took Rhoane's hand in hers and buried her fingers in Kaida's fur.

Dony smoothed a strand of hair off Taryn's forehead and sighed. "You were such a precocious child. Brave, intelligent, caring. You were a delight to have around and have surpassed all of my hopes and dreams. Not only are you worthy, my love, you are capable. Never ever forget who you are." She brushed her lips against Taryn's brow, and she heard the cracking of stone echoing through the centuries. "I'll leave you to your quest."

Dony wiped a tear and turned to go, taking her two boys with her. Gage snuck a last pet to Kaida before giving Taryn and Rhoane a cheeky wink. If they ever needed the Guardians, Taryn hoped they would come to their aid. Nowhere in her titles was

Commander of Stone Guardians or such rubbish, but she could hope.

"Since we have time to spare, I suppose we should form some sort of battle plan." Resignation echoed in Rhoane's tone.

Starting with how to manipulate time. If Myrddin could do it, how hard could it be?

CHAPTER FOURTEEN

Taryn shook out her fingers and blew on them as if they'd been burned. Kaida watched patiently as Rhoane carefully explained—again—how to fold time. Something in her brain didn't compute his words, or she was trying to rationalize what he explained. Whatever it was, she didn't get it.

She reminded herself—again—that gravity and physics were mutable when ShantiMari was involved, but she'd been raised on Earth and dismissing values ingrained into her learning was difficult. Repeating Rhoane's instructions in her mind, she lifted her hands and pinched the air—something Rhoane said was unnecessary, but it gave Taryn a visual anchor. Her fingertips smooshed together and she drew her hands apart, imagining time stretching like a rubber band.

Kaida growled and her fur stood on end. She rose, ears perked forward. *I do not like this, Darennsai. I feel as though my belly is in my mouth.*

Is that normal, Rhoane? Are animals more affected by time manipulation?

Rhoane cocked his head, his eyes clouded. She heard the familiar murmuring of his people in her mind.

I do not know. Nor do the ancients.

Taryn released her hold over time and suggested Kaida wait in the bedroom. When she was certain Kaida was two rooms away, she repeated the steps to fold time and used her ShantiMari to keep the manipulation to just their room. Her arms shook with the effort and sweat rolled down her temples, but she held fast.

Rhoane's eyes widened and he grinned. "I never thought to contain the folding. I am impressed, Darennsai."

She released her hold and panted with the effort. "How the hell did you hold it so long? That fucking killed me and it was what, a minute?"

"You will grow in strength the more you practice. My first time lasted three heartbeats, at most. Kaleigh said hers was even less."

Kaida, were you affected this time?

No answer came to them. She looked at Rhoane and to the doorway. "What if I killed her? Oh my God, Rhoane. I killed Kaida."

They ran to her bedroom and skidded to a stop in front of the bed. Kaida lay on her back with her legs flopped outward, snoring as if she hadn't a care in the world. Taryn's heart beat in her throat and she felt sick to her stomach. Kaida was safe, she reminded herself.

"You were successful in your containment. Well done." Rhoane bent at the waist and rested his hands on his knees. "I admit, I was worried for her, but she does not seem to have suffered."

"She's ridiculous." Taryn wasn't talking about just the grierbas. Her overreaction was equally as silly as Kaida's sleeping position. Her gaze flicked to the clock by her bed and a chill swirled down her spine. "Rhoane, the time…it's off. I mean, it's supposed to be, but we either went forward or backward more than five hours. Is that supposed to happen?"

She went to the window and blinked against the bright daylight. They'd gone back in time.

Rhoane tried to hide his surprise, but she saw it in the way his eyes widened and face paled. "Only if that is what you intended."

A soft knock came from the door and a moment later, Silar called out to Kaida. They heard his heavy steps in the foyer and Taryn stared at Rhoane, panic pulsing through her blood.

"We're supposed to be downstairs right now, talking to Dony and having lunch."

Silar's steps came closer and he called out to Kaida again. She twitched and rolled over with a yip. Taryn threw a shadow over herself and Rhoane a moment before Silar entered and gave Kaida a thorough scratching on her back.

"Who's a pretty girl? Hungry? Come on, lass. Let's get you fed. Your companions are waiting for you downstairs. Seems your female got herself into a fair amount of trouble." He continued talking down the hallway, his voice finally trailing off after they left the flat.

If Kaida saw them, she didn't mark it, but Taryn's heart stuttered all the same.

"Are we here, or downstairs?"

"There is only one way to find out."

They crept down the stairs to the dining area, Taryn keeping the shadows firmly in place. Even before they reached the entrance to the pub, she heard Dony telling Rhoane to drink the foul concoction she'd made. A bitter aftertaste settled on her tongue as if she'd just swallowed the drink. Even semi-conscious, it had been foul.

They peeked around the doorframe and she sucked in a breath. Rhoane cradled her and sang a lullaby. The amount of love on his face, and the words of the song, tugged on her heart. A moment later, his features twisted as if he saw a ghost.

Because he did. Standing beside Kaida was the ghostly form

of his mother Aislinn. Taryn recognized her from Rhoane's memories, but also from somewhere else. She tried to pull from her memories when or where she'd seen the Eleri queen, but it was elusive, as if it were from a dream.

A moment later, Aislinn disappeared and Taryn began to stir.

"Is this normal? I mean, being in two places at once?"

"Not that I know of. I have never had this happen before."

"If we're there, but we're also here, how do we get to the right timeline?" She pulled away from the doorway and crept back up the stairs. Dead Eleri queens aside, this wasn't something she was familiar with and she didn't know how to fix it.

"I do not know." His tone didn't fill her with confidence.

Once back inside her flat, she dropped the cloak of shadows and paced the length of the lounge.

"Can you return us to the right time?"

He shook his head. "If I try, it will only make it worse. I believe we have to wait until the past timeline catches up to this time. I hope."

"Fabulous. So, we just hang out?" She stopped her pacing at the table with the scrolls and ran a finger along the edges. "Myrddin figured it out—we can too. Let me try again."

She stood beside Rhoane and pinched the empty air in front of her before she said the words that would warp time. She concentrated on returning them to five hours later, to reset the correct timeline. Sweat beaded on her forehead and a raging headache slammed against her skull. The more she pushed, the harder her ShantiMari swirled in a tempest around them. She struggled to control both her hold on time and her power. This wasn't right. Her words warbled and the air around them vibrated with suppressed anger. At least it seemed that way. Air didn't have emotion. Or did it? Hell, she didn't know anymore. But if she tried to hold the folding for another moment, she knew for certain it would rip her apart.

She released her hold and bent at the waist, gasping for air.

"What happened?" Rhoane bent beside her, his long hair shielding his face from her view.

"I don't know. One moment, I was fine. The next, it felt like my power had turned against me, violently. It makes no sense." She flexed her fingers and opened a thread of power. Nothing nefarious lingered, nor did she feel the sheer rage of a moment earlier. Maybe it was her power reacting to something in the folding.

Her gaze slid to the window where clouds darkened the sky. Even if she'd returned them to the right time, it hadn't been so late that the sky was devoid of light. She strode to the window and swallowed her shock at what she saw.

The skyscrapers that once stood tall on either side of the pub were crumbled, as if bombs had been dropped onto them. Streets once filled with cars and pedestrians sat empty. An apocalyptic scene stretched across the landscape. Debris floated in the dark waters of the Thames.

"What have I done?"

"Is this the future, or the past?" Rhoane stared at the destruction lining the river.

"I don't know. The future, maybe? But is it the same future as the timeline we were in?" She should never have tried to manipulate time on Earth. Hadn't the experience with the scyver on the Tube taught her that? Her ShantiMari worked differently here than it did on Aelinae. "I'm scared, Rhoane."

And she was. Terrified, actually. The scene that lay before her looked as if a war had devastated all of London. Her beloved city, ruined. A glint of light caught her eye and she squinted into the darkened sky. Barely visible, but there nonetheless, was a barrier of sorts. She followed the line like a rainbow over the horizon. It reminded her of a bubble. As if someone had placed a giant glass cloche over the city.

"Should we go out there to help?" Rhoane's tone suggested he would rather poke his eyes out with his flaming sword.

"We can't stay here. If we do, we'll have lost not just London, but all of Aelinae as well. You have to help me get us back to our timeline." Tears bit the backs of her eyes. She wasn't responsible for whatever had happened to London, but she knew in her bones if they stayed, it would only make matters worse. They didn't have time to wait for their timeline to catch up. "I promise, one more folding, then I will leave all the time shenanigans to you. But, we have to do this together. I'm not strong enough to do it alone."

Rhoane's jaw tensed and his eyes hardened, but he nodded. "Focus on the exact moment we left our proper time. What were you doing, thinking, feeling? Remember everything you can and I will do the same."

Her hands shook as she raised them to pinch the empty air. If she fucked this up, who knew what awaited them or where they'd end up. Rhoane said the words necessary to fold time and she joined him. Their voices became stronger as the incantation went on and she started to believe they just might succeed.

In her mind, she saw the flat, Kaida, Rhoane, and herself as she was when she folded time. She crammed as many details into the image as she could, hoping it helped. Rhoane's ShantiMari swept past her and her power joined his in a smaller, less volatile tempest around them. Her hair lifted as if in a breeze and she felt her feet leave the floor. Rhoane's intent gaze stayed locked on her and she forced all doubt from her mind.

They would succeed. They had to.

A moment later, her feet nestled into the soft rug in her flat and their power diminished. She looked at the table with the scrolls, her precious books, and the window that showed an intact London.

"Did we do it?" They went to the bedroom were Kaida lay curled on the bed, sleeping. Her tail thumped when they entered and Taryn glanced at the clock. It flipped to the next minute and she breathed a sigh of relief. "I think we're in the right timeline."

Rhoane sat on the side of the bed and rubbed Kaida's belly. "I was not at all sure what would happen. Perhaps we should wait until we are returned to Aelinae before we proceed with any more time manipulation lessons."

"No way. Like I said, you're in charge of time shenanigans from now on. I want nothing to do with it." The image of London destroyed was too fresh in her mind. What had caused the destruction? Could it be avoided? She shook her head as if to rid herself of the thoughts. "Between an unknown future and a known horrific one, I think I prefer the unknown."

If only it were that simple. Her mishap with folding time taunted her and even though she knew she needed to focus on what she could control, it all seemed so hopeless now.

They would carry on searching for the seals, but none of them were excited for what lay beyond the door in the cellar.

CHAPTER FIFTEEN

Taryn's fingers stretched over the wooden doorframe and she said the words Myrddin had written beside the drawing of a huge tree. Green script illuminated and she had to swallow her surprise and pride that it had actually worked. She snuck a glance at Rhoane, and his wide smile bolstered her confidence. He'd never lost faith that she would be successful.

Now, if she could get them to Elvenwood all in one piece, that would be marvelous. Miraculous, even.

The three of them stepped through the doorway into the darkness and she reminded herself to breathe. This was her third time in the void and it didn't get easier. Perhaps with more trips it would, but for the moment, she fought the panic that rose to choke all thought.

Elvenwood. She put the name squarely at the front of her mind. Not knowing what the portal in Cilachaem would look like or where they'd end up, they'd dressed in clothing that was a mix of Earth and Aelinae. Comfortable pants, a bit of chain mail just in case, and their swords. Rhoane had insisted they wear Eleri boots and she hadn't argued. They were the most comfortable shoes she'd ever worn. Taryn swept a hand over her top and grinned. They looked totally kickass, if she did say so herself. Interplanetary badasses.

Her chuckle echoed in the void and she glanced at Rhoane. She could see him. Not fully, but an outline of his face.

"Rhoane?"

"Yes, mi carae?"

"Kaida?"

We can hear you, Darennsai. Does this upset you?

"Quite the opposite, in fact. I find it rather interesting."

She redoubled her grip on them. It wouldn't do to get cocky and lose them to the void. She still didn't trust that Kaldaar was gone from the eternal darkness. If this was a prank, some way of lulling her into a sense of complacency, she'd be ready.

A small light shone in the distance and Taryn focused on it, but her attention was pulled to her left, where she sensed pain and suffering. Instinctively, she turned toward it to help, but Rhoane squeezed her hand.

"That way lies something I do not think we wish to encounter." His shudder went up her arm. "I sense evil. The stench makes me ill."

"I don't smell anything. Kaida, do you?"

It is different from the man things of London. I do not think it is human at all, but it has the stink of man upon it.

"Kaida is right. Can we increase our speed, or are we hampered by a preset pace set by the void?"

"I don't know. I mean, I *am* the walker of worlds, right? Maybe we have some control over what happens here. Let's give it a go."

The first two times, she'd simply stepped into the dark and was transported—without any movement from her—but it made sense that they should be able to walk, run, skip, or whatever in the darkness. As long as she didn't try to control time, they should be fine. She hoped.

They sped forward as if they ran, but without moving their

legs. Remarkable. And terrifying. It wasn't like there was a *Portals for Dummies* handbook she could read to learn everything she'd need to know about the vast expanse of nothingness. But damn, she sure wished there was. She added it to the growing collection of how-to books she needed.

The light elongated and shimmered at their approach. Taryn sucked in a long drag of air and at her side, Rhoane did the same. Kaida sniffed the opening before stretching a paw at the undulating brightness.

"Here goes nothing. Are we ready?" She sounded more confident than she felt.

They stepped through into a damp cellar lit from a room beyond an open doorway. What was it with portals and cellars? She shook herself and patted her body to make sure nothing had been misplaced. Satisfied all her bits were where they were supposed to be, she took a hesitant step to peer into the next room.

They were in a kitchen, not modern, but familiar enough she breathed a sigh of relief. It reminded her of the kitchens in Paderau, where she'd spent many bells talking to Carga. The sharp tang of spices hit her nose and she practically swooned.

"Grhom."

"I smell it as well." Rhoane led them up the few steps and into a quiet part of the kitchens, where only a few scullery maids were cleaning pots.

At the group's sudden appearance, one of the maids startled and fell off her stool. Rhoane's ShantiMari whipped out to cushion her fall and right her on the stool. Her eyes widened and she stared first at Rhoane, and then Taryn. Finally, her gaze went to Kaida.

Taryn expected a scream or curse or maybe even the sign to ward off evil, but what she didn't expect was for the four maids to clamber off their seats to prostrate themselves at Rhoane and Taryn's feet.

They babbled in unison, but Taryn could only make out a few words. They spoke a fractured form of Eleri. The more she listened, it sounded like a lingua franca of English and Eleri.

"Please," Rhoane said in Eleri as he bent low, "there is no need for this." He touched one woman's shoulder and she rose, her eyes full of tears. "Why do you cry?"

"You have come."

Rhoane looked to Taryn, but she didn't know what it meant either.

"Can you tell us where we can find your king and queen?" Taryn spoke slowly, as if they were children, more so to not frighten them than for any other reason. The women positively vibrated with anxiety that rolled over her in waves. It wasn't a pleasant feeling.

"What'r ye' lazy sobs doin' now?" A slim woman with hair like flame stood in the doorway, her arms covered in flour. "Oy! What'r ye doin' in me kitchen? If'n ye want sommat, ye tell yer boy and he'll get it fer ye. No nobles down here. Them's the rules." She spoke the same lingua franca, but with a harsh accent that made it even harder to understand.

"I'm sorry." Taryn stepped around the women. "We weren't told the rules. I'm afraid we've gotten quite lost. Can you point the way to the throne room?"

"Och, ye aristocratties are all the same. Thinkin' ye owns the place." She waved a hand to hurry Rhoane and Taryn along. "Up'n these stairs and to the left. Can't miss it. Big ugly place, it is. Lots o' gold 'n filigree, not a lot 'o sense, if ye ask me."

Kaida brushed past the woman and rubbed her head along the cook's thigh. To Taryn's utter astonishment, the cook's features softened and she stroked Kaida's muzzle, leaving a trail of flour across her whiskers.

"Bless me heart. There's another'n like this upstairs. Got some sort o' affliction, don't he? I been makin' broth, but 'ee don't be eatin'. The prince is mighty worried about 'im. Mayhaps this'n could help."

Taryn had no idea what she was talking about, but was grateful she was no longer shouting at them.

"We'll do our best to help. Kaida thinks you smell wonderful."

A blush stained her cheeks. "It's the marzipan. Making it for the feast tomorrow night t' celebrate the wee prince's betrothal, aren't we?" She stood and wiped her hands on her apron. "Now, you git afore I call t' guards on ye." But there was no bite to her words.

On their way out, Taryn glanced toward the little room she and Rhoane had come through. Four faces poked around the doorframe, their eyes glassy. A moment later, the cook scolded them and they disappeared from her view.

She and Rhoane must've given them quite a fright. But to throw themselves on the floor? That was strange. And awkward. Perhaps not for the girls, but certainly for her.

At the top of the stairs, they turned left like the cook said, but didn't see a throne room. Dark hallways seven men wide and three times as high greeted them. They stood for a moment to orientate themselves, gazing in wonder at the stone walls. Everything was stone, as if the entire palace had been carved from rock.

"I believe we are inside a mountain," Rhoane confirmed. "There is something pulling my attention this way." He motioned down the hall, and Taryn moved in that direction.

"Is it friendly?"

"I think so, yes. Well, I hope so." He took her hand in his and led them through hallway after hallway until she was completely lost.

"This palace is even more confusing than Menurra. Are you sure you know where you're going?"

His grin was cocky and full of confidence. "Not entirely, but when did that ever stop us?"

They walked up several flights of stairs and came to an open area with ceilings that stretched to the sky. Light filtered into the space from windows too high to reach. Stone arches rose above them, graceful in their curves and stature. She knew they were stone, but they looked delicate and fragile with lacy buttresses that didn't appear strong enough to hold the weight they bore. White marble with varying veins of rose, black, and verdigris was everywhere—the floor, walls, and ceiling. Portraits hung on the walls of lords and ladies who could've been Rhoane's ancestors. They all had long hair and patrician features, and all of their ears were slightly tipped.

"I believe we have found the Elvenwood."

Taryn dragged her attention from the walls to follow Rhoane's gaze. "Oh. It's lovely."

There, inside the palace, growing through the floor and up, possibly all the way to the roof, was a tree. A grand tree with branches stretching across the arched ceiling and drooping above the heads of indifferent passersby.

They moved in unison toward it. Singing came from the tree and her heart beat faster. She knew this song. Claidholm Solais joined Ynyd Eirathnacht and the tree in beautiful harmony. Taryn's lips moved as she whispered the words. It was the song Daknys had sang to her at Ravenwood when she was recovering from Marissa's poisoning.

"Rhoane." She glanced at him and tears shimmered in his eyes.

"I know, mi carae."

He reached to touch the trunk, but hesitated.

"What's wrong?" She slid her hand over his arm until her fingers lay atop his.

"I know this tree." He tapped his chest. "In here. It is a part of me, yet I know not how."

"I feel it too." She lowered their hands and interlaced her fingers with his. "I'm afraid to touch it."

"I as well."

"Can I help you?" a snobbish voice asked from their right.

They turned to see a man dressed in a long robe that went from his throat to the tops of his silk-clad feet. Taryn glanced at the others, noting that they all wore similar clothing. Dull shades of grey and cream ghosted through the hallway.

"We are here to see King Thane," Rhoane said with authority, his face set in a stern glare that would make the legs of lesser nobles weaken.

"And you are?"

"I am Rhoane al Glennwoods ap Narthvier and this is my beloved, Taryn ap Galendrin. And who, pray tell, are you?"

The man's face went ashen and he bowed low enough to scrape his hands along the floor. "Forgive me. I will take you to the king and queen at once."

He rushed away, indicating they follow him. Taryn and Rhoane shared a shrug and went after the man. Murmuring drifted through her mind and she strove to hear their words clearly. Whispered alarms that the group sought out the king and queen bounced between voices in dizzying speed. From what Taryn could make out, the king and queen were told of their arrival and rushed to the throne room, quite displeased to be disturbed.

At a set of double doors, the snobby man paused and cocked his head. Another rush of voices clamored in her skull. He was to wait a moment while the king and queen situated themselves.

Are you hearing this as well? She sent the thought to Rhoane, who nodded.

His narrowed eyes and tense jaw indicated he was not pleased with what he heard.

Are they Eleri?

Not all of them. They call themselves elves now and have lost much of the Eleri ways, but there are a few who still hold in their hearts the skill of the ancients.

Venom dripped from every word. Taryn adjusted herself and cleared her mind. It wouldn't do well to go into their meeting with the elven sovereigns already pissed off. Rhoane was mad enough for the both of them. And although she understood why, it didn't make for a great start to their quest.

She scanned the palace for Rori's presence, getting a slight ping from somewhere, but she couldn't be certain it was the blue-haired girl. Having even one friendly face in this imposing place would've been nice. She didn't sense that the elves wished them harm, but she definitely didn't feel welcomed.

While they waited, she tried to imagine how she'd feel if she were the queen and foreigners flounced into her palace uninvited. Would she be welcoming? Fearful? A bit of both?

Until she knew what the newcomers wanted, she'd be wary.

Guards approached from behind and she glanced at the long spikes they held at waist level.

"Remove your weapons," one of them, most likely the captain, ordered.

"Not happening." Rhoane lifted his chin in silent challenge. "We are here on a matter of extreme importance and do not have time to waste with diplomatic niceties. If we wished harm to your sovereigns or their people, they would already be dead."

He spoke like a true king, his clipped Eleri commanding, yet respectful.

"Seize their weapons." The captain motioned to two men, who stepped forward.

Taryn held her hands aloft to allow access to her sword. When the man touched the hilt, he swore and snatched his hand away, blowing on his fingers. The guard beside Rhoane cast a wary glance at his sword before reaching for it. A moment later, he, too, blew on his fingers.

"Our swords are made of godsteel and do not welcome the touch of an enemy. You will allow us passage with our weapons intact and at our sides."

The captain glared at Rhoane, his jaw tensed. The snooty man who'd led them to the throne room twittered and shifted uncomfortably behind them, unsure what to do. Kaida sat calmly, her gaze swinging from the guards to the captain.

"Did you say godsteel?" he asked at last. "That is a myth."

"Then I suggest you take my sword and see for yourself. He is called Claidholm Solais." Rhoane lifted his hands the same as Taryn and winked.

What was he playing at?

The captain hesitated, then signaled to the snobby courtier. "Allow them entry. I will tell the king myself why they are still armed." He cast a worried glance at their swords. "Is this truly the Sword of Light? And is that—"

"Ynyd Eirathnacht." Taryn put a protective hand on the hilt.

Something in the way he said the name rattled her brain.

"Blade of the Night Sky. Weapons of legend." He bent low at the waist. "Forgive me, Your Eminences."

She shared a look of incomprehension with Rhoane. Whatever was happening here, she hoped it was good and not going to get them thrown in the dungeon. The throne room doors opened and she swallowed the huge lump of paralyzing doubt that lodged itself in her throat.

Dozens of faces turned toward them and she was suddenly that terrified girl standing at the threshold of her mother's throne room on her crowning day. She looked to the ceiling, hoping to see her grandfather in the rafters, but they were alone.

Absolutely, totally, and completely alone on a foreign world with questionable hostile rulers.

CHAPTER SIXTEEN

Birds chirped outside the windows, their happy tunes a mockery of the irritation Eliahnna fought to suppress. Had she ever been as carefree as the birds? The answer, sadly, was no. Growing up believing she was second in line to the Light Throne, she'd always conducted herself properly, in the manner to which she wished for the empress to be regarded. Not that she ever thought she'd ascend the throne—more so, she hoped her mother and sister might look to her as an example.

All for naught. Her mother and Marissa didn't see her as anything but a quiet erudite not to be respected, but pitied. Her entire life had been one disappointment after another—according to the empress and crown princess. But Eliahnna hadn't let their subtle insults erode her beliefs. She'd held firm to her ideals and now—well, now Marissa was dead and she, Eliahnna, was crown princess—heir to the Light Throne.

And her mother was furious over the fact.

Eliahnna studied her mother as she sat at the head of the table with her councilors vying for her attention. Ever since their trip to the Summerlands, the empress had been distracted. At first, she thought it had to do with the Danurian who demanded

Lliandra rescind the taxes that he claimed were crippling his economy—which they were—but the longer they stayed in Menurra, Eliahnna began to suspect something else disturbed her mother's mind.

Whatever it was came and went with varied intensity. Some days, her mother was her old self—happy, laughing, carrying on with the business of running a kingdom, and other days, she could barely get up from her bed. It was no secret the empress was fading. Cashiel had seen to that when he took over her ship and blocked Lliandra from using her ShantiMari, leaving the empress vulnerable and without the mask she always wore. But this was something else. Yes, her fade was part of it, but there was a darkness surrounding her mother that she couldn't name and that bothered her more than she dared to admit.

"I don't care. You'll not re-route the roads and bypass these towns." Her mother's voice rose an octave above the birds' shrill cries and Eliahnna dragged her attention back to the privy council meeting. "There are thousands of people whose livelihoods depend on that trade. If you move the routes, they will lose everything."

The passion expressed by the empress was what made her such a good ruler. Unfortunately, she didn't have the same care for her children as she did her subjects. The lord at her right threw up his hands in resignation and looked to Eliahnna for an answer.

"I believe the empress is right. We can't move the trade routes without impacting the lives of all those who live along that road. What we can do, however, is build a better infrastructure so that these towns can expand into cities, thereby increasing traffic along the roads and businesses within their city walls."

She spent the next several bells outlining the plan she and Hayden had worked on in the Summerlands. Her mother's grim expression turned from one of annoyance to interest the longer Eliahnna spoke, and by the time the meeting concluded, the councilors were turning to her more often than the empress for input.

Seasons of studying the laws of not just their kingdom, but all of the lands of Aelinae had served her well. She might be quiet, but she wasn't stupid. And now not just the privy council knew it, but her mother, too.

She extricated herself from the mob of councilors who wished to congratulate her on a successful first privy meeting, and to beg for some private time with her, and hurried through the halls to her rooms. The attention was nice, but she needed to decompress after the intensity of the meeting. She hadn't expected it to go so well, nor had she dared hope her mother would be supportive of her speaking up during the meeting. She'd been fully prepared to fight for her right to voice her opinions. With any luck, the empress might now believe she was more than ready to take on the mantle of crown princess and learn how to rule.

It was what Marissa had grown up with, but had been denied to Eliahnna, even up until that morning. She nodded to several courtiers as she sped through the huge palace, her mind whirling, her blood pumping. Being listened to was exhilarating. Not just that she'd been heard, but that the councilors seemed to respect what she had to say. That was power. Not the crown, or the title, but having the men and women closest to the empress pay attention to what she offered was…well, amazing.

She hid a giggle behind her fingers and ducked down a less crowded hallway to avoid the curious stares that always came her way. The courtiers didn't quite know what to make of her, but they would soon understand she was not to be trifled with. Her experience in the meeting saw to that.

"Are you gloating?" Ebus snickered when she startled at his sudden appearance.

The wily spy had snuck up on her. A furious blush stained her cheeks and she sneered playfully at him.

"What reason have I to gloat?"

He shrugged as if it were no concern of his, but she wasn't fooled by his nonchalance. "Oh, I don't know, perhaps because you showed those pompous twits that you're not just a pretty girl with an empty head."

"And if I was just a pretty girl? Would I be of any less value?"

"Not at all. But you'd make a lousy empress." One of the reasons Taryn's spy had gained Eliahnna's respect was that he never minced words or was obsequious to her or any of the royals. A fact her mother hated, but she valued.

"To what do I owe the honor of your visit today, Master Ebus?" She linked her arm in his and slowed her step to a more lady-like pace.

"I've asked the others to join you in your rooms." He glanced furtively at those around them. "We have things to discuss."

If he took it upon himself to gather the others, then it must be important. They hurried to her rooms, and just as promised, she met the worried faces of Faelara, Baehlon, and Tessa. A pit of sorrow lodged in her throat that Hayden and Sabina weren't there. She valued their intelligence and perspective in these meetings, but the pair whose absence cut her heart most was Taryn and Rhoane. It had been hard to leave Menurra with Taryn's maids remaining with Hayden. She'd grown so accustomed to seeing them in their meetings that she almost considered them friends. If her mother ever knew she consorted with maids, she'd probably be punished, but Taryn's casual relationships had shaped her and her sister in more ways than one—and all good.

Two newcomers surprised her and she looked to Faelara for an explanation.

"Your Highness." Fae inclined her head and smiled as if she had a great secret. "I hope you don't mind our intrusion to your private rooms, but Ebus said it's a matter of life and death." Fae's glance went to the newcomers. "With your permission, I thought having Prince Gwainne and Prince Loghan here would be beneficial to everyone."

"Please, no titles. It becomes too cumbersome remembering who everyone is and how low to bow." Gwainne's smile was meant to charm, but it turned Eliahnna's stomach.

"Can we trust him? He is bedding the empress, after all." She crossed her arms over her chest and glared at the Ullan prince.

"If he squeals, I'll stab him in the eye." Tessa brandished the dagger Taryn had given her and waved it toward Gwainne. "I don't tolerate traitors."

Poor Tessa. She hadn't yet recovered from Marissa's death, and then suffered the shocking events on the ship. She'd waited for word of Taryn by turns acting out and weeping. When Taryn finally showed up in Menurra, it was only for a few weeks before she left again. And now no one knew where she was.

Their younger sister had a strong case of idol worship for Taryn, and neither she nor Faelara knew how to cure it. For it was a disease, in a way. Tessa had created a fantasy world where she was one moment a scurrilous pirate and the next an omnipotent god. Of course, their mother ignored Tessa's peculiarities, but Eliahnna did what she could to reassure the girl she was loved, she was safe, and that Taryn would one day return for longer than a sennight.

She hoped. They all hoped. Aelinae needed Taryn. She needed Taryn.

"Tessa, darling, it isn't polite to threaten guests before they've had a chance to prove their trustworthiness. But Eliahnna does bring up a good point. Why should we allow you into our private meeting? Either one of you, for that matter." Faelara fixed the princes with one of her stares that made even Lliandra tremble. Even if the empress wouldn't admit it. Fae could be ferocious when she wanted.

"I vow on the oath I took as a healer that what transpires here will not leave this room, nor ever pass my lips." Loghan put his hand over his heart and inclined his head. "I did not help save both Taryn and Rhoane's lives only to betray them now."

Eliahnna narrowed her eyes and studied Loghan's posture. He'd told her all about the exploits in Ulla with Taryn almost dying and Rhoane arriving in time to save her, and then how his father, Amdi Agnar, had made her fight in the arena even though she wasn't yet healed. Taryn had defeated the monster his father set against her, and then went on to best not only Gwainne, but the laird as well. Ever since, his father had been stricken with a darkness in his mind. He hadn't mentioned Marissa or Zakael, but his hints let Eliahnna know that both her sister and Taryn's brother had been to Ulla. Unfortunately, he wasn't privy to why they'd been to see the laird, but knew it wasn't for anything good.

Next, she glanced to Gwainne, who made a similar oath. Now this prince, she didn't know. He'd arrived at the palace gates, spinning a tale of the Eleri goddess Verdaine and a quest, but it made little sense to Eliahnna. She'd not had time to question him further because her mother dug her claws into the man nearly the moment he presented himself to the empress.

"It is true, I have bedded the empress, but that doesn't mean my loyalties lie with her. I am a prince of Ulla. My loyalties now, and forever, are to my kingdom. If the empress wishes to pass the time with me in her bed, I am not going to deny her desires. Naked playtime is not the same as sharing secrets."

"You might think as much, but Lliandra is crafty and very powerful with ShantiMari. She can pluck all sorts of details from your mind without you even knowing." Baehlon wrapped his arm around Faelara. "She beds indiscriminately, young prince. Do not be fooled by her charms."

Gwainne held up his hands. "Fine. If what Ebus has to say is indeed a matter of life and death, and involves the welfare of my kingdom, I won't bed the empress anymore. Is that good enough for you?"

"Not in the least, you lily-livered, half-baked excuse for an Ullan. That still gives you an out if you don't like what Ebus has to say, yet you have all the information to share. I say we castrate the maggot. Then there's no chance he'll bed the wench." Tessa picked at her teeth with the tip of her dagger and made a sucking sound.

"That's quite enough, young lady. I know you miss Taryn and you're hurting, but there's no reason to be rude to Gwainne or your mother." Despite Fae's words, her eyes were soft and Eliahnna felt her pain. They all missed Taryn.

"Bind me," Gwainne said. "Just, not this little one, and not with that dagger. But bind me to my word. Should I break my promise, trust me, the empress won't want anything to do with me or my manhood."

Tessa snickered, followed by a grunt from Ebus. Faelara and Baehlon agreed that was an admirable compromise and Eliahnna added her ShantiMari to Fae's to set Gwainne's oath. She wasn't sure what consequence Fae set, but for herself, she added a nasty little twist if Gwainne betrayed them. It involved massive amounts of ooze from somewhere he ought not be oozing.

Once everyone was settled, Gian entered with Duke Anje. The faerie immediately curled beside Tessa, and they chatted for a moment with their finger language. Eliahnna didn't know as much as she should, but she caught a few references to Taryn and Rhoane, and how much he, too, missed them. Kaida as well. Gian's sign for the grierbas was two fingers on either side of his mouth and a snarl. It made her smile to see the pair supporting each other, even if it was a difficult situation for them both.

"As most of you know, Gian has a life debt with Taryn," Ebus started and they all shifted their attention to the thief. He held up a hand. "Don't ask me what that means, because I don't know and if you ask him, he won't tell you. What I do know is, it allows him to see and hear things not meant to be heard—if it involves the welfare of the *Darennsai*. What I'm about to share with you will not be easy to hear, nor will you wish to believe it, but I witnessed part of this discussion myself. Although I couldn't hear their words, I am adept enough at reading lips that I corroborated Gian's story."

"Are you deliberately trying to stall, or would you like to get to the matter before I die of old age?" It wouldn't be a meeting without Baehlon's grousing, but in this instance, Eliahnna agreed with the knight.

"I suppose I am stalling." Ebus scrubbed his face with his palms and looked to Gian. The faerie gave him a solemn nod and he started his tale. "We were in the garden, eavesdropping on the courtiers as usual, when Myrddin and Brandt strolled beneath the branch where we were hiding. They were shielded, but we could see them. Gian thinks it has to do with his life debt. In any case, I believe Myrddin wished for us to know his terrible truth."

As he spoke, the color drained from Eliahnna's face and her hands went cold. Then her heart turned to ice, her tummy did somersaults, and finally, her whole body trembled. Prince Loghan sat beside her and wrapped a protective arm around her shoulders. She leaned into him for support, not wanting to believe what Ebus told them, but knowing in the depths of her being that he spoke true.

Myrddin had betrayed them all. From the very start, he'd been working for Kaldaar to upset the balance of Aelinae. Not only that, but he'd manipulated Taryn and Rhoane to leave their world. Ebus said it was at Nadra's behest, but that was too much for her to comprehend. Why would their goddess want them gone from Aelinae? Hadn't they just gotten Taryn back from wherever she was raised? She shoved her emotions deep within. An empress does not let her feelings show on her face. Ever. But gods, it was difficult to keep from gnashing her teeth and wringing her hands. She wished to rail against the gods and break every last expensive vase in her rooms. Instead, she sat passively, her fingers knotted in her lap the only outward display of her confusion and rage.

Eliahnna focused on Faelara and Baehlon. They didn't look as concerned as they should. Did they know Myrddin had betrayed them? Or did they already know about Taryn and Rhoane?

"It appears I need to have a chat with my father." Faelara stared out the window, her lips tight. "I can forgive him for not seeing me while he was here, but if he helped Myrddin with his devious plans… That I will never tolerate."

"Before you confront Brandt, you should know that I believe Myrddin was confessing. I think he's trying to help Taryn." Ebus's shoulder twitched in a slight shrug and he scratched at his neck. "Gian and I discussed it at length before coming to you. Myrddin said this is their final test before becoming what they must, whatever that means. And also that he couldn't tell Taryn he betrayed her, but hoped Brandt would. He refused, of course."

"What they are meant to become?" Loghan cocked his head. "What does that mean?"

"It means they are to become gods." Anje spoke and everyone turned toward him. Several mouths gaped open at the blunt admission. "It's always been their fate. Taryn wasn't aware of it until recently, but Rhoane has always known." His dark eyes shimmered in the afternoon light. "I suppose I've always known, too. It's why Valterys and Zakael were so desperate to control her powers. They wanted what she didn't even know she possessed."

"Our sister is a god?" Tessa's cheeks plumped with her wide smile. "Wicked. Now no one will dare try to hurt our family ever again."

"Darling," Faelara sat beside Tessa and wrapped her in her arms, "I'm afraid it will get much worse before it gets better."

It was the harsh truth none of them wished to accept. Eliahnna's mind whirled with plans.

"Gwainne, continue bedding Mother. But now, it is you who will be the one plucking information from her mind. Do it carefully. She isn't as daft as she pretends. Loghan, you, Faelara, and Baehlon will continue with your trip to Ulla. We can't let Myrddin know we suspect him. Tessa, you must promise not to let your anger get the best of you. If you're to lead my army one day, you must learn to control your temper."

Tessa looked up at her with tears streaming down her face. "You remind me of Mother." She swiped at her wet cheeks with a fist. "But in a good way. You're very empressy right now."

"And what will you do?" Gwainne asked, and they all turned toward her for an answer.

Eliahnna clasped the wooden snippet she always wore and closed her eyes. She would send word to her secret love and pray it wasn't too late.

CHAPTER SEVENTEEN

Taryn and Rhoane stood at the front of the vast room that was obviously meant to impress and intimidate. The king and queen sat upon their thrones, looking as if they both had a broomstick up their asses. Gold crowns rested on heads with long golden hair hanging like a silken waterfall down their backs. They wore robes like the rest of the court, but theirs were expensive gold brocade. The only color on their pale faces was a hint of the queen's pink lips and the king's dark-blue eyes. The pair reminded Taryn of expensive wallpaper—pretty to look at, but ultimately as boring as paste.

The monarchs hadn't acknowledged Taryn and Rhoane with words, but their sneers said all she needed to know. The queen seemed to take issue with Kaida, giving the grierbas furtive glances laced with disgust. The king glared at the back of the room as if waiting for something or someone.

Taryn kept her mind distracted so that she wouldn't do or say something that might get them executed, but it was difficult. Her season with Lliandra had taught her to have patience with selfish overlords, but damn. Being ignored in front of an entire court chafed at more than her patience. Not her pride. For that, she'd have to give a crap about this king and queen. Thus far, they'd given her little reason to show respect. No, their behavior chafed at her sense of decency. Rulers or not, their conduct was childish and rude.

Their thrones, however, were magnificent. Made from wood with intricate carvings and delicate scrollwork, they would've made Lliandra envious. But it wasn't the thrones themselves that took Taryn's breath away—it was in the way the white marble held the chairs aloft as if they floated. How the sculptors were able to make marble look weightless was remarkable.

Branches rose from the backs of the chair and more marble— this with gold veining—acted as a backdrop. The effect was truly stunning. As if the thrones were held on high, the king and queen gods.

But they weren't. The beauty of the thrones aside, Taryn reminded herself she was dealing with mortals. At least, she hoped she was. She'd had quite enough of battling gods for a while. A door opened in the back of the room, at least a football pitch in distance, and the sound of footsteps echoed in the silent hall.

Rhoane's fingertips tapped out the steps on the hilt of his sword while Taryn gazed at the paintings and frescoes that covered every inch of the walls and ceilings. It reminded her of the Menurran palace, which then made her think of the near identical mosaics they'd discovered in London.

How connected were the worlds? Dony said Stone Guardians were all over, and obviously Myrddin had found a way to travel between the worlds, but how much of the culture of Cilachaem was borrowed from other cultures and vice versa? Were they living in a closed ecosystem? Or were the worlds parallel, happening at the same time, but unknown to others? Cilachaem and Earth seemed to fit that model. What about Aelinae?

Her head throbbed with the infinite possibilities. And here they were, at the center of it all, trying not to brick it.

"There you are, my darlings." Queen Helena waved at the approaching group. "The Crown Prince Therronysus, and his brother Prince Theodonys."

Taryn and Rhoane turned to face the newcomers. Two men, who had to be related to the king and queen with shining golden hair, walked with several others. Rhoane sucked in a breath with a tsk. One of the princes wore their hair short as if he were sheanna, but that wasn't what caught Taryn's attention—angry red welts scarred his cheek in the shape of a flame, or perhaps even a dragon's wing. A flutter of recognition tickled her mind.

She flicked her attention to the others and sighed with relief to see Rori walking hand-in-hand with the scarred man. The Eleri of the Narthvier were gorgeous, but these elves were even more breathtakingly attractive, with their tipped ears and glossy hair. Beside Rori was a man who didn't fit the mold of the other elves. Handsome, yes, with dark hair and deep-brown eyes, his ears we not even a little bit pointed. Power wafted from him, but not from ShantiMari. He was lethally confident in his strides and his intent gaze studied her as they approached. She had a sense they'd met before, but couldn't place his face or name. He flicked a glance to Kaida and then back to Taryn as if he, too, were trying to remember how they'd met. A huge black dog—not quite as large as Kaida, but close—shuffled beside the group. Something about him tugged at Taryn, but she was too distracted to concentrate on what it was.

Rhoane, the dog—he's in pain.

I sense it as well. Although, I do not believe he is a dog.

Nor do I, but I don't know what he is.

He is a lycan, Darennsai. His ShantiMari was stolen from him by the one that created the scyvers. Kaida's thought was wrapped in sadness—and anger.

Taryn swallowed a gasp and brought her attention to the two

princes, who placed their right hands over their hearts and bent low. She smiled warmly, though her heart was aching for the lycan, and inclined her head. Rhoane kissed his thumb before placing it first to his forehead, and then to his heart in the traditional Eleri greeting. The princes were dressed similar to the other elves, but like the king and queen, their robes were decorated with gold and silver thread. Rori's garment was in the same vein, but not as blocky or ugly. And her blue hair certainly set her apart from the rest of the courtiers.

Taryn curtseyed to the king and queen, feeling it appropriate to at last address them now that the others had arrived. "It's an honor, Your Majesties. I'm Taryn. He's Rhoane." She didn't elaborate or use any of their titles. The snooty man's reaction to their names was enough for her to use caution. She reached for Kaida and pet her head. "And this is Kaida. She's a grierbas." She waited for them to acknowledge her with inclined heads before turning to Rori. "So, we meet again. I was hoping you would be here."

Rori left her little group and sauntered to Taryn and Rhoane. "It's nice to see you again. Hey, Kaida. Hey, Rhoane." Her informal greeting earned her several gasps from the uptight courtiers and Taryn chuckled. Rori knelt in front of Kaida, who greeted her with a wagging tail and long lick of her tongue against the girl's face.

"I hope your friend is all right. We tried to meet with her, but she hadn't returned. I hope she understands our time is limited and couldn't wait more than a day." Taryn joined Rori in scratching Kaida's neck. She wasn't sure whether mentioning Nikala by name would cause problems and hoped Rori understood her obliqueness.

Rori nodded, but her attention was on Taryn's ghost tattoos that shimmered lightly beneath her Glamour. She shared a look with the short-haired prince, and he flicked a glance first at Taryn's wrist, then Rhoane's.

"It's an honor to have you here. How may we be of service?" Rori's prince asked.

Taryn guessed he was the Crown Prince Therronysus, which was quite the mouthful to say. She hoped he had a nickname like Ted or something.

"We are in search of seals, Your Highness." Rhoane bowed low to him, then turned and bowed even lower to the king and queen. "If Your Majesties would be so kind, we would like to search your archives for any information that might lead us to a seal that looks like this." Rhoane flicked his wrist and made a glowing picture of the Seal of Ardyn dance on the air. "We have information that leads us to believe there is a seal here on Cilachaem."

The courtiers gasped and murmured among themselves. Taryn groaned. They'd both forgotten Rori's warning that they didn't call it Cilachaem anymore.

The king glared with open hostility meant to make her knees quake, but it just made him look a little sad. When would rulers realize bullying wasn't the way to lead?

"We do not speak that name here. You are in Elvenwood, sir, and would do well to remember who sits upon this throne." King Thane's voice boomed to the back of the room.

Fuck.

Rhoane bristled at her side, and she placed a calming hand on him. Truly, they hadn't meant to insult the monarchs within the first few minutes of being there, but she and Rhoane had both grown weary of placating egos. Nor did they have time to coddle and curry favor. The queen sat impassive, yet judgmental beside her husband, and Taryn's patience frayed.

Her Glamour brightened with her anger, and Rhoane put a hand on her forearm. At his touch, their tattoos lifted and floated in the air around them, not completely unusual, but alarming all the same. Why now? Why here? What were these people to cause their tattoos to show themselves?

"Be still, *mi carae*. They are ignorant of their own machinations." Rhoane's soothing words were meant to calm her, but the king rose from his throne and glowered at them with such malevolence and hatred, it was like a physical blow.

"Do not silence me, boy. You will—"

"Silence, petty king!" Taryn snapped, her willingness to placate gone.

Oh hell no. No one, king or otherwise, spoke to her beloved with such disrespect. They could treat her like shit, but how dare this petulant excuse for a king call her love a boy. Rhoane was a million times the man Thane would ever be. She drew her sword and held it aloft, ignoring the gasps and muffled cries of those nearby. They'd gone too far and needed a reminder of who she was. A crack of her anger flashed like lightning to the ceiling. She advanced on the king, her sword glowing as brightly as her flesh.

"I have battled gods, you pathetic excuse of an Eleri. Do not tell me what I will or will not do. I am here asking for help, not to play whose power is greater. Hint: you'll lose." Her silvery hair crackled as it floated around her and her feet hovered above the tiled floor.

Power coursed through her—great and terrible strength that could fell kingdoms and build worlds. Stars shone beneath her flesh and she had to remind herself to breathe, to control her anger. Technically, they didn't need the king and queen's help, but it would certainly make their search go smoother. But damn, she was tired. So tired—of playing stupid games, of chaos all around, and of never really knowing whether what they were doing was helping or hurting.

Behind her, she heard whispers and gasps, but she kept her focus trained on the man frothing at the lips and undulating like a serpent. To his left, the queen lost what little color her face had and she sat stiffly with hands on armrests, her body buzzing with anxiety that wafted to Taryn like waves crashing on the shore.

The king's expression turned stormy as he gesticulated wildly.

"Nae, lass. I will not lose. Not to some upstart who thinks a fancy sword is enough to frighten me. My forefathers have sat upon this throne longer than any of these families have been in existence. You have no right to come into my palace and threaten me."

A full season of dealing with her mother and the pernicious gods had taught her well. She refused to back down to this pathetic excuse for a ruler. Rhoane's ShantiMari buttressed against hers, and she wrapped it around her like a caress. He had her back should anything turn sour. Which, with any luck, it wouldn't, but luck hadn't been on her side of late.

"And my ancestors are descended from gods." Enough. She could toy with the insolent brat all day, but it wouldn't get them what they needed. With a sigh, she lowered to the floor. The glow evaporated from around her body and the symbols settled back into ghost tattoos on her wrist. She let go of her rage and tried for a softer approach. How could she despise bullies and yet act like one? "You're right. What was I thinking? Forgive me, Your Majesty." She inclined her head and a cumulative breath was released in the vast space.

The prince she believed to be Therronysus strode to her side and placed his hand over his heart. The brave, possibly stupid, creature earned a modicum of respect from her. He showed no fear in approaching a shimmering, starry-skinned woman who'd just insulted his parents. In fact, she rather liked this rash man.

"Father, perhaps it would be best if we allowed the travelers to tell us how it is they found a way to Elvenwood, and why these seals are of such importance. Perhaps then, we could aid them in their search. Since Hensen is permanently indisposed, I would be happy to assist."

"As would I, Your Majesties," a pretty woman with crimson hair who'd been standing with the prince added.

The other prince joined his voice to theirs, but Taryn noticed the handsome man with dark hair said nothing. A grey cat slunk over to where the lycan sat with Kaida and rubbed along the grierbas's foreleg. What was going on with people and critters loving on the blasted beast? Taryn couldn't remember a time when Kaida had allowed this much nuzzling, except for when she was a puppy and would snuggle with Tessa and Eliahnna. Was it Elvenwood, or something else affecting Kaida? She made a mental note to ask her once the threat in the throne room subsided.

Even though she'd lowered her tone, the king was still irate.

"What did you say about Hensen?" The king sat on his throne, his eyes narrowed to tiny slits, but that didn't stop his rage from shining through. "Indisposed?"

Therronysus lifted his chin and squared his shoulders. Oh, yes, she liked this rash madman. Anyone willing to take on the ire of the king was her ally.

"It is perhaps a matter best discussed in private."

"You will discuss it now. Has everyone in Elvenwood declared this defy the king day? Well, I'll have none of it. Speak, boy! Tell me what has happened to Hensen."

Tension prickled in the room and Taryn slowly stepped back until she was even with Rhoane. Whatever this new development was, it didn't involve them and she couldn't get caught in the crossfire. She'd be wary and observant, but this seemed to be a family matter best resolved without her interference. The gods knew she had enough family drama on Aelinae to last several lifetimes. Besides, she might learn something watching how these people interacted.

The prince bowed to his father. "As my king commands. Hensen was using dark magic in the library. A black stain covered the forbidden section and when I impaled it with my sword, Hensen, erm, well, he melted, sire."

"Melted?" The queen leaned forward, her face a study in misery.

"You killed my servant?" King Thane rose again, madness in

his dark eyes. "Hensen was loyal to us, you idiot. Why did you kill him?"

Taryn slipped her right hand into Rhoane's and her left into Kaida's fur. At the mention of dark magic, the hairs on the back of her neck pricked and her nerves snapped against her skin. Though glad they missed the melted guy, it appeared they'd walked into a hornet's nest. Should she have need, she'd whisk her two loves back to the kitchen, where they could use the doorway to leave this godforsaken palace.

The king raised his hand and a glowing orb formed. Thane's lips moved, but Taryn couldn't make out the words he spoke. It was eerily similar to when she'd first arrived on Aelinae and Zakael had killed Brandt. She shut the memory away, not wanting to get lost in the emotional turmoil that day had wreaked. Seeing the king's intense focus, she was certain he whispered a curse. Why would the king attack his own son with a cursed fireball? What the hell was wrong with this family?

That almost made her laugh. Seeing as her own family was batshit crazy, maybe it was a royalty thing—to be king or queen meant being a little mad.

Do we intervene, mi carae?

I'm afraid of what might happen if we do. The prince looks capable of protecting himself. I've got you and Kaida, but if you could keep an eye on the others, I'd appreciate it.

The queen half-rose from her seat. "Thane, stop this at once!"

The king was too far gone in his spell to hear or care. Behind the king, a dark shadow hovered. Her heart dipped, but it wasn't Kaldaar. This shadow looked like an ordinary man with dark hair, bearded, but with a damaged face. Red scars spiderwebbed across his neck and cheeks. A wave of hatred roiled from the figure.

Is he here? Or is this an apparition?

No idea, but he's vile, of that I'm certain.

I recognize him. From the woman on the train. I believe he is the one who created the scyvers.

What the bloody hell is he doing here? Rhoane, what's going on?

I wish I knew.

Captured faeries on Earth, the man responsible for the scyvers on Cilachaem—how were they connected and how did they affect Aelinae? Was it Kaldaar's doing? She imagined him jumping from world to world, infecting each with his malice. They had to stop him. Whatever it took, they had to prevent Kaldaar from poisoning any more worlds.

The shadow stared past the prince to the handsome man who'd entered with Rori. Their coloring wasn't the only similarities Taryn noted—they reminded her of Valterys and Zakael. A shudder wracked her from head to toe and Rhoane's grip tightened on her hand. Her sword hung awkwardly between their clasped fingers, but easy enough to snatch if need be. The throne room darkened with King Thane's muttering and the fireball spun with ferocious speed, eager to be freed.

At the crack of magic being unloosed, the prince reached for his sword. Taryn threw a blanket of protective ShantiMari over those nearest to the prince and she felt Rhoane's power spread through the room.

The fireball sped toward the prince, who swung at it with his sword in one long, powerful stroke. A shriek tore through her hearing as the sword sliced the fireball in two. The king's Shanti-Mari fizzled and curled in on itself like a paper burning to ash. The prince stomped on the embers until every last one was crushed beneath his boot.

Therronysus held his sword high, much as Taryn had done a few minutes earlier. A look of triumph and challenge filled his eyes. She squeezed Rhoane's fingers. They definitely needed this guy on their side.

The shadow disappeared and the king wobbled a moment before steadying himself against the throne.

"Get out. All of you. Get out of my kingdom and don't ever

return." Thane pointed to each of them in turn, starting with Therronysus, then to the other prince, the pretty redhead, and next to Taryn, and Rhoane. He jabbed a finger at the dark-haired man and Rori as if to emphasize they most of all needed to leave. The handsome chap whispered in Rori's ear, then strode from the throne room without looking back. Whoever he was, he gave about as many fucks as Taryn for the king's tantrum. He might also make a good ally.

"No, Father." Therronysus stood to his full height and faced his parents. "This is our home. We will not leave the kingdom to you and your whims." He sheathed his sword and took a step forward, his hands out, palms up. "What chaos have you brought, Father? What have you done that cannot be undone?" His tone was submissive, calming. To his mother, he said, "We will stay and repair whatever destruction you've caused."

The king sat upon his grand throne, fuming and sputtering, with droplets of spittle flying through the air. The courtiers cowered to the edges of the great room. They were caught between the king and heir apparent. Their loyalty should be solely to the king, but Taryn sensed their fear and discontent. What had King Thane been doing, indeed.

Not her circus, not her monkeys. She forgot where she'd heard that saying, but it fit far too well at the moment. This wasn't her problem to fix. This wasn't even her world or her kingdom or her family. Except, of the former, it might be? She shook her head in disbelief. They weren't gods yet. If they were killed, would Cilachaem cease to exist?

Was this part of Kaldaar's plan? She didn't sense the god in Elvenwood, but she wouldn't put anything past him. Seeing King Thane's irrational rage was a little too familiar. Valterys, Zakael, Marissa, Amdi, and her personal favorite, Cashiel had all exhibited similar anger toward her.

Perhaps her very presence was a trigger to them. As if Kaldaar had implanted a response that automatically activated if or when she got near.

Her mind cycled to Nikala and the way she'd reacted to their ShantiMari. Taryn's thoughts spun with possibility. How many more would she set off? And, if she was the trigger, how did she reset the code?

CHAPTER EIGHTEEN

Rhoane bent over the ancient manuscript and squinted at the elaborate scrawl. Damned scribes were more enamored with their artistry than with the words they wrote. It was his fifth time trying to decipher the unusual spellings and his frustration was at its limit.

Nothing about their day had gone as planned. Starting with Taryn's exhaustion from using too much power on Earth, and ending with them poring over stacks of books and parchments in an attempt to find a seal. His ears still rang from the queen's screeching. She'd shouted and stomped her foot, all the while the king seethed with rage. Eventually, and with both the princes' help, the monarchs relented and allowed Taryn and Rhoane to search the library. Albeit, with a guard of ten fierce-looking soldiers standing ready.

Rhoane glanced at the sharp pikes the guards gripped as if prepared to stick them like a pig at any moment. He shook his head at the idiocy of some people. Just as the queen's tantrum had been unnecessary, so too were the guards.

Taryn adjusted the collar on her robe and rolled her shoulders. They'd adapted their outfits to clothing more fitting the elven palace, with Taryn wearing a soft-blue cape that went from throat to toes and pants of the same color. Unlike the elven robes, hers opened at the waist to flare out behind her like darathi wings. Rhoane's robe of jade was more in line with what the princes wore, but he, too, wore pants beneath his long tunic. Hell, the princes might be wearing trousers; he really didn't know. He'd just assumed they weren't. Considering his experience with assuming, he should've known better.

"Everything is so stuffy here. It's hard to breathe." Taryn tugged on the collar and made a face.

"Well, we *are* inside a mountain. Would you like some fresh air?"

"In a little bit. I need to decipher this passage first." She bent her head to study the page in front of her, and he returned to his frustrating manuscript.

The two princes joined them at the table, their voices lowered in conversation. They spoke about Hensen and the dark stain, but Rhoane deliberately shut out their conversation. He and Taryn had agreed not to get involved in whatever family squabble was happening. Same with the situation on Earth: they decided they had to focus on their objective first.

Each world they visited would have the possibility of turmoil. It wasn't for them to fix every problem—not that they thought they could, but it pained their hearts not to do so. He'd promised her that after balance was restored on Aelinae, and the threats of Rykoto and Kaldaar were eliminated, they could return and offer assistance. It was his fervent desire that all the realms find peace, sooner rather than later.

From the corner of his eye, he caught Taryn grinning and peered in the direction of her focus. Rori sat with Kaida near a table laden with books. The great black beast panted beside her, and the strange grey cat looked as if he were carrying on a conversation with the three of them.

"Prince Therronysus," Taryn began, but the prince stopped her.

"Please, call me Therron."

"Thank the gods. Your names are rather formal, but I guess that's par for the palace." She looked as if she'd say more, her eyes narrowed in that way that made his pulse race. Her beautiful brain was working through something, but in a flash, her expression changed and she tilted her head behind her. "What's back there? I sense suffering and anger and something I can't quite put a finger on."

"It's vile, isn't it?" Therron moved in close. "Just yesterday, a stain appeared. When I impaled it with my sword, our librarian Hensen melted into a puddle of black goo and feathers. Did you notice the shadow standing behind my father in the throne room?"

So much for not interfering. Rhoane sighed and reminded himself that Taryn's heart was full of kindness.

"Do you think your father is being controlled by a Telraicht-Noir Master?" Rhoane kept his voice low, but these were elves. Their hearing might be as good as his.

"A what?"

"They are followers of Kaldaar and practice forbidden ShantiMari."

"You lost me there. I don't know who was behind my father, but whoever it is, I'm certain he's responsible for Rori's encounter in the in-between."

Taryn glanced at the blue-haired girl. "We felt something in the void—a presence—but we didn't see what it was. It wasn't friendly, of that I was certain."

"She claims it was a snake-dragon-demon. It bit her shoulder and when she came through my doorway, she bore the fang in her flesh."

Rhoane sucked in a breath. "You are saying she was bitten by this demon and has already recovered?"

"Exactly. Eiodian, our most skilled healer, is quite perplexed. She and her brother—the gentleman who was in the throne room with us, but left after Father's outburst—they are remarkably fast at healing. He arrived here from the human realm not more than a sennight past, suffering from a wound most would consider fatal. Yet he, too, is recovered."

Taryn gazed at Rori, her eyes narrowed and bottom lip caught between her teeth.

"Do you think Myrddin hid the seal in the void?" Rhoane pulled her attention away from Rori and back to their immediate concern.

"I hope not, but if so, we'll have to go in there to claim it." She turned to Therron. "Do you know where in the void Rori was when she was attacked? Which portal did she use?"

Therron's jaw tensed and he glanced at the guards. "I can help, but not here. We'll meet later and I'll explain."

He drifted off toward Rori, and they were left to stare after him.

"Is everyone at this palace weird? Or is it just us?"

"Perhaps it is a mixture of both."

"So diplomatic." She nudged his shoulder with her own. "I would swear I've met not just Rori before, but Therron, too. Rori from that vision I had, and Therron, I don't know from where. It's a tickle in my memory, but slips through my fingers if I try to grasp it too hard." Her groan sounded as frustrated as he felt. "I'm getting nowhere. How about you? Want to go explore and find some fresh air?"

"I would love to." Rhoane stepped around the large table and the guards shifted. "Should we tell them or leave them to mutter to themselves?"

They managed only a few steps when Therron and Rori approached. He'd not had a chance to speak to the pretty blue-haired girl, but as she stood before him, eyes downcast, anxiety rolled off her and she fidgeted with something in her hand.

"Have you found something?" Rhoane cocked his head, eyes searching Therron's.

Rori held out her open palm to show three amulets and Taryn gasped.

One was the pendant Nikala had been wearing and the other two were new. Not as elaborate as Nikala's, but beautiful craftsmanship all the same.

"Do you see the little symbols etched into the glass? Do you know what they mean?" Rori bit her lip, as if asking had been difficult. Kaida sat at her side and nudged Rori's hand until she petted the grierbas.

He'd never seen the beast take to someone as quickly as she had Rori. He took the pendants from her and inspected them one by one. Each had decorative coverings over the glass, with a tiny stamped piece of silver around the neck.

"These markings are crude, but legible." His ghost tattoos shimmered beneath his skin and he understood why Rori had asked him. The symbols stamped on the silver were similar to the runes etched in his skin. "This, I believe, is the rune for Eleri. Or, as you say, elf." He handed Rori an amulet decorated with vines and leaves and inspected the most elaborate amulet—the one Nikala had been wearing in London. Gold and silver strands wrapped around the glass in curls that looked like the tiny veins seen on air faerie wings. "This means faerie." He held the last one between his fingertips. Dread pooled in his belly. Unlike the first two amulets that glowed softly from within, the interior of this glass was entirely black.

"And that last one?" Rori urged.

Rhoane glanced at Taryn and saw by her frown she already knew what was inside.

"This one represents a *darathi vorsi*, what you'd call a dragon."

Rori nearly dropped the pendant. "Cilachaem doesn't have dragons."

"So you've said. But either Rhoane's mistaken, which I highly doubt, or someone found a dragon here." Taryn rolled her bottom lip between her teeth, her brows dipped in a V.

"Or," his eyes bore into Taryn's, "they found one on another world." Rhoane slipped his hand beneath his love's. She squeezed his fingers and he felt the slight tremor in her grip.

"Snickertits. I hadn't considered that as a possibility. Is there any chance you can go to the Seelie Court? Queen Eirlys has the rest of the amulets and I'm sure she'd like to know what's inside." Rori glanced from Taryn to Rhoane, her look hopeful.

"We cannot afford the time, I am afraid." He was truly sorry to deny them, but each moment they were away from Aelinae was a chance for Kaldaar to strengthen his hold.

"How many are there?" Taryn's words warbled and he felt her emotions as if they were his own. She was scared, but also incensed that someone would do this.

"Dozens." Rori looked to Therron and he nodded. "I was imprisoned in one and escaped, but I think I'm the only one who has. We don't know how to release them."

Rhoane already knew Rori had been imprisoned in one of the glass prisons—Taryn had shared the conversation she overheard between Rori and Nikala, but he didn't know they couldn't free those trapped inside. The fear he'd sensed from the woman inside Nikala's amulet had been potent enough to immobilize even a seasoned soldier. What he'd thought was a one-off was becoming a swath of living creatures captured in the glass vials. He understood and shared Taryn's frustration that they couldn't spare the time or energy to help.

Taryn reached for Rori's hand and gripped it in her own. "When I saw you in the vision, you had a sleeping fae in your pocket. Was she also a prisoner?"

"She's Queen Eirlys's daughter." A look passed between Rori and Taryn.

The sleeping fae was the girl Taryn recognized as her daughter. He blew out a breath and looked to the rafters for answers. A large domed skylight showed the cloudy skies overhead and his darathi longed to stretch his wings. Soon. Perhaps there was a way to see Queen Eirlys without taking too much time away from their search. Better yet, the Seelie queen might shed some light on their past. Or was it their future?

"There's a book on Eleri runes in the forbidden section." The crimson-haired girl from the throne room stepped close to their little circle. "I'm Rainne." She curtseyed prettily and tucked a lock of hair behind her ear. "Lady Delarainne, actually, but I prefer Rainne. That's my cat, Pora."

Taryn squinted at the wee beastie. "He's an odd little thing, isn't he?"

"Quite. But that book." She drifted to the forbidden section as if she owned the library.

The guards shifted and looked at one another, but didn't stop her. Therron chuckled and joined Rainne in the back of the nook Rhoane and Taryn had been forbidden from entering. After a minute of searching, they came back with not one but three volumes.

"It's in Eleri, though. Can you read it?" Rainne handed the book to Rori.

"I can't. Can you, Therron?"

He flipped through the pages and tilted his head side to side. "Enough. If not, perhaps my brother Theo can. We had a tutor when we were lads who taught us the old ways."

Prince Theo sidled next to Rainne and peered over his brother's shoulder. "Mother can decipher those. She pretends to eschew the old ways, but she's quite keen on our history."

Rhoane glanced at Taryn, and she grinned, mischievousness dancing in her eyes.

I know that look. What are you planning, mi carae?

Nothing. I promise. It's just the way they refer to anything Eleri as the old ways. It's surreal to be standing here listening to young Eleri speak of a planet we supposedly created, as old. How does that even happen?

He'd been asking himself the same question. What concerned him most at the moment was the possibility that someone had traveled to other worlds, capturing creatures in those tiny glass bottles. Why? And if Cilachaem didn't have dragons, then where did they come from? Were they the missing darathi vorsi of Aelinae?

His blood heated with his anger and he flexed his fists as the thoughts came fast and furious. Had Cilachaem ever had dragons and if so, where were they now? If the elves of Elvenwood had forgotten Eleri ways, could that happen to the Eleri on Aelinae? Aelinae had already lost her dragons; was this the natural progression of things?

Eleri were not only the caretakers of the darathi vorsi—hell, all darathi—they were also the guardians of that world. Somewhere in Aelinae's past, the Eleri had forgotten who they were. His ancestors might have guarded all of Aelinae, but the current living Eleri thought themselves better than the other races on their world.

Not unlike the elves of Elvenwood. He studied the group as they discussed how best to get Queen Helena to help and his heart pounded a steady death march in his ears. If he and Taryn had created Cilachaem, was it a success? Or had they failed?

Were calamities like Kaldaar the natural progression of a world, and no amount of fighting the inevitable would change it? Or did they still hold hope in their mission?

There is always hope, mi carae. Taryn's thought brushed his troubled mind.

His gaze went to the two princes. *They are the hope for this world and we are the hope for ours.*

He took her hand in his, ready to be out of the stuffy confines of the mountain. No more than a few steps later, Kaida howled a yearning, piercing cry as if her life were ending.

CHAPTER NINETEEN

The very air in the room stopped at the sound of Kaida's wail. Taryn's skin prickled and her ShantiMari whipped toward her friend. Never in her time with the grierbas had she ever heard her make such a sorrowful, pain-filled sound, and it scared the fuck out of her.

"What is it, Kaida?" Taryn knelt and immediately checked her skin for cuts while her power went through Kaida's internal organs.

Not me, Darennsai. The lycan—he is dying. Help him, please.

"Rhoane, he needs us." Taryn pointed to the black beast who panted heavily and swayed from side to side. "Put him over there." She pointed to a large ottoman. "Thank you, my friend. We will do what we can for him." Taryn nuzzled Kaida, her skin prickling with the flood of relief that sped through her veins. The emotion was short lived as a storm of anxiety nipped at the tail end of any joy she might've had. Blinking away her worry and the traitorous tears that bit the backs of her eyes, she turned toward the lycan.

"Can you heal him?" Rainne hung back, her eyes filled with distress, and her hands flexing as if reaching for something.

"We'll do our best, but you are of this world—your Shanti-Mari will add strength to ours." Taryn tilted her head toward the group.

"No. I can't. I might hurt him worse." Rainne backed up several steps and shook her head.

"If you change your mind, you're welcome to join us." Taryn thought she saw faint green veins travel the length of Rainne's forehead and neck, but when she looked closer, the girl was as pale as ever.

Theo held Rainne in his arms, his expression equally as worried and defeated as hers. Kaida howled again, and Taryn left the couple, determined not to get involved while doing exactly that. It reminded her of one time she and Brandt went to Christmas dinner at his friend's house. They were outsiders looking in on years of family history that didn't involve them, but by the end of the night they were part of. Except here, she felt responsible. Which made no sense at all.

She knelt at the ottoman with Rori between her and Rhoane. The lycan huffed with labored breaths that came in rapid spurts. Pora hissed and yowled as he paced the perimeter of their legs. Therron knelt opposite Rori, his concern focused on the girl more than the lycan.

Rhoane, can you heal the beast?

I can try. Shall we use our swords?

Taryn's hand wavered over the hilt of Ynyd Eirathnacht. *I don't think so. At least, not at first. We don't know what godsteel does to a lycan.*

I sense two beings in this one. What is he?

Lycans are like us, but instead of darathi vorsi, he's a wolf. She'd leave it there for the moment. Trying to explain werewolves to him might do his head in. As it was, they had enough to deal with already.

Rhoane's eyes widened as he studied the black beast. She settled herself and placed her hands close to Rori's. Being careful not to let too much ShantiMari loose and set off her glowing, floating-above-the-floor thing, she slid her power to the lycan and the rest of the group. Rhoane's ShantiMari joined hers, and she leaned into it.

Rori's thoughts bounced around the group, open and vulnerable to their hearing. Taryn sent a thread of power to the girl and also to Therron. The scar on his cheek looked freshly made and she heard the soft rustling of dragon's wings in her mind. She shared a glance with Rhoane and saw that he, too, heard the familiar sound.

As Rhoane began a healing chant, the lycan kicked out. Against the song or the touch of their ShantiMari, she wasn't sure, but it distressed him immensely. Instead of pulling away, she strengthened her power and reached for the others to join her ShantiMari. Therron's wove between hers and Rhoane's threads, but Rori's power was shielded from them. Taryn suspected not from her own doing. She coaxed Rori to open up and release all that she had, but that only confused the poor girl.

While keeping a connection to Rori to help her release what was blocking her full powers, Taryn searched the lycan for signs of distress. If they could understand how his ShantiMari was stolen from him, then maybe they could restore not only his power, but his ability to shift back into his human form.

A shudder went through her as she searched his memories. Of the one who stole his power, she saw only a shadow, much like the one in the throne room behind the king. Pure hatred oozed from the image and the lycan whimpered. Kaida yipped and nipped at his neck in what Taryn hoped was a healing thing sentient beasts did to help each other. Pora hissed and whipped his tail as if he were half a heartbeat away from shredding all of their faces with his claws.

Help me heal you. Where does it hurt most?

The lycan groaned and stretched, and Taryn saw a bloodied and bruised stump inside the lycan's mind. It wasn't an actual stump, but how the lycan pictured the loss of his ShantiMari. Bile surged up her throat and she gagged against the sickness. Who would do this to a living being?

Rhoane's song rose in timbre and his power flooded where Taryn touched the lycan's fur.

I'm fine. Keep healing the lycan. Here, can you sense it?

I can, mi carae. This will be difficult, but I believe with Rori and Therron's help we will succeed. Kaida, what does he need besides our power?

I do not know, Surtentse. He wavers between wishing to be healed and wishing for death.

Taryn understood his feelings all too well. The bloody stump in his mind opened the barely healed memory of when Zakael had cut her off from her power. She'd felt lost and broken. A singe of guilt cut her heart. That must've been how Rhoane felt after Marissa raped him.

What cured him, and what gave Taryn the strength she'd needed to continue was love. It sounded so simple to her now, but true. Unconditional love had saved Rhoane from being lost to his brokenness. Who did the lycan have to love him?

She glanced at Pora and Kaida, then at Therron and Rori. And finally, at her betrothed. They were fighting for this beast they didn't know because somewhere, they all knew how it felt to be stepped on, bullied, and broken.

Therron's ShantiMari brushed against hers, and she saw an image of herself as a child, perhaps five or six, in a golden room talking to Therron. Their eyes met and he looked equally as baffled as she—it wasn't a vision, but a memory. His, but also hers. She *remembered* him. Of course, the elf she'd dreamt of as a child was Therron. Somehow, they'd communicated between Earth and Cilachaem, but how? And why? She glanced at his scar and saw in it darkness, but beyond that, a sky filled with darathi vorsi. Her gaze flicked to his eyes, which continued to watch her with wary curiosity. He didn't know who he was, or his destiny. How, exactly, was his future tied to Aelinae?

Rhoane's song lowered and Taryn returned her focus to their healing. Rori held back and she urged her to unlock the hidden part of herself that was shielded behind layers and layers of powerful wards. What could be so dangerous it needed excessive warding? She slipped her ShantiMari through Rori's blood and up to her brain. Her thoughts were scattered and she was scared, but there, lurking in the midst of her memories, was Rori's secret. She was a fucking unicorn.

Not a prancing rainbow of sparkles, but a creature of such pureness it brought tears to Taryn's eyes. And Rori had no clue. Just like Therron didn't know he had a dragon soul.

They'd need everything the pair had to save the lycan. Rhoane prodded Therron to unleash his inner darathi vorsi and Taryn urged Rori to unlock her unicorn. Even saying that to herself made her giggle. If dragons and elves were real, why not unicorns?

Rori struggled to believe her, but Taryn sensed her effort to break through what was holding her back. A deluge of memories roared through Rori's mind, drowning Taryn, but she kept a firm grasp as the emotions swirled and tilted. They poured into the lycan, with all of Rori's fear and love and uncertainty.

Taryn opened her ShantiMari to corral all of their power and funnel it to that place in the lycan's mind where he was most injured and aggrieved. A spark lit from the stump, tiny at first, and then glowing as bright as a star. Rhoane's ShantiMari cloaked them and he finished his song with an Eleri blessing.

The lycan settled and his breathing came in even drags. His head lifted off the ottoman and he looked at Taryn with a sense of deep gratitude. She nodded and rose, her legs stiff from kneeling for so long. Several servants came to take the lycan away and she turned to follow.

Rhoane took her hand in his, and she felt the trembling of his muscles as if it were her own. The healing had exhausted them, but it was more than that. It was what they'd discovered about themselves and the others. Perhaps it wasn't a healing only for the lycan.

"They are taking him to the healing wards," Theo explained and Taryn nodded.

"I'd like to make sure he's comfortable, if you don't mind."

"I'm sure Eiodian would like to talk to you both. He's our chief healer and was quite vexed at the beast's condition."

"Lead the way." Taryn glanced over her shoulder, to where Rori and Therron shared a kiss.

They could talk later, after they'd had a chance to recover from the healing and their discoveries. Whether or not Therron consciously remembered her, she was more than curious to know how it was she had been able to communicate with him and if he'd been on Cilachaem or Earth.

As they walked through the open hall where granite columns soared toward the ceiling and the enormous tree grew as if trees growing inside a palace were normal, Taryn's skin itched as if bugs crawled all over her. She veered toward the tree and the itching increased.

Rhoane stepped forward, his hand outstretched as if to touch the bark, but suddenly doubled over and cried out.

Taryn lunged and pulled him to her, away from the tree. "What is it, *mi carae?*"

His face had lost all color and blue veins stuck up on his forehead. "The tree is sick."

He forced the words out, and she kept moving them toward the other side of the room. The veins diminished and color slowly returned to his cheeks.

"We will have Eiodian look at him. Come." Theo didn't look confident as he spoke. His gaze flicked from Rhoane to the tree and back.

"Is there something we should know about that tree?" Taryn wasn't in the mood to play games. "Why would it hurt Rhoane?"

"I don't know. The Elvenwood was first planted when the world was created." Theo looked to Rainne, and she swallowed with a quick shake of her head. "By you."

What the actual fuck?

A branch lowered and a tendril caressed her cheek. She flinched and reached for her sword.

"Nay, lass." Theo put his hand over hers and for a moment she could've sworn it was Rhoane who spoke.

The tendril stroked along her jaw and dropped a nut into her open palm before swinging toward Rhoane's face. His eyes widened with an anxious wildness before rolling up and only the whites were visible.

"Rhoane!" Taryn grabbed him around the waist and hurled him toward the stairs, but the branch stopped her movement.

A second, slimmer branch lowered toward Rhoane's hand and he reached for it, despite Taryn mentally willing him to leave the damned thing alone. The branches retracted to settle near the ceiling. The entire episode happened in only a few moments, enough not to alarm those around them, but Taryn felt a shift, as if something monumental had taken place.

She stared at the benign branches above them and then pulled her gaze to Rhoane's face. He was looking at his hand with a sense of bafflement. Gripped in his fist was a lone leaf. She held her hand beside his and showed him the caramel-colored nut the tree had given her. No bigger than her thumbnail, it looked innocent lying on her palm.

"I know these. This seed, that leaf—they're the same as the Weirren."

"Cllynellren. That is the ancient name of the great tree of the Weirren."

Taryn worried the nut between her thumb and forefinger. Was it a warning, or a wish?

CHAPTER TWENTY

Eoghan stood on the highest balcony of the Weirren and looked out over the Narthvier toward the south. Toward Talaith and his love. His fingers played with a seed the tree had dropped and he pictured the carving he could make once it hardened. He'd send it to Eliahnna as a token of his affection and to let her know he was thinking of her. As always.

The honey-hued nut ducked under and over his fingers as he planned what he'd inscribe into the flesh. An image of Taryn and Rhoane burned into his mind and he shuddered against it. The seed faltered but didn't fall from his grip, and he stared at the thing as if it were possessed.

Rhoane was sick. Far away, too far for Eoghan to reach, his brother was unwell. It had something to do with the Weirren, but what? He closed his eyes and held the seed to his lips, begging the vision to continue, but the connection was lost. All that remained was a sense of urgency and melancholy. The dichotomous emotions banged against his heart. Were they Rhoane's? Or something else?

A second vision struck him, and he swayed with the overwhelming love that flooded through his senses. Eliahnna. He gripped the iron railing that kept him from falling from the perilous height and struggled to clear his mind to receive her message. They'd discovered quite by accident that if she held the wood snippet he'd given her and concentrated solely on Eoghan, they could mentally communicate across the many leagues separating them. Of course, if they were closer together, she wouldn't need the snippet. But at such a large distance, it was necessary.

When he'd made the trinket, he'd only wished to give her a reminder that he was fond of her, but that fondness had grown on both their parts with secret letters that eventually turned into them being able to speak across the lands using only their minds. And now, he could speak to her and she him, even without the wood snippet.

Eoghan? Are you able to talk? There are…things you must know. Eliahnna's usually calm voice battered his skull.

I am here. What is it, my love?

Her sigh was like a gentle breeze. *Thank Nadra. There is so much, but where do I start?*

He could picture her wringing her hands, her blueish green eyes large in her lovely face. *Start with the most vexing problem and we will solve it together.*

That's the problem. They're all fairly terrible.

He heard her take a deep, cleansing breath and then she proceeded to tell him of betrayals and godly possessions, ending with the revelation that Taryn and Rhoane weren't on Aelinae.

Eoghan stared at the lengthening shadows as he listened, not quite wanting to believe everything she shared, but knowing in his bones what she said was true. He'd felt a disconnect from his brother for the past sennight, but attributed it to the fact Rhoane was in the Summerlands for his friends' wedding. Turned out, Eoghan was right to worry.

He gripped the seed in his fist and pounded the railing at his stupidity. Why hadn't he shared his concerns with his father? Because he wouldn't have believed him. The king had a blind spot with anything having to do with Rhoane. Especially if it involved Taryn.

How can I help? Eoghan's mind spun with ideas and schemes, all of which his father wouldn't allow. But he'd find a way to protect the woman he loved.

His gaze went to the sky and for one mad, glorious moment, he imagined flying south to Talaith. It was folly to daydream impossibilities, though. He'd never been out of the Narthvier. How would he find his way to Eliahnna?

Just knowing you're there and you support me means everything. Despite Eliahnna's claim, he couldn't help but feel guilty that he wasn't with her when she needed him.

They said their farewells and he stood at the railing for several long moments, contemplating his wild scheme. Nothing was stopping him from leaving the vier. Well, if he considered betraying his father—the king—nothing, then he was free to leave that very moment. Unfortunately, King Stephan didn't take lightly to Eleri who left the safety of the Narthvier.

"If those furrows were any deeper, I could plant potatoes for the winter in them." Carga slid beside him and wrapped her arm around his waist. She smelled of herbs and onions.

"Have you come home to cook for Father again? You spoil the old man." He meant it as a jest, but her sudden arrival spiked his heartrate. She was supposed to be at Verdaine's temple, training the novices. Although, it was true everyone loved her cooking, not just their father.

"I have not been sleeping well these past few weeks." She rubbed his arm and rested her head on his shoulder. "I fear for our brother and his beloved."

His stomach flipped and he sucked in a breath. "I have had word from Eliahnna. There is much to tell, and I fear you will not like the telling of it."

She stared up at him, her pretty heart-shaped face full of concern. "Tell me everything, Eoghan. Leave nothing out."

He palmed the little nut and pulled her close before he reiterated what Eliahnna had told him. When he came to the part about Myrddin's betrayal, he stumbled. The mage had always been a friend of the Eleri. His father would not take the news well at all, possibly even going so far as to lock down the forest, letting no one in or out. Eoghan's heart pinched and he shuddered at the realization that he would be trapped in the Narthvier.

"I must go to Eliahnna."

Carga turned to face him, her eyes narrowed. "Yes, that is your path. But Father will not allow it. How do you plan to convince him to let you leave?"

The twist of her lips was clue enough she was testing him, but the spark in her jade eyes hinted at a bit of mirth.

"Does the idea of our father shouting at me bring you so much joy?"

"Not at all, brother. But seeing you blossom over this past season does. It is obvious to all who know you how much you care for the Aelan princess. Go to her, but be wary. She will be empress soon and sit on the Light Throne. You know well what that means."

Eoghan shook his head. "She will not be like her mother. Eliahnna means to bring a new era to the east. All children born to her will live at the palace, male or female, and she will not choose her lovers indiscriminately."

Carga's smile widened. "I see. And will you be her paramour, my brother? For I doubt the councilors will allow you to be emperor."

"I will be whatever Eliahnna needs me to be. Protector, lover, husband—she will have my support and my loyalty."

"You have it bad, brother. I wish you luck on your journey." She turned his hand over and opened his palm to reveal the nut. "What is this?"

"A seed from the tree." His gaze went from the huge trunk to the branches overhead. "I was going to make a carving for Eliahnna out of it."

"You have a romantic's heart, mi carae. Never lose that." She examined the nut and held it to her lips.

Murmuring from the ancients drifted through his mind. The whisperings were such a constant that he barely registered them, but when Carga's thoughts brushed his own, a rush of anticipation swept through him. She was blessing the nut, but not only that—she placed a protective ward into the seed.

"Not just a protection, darling." She handed him the nut and winked. "May you and your princess have many seasons of happiness together." She linked her arm through his and breathed deeply. "Did you know the roots of the cllynellren tree reach all the way to Lan Gyllarelle and beyond? I have heard rumors that the roots grow beneath all of the kingdoms, stretching to the seas and even the far-reaching islands. That would be wonderous, would it not?"

"Indeed, it would." He placed his hand on the trunk and whispered an old Eleri saying to bless the tree. "Roots that stretch beneath the land, leaves that touch the skies, linking the terrarae and stars. Incredible." This tree was the first planted on Aelinae by his ancestors. It was as much a part of Eleri lives as was breathing air.

One of Carga's famous sly smiles adorned her lips. "Let us tell Father what we know."

Her hand grazed his when she reached to caress the tree. In that brief moment, he saw beyond their surroundings to a room full of marble. A second tree, brother to the cllynellren, grew from the floor and up through the ceiling. He blinked and the image was gone, but that damned knowing grin was still on his sister's lips.

"What does it mean?"

Carga's shoulders lifted and the silken dress she wore floated around her like wings. "I do not know all the secrets. Some are meant for you to discover. Now come, Father is waiting."

He puzzled over her cryptic answer all the way to their father's study. Bressal and Janeira were there as well, which made his stomach pinch with heightened anxiety. For the king to ask his heir and fiercest warrior to join them meant this was not a simple conversation.

Carga took the lead and told their father everything Eliahnna had said to Eoghan, elaborating on some details he'd tried to minimize, like the fact that Gwainne was in Talaith with his brother Loghan. The king's last meeting with the Ullan prince had not gone well, and Eoghan thought it best to keep Gwainne's name from the retelling, but Carga had other ideas. Not only did she embellish the story, she told their father that it was imperative that they send Eoghan to Talaith as an Eleri ambassador.

His head jerked up at that and he glared at his sister. Not because he didn't want to go, but he had a plan for asking their father permission to leave. He didn't need his sister speaking for him, and yet, that was exactly what was happening.

His father listened to Carga without interrupting, his face stern yet still. Although he didn't show outward emotion, Eoghan saw the tap, tap, tapping of his fingers on the arm of his chair, and heard his shallow drags of breath. When Carga finished, the king looked first to Bressal, and then to Janeira. Of the two, he'd take Janeira's advice over his heir, and Eoghan silently pleaded with the warrior to not offer extremes.

"We should close the borders, now, my king. Expel anyone not friendly to the throne. Including any faeries with ties to the outsiders." Janeira placed a fist over her heart. "I will see to clearing the Narthvier myself, if that is your wish."

Eoghan shook his head. And they called him rash.

"Father, I do not believe we need to close the borders. Let me go to Talaith as an ambassador as our sister has said, and allow me to assess the situation."

His father glared at him as if he'd lost his mind. "I should send you, my youngest son, to the Aelans? You, who have no negotiating skills, have never hinted at wishing to understand diplomacy, and if I recall, have never been beyond the final veil. What do you hope to accomplish with Empress Lliandra? Do you think to woo her with your Eleri charms? Do you perhaps hope to uncover the depths of Myrddin's treachery?" The king leaned forward with a sneer. "Or do you simply wish to be near the princess? Do not think I have not heard of your correspondence with the crown princess. I forbid it, Eoghan. I have already lost one son to the Aelans. I refuse to lose another to those filthy puppets. I am angry that Myrddin has betrayed us, yes, and he will be dealt with, but I will not lose any Eleri to the Aelans' stupidity. And that includes you, my son."

Every word was like a punch to his gut, and Eoghan staggered beneath the vitriol lacing his father's words. Even Carga appeared shocked by their father's outrage. Bressal, damn him, looked pleased as punch. Of course he would. He hated the Aelans even more than the king did.

"I will see to securing the veils immediately, Your Majesty." Bressal bowed to their father and exited the room with Janeira beside him.

As she passed, she glanced to the ceiling and then winked. Eoghan stared after her, not quite comprehending what she meant. What he did know was that they'd already discussed a plan before he and Carga entered the study.

"How long have you known about Taryn and Rhoane being gone? And who told you?" Eoghan turned to face his father, Janeira's strange message still pinging his brain.

"I learned about them when Carga informed me just now."

"No sooner? It is just…you seemed to already have a plan in place for closing the border."

The king steepled his fingers and blew out a breath. "It is something we have discussed previously, yes. After Prince

Gwainne's surprise arrival, we decided it was time we protect the Eleri. It is the only way I can be assured of our survival. The east and west are heading for war, and I will not allow my people to be caught in the middle. Not again. Not for those Fadair."

"Father, we have talked about this. Aelans are not our enemy. None of the races on Aelinae are. We have to work together to heal our world, not close ourselves off. This is exactly what I warned would happen." Carga stood in front of the king and lifted her chin. "What if this is what Kaldaar and Rykoto want? What if they planned it this way to manipulate you into hiding in your forest? Do you not care that they are responsible for breaking our world? That they are the ones who cast our darathi from Aelinae? We must not let them win. If we do, all of Aelinae is lost."

Their father waved his hand, as if he couldn't be bothered with facts. "We have already lost. Now, go. I have made my decision and will not yield."

Carga took Eoghan's hand and led him out of the study. He glanced at the king, hoping he would laugh and say he was only kidding. How could he have given up so easily? They had to fight alongside the Aelans if they had any hope of returning balance to Aelinae. Why would his father think they'd already lost?

"Because he mourns our mother. When she died, he blamed himself, but instead of dealing with the loss, he took his anger out on Rhoane. It was a dark time for all Eleri." Carga rushed them through the halls, toward their sleeping quarters.

"I remember." He'd been little more than sixty seasons then, not yet an adult, but not a child.

Still, the memory was hazy in his mind. He'd been exploring the forest the day she died, but heard the horrifying details from those who were present. Rhoane had refused to leave the Weirren to fulfill his promise to Verdaine and seek out the Darennsai. He and their mother had fought, with the argument ending in flames —literally. According to the witnesses, the queen became a dancing white flame, then shrieked before collapsing. Verdaine came to take the queen to Dal Tara, and Rhoane left the Narthvier.

There was much more he'd forgotten. Nuance and detail that was lost to memory, but the queen's departure from court had affected everyone. The king never truly recovered, nor did he ever forgive Verdaine for tearing his family apart.

Carga stopped in front of his rooms and ushered him inside. After she closed the door behind them, she swept the empty area with a grunt.

"Take only what you can carry. Fly to Paderau. At the palace, speak only to Lord Tinsley. Tell him I sent you. You can trust Tinsley with your life. Rest there, but do not linger. You must get to Talaith as quickly as possible. Tell your love what has transpired here." She cocked her head and listened a moment. "They have already sealed the first three veils. You cannot escape through the forest. Rykoto's balls, I had hoped Bressal would dawdle, but he has been waiting for just such an opportunity. He must have had soldiers stationed and waiting."

She paced the room, eyes narrowed, a slim finger tapping her lips.

"You heard Father. I have never been out of the vier. I will get lost."

"Yes, you will. And then you will find your way. If you ever hope to grow beyond this mighty tree, you must do this, Eoghan. It is for the benefit of all Aelinae that you leave the Weirren tonight. But, how?"

She was right. He had to warn Eliahnna, and not through mind-speak. His place was by her side, but that meant turning his back on his family and disobeying his king. He would be sheanna and possibly never allowed back into the Narthvier. Although his heart knew what must be done, it also ached with what he would be losing.

"This must be how Rhoane felt when he left to fulfill his oath to Verdaine." He tapped his chest. "It hurts."

"I know, brother. It will always hurt. Even when you are Purified, it will hurt. There will be people you love who you must leave in order to do what is best. It is never easy, nor does it get easier, but it must be done." Her eyes shimmered with unshed tears and he wondered for a brief moment who she left behind outside the safety of their veils. She'd lived with the Aelans for almost twenty-five seasons; surely there were people she loved that she had to leave.

He didn't take much. A few changes of clothing, small mementos of his family, two daggers—nothing of much value. He realized his worldly possessions weren't in things, but in people. The sound of his father's laughter, the light that always shone in his sister's eyes.

As terrified as he was to leave home, he was equally as excited. This was the adventure he'd always wanted, but had been denied. Whatever waited for him on the other side of the Narthvier, he certainly wasn't ready for, but would take on with the confidence of an Eleri prince.

But how did he get to the other side of the forest with his brother sealing all the veils? His gaze flicked wildly from one end of his room to the other, his mind churning. Janeira's strange message popped into his mind and he ran to the small terrace outside his sitting room.

"Have you figured it out?" Carga stood at his side, that cheeky grin lighting her pretty face.

"You knew all along, did you not?"

She giggled and rose to kiss his cheek. "Fly with Verdaine's blessing, my brother. When next we meet, may it be in sweetness and not sorrow." She pressed her forehead against his.

"When next we meet." He finished the saying and wrapped her in a tight embrace. "I will not fail you."

"I know you will not. You are exactly what Aelinae needs

right now." She unfolded herself from his hug and motioned upward. "You do not have long. They are preparing to seal the treetops. Go now."

It had been ages since he transformed into a bird and flew above the trees, but not so long that he had forgotten how. Taking care not to forget a feather or foot, he concentrated on the form of a levon and transformed into the bird. Carga clapped and urged him on, cheering when he took flight off his terrace into the dusky sky.

Up here, the world was quiet and still, but his heart wasn't. Rhoane had once left the Narthvier in search of his future. Eoghan hoped he had a bit of his brother's courage and grace to face whatever waited for him on the other side of the border. He turned toward the south and the unknown.

By the time they reached the healing wards, Rhoane's sickness was gone. His head felt light, but that could've been due to being exhausted. Kaida and Pora lay curled at the end of the pallet where they'd put the lycan. She lifted her head at their approach, her great golden eyes filled with concern. The lycan was healing, but seeing the brutality done to him, and remembering what Cashiel had done to Taryn, scared her. Would someone do that to her one day? Were all sentient creatures in danger?

Her questions tumbled through his mind and he did his best to reassure her that she was safe, that she had him and Taryn to protect her, but he understood her worry. Seeing what the lycan had suffered had hurt him in ways he didn't know possible. He, an assassin and prince, a man who had witnessed cruelty on every level, and who had dispensed his fair share of heinous deeds, had recoiled at what had been done to the lycan—making him more a beast now than a man.

Rhoane strove to return the male part to his soul, but how was he supposed to do that when it had been all but cauterized? He gave Kaida a pet and scratched Pora beneath his chin, earning a deep purr from the wee beastie. The cat was also worried, but not for the same reasons as Kaida. He promised to keep the cat's secret and also assured him he was protected as long as he stayed close to Theo and Rainne.

Sentient creatures. Wasn't that what they all were? He knelt at the side of the lycan and stroked his silky black fur. Beneath his fingertips, he sensed their combined powers knitting a web of strength that he hoped would be enough to restore him completely—man and beast.

"This is Eiodian, our best healer," Theo said from behind Rhoane.

He gave a last pat to the lycan before rising to greet the healer. When their eyes met, a sense of familiarity rushed through Rhoane's senses and he was overcome by homesickness so powerful it felt as though he'd been punched in the gut. As tall as Rhoane, his dark skin was a contrast to the white of his wide smile. Black braids piled on his head to trail behind him and Rhoane half expected to hear little bells chiming from their ends. Not as bulky as Baehlon, but the two could've been brothers.

The healer sucked in a breath and bowed low. When he rose, he touched his thumb to his heart, then his forehead, and finally to his lips. "Tel raiden besodden carmallae, mi Surtentse."

"Tel railacht nodden hesplenalde." Rhoane inclined his head to the healer, surprised he knew the Eleri greeting.

"And you must be the Darennsai." His gaze traveled to Taryn. A golden glow came from his brown eyes and his smile grew larger. "Rori dreamed of you in her illness. I am honored to make your acquaintance."

"As am I, Healer." Taryn inclined her head with a quick glance at Rhoane that said she recognized the similarities between Eiodian and Baehlon as well.

They discussed the lycan's progress, with promises from the healer to keep them updated should anything change. Thus far, he was pleased with what the group had accomplished and admitted it was beyond his scope of healing. Gratitude spilled from his words. Perhaps he, too, feared the uncomfortable realization that ShantiMari could be stolen with brutal efficiency.

Taryn asked whether they had any beds available for her and Rhoane to rest, since the king and queen had yet to offer them accommodations.

"We can retire to my rooms while we sort out the details," Theo offered. "I was hoping to discuss something with the both of you. I'll have food sent up as well."

Kaida wished to stay with the lycan and so they bid farewell to Eiodian to follow Theo. They traversed hallways and stairs, turning in every which direction, but Rhoane always knew where the Elvenwood was. He ran a thumb over the leaf and studied it as they walked. Unremarkable in color or veining, it looked the same as the leaves at the Weirren. What was the tree trying to tell him? When he'd been close to it and felt horrifically ill, he knew it was the tree's sickness infecting him, but there was something more.

What bothered him most was that he couldn't speak to the elvenwood. Never in his long life had he not been able to communicate with nature. But this tree eluded him. Was it intentional on the tree's part, or was something preventing him?

They crossed one of the many walkways that crisscrossed the halls and Rhoane looked at the emptiness above him. His Artagh cousins who called Haversham home would love this mountain palace, but Rhoane had grown up in the openness of the Narthvier. Being closed in did not settle his heart.

Thankfully, Theo's rooms were as spacious as Rhoane's at the Weirren and just as luxuriously appointed. It was hard to tell he was inside a mountain with all the soft furnishings and tapestries. Theo led them to a balcony that overlooked a great canyon and the city beyond.

Rhoane gulped in fresh air and lifted his face to the sky. He'd never been so happy to see open space in his life. As long as he kept the mountain to his back, he'd be fine. Except, the balcony followed the natural curve of the ridge and it was impossible to fully escape the rocks in his perimeter.

"This is gorgeous." Taryn leaned precariously over a marble banister that kept her from falling to her death.

Bridges spanned the width of the canyon and a waterfall spilled from a great height to their right. In the late afternoon sun, shadows lurked over the city streets, but made the tops of the buildings glitter like diamonds. It reminded him of the Crystal Palace in Talaith.

"We can take you to the city later, if you'd like," Theo offered.

"As tempting as that is, we need to find the seals." Taryn turned from the spectacular view. "I'm sorry." Her gaze drifted over the mountain and to the other side of the balcony. "Is that a telescope?"

"Would you like to see? I've been charting the stars." Excitement bounded from Theo and he led Taryn to the odd contraption.

Rhoane had seen them before—Brandt had one in Talaith and Myrddin had several—but he'd never understood the appeal. He kept his feet firmly on the terrarae. Others could explore the stars.

"I'm afraid we've lost them for hours." Rainne stood with her back to the canyon and nibbled on a nail. "What's so important about these seals?"

Rhoane joined her, but kept the mountain to his back. "They are keeping a cruel god locked in his prison."

"Your world, is it a savage place? I mean, if you have to imprison gods, I can only imagine what life for the inhabitants is like."

"Aelinae is peaceful, for the most part. Especially since the Great War—that is when Rykoto was sealed in his temple and Kaldaar exiled to the edge of nothingness. But now, Kaldaar has returned and Rykoto's prison is vulnerable." Rhoane glanced at Taryn with a sigh. "She is the hope of our world."

"No, Surtentse." Rainne placed her hands atop of his. "You both are. I've read the histories. If you failed, there wouldn't be a Cilachaem." She bit her lip and looked to where Theo chatted animatedly to Taryn. "I don't understand how you can be here, now, warm with flesh, when you are the creators of this world." She flicked a glance at her hands and blushed. "Forgive me, Your, erm, do I call you Your Eminence? Your Godliness? I'm afraid I don't know the protocol."

Rhoane chuckled and patted her hand. "Nor do I, Lady Rainne. Just call me Rhoane. As to your other query, we do not understand it, either. I have always known Taryn would ascend to Dal Tara—the home of the gods. But I only realized recently that I would as well. In truth, I do not think we believe it, though I have no doubt Taryn is worthy of being a goddess."

"I'm sure you're worthy, too. You saved that lycan." She shrugged and chewed a nail. "Maybe your swords can help your search. Like divining sticks or the like."

"Perhaps." Rhoane drew his sword and Rainne sucked in a breath.

"Do you know what the blade says?" She reached a finger toward the scrolling words and hesitated. "May I?"

"Please." He held the blade steady to prevent her from cutting herself.

"My ogress would've loved this." As if realizing what she said, she slapped a hand over her mouth. "Forget I said that." Her mumbled words came from behind her hand and her eyes filled with fear.

"I heard nothing," he assured her, but his mind clamored for more information.

An ogress? It might explain the pale jade that came and went from her features. He wasn't altogether sure he'd seen the shading, but was damn curious to know everything about this ogress of hers.

"Theo?" Queen Helena called from inside, and Rainne stepped back as if bitten by an asp. "Theo! Where are you, darling? I need your help. Your father has banished Therron and that wretched girl. I need you to go find your brother and bring him home to talk some sense into your father." She burst through the open doorway and skidded to a halt. "What the blazes are you doing here?"

Rhoane had no idea whether she meant him or Rainne and, frankly, didn't care. He fixed her with a raised brow and narrowed-eyed stare that he'd learned from his mother. The queen faltered a moment, but then brushed past him to her son.

"Darling, stop playing with your toys. This is important. Your father's lost his mind completely. Go find your brother and bring him home this moment. With or without the girl." She waved a hand as if it were of no consequence, but everyone there understood that she'd prefer if Rori didn't come back with her son.

"Mother, whatever Father's done is for you to resolve, not me. Therron is a grown man."

A servant entered, carrying a silver tray with three letters. He approached Theo first, then Rainne, and finally Taryn, who looked surprised to receive a note. The queen drummed her fingers on her crossed arms while she waited for the others to read their letters.

Taryn was the first to look up. "Rori asked that we meet her at the Seelie Palace. Where is that?"

"I should've known. Never trust a faerie." Queen Helena turned on her son. "Go there at once, Theo. Bring Therron to me. This disobedience will not be tolerated."

"What disobedience, Your Majesty? Your husband asked Therron to leave and he did." Rhoane knew better than to get involved in family squabbles, but this family seemed to be chasing its tail.

"Don't you patronize me, boy. You're not the ruler here. I am.
I will not have you—"

"Your Majesty," Taryn interrupted, "point us in the direction
of the Seelie Palace and we'll go talk to your son. Lady Rainne,
Prince Theo, will you keep our Kaida safe while we're gone?"

"It will be my honor. But I should warn you, Queen Eirlys
doesn't take kindly to strangers using her Room of Mirrors. Her
doorways. For the in-between," Theo explained.

"Then we'll have to arrive by another means. Is there a
Shoogly Dragon near her palace? Or a doorway close enough that
won't cause alarm?"

"Taryn, there is another way." Rhoane sheathed his sword and
took her hand in his. "One that would allow us to see the kingdoms and search for the seals at the same time."

She squinted as if to better understand and then grinned with
cheeky mischievousness. "Much better plan. If you all will excuse
us, we'll leave you to discuss your private matters. We should be
back in the morning."

As she spoke, Taryn walked backward toward the balustrade.
When her back bumped up against it, she gave a little wave and
climbed onto the marble.

"What do you think you're doing?" A note of hysteria entered
the queen's voice.

"Your Majesty, thank you for your hospitality." Rhoane seared
her with a scathing look. "I expect to find Kaida well and the
lycan recovering when we return." It was more than an idle
threat. He didn't like leaving the grierbas with these people, but
she wished to stay with the lycan. "If we do not find the seal on
our journey, we will continue the search here on the morrow."

Rhoane joined Taryn atop the balustrade and nodded to
Theo and Rainne before leaping into the air.

Startled gasps followed and Rhoane let out a burst of laughter. Damn, that felt good. Who knew plummeting to one's death
could be so freeing?

CHAPTER TWENTY-TWO

Taryn's dragon roared at the change and a plume of fire shot from her snout. Beside her, Rhoane's gorgeous moss-green dragon spun and dove deeper into the canyon. She raced after him, letting the cares and worries of the past few weeks slide off her like the wind over her wings. For just this moment, they were free.

Rhoane sped toward the waterfall and she grinned. A second later, she whipped past him to reach the falls first, but he kept pace with her. The spray of cold water against her scales refreshed her lagging energy. Up they went, spiraling in and out of the fall until they crested the top.

To their left, the sun hovered over the horizon. Rhoane turned them around until they were, hopefully, flying south. They dipped lower as they passed Theo's rooms, and Taryn suppressed a giggle at their astonished faces. Even the haughty queen looked as if she'd seen something quite remarkable. If Taryn wasn't mistaken, tears shimmered in her eyes.

Served her right—her and her husband. Their egos had grown bigger than their crowns. As much as Taryn would love to teach them a lesson in humility, she had neither the time nor the patience. One day, Therron would rule Elvenwood and she had to hope he would be a better leader for his people.

They flew onward, their wings making soft hushes with each beat. Taryn inclined her head to Rainne and Theo. That was an interesting pair. Theo's fascination with the stars far outstripped even Brandt's enthusiasm. He'd charted the night sky since he was a young lad, noting additions and subtractions of planets as they came and went. He'd asked Taryn which one was Aelinae and she hadn't been able to answer. Were they even in the same galaxy?

Every time he said, "You and Rhoane created Cilachaem," her belly pinched and she felt slightly ill. Even if they had, how were they able to be there as living flesh? What really did her head in was the possibility of messing something up. What if what they did today changed the world? Was healing the lycan somehow going to erase another part of Cilachaem's history?

She shared her thoughts with Rhoane, and he agreed they should be minimally involved. The shadow behind the king was worrisome, but the longer they were in the palace, the more confident she was that it wasn't Kaldaar manipulating him. They'd find Therron, identify the amulets, and search for the seals. If they couldn't find them in Faerie, they would finish their search of the elven palace.

Rainne asked if the swords could help in our search. I never thought to give it a try, but it might work.

Do you know a song about finding lost items? Is that how it works? Or do we simply ask?

How were they supposed to be gods when they couldn't even find a bloody seal?

I will scour through the Eleri songs I know. This kingdom is rather attractive from the sky.

They flew over lush green valleys and sapphire lakes, across meadows and forests, and saw only a few towns. Granted, they skirted any large groupings of buildings for fear of scaring the inhabitants. An arrow through the heart hurt a dragon just as much as it did a woman.

The sun slipped lower and Taryn's breath caught. *Rhoane, look over there.*

Silhouetted against a brilliant jeweled sky, the Elvenwood mountains cut a magnificent skyline. More beautiful than London or New York, even. She banked right and circled around to see the full effect.

It is stunning.

That's exactly what I was thinking. Enchanting, even. She ran the tip of her wing across his and smiled when he shuddered. *We are fortunate to spend these moments together, mi carae. We must never forget that.*

I bless Verdaine every day for you. For us.

They turned south and continued searching for the Seelie Palace.

Any idea where we're going?

Some. Not as much as I would like, but Therron is Eleri. That should not be too difficult to track.

Not the brilliant plan she was hoping for. She probably should've at least looked at a map before leaping off the balustrade like a circus performer. They flew along the edge of a city and Taryn's attention was pulled toward a building near the center. Her dragon senses recognized something there, but she wasn't entirely sure what. Not Therron or Rori, but strong ShantiMari.

They landed in a grove of trees just outside of the city and shifted into more suitable, Eleri forms. Their clothing changed from the stuffy Elvenwood robes to what they'd worn when they left London. A cross between medieval badass and jeans and T-shirts. Definitely comfortable.

She patted the sword at her side and took a deep breath.

With a grin to Rhoane, she unsheathed it and held it out before her. "Show me where the Seal of Ardyn is hidden."

The sword did nothing.

"I guess we have to sing to it. Did you come up with a song yet?"

Rhoane shook his head and looked skyward as if the clouds could provide answers. "Eleri have many songs. Some I have forgotten and am trying to recall, but it is not easy. Carga would know instantly. She always held more of our history in her mind than I ever could."

"I miss her too." Taryn took Rhoane's hand in hers. "We'll see them again soon."

"I hope so, mi carae. I hope so."

Taryn reached for Kaida and swallowed a sob that rose in her throat. She knew Kaida wanted to stay with the lycan, but it wasn't the same being without her. Her hand felt lost without her fur warming it.

"This sucks."

"It does indeed. The sooner we find the seals, the quicker we return to Aelinae. What are we looking for here?"

Taryn bit her lip and seriously debated her life choices. She was still far too impetuous. "I don't know. ShantiMari, but how or what, I couldn't tell. Just that there was a big hit of it in one of these buildings."

They passed beneath the city gates and scanned the area for signs of power. ShantiMari threads were everywhere, but none large enough to draw her attention. People roamed the cobbled streets, unhurried and unbothered by two strangers. As they passed, many nodded in their direction or smiled. The friendliness of the citizens and the city itself reminded her of Celyn Eryri, where her mother held the Light Celebrations every season.

Alongside the human-looking dwellers, giants, trolls, ogres, brownies, sprites, and a few unrecognizable creatures went about their day in peaceful cohabitation. The winged sprites whizzed past, with little *zings* following behind them.

"It's enchanting."

"Aye." Rhoane's gaze flicked from left to right. "Has a familiar feel to it, too."

"Look, over there." Taryn pointed to a pub with a sign hanging above the door. "Shoogly Dragon, just like Dony said."

It was where the hit of power came from. As they approached, her skin itched as if she had a rash. A shudder wormed its way down her back and she wrinkled her nose against a blast of rotten eggs.

"Can you smell that?"

"I smell scents of a city—perspiration, dirt, ale, fried onions. It is not pleasant, but not horrible."

"This is definitely more than horrible. I hope the pub doesn't try to kill us."

Inside, tables filled the main area of the room with a large bar in the back and booths around the perimeter. It could've been any pub in any part of England, with a medieval decorating aesthetic, but it wasn't all that unusual. And it certainly didn't try to kill them. Thank the gods.

An early evening crowd of boisterous people in every shade and shape took up many of the tables, and Taryn scanned the room for the source of power. Time slowed and the pub became a hazy backdrop.

"Are you doing this?" Taryn reached for Rhoane's hand and gripped it hard.

"I am not. Look there, by the window."

Taryn followed his gaze and cold shivers cut across her skin. Myrddin—or a man who looked very much like him—sat at a table with a stunning creature with glossy golden hair and slightly pointed ears. An elf or Eleri, or whatever they called themselves.

She and Rhoane watched like silent observers as Myrddin and the elf argued, their faces and hands animated.

"Can you hear them?"

Rhoane shook his head and squinted at the pair. "By their body language, the Eleri is not pleased that Myrddin is commanding him to do something."

The one who looked like Myrddin pulled two parcels from inside his tunic and placed them on the table. The Eleri's eyes widened and a grin pulled his lips into a vicious smile. If this was Myrddin's memory and she triggered it by entering the pub, why would he want her to see it?

Myrddin slid the parcels across the table and kept his fingers atop the larger one. The Eleri snatched the smaller of the two and opened it with greedy fingers. A silver ring with a large onyx stone winked in the candlelight. At her side, Rhoane shuddered and she felt his disgust for the thing. Myrddin tapped the wrapped package and leaned forward until his face was inches from the Eleri's.

Taryn strained to hear but they were in a sound vacuum, where all she heard was the beating of her own heart. No pub sounds penetrated the bubble, not even from those seated closest to her. She could see the others in the pub, but through a hazy veil. They moved at normal speed, but didn't seem to know she and Rhoane stood in their midst. Nor were they disturbed by the Eleri and Myrddin.

He pushed the parcel into the Eleri's eager hands and sat back, a satisfied smile on his lips. He tugged at his beard, so similar to the man she knew on Aelinae. The Eleri tucked the palm-sized package into his robe and rose. Without another word, he strode through the pub, straight through several tables and the people sitting there, to a doorway to the left of the bar.

Taryn watched in horrified fascination as he spun his hands in a wide circle to make a portal. A heartbeat later, he stepped into the swirling air and disappeared. Her gaze snapped back to Myrddin.

He stroked his beard, a pensive look on his face. A moment

later, he turned and met her steady gaze. Blue eyes that she'd come to associate with mischief and friendship bore into her with a silent challenge. *Catch me*, it said. *If you dare.*

CHAPTER TWENTY-THREE

Myrddin rushed through the halls of the Crystal Palace as if his ass were on fire. In a way, it was. Another sharp pain cut into his heart, and he leaned against a marble pillar for support. He hadn't expected Taryn to find the Shoogly Dragon in Cere quite so quickly. He thought he had a sennight, at least. Possibly even a fortnight. But she found the pub in less than three days.

What a fool he'd been for convincing himself she wasn't all that clever. No worries. The timeline was moved up, but that wasn't a catastrophe. He'd given her six moonturns to find the seals; now he'd adjust for half that amount of time. This first one could've been a fluke. A happy accident that she stumbled into. He'd prepare himself for every contingency, just in case. It wouldn't do to have her return before Kaldaar was ready.

At Lliandra's door, he smoothed his sweaty palms down his trousers and adjusted the crimson silk doublet he wore. The empress would not be pleased with him interrupting her after-noon meetings, but he had to spur her to action.

The guards allowed him entry without question, and Myrddin grinned at their naivete. He'd fooled everyone. For five millennia, he fooled them all. Even his god. His belly tightened and his steps slowed. He'd have to visit Kaldaar before the god became too petulant with his errant servant, but not until he'd settled things at Talaith.

Lliandra wasn't in her sitting room, which meant she was most likely in her bed and not alone. Myrddin paced the huge windows that faced the Summer Seas without seeing the tranquil blue-green of the water or the vibrant pinks and oranges of dusk. He saw his head on a platter if he barged into Lliandra's rooms, shouting about sending Faelara and Baehlon away.

A door opened in the distance and Myrddin breathed a sigh of relief. A few moments later, Prince Gwainne strolled into the sitting room like a fucking peacock. Insolent brat. He'd lapped up Lliandra's fake charm and bedded her without so much as a flicker of hesitation.

"Master Myrddin, I was hoping to find you so that we might discuss a few private matters. Are you available tomorrow? We could break our fast together."

Myrddin smelled the lad's lust mingled with Lliandra's and it made his stomach turn. It annoyed him that the prince had been just the thing she needed to break out of her melancholy and dark mood. Nothing Myrddin had done helped, but one fuck from this…Ullan, and Lliandra's fever broke. Her smiles should've been enough for Myrddin to forgive the lad, but his old heart was jealous. Such a pathetic emotion that served no one, but he was impotent to keep the vicious thoughts from his mind.

"What is so important to drag you away from the empress's bed to speak with me?"

His cheeky grin made him even more handsome, and Myrddin had to keep himself from smacking the boy.

"Ullan business. My brother will join us, if you don't mind."

Why would he mind? Two Ullan princes wishing to discuss their kingdom's business without provocation or manipulation? How did he get so lucky?

"It would be my pleasure. If you'll excuse me, I need to speak with the empress." Myrddin made a quick bow to the prince and pivoted away.

"She's not quite presentable, I'm afraid."

"Are they ever after a good routing?" Myrddin laughed as he strode to Lliandra's bedchamber, even though he felt anything but merry.

Fucking prince, thinking he could dissuade Myrddin from seeing Lliandra. As if. He hadn't been her closest advisor for near on four hundred seasons without learning a thing or two. Without knocking, he entered her private quarters and winced at the stench. He knew what that meant and cursed the Ullan boy for having the audacity to violate Lliandra in ways only Myrddin should enjoy.

"Myrddin, be a love and run me a bath. I'm afraid Gwainne was rather robust in his duties and I feel I'll never be clean again."

"Were you ever, my love?" He nuzzled her neck to hide his grimace. "I should take you now so that you would forget the Ullan."

"Naughty." She lay back and let her legs fall open with a casual invitation. "Add your seed to his—let us create a new Eirielle."

Thirty-six seasons past Taryn's birthing date, and she was still insistent they make a new anomaly. A better child of prophecy. An Eirielle she could control.

It was useless. There was and would only ever be one—Taryn.

"Of course, my love." He growled against her soft skin and unfastened his breeches. As long as he kept his nose near her flesh, he couldn't smell Gwainne's repulsive Ullan scent.

Bloody desert dwellers and their spiced oils. They wore it in their hair, on their bodies—hell, they probably wiped their asses with scented leaves.

Lliandra gasped when he rammed his cock into her pussy. She would get everything she asked for and then some. Gwainne might've worked the empress hard, but it was Myrddin who would leave her breathless and fulfilled. Literally.

She pawed at his doublet and he stripped it off in one smooth movement. It was only a brief tightening of her eyes, but he saw the disappointment that lingered there. Myrddin was no longer young with chiseled abs. Lliandra craved youth more than jewels or even power. To her, youth *was* power. A little ironic considering her quim was no longer tight and her body lacked the firmness it had when she was newly crowned.

They were both growing old—too old to play these insipid games.

Myrddin might not have the youth or stamina of the Ullan prince, but he had something far better. In all his seasons, he'd only shared his ShantiMari with one woman—Lliandra. As she writhed beneath him, fighting for her release, he loosened a cord of his power and enveloped the empress with his unique blend of ShantiMari.

Somewhere between Dark and Telraicht-Noir, he'd spent two thousand seasons blending and mixing the two until they formed an unbreakable chain. Every source of power had a weakness, but Myrddin had found his and strengthened it until not even Kaldaar could penetrate his defenses.

His power oozed into her orifices and melted into her pores until he was as much a part of her as her own blood. Her veins bulged deep blue and she gasped against the intrusion while simultaneously bucking her hips for more. Ever the good servant, Myrddin rammed a fist-sized thread of power into her asshole and ploughed her hard.

Lliandra shrieked around the cord of ShantiMari filling her mouth and shuddered with her release. Her arms flopped to the side as if to say they were finished and Myrddin chuckled.

"Oh, darling. We have only just begun."

A frightened yet delighted gleam lit her eyes.

More than a bell later, Myrddin reclined in a hot bath, totally satiated. Lliandra ran her foot along the inside of his calf and sighed.

"What am I to do with Eliahnna? The girl's useless."

"Send her to foster with King Stephan." It was the opening he needed, but had yet to decide on a course for asking.

"You think so? I was more inclined to send her to Zakael. He absolutely ruined Marissa, and I'm certain he would love to take advantage of Eliahnna. The girl's too soft. Zakael would strengthen her in no time."

Caer Idris was the last place he wanted Eliahnna. "You could send her with Faelara and Baehlon to Ulla." He sat up and pressed his hand to Lliandra's mound. She moaned and he flicked her little bud twice before adding, "Why delay their trip? If you send the princess with a knight protector, surely you don't need the entire ensemble to accompany them? They'd be much faster with just the five traveling. Ten if you feel you must send guards."

"You're jealous." A sly smile spread across her face and he saw a glimmer of the real features beneath her youthful mask. It was ridiculous that she continued the farce. Everyone saw the real empress when Cashiel had stripped her of her power. No one cared but Lliandra.

"Perhaps. The Ullans are renowned for their lovemaking skills."

"Don't you mean healing skills?"

"Is there a difference? Are you going to tell me Gwainne is a healer now?" He snorted and pushed three fingers into her channel. She pulsed around him with a moan.

"There's no reason to be jealous. You know I've only truly loved you." She arched and bit her lower lip. "There. Ahhh, yes. More."

"You love me, but you'll bed any man with a hard prick."

"Not true. I'll bed any man with a title and a hard prick."

She panted into her words and pressed her hips into his hand for more. He withdrew his fingers and smoothed his beard. Her whimpers were music to his ears.

"I think the princess should leave tomorrow. Along with Baehlon, the princes, and Faelara."

"Yes, yes, whatever you say. Just finish what you started."

He sloshed across the tub that was large enough to fit six comfortably, and often had, to obey her command. His tongue lashed across her lips and he sucked them into his mouth at the same time he pushed his fingers into her pussy. While his thumb flicked her bud, his tongue ravaged her mouth and fingers worked her nethers.

"You're a wise and benevolent empress, my love." His Shanti-Mari spun to her mind. The darkness he'd sensed since Menurra was little more than a speck. Whether it was his fucking that banished it, or something else, would have to be investigated further later. First and foremost, he needed Lliandra to commit to his plan. "What a brilliant idea to send Eliahnna to the Ullans. Tessa will go to Paderau to foster with Duke Anje for a season or two. You are a good mother to your daughters."

"Yes." She lay her head on the tiled edge of the bath and he seized upon the exposed flesh. "They should all leave so that you and I have more time for this. Just us, my love. Don't ever leave me. Stay with me. Always."

"Always."

She pulsed and convulsed with her release, swearing she'd never love anyone but him. Myrddin kissed her more tenderly than any of her past lovers had. They might've believed they loved Lliandra, but no one had loved her more than Myrddin. She was his, had always been his.

A flicker at the edge of his vision caught his attention and with a sinking heart, he turned away from his love to the hulking shadow in the corner. Even before he saw the ravaged face, he knew that presence. It was the same darkness that had been in

Lliandra's mind. He'd suspected what it was, but hadn't wanted to confront that reality. And now, here it was.

"Care to share?" Kaldaar stepped from the shadows and extended a bony hand. "You smell delicious."

Lliandra's satisfied smile vanished and she glared at the god. "I told you to wait."

She pushed herself out from beneath Myrddin and stepped out of the bath with her hand extended for Kaldaar to assist. Myrddin studied the pair, an awful realization shrinking his balls.

He'd been betrayed. Utterly and cruelly by not just his god, but the woman he loved.

CHAPTER TWENTY-FOUR

Was the image of Myrddin a ghost? Or a vision? Or perhaps a memory Taryn had activated by entering the pub. If only she knew when she'd trigger something—like maybe an alarm could sound, or a bell ring—anything that would alert her to potential danger. Or potential madness. What did the vision with Myrddin mean?

"Are you lost, lassie?"

Sound rushed back and Taryn startled at the woman's question. Was she lost? Definitely. Could she ever find her way? Possibly. Was all of this more confusing than her first days on Aelinae? Without a doubt. The thin veil separating Myrddin's past and her present dissipated and she saw everything in the pub with a clear crispness.

She turned and blinked into the broad chest of a man. Her gaze traveled upward to his round face and wide smile.

"Are you a giant?" she half-whispered.

"So me mam tells me." A chuckle rumbled from his chest.

"I'm sorry, that was rude. I've never met a giant before. It's a pleasure to make your acquaintance."

"I like 'er, Meg. She's got manners."

"You look like you could use a strong ale. Both of you. Come, let's get you sorted." The woman led them to a corner table, where they could see much of the pub.

"We don't have any money." Taryn glanced over her shoulder to where Myrddin had been in the image, but it was empty.

"Not to worry, lass. Tug'n me have a few coppers to spare."

"Thank you for your offer, but we are short on time." Rhoane sounded as distracted as she felt.

"Aren't we always. Never enough time, but always time to spare when needed, eh? Now, sit. There you go." Meg slid into the booth and Tug sat on a chair at the end of the table. "Let's start with introductions. I'm Meg, this here's Tug. Who be you?"

"I am Rhoane, and this is Taryn. We are looking for the Seelie Palace."

"Well now, you're in luck. We just happen to know a way to the palace that won't get you shot by one of the queen's assassins. They're wicked good with a bow and arrow, if you know what I mean." She gave a saucy wink. "Stitched up more than a few fair of their targets, haven't I?"

"Meg is the best healer in all of Faerie. Probably the elven kingdom, too." Tug puffed his chest as if he were the healer and not his friend.

Actually, the way he gazed adoringly at Meg, Taryn suspected they were more than friends. He had to be at least seven feet tall, and Meg at most five two, but age and height meant nothing to love. Meg tucked a strand of auburn hair behind her ear and a sweet blush crept up her cheek, making her look younger than Taryn suspected she actually was.

"We just came from Elvenwood and their healers are indeed magnificent. It is a great compliment you pay your lady, friend." Rhoane reclined against the seat, his body relaxed. Even though he'd just met them, Taryn sensed he trusted these people.

"Did you happen to see a rapscallion who goes by the name

Rori?" Meg's eyes darted around the room, worry edged into her features.

"We did." The concern wafting off Meg kept Taryn from saying more.

She repeated her mantra that whatever was happening on Cilachaem was not for her and Rhoane to solve, and in fact doing so might upset the balance of this world.

"Was she well? I had horrible nightmares about her." Meg peered at Taryn as if she were a bug to be studied and Meg's eyes widened with alarm or fright or awe, Taryn couldn't be sure. "You're her, aren't you? The silver-haired woman from Rori's fever ramblings."

"I, erm, maybe? I saw Rori once in an illusion, but I don't know about any fevers."

Meg fluttered her hands at Tug. "Get up, lad. We're going to see Eirlys."

"But we haven't had our ale." Tug pouted as he stood.

"We'll get some at the palace. You'll like the queen's brew, dear. I promise. Now, quickly, come, come. That's it. Follow me." Meg hurried them through the pub with a wave to the barkeep as they passed. His gaze followed them, but only in a half-interested sort of way.

At the hallway where the elf with golden hair had made his portal, Taryn paused. She sniffed the air, but no ShantiMari lingered, nor could she see any threads of power. Rhoane felt the empty air and huffed his disappointment. She felt it, too. The possibility of making portals out of thin air, anywhere they needed sounded too good to be true.

"What're ye waitin' for?" Meg waved them toward a door leading to the cellars. Or what Taryn hoped were the cellars and not actually a trap that would take them straight to hell.

She reached for Kaida and once again felt an ache in her heart that she wasn't with them. She'd always thought of herself as Kaida's protector, but the grierbas's absence showed her that in reality, she depended on Kaida's protection far too much. Kaida could sniff out what Taryn and even Rhoane couldn't. And she had a wicked good sense of who to trust, something that Taryn struggled with. She chose to believe everyone was inherently good, even though her family often contradicted that belief. Kaida saw people as they were, not as she'd like them to be.

And right then, Taryn could've used some of Kaida's trust sensors. Rhoane might trust the pair, but she wasn't sure she could. They claimed to know Rori, but were they friends?

The foursome clambered down stone steps that wound in a half circle to an empty room that smelled of damp and centuries of must. A slick coating of dirt covered stone pavers. Several torches provided light and shadows danced up the walls to a vaulted brick ceiling. With barely a hand's width to spare, Tug hunched over the little group, as if trying to make himself smaller.

"I don' like it 'ere, Meg. Ye know I gets the clusterphrobias."

"I know, dear. This will only take a moment, then we'll be at Eirlys's palace. Take my hand, there's a good boy." Meg stood in front of a solitary door and placed her free hand in the center of the wood.

Rhoane leaned forward to watch what she was doing, and Taryn paid close attention as well. A familiar tingling went up her arms and she recalled the morning she and Brandt had traveled from the pub in London to Aelinae. His words and actions had been similar to Meg's. A little too similar. Almost word for word, except where Brandt would've said Aelinae—Nadra's cavern to be exact—Meg said, "Seelie domunae regis slante locus speculorumae."

The words were Latin, mostly. It had been too long since Taryn had studied the archaic language, but she recalled enough to make out that Meg was opening a portal to a room of mirrors in the Seelie Palace. At least, she hoped so.

A pale-orange glow emanated from the wood and Rhoane

put his arm around Taryn's waist. A moment later, the door disappeared and a gaping blackness beckoned. Her stomach dipped and she drew a deep breath before following Meg and Tug into the void.

A minute, perhaps two later, they emerged into a room made entirely of mirrors. She sucked in a breath and gazed at the ornate frames on each one.

"An actual Room of Mirrors." A vision struck her of a little girl with golden hair standing about where she stood now. The little girl was asking Therron if Rori were Eleri, too. "I've been here before." Taryn glanced at Rhoane. "When I was a child, or I presented myself as a child. I spoke to Therron here, in this room. He was with Rori." She rubbed her forehead. "This place is doing a number on my sanity." Was it her past or future self that had spoken to Therron?

"Rori only just met Therron not a fortnight past." Meg's probing gaze flicked from Taryn to Rhoane. "Seems to me you've been busy here of late, but perhaps you aren't yet who you're meant to be."

Taryn held up a hand. "Stop right there. I'm beyond knackered, hungry, and annoyed. Maybe when I've had a decent night's sleep, a full belly, and get some answers I'll be in the mood to entertain your riddles, but not right now."

"Aye, lass. We'll get you sorted. Let's go find our missing spy, shall we?" Meg walked to one of the mirrors and turned a decorative knob cleverly hidden in the many swirls and curlicues of the frame.

No one stopped them when they emerged from the room, nor did they get questioned as they strode through the palace. If a giant were to rock on up to the Crystal Palace, Lliandra would have kittens, but here he wasn't an oddity. Despite the bad behavior of the elven monarchs, Taryn quite liked this world.

"Meg!" An attractive girl with sandy-blonde hair and huge sea-green eyes threw her arms around the healer. "It's so good to see you again. Are you here on official business?" Even though she spoke to Meg, the girl's intrigued glances were for Taryn and Rhoane.

"I'm escorting these two to the queen, if you really must know."

"Who are they? Are they spies? Have they come looking for Rori? Did you know she was here with that gorgeous elf, but they left a short time ago. The queen had another visitor. He—"

Meg held a finger to the girl's lips. "Esme, I know you love a good intrigue, but we really don't have the time. Where is the queen now?"

"In her quarters. May I come with you?"

"If you must." Meg sighed and rolled her eyes at Taryn. "This is Lady Esme Daj Valen. Sweet girl, but a bit gossipy. It's the burden of living in the palace and being bored witless."

"Meg! You're a scandal is what you are." But Esme grinned with affection and hugged the healer.

"Valen?" Taryn's throat tightened and Rhoane took her hand in his. "Is that a common name?" Why would she have Hayden's surname?

Esme shrugged. "I guess. I mean, all of my family are Daj Valens and we can trace our lineage to the beginning of the Seelie Court."

Taryn blinked back the tears that stung her eyes. "It's a beautiful name. As is Esme. I'm Taryn."

"And I am Rhoane."

Esme squinted in their direction. "You look elven, but… different. Are you spies? Have you been sent by King Thane to assassinate the queen?"

"You seem a little obsessed with spies and assassins. I assure you, we're neither. Well, Rhoane has been an assassin, but that was long ago and we don't speak of it." She meant it as a joke, but a splinter of painful truth lodged into her mind. Kaldaar had taunted her at the runyon tree, implying something untoward about Rhoane and Zakael's mother. She shoved the thought to the far reaches of her brain where hopefully it would linger, never to surface again.

Meg leaned in to whisper to Taryn and Rhoane, "Esme's betrothed was killed a short time ago by a known assassin and spy. Since then, she's been rather preoccupied with sorting who is friend or foe. Her trust meter is broken, you could say."

"How rude! We fae have excellent hearing, Meg. A witch only recently on the queen's good side would do well to remember that." Esme tossed a lock of hair over her shoulder. "She's not wrong, though. Turns out, my betrothed wasn't as loving as he purported to be. When Rori killed him, I'll admit, I was devastated, but then I learned he was working for that Acelyne witch and my affections for him vanished." She snapped her fingers. "Like that."

Taryn had no idea what she was talking about, but nodded as she rambled the entire way to the queen's chambers. At the double doors, she paused her chatter long enough to ask the guards to allow them entry. Taryn and Rhoane surveyed the area, noting the colorful mosaics that resembled the one in Menurra and the other at the museum in London. There were slight differences, as if the one in the Seelie Palace were part of a triptych with the other two.

Another riddle.

Rhoane swirled his wrist as he'd done at the museum and she felt his power curl along her body. He was capturing these murals to compare with the others. Brilliant man. Just as he finished with a flourish of his fingers, Esme called them over.

The queen had been waiting for their arrival and was quite eager to see them.

CHAPTER TWENTY-FIVE

Zakael scanned the horizon for signs of life, secretly hoping to find none. If there weren't creatures to capture, surely Kaldaar couldn't fault him for returning empty-handed. It wasn't that he cared one way or the other what happened to the stupid brutes. Not at all. It was more that he hated the way Kaldaar assumed Zakael would do his bidding. Not since he was a young lad had he been ordered about and truly, it chafed.

He had to find a way to convince Kaldaar that they were partners. Equals in the ruination of Aelinae. If they worked together, Kaldaar could get his revenge and Zakael could rule the entire world. But Kaldaar wouldn't listen to his schemes.

"What do I need you for?" He sneered when Zakael brought it up. "I am a god, and you are nothing but a spoiled child."

That had hurt. Marissa had been spoiled—given everything, worked for nothing. Zakael had to fight for everything he'd ever had. Valterys was a benevolent dictator—in his rule and as a father. He rarely gave anything without wanting something in return. Once Zakael's mother Troyanna died, he'd been at the mercy of his father's whims. He shuddered with the memory of that first foray to the dungeons, when his father had scrutinized him for any signs of weakness.

He'd kept his features neutral while inside his belly, sickness churned with terrifying speed. What he saw that day changed him forever. Whatever innocence he'd had left at only eight seasons of age was mutilated as brutally as the men in Valterys's dungeons.

After that, Zakael became a frequent visitor to the dark tunnels, studying his father and the masters who tortured prisoners. He was an excellent pupil, his father had boasted to the masters. But to the courtiers, he presented a different story about his gifted son. Over cups of wine, the overlord deftly manipulated conversations away from Zakael's lust for all things depraved, instead bragging about his accomplishments with women and pointing out how charming a dancer his son was. In time, Zakael sensed that his father feared his unhealthy obsession with the torture chambers. But if Valterys hated the malignancy in his son, he had to remember it was he who had created it. Once the seeds had been planted, Zakael flourished greater than any of them could've predicted.

And now he was the puppet of a deranged god precisely because of his gifts. To his left, near the swamps he remembered from his last trip to the strange world, he saw movement. He rolled his shoulders and flexed his hands in preparation for a fight.

The last time, he'd only captured five of the ape-ram beasts and that had nearly exhausted all of his power. But he was overlord now, with vast amounts of ShantiMari at his disposal. He'd trap the creatures in a net of power and force them through the portal to the cages waiting on the other end. First, he had to get their attention.

He cloaked himself in shadow and strode toward the rain forest that enclosed the swamps they called home. The creatures lived in the trees in houses that looked like mushrooms, with their leafy roofs hovering over crudely made walls. He knew from experience that inside those buildings were hammocks where the creatures slept and roughly hewn furniture. They lived like the beasts they were, without any of the comforts Zakael took for granted. They didn't seem to cook, nor did they bother with clothing, relying on their fur to keep them warm.

They had offspring, so they must have some way of procreating, but the very thought of fucking one of them made him physically ill. It wasn't for him to deem their worthiness based on how attractive they were. As long as they could wield a weapon, Kaldaar had need of them. Male or female, he was told to bring them all to Aelinae.

Several faces peeked out from the doors cut into the branches and he gripped his shadows tighter. They shouldn't be able to see him, yet he felt watched as he came closer. A raw tingling went up his arms to nestle at the base of his neck and he loosened several threads of his ShantiMari.

Something wasn't right. It was too quiet. The last time he'd come to the world, there was music and dancing high up in the trees. Now, only the sounds of birds chirping and a nearby river greeted him. Even the forest critters that had raced between his steps were hiding.

His booted foot stepped forward over a fallen branch and he stumbled onto a patch of leaves. An ominous crack sounded and a moment later, he plummeted into a cleverly hidden hole. His power stretched out, stopping his fall. Sunshine struggled through the trees to illuminate several horrendous-looking spikes not more than a hand's width from his feet. A moment too late and he would've been skewered on the dastardly things.

Using his power, he climbed out of the hole onto the leaf-covered ground and panted with the effort, happy to be alive. What were the stupid beasts trying to trap? As far as he knew, there were only the ape-ram creatures on this part of the world.

Perhaps a new species had invaded the area since he'd last been there.

He rolled over in time to see a club slashing toward his face. He cursed and scrambled to the side, barely missing the spiky end.

"Whoa, whoa, stop!" He held his hands up to show he had no weapons. "I mean you no harm."

"You have returned to steal our men." A woman loomed over him, her horns curling around her face. Her extremely angry face. "I remember you well. What have you done with my husband?"

Her words came out as grunts, but he understood them from when he forced his ShantiMari into the minds of the men he'd captured before.

Zakael struggled to stand, but a blow to the back of his legs felled him like a tree. He came down hard on his knees, swearing at the shooting pain and the stupid beasts who dared attack him. He whipped his hands out, spraying his power in a wide circle, uncaring who it touched. Their screams rent the air and birds flapped from the trees, their cries adding to the torments of the ones he killed. Within minutes, a dozen of the ape-rams lay dead on the verdant ground. Blood oozed from their shredded bodies and he scrunched his nose at the stench they made.

He breathed heavily, anger roiling through his blood, infusing him with vengeance. How dare they? How dare Kaldaar? How dare Taryn? How dare Valterys? And Lliandra, and Marissa—how dare them all to defy him?

Zakael stood on shaking legs and looked skyward toward the treetops. They would pay, all of them. His ShantiMari snaked out to invade the crude houses, snatching anything with a pulse. Males, females, children, critters that foraged beneath the trees: he grabbed them all and shoved them toward his waiting portal.

Their wails went unheard as he ripped them from their homes. If Kaldaar wanted disposable lives to use as soldiers, Zakael would give the god what he'd asked for. After this world, he'd go to the others and take them just as brutally. And through it all, he'd feel nothing for the beasts. Nothing.

Valterys might've planted the seeds of villainy in Zakael, but he'd nurtured those fledgling sprouts until he'd become an unrepentant sadist. Taryn had been foolish to let him live, but he was no fool.

He'd destroy everything and everyone she ever loved. Then he'd destroy her.

As the cries died down, he turned from the wreckage he'd made and started for the portal, his mind already planning his next assault. A boy crept from behind a thick vine to crouch beside the woman who'd said she recognized Zakael. Intrigued, he paused a moment before snatching the child for Kaldaar.

"Mama." Soft cries came from the lad and he held his mother's hand as tears slipped down his fat, furry cheeks. His horns glowed with an inner light, by turns reddish brown and green.

Zakael put a hand over his heart to stop the pinching he felt. Aside from the strange horns, the boy reminded him of when he was perhaps that age and sat at the side of his mother's bed, clasping her dead hand and begging the gods to please, please bring her back to life.

Sentimentality never bode well. He flicked his finger and a shard of power stabbed the boy in the chest. He didn't even have time to cry out before his lifeless body joined his mother's. Zakael spat a curse and spun around to avoid seeing the way the little boy's hand gripped his mother's.

The pinch in his heart turned to a tear and he gasped at the pain it brought, but also the memory of his mother. His life would've been completely different if his mother had lived. Yet, if she had, Taryn never would have been born.

He returned his hand to his chest and breathed deeply of the putrid stench to remind himself who he was.

Between his thoughts, an image of his half-sister tormented him. She wouldn't approve of his wholesale slaughter, but then she was born for kindness, wasn't she? She hadn't been torn from her mother at an early age and plunged into a world of brutality and torture.

Zakael fell to his knees and wheezed against the thick air. How wrong he was. Not only had she been taken from her mother, she'd suffered abuse from her mother, father, half-sister, half-brother, and himself. And yet, despite it all, including the horrendous beating Cashiel had given her, she showed grace.

She should've killed him several times, but she didn't. Why?

What about him was worth saving? He glared at the empty sky and dared the gods to strike him down. Nothing about him was worth saving. Not a bloody damn thing.

His gaze swept the lush greens of the rain forest. There was beauty everywhere, if he only stopped to see it. Perhaps that's what Taryn saw in him—some inner goodness that he'd buried so deep and pushed so far to the back of his being that he'd forgotten it was there.

"Ha!" His laughter cackled over the unnatural stillness his slaughter had brought.

If she saw goodness in him, it was her imagination. And would be her downfall. Only fools hoped for something that didn't exist.

CHAPTER TWENTY-SIX

Taryn took a deep breath and mentally prepared herself for yet another selfish ruler. Her altercation with King Thane was still too raw. She hadn't had time to process everything yet and didn't have the mental or emotional capacity to deal with an outburst. In fact, she barely had the energy to stand. She and Rhoane had been awake since early morning London time, which made it almost a full twenty-four hours with no sleep and very little food. Her belly grumbled as if she needed validation.

Maybe it wasn't just King Thane's fault she'd exploded in his throne room. Mostly his, but she was willing to give him some leeway. A hungry Taryn wasn't the kindest Taryn. And an exhausted and hungry Taryn was even less patient. Hopefully Queen Eirlys would be more hospitable in the way of food, drink, and a bed. Sleep would be lovely. A week of sleep without the stress and worry about having to save a world, not upset the balance of another world, and definitely without any petulant rulers or gods would be bliss.

Two halberds crossed in front of her face and she jolted from her musings to stare at them as if she'd never seen a blade-topped pike before. The detail of the blade was exquisite and any other time she might've inquired about the craftsmanship, but the halberds were blocking the way to possible food and drink.

"No swords allowed in the queen's chambers," one of the guards said.

"Then tell the queen we are sorry to have missed her." Rhoane turned on his heel and strode down the hallway, his boots making angry *thunks* on the wood floor.

Taryn blinked at the halberd, and then at the guard. Food, glorious food was just a few steps away. Maybe. Even if not, they could sit, maybe nap. With a last longing sigh, she followed Rhoane.

"Where do you think you're going?" a woman called after them, and Taryn slowed her step. "You don't have my permission to leave."

Taryn and Rhoane turned in unison. Her permission? They didn't need her permission for anything. Taryn's irritation pricked at the ends of her nerves, and she reminded herself lashing out wasn't being kind. But she was so fucking hungry.

"We were told we could not enter with our swords." Rhoane stood beside Taryn, his chin lifted.

"Yes, that's true. Give them to my guards." She spoke with authority, and a hint of annoyance laced her words. She hadn't introduced herself, so Taryn could only assume she was the queen.

"We can't do that." Taryn placed her hand on the hilt of her sword.

"You would deny the Seelie queen an audience over a blade? What makes them so special?"

Taryn withdrew her sword and the guards advanced on her with their halberds extended.

"Stand down. Let the girl speak."

The guards halted immediately, cementing Taryn's suspicions that this was, in fact, the queen.

"They were gifted to us by the gods of our world. Claidholm

Solais by Verdaine, Goddess of the Eleri," Taryn indicated Rhoane's sword, "and Ynyd Eirathnacht by Ohlin, the Great Father of Aelinae." She held her blade out for the others to see. The gems sparkled, but the dragons remained curiously still. "They do not tolerate others touching them, nor do they suffer fools. But I promise I will not harm you or your guards if you promise the same."

"You speak in riddles, which I find tiresome. I will hold you to your word. No harm shall come to you unless provoked." She peered at them with narrowed eyes. "You look familiar. Do I know you?"

"I am Rhoane al Glennwoods ap Narthvier, and this is Taryn ap Galendrin. I do not believe we have ever met. Did you perhaps meet in an illusion, Taryn?"

She shook her head, even though the woman did seem familiar. Rich brown skin, hair the color of night, and soft lavender eyes that bespoke of kindness. And…wings? Taryn stared at the diaphanous wings that fluttered behind her. Opalescent veins winked in the fading sunlight.

A faerie queen. Taryn sucked in a breath, too in awe to speak.

"I will grant you an audience, but be warned, I am not in the mood for nonsense or trickery."

It was then Taryn saw the others crouched in the doorway, eavesdropping. They scampered away the moment the queen turned toward her rooms. The guards ignored the others and took their position by the doorway with a scowl for Taryn and Rhoane. She smiled sweetly at them as she passed. They were only doing their job. It wasn't personal.

Inside the lavishly appointed rooms, the queen beckoned them to sit.

"I am Queen Eirlys, ruler of the Seelie kingdom of Faerie. I have heard much about you, Taryn, but was not told of your breathtaking beauty. I did not, however, hear much about you, Rhoane. A pity, for you are quite attractive." Her gaze raked over

Rhoane as if she were deciding whether she should eat him or bed him.

Rhoane shifted and cleared his throat. "It is an honor, Your Majesty." He bowed and Taryn noted the curtness of his tone.

Eirlys raised a brow. "So formal. And though I've said little, I feel I have insulted you somehow."

"I am sorry to give you that impression. We are tired and hungry and though your compliments are nice, they are unnecessary. We are in need of information, nothing more." He took Taryn's hand and a wave of his guilt slid up her arm. He'd sensed Eirlys's attraction to him as well.

Marissa was ancient history, she reminded herself, but the scars lingered.

The queen beckoned a servant to have food brought before turning on them with a sharp gaze. The flirty woman was replaced with a queen accustomed to getting her way.

"Why don't you start by telling me why the two of you are in my kingdom. What was the purpose of your visit to Elvenwood? Tensions are high between the kingdoms right now and travelers are suspect."

Taryn rubbed her temple to fight off the beginnings of a headache. A buzzing or murmuring irritated the back of her brain, but she couldn't shut it out. Different from the usual hum of power she heard, this was as if a thousand voices were all speaking at once and every last one of them was crammed inside her skull.

The queen and Rhoane discussed their purpose for being on Cilachaem, and he explained the seals while Taryn tried to sort out her mind. Vaguely aware she was being rude, she nodded and made little grunts of agreement when Rhoane spoke.

She surveyed the room for clues as to what might be causing the clamoring, but saw nothing unusual. Threads of ShantiMari were everywhere: some strong and robust, others tattered with age. A pale golden thread circled the queen and

Taryn focused on it. She kept her own power close, not wanting to alarm the queen or get them thrown in the dungeons on spurious charges.

A snag of their conversation pulled her attention away from the little thread. "Rhoane can help you decipher the symbols on the amulets. They're Eleri runes." She held her hand up for Eirlys to see. "These are bonds given to us by our gods. They're the same as on the amulets. Well, not the same, same, but Eleri runes like these."

The queen reached for her hand and when their skin touched, a shock of recognition whipped up her arm. If Eirlys felt anything, she didn't register it on her face. She peered at Taryn's wrist, turning it this way and that before clucking.

"I would appreciate your help in the matter." Eirlys pulled away, but the sense of remembrance remained.

"What is in your pocket?" Taryn pointed to the queen's heart. "I feel it calling me."

Eirlys put a protective hand over her chest. "It's not your concern."

The voices became louder and then hushed. Taryn watched the queen, studying the way her pupils darkened and lips tightened. She heard the voices, too.

"They are my people," Eirlys said. "I have the thoughts of all my citizens in my head every hour of every day." The queen grinned. "Most days I can tune it out, but your arrival has them quite excited."

"And how is it you heard my thought? I'm not one of your subjects."

"No," Eirlys laughed, "you certainly are not. I didn't hear your thoughts. You spoke aloud."

"I did?" She looked at Rhoane and he nodded. "Why can I hear them?"

The queen's eyes widened and she turned to Rhoane. "She doesn't know?"

"It is a new development—for both of us. We have not had time to properly understand what it means."

They meant Taryn and Rhoane's eventual godhood. It wasn't a topic she was comfortable discussing, nor did it explain why she could hear the voices. Thankfully, food arrived and the subject was dropped. She'd ask Rhoane about it later. Her immediate need was to satisfy her belly.

At the sight of a full feast, she almost cheered as if she were at a football match. Almost. She did give a slight, "Whoop!" that earned her a scowl from the queen, but she didn't care. She was beyond shattered and ravenous enough she could eat the entire feast and a good portion of the table, too.

Meg, Tug, and Esme joined them at the queen's table, which should've surprised her, but didn't. They'd been quiet while Rhoane explained their purpose for being on Cilachaem and quite honestly, Taryn had forgotten they were there. But now, sitting across from Tug, she was happy to have the others divert the queen's attention from her.

Tug adjusted himself to sit across two chairs and gave a happy little harrumph when he was settled. The beautifully crafted table made of long oak planks could easily have seated thirty. All during the meal, Taryn's attention was drawn to the queen's breast, where the pale golden ShantiMari was strongest. Just after dessert, with a full belly and raging migraine, she broached the subject again.

"Please, Your Majesty, I would very much like to see what's in your pocket. I promise no harm will come to you or what's in there."

Eirlys rose and beckoned the others stay, but that Taryn and Rhoane should follow her. Esme scowled and crossed her arms, but Meg and Tug seemed nonplussed to be left out. With the way Meg grinned, Taryn had a feeling she knew exactly what was happening with the queen. She recalled someone had mentioned Meg was a witch. At the doorway, she glanced at the auburn-haired lady. Meg gave a saucy wink and giggled as she poured more wine. What the hell did that mean?

Eirlys directed them into a private sitting room and closed the door. Her ShantiMari spread outward and Taryn cocked her head, curious what the queen needed to protect. A moment later, she had her answer.

The queen withdrew a sleeping faerie from her pocket. No bigger than a thumb and with golden hair cascading down her back. Translucent wings wrapped around her curled body. Tears stung Taryn's eyes and her heart pinched to see the wee lass.

"What happened to her?" Taryn stroked the fae gently, at once needing to feel her life-force, but not wanting to disturb her slumber.

"She was in one of those amulets with Rori. When she broke free, my sweet Arianna didn't wake up. We don't know how to free them or wake them from their eternal sleep." Eirlys nuzzled the princess against her cheek. "She's my only child and the love of my life. I don't know what I'd do without her. Is there anything you can do for her?"

Fresh tears slipped over Taryn's cheeks and her breathing deepened. She flexed her hand where Kaida should've been. The anguish she felt at being separated from Kaida was almost unbearable; she couldn't imagine what Eirlys was going through.

"I wish we could help, but I'm afraid we don't know how to free them, either." Taryn's heart raced and the air thickened until she was gasping for breath. Panic whipped up her spine to pool at the base of her head where the migraine was fiercest and the voices continued their torment. Fresh voices added to the din, screams and cries as if an entire city were being slaughtered.

Where it was, she wasn't sure. Not on Cilachaem, nor on Aelinae, but somewhere close. One of the portals on Myrddin's map, perhaps. All she had were images of carnage and a flash of Zakael's tormented face. Was he injured? Or was he the one doing the butchering? An image of swamps and a rain forest tore through her skull. She knew the place, but how?

"*Darennsai*, what is it?"

"I'm fine. Just too much wine and rich food. I think I'll walk in the garden, if you don't mind. You can help the queen with the runes." Taryn kissed Rhoane on the cheek. "I'm good. Seriously."

His expression said he didn't believe her, and she couldn't blame him. She was anything but fine.

CHAPTER TWENTY-SEVEN

It took five wrong turns, three guards surreptitiously following her, and a kindly elder courtier to find the gardens. Taryn burst through the doors to the outside as if she'd never breathed fresh air in her life. She gulped in breaths and strode from one end of the path to the other, all the while fighting off a panic attack. Why here? Why now?

Hadn't she been through more stressful events? Why did seeing the sleeping fae set her off? Or was it the strange images of Zakael and the foreign world? Where was that and why was it so familiar? Taryn scraped her hair off her face and wound it into a messy bun. A thread of her power kept it secured and off her neck. She shook out her hands and flexed her fingers. Usually when she was on edge, she'd train, but she somehow doubted Queen Eirlys would welcome Taryn and her sword anywhere near her soldiers.

In the open air and away from the queen, the voices quieted, but were still a constant buzz like a gnat that she couldn't rid herself of. Globes of drossfire lit the garden path and she strolled beside neat hedges that bordered roses. Their floral scent filled the air and she breathed deep, cleansing her soul with the fragrance.

Blooms of every color filled this part of the garden. A stunning white rose with black veins caught her eye and she bent to smell its petals. Powdery softness tickled her nose, but the longer she inhaled, the scent changed. A crisp hit of cologne and tobacco stung her senses—the scent reminded her of Brandt. Tears welled in her eyes and she blinked them away. Several drops fell onto the rose she hovered over. Where they touched, the petals turned clear and hardened like a crystal.

She stood, her legs shaking and mind racing. Nadra's tear had turned to crystal in the cavern after Brandt's death. Was that the tear the prophecy mentioned? The crystal was in her rooms in Talaith, nestled in a wooden box with her looking glass and a few other trinkets. No one but her knew what the crystal was, but what if someone figured it out and stole it? She put a hand over her heart to steady the rapid beating and told herself the crystal was fine. She'd placed wards on her belongings before they left for the Summerlands. It was fine. She was fine. Everything was fine.

She bent and used her power to clip the rose from its stem and held it to her nose. Brandt's scent remained, but faded.

"You risk the queen's wrath by picking her roses. She'll have you thrown into the dungeon or exiled if you're caught," a deep, definitely male voice warned from her left.

She turned with the rose, hiding a smile. "She could try."

The breathtakingly handsome man with a shock of white hair and dark skin grinned. His light eyes—grey perhaps—watched her with keen interest.

"You must be the girl everyone is talking about. The special one."

"I suppose that depends on what you mean by special." She tucked the rose into a pocket and secured it with her ShantiMari. She'd hate to lose it, and not because the queen deemed it valuable.

"You really ought not do that. These roses are protected by the queen's magic. I wasn't being trite with my warning."

"I appreciate your concern, but this rose is dearer to me than it could ever be to the queen. She has hundreds of them, and I only have this one. It's quite unusual. What's it called?" Her hand hovered over the pocket with the rose as if she were protecting Brandt himself.

"Remembrance. As I'm sure you've discovered, the scent of the rose becomes that of your dearest departed. That's why these are under the queen's guardianship." He inclined his head and bowed. "I will leave you to your fate." A swath of burgundy silk flowed from the tails of his dinner coat. His footsteps crunched against the gravel and faded when he turned behind a tall hedge.

For half a second, she debated putting the rose back, but what good would that do? She'd already cut it from the bush. If Eirlys ranted at her, she'd take the punishment, but refuse to give up the rose.

Not wanting to court temptation, Taryn turned away from the roses and walked between neatly kept beds of flowers that didn't entice her to steal. At the end of the long row, a bench overlooked a pond and she stood for a moment to appreciate the beauty. Birds sang the last of their songs before tucking in, and bugs chirped the coming of nighttime.

She lifted her face to the twilight sky and searched for stars she might recognize. Theo had shown her a few constellations with his telescope, but it had been too light to see much else. With a night as clear as this, the view from the scope would be incredible. If only they could return to Elvenwood immediately... But Rhoane was helping with the amulets, and she should really be searching for the seal.

She pulled her sword from its scabbard and held it out like a divining stick. "Please, Ynyd Eirathnacht, please help me find the seal."

Eyes closed to better focus, she repeated the request in her mind. The sword didn't burst into song, but it did vibrate. Although, that could've been from her exhaustion and tired arms.

"Where is the seal?" She tried for a simpler question.

Suddenly, Ynyd Eirathnacht whipped her around.

"Oy! Best be careful with that. Ye could hurt someone awful if yer not careful."

Taryn opened her eyes with an apology on her lips. Tug stood at the end of her sword, the tip nearly embedded in his tunic. "I am so sorry. I thought I was alone."

"And ye were. Until I showed up. Then ye weren't."

"What's in this direction?" The sword had turned her around so that she was facing away from the pond and away from the palace.

Tug peered in the direction she indicated. "A coupla cities. Cere, the place we found ye at the Shoogly Dragon."

"And beyond that?" Maybe the seal was at that pub, or somewhere in Cere, but she had a suspicion it was farther away.

"Dunno. Guess Elvenwood at some point. I ain't never been, so's I can't says fer sure. Rori'd know. Or Meg. I 'spose the queen could tell ye."

"No need. You've been a great help." She sagged beneath the weight of responsibility, exhaustion, and dread at having to return to Elvenwood to search for the seal. She was hoping they could swoop in, grab Kaida, and leave without having to deal with the mercurial monarchs.

"Ye look shattered. If'n ye don't mind, I could sit with ye a spell. I like the view from here." He helped her to the bench and she sank onto the hard concrete.

Tug sat beside her, his bulk providing both welcome support and warmth. With the coming of night, a chilly breeze picked up and she shivered against it. Tug wrapped his arm around her with a questioning gaze.

"Don't mean nothin' by it, just thought mayhaps ye be cold."

"You're the sweetest giant I've ever met. Thank you."

"Do ye know many giants?"

"Just the one." She grinned at him and he laughed.

"I like ye, Taryn ap Galendrin. I don't care if'n they says ye be a goddess or a goat. Yer alright by me."

They sat quietly for a while, Taryn lost to her thoughts. The libraries here and at Elvenwood most likely had books or scrolls about her and Rhoane, but did she want to read them? Panic buzzed in the small of her back and snapped against her spine, threatening to spiral out to another attack.

"Why're these seals so important to ye?" Tug broke the silence and she startled at the sound of his voice against the hush of night.

"On our world, Aelinae, there are two gods who wish harm to all the people. One of these gods is called Rykoto. A nasty piece of work who did terrible things, and is paying for his crimes by being imprisoned in a temple. The seals help keep him confined."

"And if ye don't find them, does he go free?"

"I don't know. Maybe? It's complicated." That prick of dread at the base of her spine became a stab against her heart. "If we fail, our world will suffer and all the people there will know anguish. We can't fail." Tears threatened and she sniffed against them.

Fail, fail, fail. The word echoed in her mind. They'd failed in London. They'd failed here so far. How many more failures until she admitted defeat? What were they doing here, anyway? Wasting time chasing their tails when they should be back home fighting Kaldaar. She was as useless as Lliandra accused her of being. She wasn't a goddess. She would fail Cilachaem just as she'd failed Aelinae.

"I don't think ye'll fail. Yer too strong fer that. Ye and yer mate, Rhoane. Hims real smart, too. Been tellin' the queen all about them symbols and what's what with the amulets. Told her Rori'll sort 'em when she gets back, didn't he?"

"Bless you, Tug. I wish I had your confidence. I'm just so damn worried that I'll do something to endanger your future. I mean, if we created this world, how can we be here, now, in the flesh?"

"I 'spose when yer a goddess, time don't mean the same thing."

"Perhaps you're right. I mean, gods can do anything, right? Why not move between worlds and timelines?" Excitement buzzed in her belly.

Nadra had once told her that when you're a god, physics is a matter of semantics. Why not time as well? The implications of what was possible nearly blew her mind. She was thinking like an Aelan—like a mortal. But how did she stop thinking in finite terms? That was the problem.

"Can't ye just ask yer magic to help ye find these seals? Ye do have magic, doncha?"

"You're bloody brilliant." She twisted on the bench and stretched to kiss him on the cheek. Why didn't she think of that? Too busy worrying about failing. Which was the highest form of idiocy she could imagine. "Let's go see if they're done with the amulets. Can you show me the library on the way?"

With Tug leading the way, they didn't get lost once. In the library, Taryn decided to give Tug's simple yet genius plan a try. About five times smaller than the huge rooms at Elvenwood, it didn't take long for her ShantiMari to cover all of the books. She asked for references to Aelinae, but came up empty. Next, she asked about Myrddin or Merlin and several lights pinged on different shelves. Tug retrieved whatever he found glowing and brought them to her. Finally, she asked about the seals. Again, she was left wanting.

It didn't matter. Tug had given her the means by which to search Elvenwood and the remaining worlds. They scanned the scrolls and books, reading snippets about Myrddin's time at the Faerie Courts, especially his lengthy stay with the Unseelie queen who, if the tales were to be believed, was quite taken by the wizard and heartbroken when he left. Nowhere did the tales mention his reason for being in Faerie or why he left.

Tug watched her as she chewed her bottom lip, thinking. "One more search." She asked her power to find any mention of the Eirielle, the *Darennsai,* or the Chosen One.

A lone light glowed and Tug raced to grab the scroll for her. The single page was written in the same hand as Myrddin's maps. Unlike the other books and scrolls that were written in the lingua franca of Elennish and Eleri, this page was solely written in Elennish. She skimmed the words, her heart beating loud enough she could scarcely hear beyond the thumping. The entire page was a letter meant just for her. For the Eirielle, to be exact.

"He's set a trap for me." She tilted her head left to right. "I suppose I should've suspected that. But what would he do? Make me sick? Strike me down? Send a demon after me? What kinds of wards could he put on the seals that would last possibly thousands of years?"

"Are ye askin' me or just talkin' to yerself?"

"Mostly talking to myself, but I welcome your thoughts."

Tug rubbed his chin and nodded. His black hair stuck straight up and danced with the movement. "I've found, the best way to hurt somun is to take somethin' precious from 'em. Or get in their head somethin' awful." Tears shimmered in his soft brown eyes and she took his hand in hers.

"I'm sorry, Tug. I didn't mean to upset you."

He wiped his tears and sniffed. "Naw, ye didn't. I was just missin' Rori is all. She's me best mate, but I have Meg, too."

"It's good to have friends and loved ones close, but it's hard when they're far away. I have a companion who stayed at Elvenwood to see after the lycan, and I miss her very much."

"That was a nice thing ye did fer the beast. Meg was sore upset she couldna heal 'im."

"I'm not sure we did, but we can hope. Thank you for being

here. Truly. You've been a tremendous help." She patted his big hand and gave it a reassuring squeeze.

"So this is where you've been hiding. I suppose I should've guessed when Rhoane told me you have a thing for libraries." The queen's tone was snide and possessive.

Taryn's gut pinched, and she looked to Rhoane for an explanation. *A thing for libraries* didn't sound like something he'd say. His expression said he was just as confused as she.

"Did you find anything, *mi carae*?" He was at her side in a few short steps and slid her hand into his. Their runes sparked to life and shimmered with a soft glow.

Ease rippled over her, but her heart was still unsettled. "We did." She showed him the page Myrddin had written to the Eirielle, and his jaw tensed. "I searched the palace and the seal isn't here. We should return to Elvenwood."

"Nonsense. You should stay here for the night. You both look like you could use the rest." The queen took the page from Rhoane and frowned. "I can't read this. What does it say?"

"That the Eirielle—Taryn—is in danger. When she is close to the seal, she will know it by experiencing some sort of horror." Rhoane retrieved the page and rolled it tightly before tucking it inside his tunic. "You have no need for this scroll, but we do. Taryn is right. If the seal is at Elvenwood, we must return there immediately."

"But you're not absolutely certain it's there, are you? Stay the night. Keep an old queen company."

"Your Majesty." Esme spoke up and Taryn noticed she and Meg had entered with the queen, but stood off to the side where she couldn't see them. "We have pressing matters of our own. Perhaps it's best to wish them well on their journey and focus on the kingdom."

Meg agreed and flashed a glance to Tug, who added his voice to theirs. More chaos. Like in London, something was happening on Cilachaem that affected them peripherally. This could be

Myrddin's doing—throwing random obstructions in their way to delay or frustrate them.

As much as she needed sleep, it was imperative they find the seal and leave this world before even more turmoil tried to trap them. Every moment spent here was a chance for them to upset the balance. And that might be exactly what Myrddin was hoping to accomplish. Kaldaar thrived on chaos, and what better vehicle to introduce it or stoke the flames already lit on other worlds than her bumbling around, looking for seals?

What if it was all for naught and they didn't need the seals to keep Rykoto imprisoned? The maps, the notes from Myrddin, the page she'd found in the Seelie library: they all could be part of some elaborate scheme to keep her away from Aelinae while Kaldaar grew stronger.

"We have to go, now. Thank you, Tug, for everything. Your Majesty." She curtseyed low to the queen before thanking Esme and Meg for their help with the amulets.

Against the queen's wishes, and ignoring her commands, they hurried to the pond. Along the way, Taryn explained to Rhoane her twisty thoughts.

"It might be a game, another puzzle for you to solve, or it could be exactly what it seems—we must find the missing seals to keep Rykoto imprisoned. Either way, we will not know until we return to Aelinae with them or without. What is your choice?"

Taryn chewed on her bottom lip and paced a tight circle around the bench. "I think we should find them just in case I'm wrong and it's not a convoluted trap."

"I agree. It might not be what it appears, mi carae. Myrddin could be helping us, but making it look like he is setting a trap. It could be that this is a test and should you pass, it will make defeating both Rykoto and Kaldaar easier. We simply do not know." He kissed her brow and held her face between his hands. "I do know that you will not be alone. Kaida and I are with you, always."

"Let's go get our friend. Should we fly or use a doorway?"

"Our darathi will refresh our energy."

They shifted and he was right—she immediately felt the rush of dragon power that came with unleashing her inner darathi. Torches lit the outer palace walls and she spied four figures standing in the garden near the unusual rosebushes. Tug's wide smile made his face even rounder and he lifted a big hand to wave at them. Queen Eirlys, Meg, and Esme stared up in awe. She snorted a flame and banked north in the direction her sword had pointed earlier. Toward Elvenwood, where she was confident they'd find the seal.

Rhoane ghosted beside her, his wing tip periodically scratching across her scales as they flew over towns, meadows, and a dark-blue ocean. With the wind in her face and her love by her side, she felt alive, rejuvenated. Invincible. They could fly all night and she wouldn't tire of it, but they had a duty to Aelinae.

I needed this, mi carae. Thank you. The fresh air cleared the doubt from her mind and settled her nerves.

It has calmed my heart as well. Let us hope the serenity continues.

The spires of Elvenwood came into view and she grasped Rhoane's words like a lifeline. They could use some calm in their lives. The sound of whispered voices reached her dragon hearing and she heard a snap come from the battlements. A moment later, something whizzed past her head.

They're shooting at us. Go higher! She sent the frantic thought to Rhoane and beat her wings to get out of the arrows' range.

They'd been waiting for her and Rhoane to return. Bloody bastards. From the constant barrage of arrows, it was clear the fuckers were trying to kill them.

CHAPTER TWENTY-EIGHT

An arrow shot past his head and Rhoane banked right, a fraction too late, seeing a second arrow aimed directly at him. He beat his wings harder, but it did no good. Pain seared through his wing and he roared a curse that came out a flame of rage. They were too low and the soldiers too skilled. He scanned the top of the palace and saw figures along not just the battlements, but the top of the mountain, too.

It was an ambush. He jerked his gaze to the other side of the canyon and saw even more soldiers.

Kaida, we are under attack. Are you safe?

I am with the prince and his lady in his rooms. He worried this might happen.

Stay there. We will be with you shortly.

Soldiers are waiting for you. Be careful, my Surtentse.

Rhoane dodged another volley of arrows and blew more flames from his snout. They could outfly the attack, but that would leave Kaida alone in the palace and he wasn't leaving Elvenwood without the grierbas. They were using her as bait to trap, or even kill, him and Taryn. The elven rulers would regret their rash decision, but first, he had to get into the palace.

Taryn, I have an idea. It is madness, but if it works, we can rescue Kaida.

I'm up for whatever you got. All I can think of is bringing the entire fucking mountain down on the king and queen.

Best not be hasty, mi carae, he warned, and her chuckle caressed his mind. *I am going to slow time. When I do, we will transform back into our male and female forms. As soon as we are no longer darathi, you will transport us inside the palace.*

Whoa. When you said mad, I didn't think you meant completely barking. You do realize we could die, right? She gasped and her dragon dove low to avoid a flaming ball the size of his fist. *What the hell? Let's do this.*

She sounded as confident as him, which wasn't much at all. It was the only plan he could think of, given the circumstances. His wing burned from the arrow wound and it was only a matter of time before he lost use of the appendage.

Rhoane drifted close to her darathi and flipped until he was beneath her. He closed his eyes and said the words necessary to slow time. Taryn gripped his talons in hers and they spiraled down together.

Time stretched until a second was as long as he needed it to be.

Now, my love.

They transformed into their Aelan and Eleri forms, their hands clasped. Taryn wrapped her arms around him and everything went black. A heartbeat later, they stood in the forbidden section of Elvenwood's library. Blinking against the sudden candlelight, they both nervously chuckled.

"I can't believe that worked." Taryn felt his face and kissed him hard. "Let's not ever do that again."

"Agreed."

At this time of night, the rooms were deserted, but a gossamer image of a woman lingered in the corner of the nook.

When he looked in her direction, she disappeared. A hazy film covered the room from his manipulating time.

"Shall I continue to stretch the minutes, or return to normal?"

"Normal. I want them to see us and know we cannot be defeated." Taryn's jaw tightened and he nodded.

He released his control of time and the film lifted. Taryn scanned the bookshelves, her eyes narrowed.

"A pity we can't do a quick search, but that would draw their attention."

He took her hand in his and gently urged her forward, hiding a wince at the pain that shot through his shoulder. "Once we know Kaida is safe, we will find the seal."

"You're right. I just have this strange feeling we're close."

Outside the library, the halls were quiet. Too quiet. Most of the soldiers were at the top of the palace, but surely the monarchs had prepared for anything. Or maybe not. They crept through the hallways to the vast area with the elvenwood tree. Burning pain shot from his shoulder to his brain and settled in his gut. He doubled over and gagged against the sickness that rose in his throat.

"Rhoane!" Taryn whispered the word, but it echoed in the open space. "What is it?"

Her ShantiMari immediately circled him, but the touch of it was like poison.

"No, no power." He gasped the words and stumbled forward. "It…hurts."

"No, no, no, not again. Is this leftover poison from the runyon tree?" Her hand hovered above him, as if she were afraid to touch him.

"Something. Different." He couldn't breathe or think or hold his weight. With a wheeze, he fell over and curled into a ball.

The similarities to the runyon tree poison were too close to ignore. He inched his way toward the elvenwood. Each skootch forward brought a fresh bout of anguish, but he kept moving.

"The elvenwood? Is that what's doing this?" Taryn unsheathed her sword, but Rhoane shook his head.

"The tree is in anguish. I feel its pain mingled with my own. Something is killing it from the inside." It took all of his strength to say the words and he lay panting on the cool marble.

Taryn's eyes flicked from him to the tree and back. "Why can't I feel it?"

The sound of footsteps running in their direction came from one of the galleries, and Rhoane urged Taryn to drag him to the tree. She grabbed hold of his tunic and sucked in a breath.

"You're bleeding. We need to get you to Eiodian."

"Tree."

She hesitated only a moment before gripping his shirt and pulling with all her might. He tried using his own ShantiMari to help, but the touch of his power was like pouring boiling water across his body.

"Stop right there!" Queen Helena shouted at them from a short distance away.

A blast of Taryn's power singed his skin as she made a barrier to keep the queen and her soldiers from reaching them. Just a few more paces and they'd reach the tree. Taryn tugged harder, her grunts a hammer to his heart.

"Stay with me, my love. We're almost there."

One more pull and his head butted against the trunk of the elvenwood.

"What now?"

"Not know." Words stuck in his throat and his vision became clouded. Sickness churned in his belly as quickly as his thoughts muddled his mind.

A crumpled white rose with black veins fell from Taryn's shirt, and she leaned her head against the tree's trunk. Tears rolled over her cheeks to drip from her chin to the marble beside his head. Several landed on the petals and he stared at the drops, fascinated by the rose, yet equally terrified of what was happening.

Outside the barrier, soldiers shouted and he heard Kaida's barks above the din.

"Inside," Rhoane croaked and pushed himself to a sitting position. "We must go in the tree."

"No, Rhoane. The last time that happened, Kaldaar tried to trap you for all eternity. I can't lose you again."

"You will not, mi carae. Listen to Kaida." He lowered his head to indicate the grierbas.

She stood beside Theo and Rainne, her eyes glowing golden. The queen's soldiers slashed at the invisible barrier with their swords while Helena glared at him and Taryn. She was scared, but not of them. He twisted until his face was a breath away from the bark. The tree was sick and she feared for her kingdom if the tree fell. Was she pushing her thoughts into his mind, or was it the tree telling him this?

"Take my hand." He flopped his arm toward Taryn, and she gently took his hand in hers. "Inside. We are safe."

Fresh tears poured from her lovely deep-blue eyes and she bit her lip, unsure. "I love you, Rhoane. I trust you."

Still holding his hand, she pressed her body into the tree trunk. A moment later, they both stood in the center of the tree. As big as his father's great hall, the hollow interior stretched upward, with rings marking the tree's age along the walls. Similar to the Weirren, a pinch of homesickness startled his heart.

"Rhoane, there." Taryn pointed to a shining silver disk floating above their heads.

Farther up, moonlight streamed through the tree's branches and the cries of night creatures could be heard. He took a step toward the seal and a bout of cramps ravaged his gut before traveling down his legs. Strength failed him and his knees hit the ground hard, rattling pain up to his skull.

Taryn reached for him, but he waved her off. "Get the seal."

"But you're hurt."

He pointed at the shining disk and gasped in labored breaths. She wavered a moment before taking a step. His hand ripped from his arm and plopped onto the dirt. He stared at the bloody stump, too stunned to react. Taryn took another step and his other hand followed the first.

"Fuck, Rhoane!" She stared in horror at his butchered wrists. "The seal can wait. We have to get you out of here."

"No." He gagged against a fresh wave of sickness. "Finish this. Just, take bigger steps, please." He tried for a wan smile and failed.

"My steps caused that?"

He nodded and hunched over the lifeless hands to block them from her view.

"His note said I would suffer. Why is this happening to you?"

He chuckled and met her worried gaze. "Are you not suffering now?"

"Dammit." She scraped her hair off her face and swore again before shaking out her hands and blowing out a long breath. "What if this isn't real? Maybe it's an illusion to make us think you're losing limbs with each step I take."

"We will not know until you retrieve the seal." Every syllable tore at his throat and he tasted blood with each swallow.

"I hate this. Myrddin was Brandt's best friend. What a dick." She arched her back and gazed upward, her lips pinched to thin white lines. "I'm trying to think of what I can do that won't kill you." She gave him a haggard smile. "Got any ideas?"

He wheezed and nodded, unable to form words. Tears sparkled in her eyes and it killed him to see her agonize over him. Myrddin couldn't have known he would be with Taryn when she searched for the seals. Or had he? If so, then he'd planned his deception brilliantly. Taryn would've slogged through the tree, taking on grievous injury one after another, but seeing her beloved suffer stopped her from reaching the seal. It put fear into her actions. Myrddin had counted on that.

Rhoane lifted his mutilated arm and positioned it facing the seal. "I carry you."

His ShantiMari flowed from his stump to surround her. Her eyes went wide and tears rolled gently down her face.

"Rhoane, no. It could kill you."

"Or save us."

He closed his eyes and channeled his power to lift her up. Sweat dripped from his forehead and his arm shook with the effort, but he wouldn't fail her. Claidholm Solais burst into song and he opened his eyes to see her stretching toward the seal. Beams of moonlight haloed around her and she looked every inch a goddess at that moment. Radiant. Determined.

Stars danced around her as if she were the sun to their orbit. And she was. At least, she was his sun and moon and stars. She was his everything.

And you are my everything, mi carae.

A lump of affection rumbled up his chest and he redoubled his focus to keep her aloft. It was then he saw tiny glistening threads of deepest obsidian webbed from one side of the tree to the other.

Telraicht-Noir ShantiMari.

With his free arm, he plunged the bloody stump into the dirt and coaxed new roots to grow. They sprouted from the ground toward Taryn to make a nest of sorts around her and the seal. Ynyd Eirathnacht joined his sword in a harmony that filled the tree with exultation. The song they sang was one he knew from his childhood. As ancient as the roots of the Weirren, it was a melody his mother would often hum. A song of rebirth. Of Light and Dark and all that existed between the two.

Rhoane wrapped his roots around Taryn until she was ensconced in his protective embrace. Nothing would harm her. Not while he lived.

The songs hushed and time stood still for one long heartbeat. Taryn's fingertips touched the seal and she clasped them around the silver disk.

There was a soft hush, followed by the shattering of glass. Not glass—the black webbing splintered into thousands of shards and hung in the empty air.

He blew a breath as strong as if he were his darathi. Flame as bright as the sun flared from his lips. The obsidian shards melted and he whisked the remnants through the top of the tree to the sky, above where the ashes of Myrddin's power were scattered among the stars.

His heartbeat rammed in his skull and his body ached from the effort, but he couldn't rest until Taryn was safe. He pulled the nest toward him and she stepped from the roots with the seal in her hands. Face ashen, eyes huge, she rushed to his side.

"You mad, mad man. I love you." She pressed her lips to his and lifted him with the strength of a giant. "I've got you."

A moment later, they burst from the tree to land on the hard marble floor of the elven palace. The wound on his shoulder objected violently and he swore against the jag of pain that radiated down his arm.

"Move and you die."

Before he could adjust his position to see who spoke, a dozen sword tips moved to within a breath of his face.

CHAPTER TWENTY-NINE

Holy fuck, that hurt. Taryn lay on her back, panting as if she'd spent three bells training with Anje's soldiers. She held the seal in a death grip, too afraid to loosen her fingertips for fear Myrddin's ShantiMari might snatch it away. He was clever, that traitorous asshole. When she saw him next, he was in for a world of hurt.

How could she have been so stupid to believe he was a friend? And Brandt! Thank the gods her grandfather wasn't around to know of Myrddin's betrayal.

She squinted at the sword tips that suddenly appeared an inch in front of her face and debated her choices. It wasn't the guards' fault; it was their sovereigns'.

"Move and you die." Queen Helena sneered from behind the guards.

To her right, Rhoane lifted his once-mangled arm to press a fingertip against the nearest blade. "Is this really necessary?"

"Rhoane, your hand—it's healed." She reached for him and clasped his whole, unharmed hand in hers.

Confusion and delight flooded his gorgeous eyes and he rolled toward her. "The cramping and sickness are gone as well."

Kaida broke through the guards and licked both of their faces. Her whimpers and yips mimicked the fear and relief that whirled through Taryn's own heart. She rolled to a kneeling position and the guards shuffled to accommodate her movements. The ground rumbled and she grabbed Kaida with one hand and Rhoane with the other.

"The tree." Rhoane gazed wide-eyed at the elvenwood.

The trunk shivered and expanded. What was once the width of two grown men tripled in size within the space of a single breath.

"What are you doing? Stop it at once," the queen commanded. But it wasn't Taryn or Rhoane making the tree grow. Helena shrieked for her guards to kill them, but the soldiers hesitated.

Their wild eyes pinged between the tree, their queen, and Taryn's little group. The rumbling stopped suddenly and their faces turned from worry to wonder. Several leaves fell from the branches, but no other damage was done. No tiles were broken or columns felled. The only change in the great room was the size of the tree.

Queen Helena advanced on them, but a branch swooped low to block her path. Another branch lifted Taryn and Rhoane to standing and curled them against the trunk. The song their swords had sung inside the tree played not in her mind, but in the very tree itself. She gazed at the lush green leaves sprouting from new branches and sucked in a breath. Emerging between the leaves were flowers the size of a dinner plate. Clear as a polished diamond, with tiny opalescent veins running through the petals and along the edges.

The tree lowered one of the blooms to the queen and another to Taryn. She recalled the white rose she stole from the Seelie Palace, and shoved a hand inside her empty pocket.

"You dropped it before we went into the tree." Rhoane took

the flower and held it cupped in his hands. "The tree absorbed it, along with your tears."

"You've healed the elvenwood," Helena whispered. "You have our everlasting gratitude." She curtseyed low, nearly to the floor.

Her guards sheathed their swords and stood at attention.

"You are remarkable, mi carae." Rhoane handed her the rose and kissed her gently on the lips.

"*We* are remarkable."

They'd defeated Myrddin's traps and healed the tree together. Thank the gods for Rhoane's basket. Without it, she might not have succeeded. His power woven through every fiber of the roots had shielded her from the worst of Myrddin's Telraicht-Noir Shan-tiMari. It had oozed into her skin, searching for her own dark powers—not to command, but to destroy. She'd suffered Myrddin's power eating away at her like fire ants gnawing on a greasy bone.

Still, she wasn't sure how much of what they'd just experienced was illusion and what was real. Even after expanding, the tree's trunk wasn't nearly as wide as the room they were in, but spatial manipulation wasn't difficult. After five thousand years to practice, Myrddin had plenty of time to perfect his illusions and tests. Hopefully, they wouldn't all be as horrible as this one.

"Tomorrow night, you will join us at the feast and afterward, you will tell us how you healed our sacred tree." Helena waved her hand imperiously.

Taryn extricated herself from the tree branch's embrace and strolled to where the queen stood with her guard. She lifted her chin to Theo and Rainne, who hovered just outside the ring of soldiers. Their expressions were veiled, but she felt their anxiety. The feast was for them, to announce his betrothal to Rainne. In the short time they'd tinkered with his telescope, he'd shared that and more about the king and queen's reluctance to accept Rainne into the family. If she and Rhoane denied the invitation, it would reflect poorly on the couple.

"We will attend the feast to honor Prince Theo and his Lady Delarainne. Once we have properly rested, we will discuss the tree's health and many other failings of the Eleri clans of Elvenwood." Taryn stood to her full height, which was perhaps an inch shorter than the queen. She would not be commanded by this woman or any other. Not ever again.

Helena's eyes narrowed and lips parted as if to rebuke Taryn, but they turned to a smile instead. "As you wish. I will have a room prepared for you." She lifted the rose to her nose and inhaled. "It smells of my mother." Tears sparkled in her eyes.

"It comes from a rose I stole from the Seelie Palace—something the faerie queen does not know—and is called a Remembrance Rose. Although, the one I took was white with—"

"Black veins. I know this flower. Eirlys showed it to me on a state visit not long ago. She had wards and protections in place to keep anyone from touching them, they were so precious. How is it you obtained one?"

"I simply cut the stalk with my ShantiMari." She ran a finger along the top of the petals. "I'm sure it has some deeper meaning, but I'm so tired I barely know my own name."

They were led to a suite of rooms that rivaled Lliandra's in their splendor. Taryn would appreciate the lovely furnishings later. All she cared about was the bath she heard running in the distance. She hoped it was meant for her and not her mind playing tricks. It would be quite the letdown to discover it was actually a waterfall outside their rooms. The way her day was going, she feared it might well be. Or worse, these weren't their rooms, but a convenient bypass for the queen to toss them over the edge of the canyon.

She was losing it. Truly and deeply, she was mad.

Once their escort had left, Rhoane directed her to the bathing room, where a magnificent tub big enough for both her and Rhoane, plus Kaida, sat waiting. She stripped her clothes and was in the soothing warmth before Rhoane had a chance to unfasten his sword belt. Kaida waited for them outside, but kept close in case she was needed. While Taryn and Rhoane bathed, she told them of the lycan's progress. He was healing and even showing signs of reclaiming the male part of his being.

Kaida's worry that she might be ripped apart crowded her thoughts, and Taryn did her best to reassure the grierbas that no one would strip her awareness from her soul. But there was no way to be certain it couldn't happen. Someone had found a way to steal the lycan's ShantiMari so completely that he was broken almost beyond repair. Same with the scyvers.

Zakael was cruel, but could he do something like that? What about beasts like Enghor? Did Zakael take them forcibly from their home worlds and bring them to Aelinae as playthings for Amdi, or for a greater, albeit more sinister purpose? The image of Zakael and swamps crowded her skull. Bile splashed the back of her mouth and she remembered why the world looked familiar.

"I promised Enghor I would tell his wife he died honorably." She blinked back tears and hoped her vision had been wrong. "At the Seelie Palace, when I left suddenly for the gardens, it was because I had a vision of Zakael devastating swamps. I fear that might be Enghor's home. Any idea what world he came from?" Taryn dried her hair and gazed across the canyon to the city of Elvenwood. So much destruction amid so much beauty.

Lights flickered in several windows, but most of the buildings were dark. It had to be close to midnight, but with all their hopping from place to place, she had lost track of the day and the hour.

Rhoane sidled up behind her and wrapped his arms around her waist. "I do not. If Zakael is causing harm, there is nothing we can do about it right now. We need sleep. Tomorrow we will plan our next move. Your promise will be fulfilled, but not tonight."

He was right, as usual. "First, I need to heal your wound."

She dropped the towel and turned his naked body until his back was to her. "This might hurt a bit."

It always did, but he never complained. She felt his pain as if it were her own and knew the moment the arrow had sliced through the tough membrane of his wing. She ran her fingertips over the cut and channeled her ShantiMari into his skin.

"You know, we could do this the Ullan way." She playfully nipped his shoulder and he flinched. Gods, she'd forgotten he was jealous of Loghan. "I'm sorry, Rhoane."

An image of her lying on the table in the healer's tent with a very naked Loghan at her side seared her mind. It was Rhoane's memory of how he'd found her in Ulla, near death and about to be defiled by the Ullan healer. The sheer amount of anger, pain, and fear that coursed through her brain was staggering. She'd been on the brink of death and it was the only way Loghan had known to heal her. In the end, it was Rhoane who had saved her. She focused on those memories. Of when Rhoane made love to her for several bells and brought her back to life. It was that love she funneled into him now to heal not only him, but his dragon as well.

The wound knit together beneath her touch and a few minutes later, it was difficult to tell there had ever been broken skin. A thin scar was all that remained. She kissed his back and he didn't flinch at her touch. He turned to face her, an apology in his eyes, but she kissed him to let him know no apology was necessary. They'd shared enough sorrow.

She swayed with exhaustion and he led her to the ridiculously huge bed, where Kaida lay sprawled on one side, with plenty of room for Taryn and Rhoane leftover on the other. It brought forth happy memories of when Kaida was a puppy and would sleep with her or the other princesses. Those were days of innocence and part of her longed for them.

"Good night, my loves." She snuggled beneath the covers and curled into Rhoane's warmth.

She might not be innocent anymore, but she could appreciate what she had. For tonight, that included a roof over her head and a stunningly comfortable bed.

When Rhoane woke her the next morning, she wasn't all that surprised to find it was closer to lunch than breakfast. Her body needed the extra rest. He brought her food on gilded plates that made her whistle at the extravagance. The queen was certainly trying to impress them. Which would've been far more appreciated if the queen also hadn't been trying to kill them less than twelve hours earlier. Bloody elf and her mercurial moods.

They lounged around their rooms for most of the day, only venturing as far as the balcony. Twice Rhoane took Kaida to the garden where she could run and stretch her legs, but Taryn stayed inside, studying Myrddin's papers. She leafed through them, rereading passages she'd already committed to memory. If only he'd left clues to which worlds he'd hid the seals, but the lying bastard hadn't.

On her third pass skimming the page with Cilachaem's information, she paused, unsure whether her eyes were playing tricks on her. A tiny smudge was squiggled next to the word Cilachaem. It hadn't been there before, she was certain of it. She checked her hands for dirt and wiped them on her pants, but she didn't think the smudge came from her. She hadn't touched that part of the paper.

Rhoane and Kaida entered, his cheeks pinked by the fresh air and her fur fluffed.

"Was it windy?" She peered out the open balcony doors. "Seems like a nice day out."

"Theo took us to the top of his tower. He has a larger telescope up there. He is quite keen to learn more about Aelinae, and I did not want to disappoint him with my ignorance of the stars."

"If it makes you feel any better, he asked me too and I couldn't give him an answer." She shrugged and scrunched her face. "I'm Keeper of Stars, not knower of all constellations of every world."

Rhoane chuckled and kissed her forehead. "It is almost time for the feast. Do you need assistance getting dressed?"

They arrived at the feast looking properly elven in their coordinating robes of dusty grey. The queen had them delivered while Taryn and Rhoane were preparing for the evening. Although she thought they were more suited for monks hidden away high in the mountains, Rhoane wasn't all that fussed about the drab outfits. Underneath the long robes, they both wore soft cotton pants and Eleri boots. They would appease the queen only as much as necessary.

Kaida sat beside them at their assigned seats—not at the high table, thank the gods—and watched the proceedings with seemingly lackadaisical attention, but Taryn knew better. The grierbas was a master at appearing indifferent when she was anything but. Kaida wasn't the only one surveying the guests. Taryn and Rhoane kept alert to the goings-on while the nobles and courtiers watched them with veiled interest.

Every so often, a whisper hidden behind a hand or fan would reach Taryn's hearing. Most of those present were curious about the couple and only a blessed few were outright hostile to have them in their presence. It was the same everywhere they went, apparently. Except in Menurra. Queen Prateeni and King Faisal's court was the one of two places she felt accepted and could relax. Paderau was her first home on Aelinae and would always be where she felt she belonged, but she wouldn't mind living in the Summerlands.

Thinking about Menurra inevitably made her long for home and miss her friends. Especially Hayden. He was the brother she never had. Hell, if she'd been raised on Aelinae, they would've grown up together. With only a few days separating their births, they were practically twins. Except Hayden wasn't her twin. Gavyn was, and he'd been cruelly twisted and used against her.

She reached for Rhoane's hand and gave it a squeeze. With them away from Aelinae, she could only hope Kaldaar didn't try to corrupt Hayden again. He'd nearly succeeded once and although Nadra assured her he couldn't do it again, she worried. Worried for all of them.

She leaned over to whisper in Rhoane's ear. "What are we doing here? We should be in Talaith planning our defeat of Kaldaar, not eating rich foods and listening to gossip as if we haven't a care in the world."

"And we will. Once we have secured the seals, we can be assured Rykoto will not be free to join his brother. Just a few more days, mi carae. Let us dance and forget our troubles." He rose and bowed to the high table before leading Taryn to the dance floor, where several dozen elves lined up for a quadrille.

For the next three hours, she danced and drank and tried to forget her troubles, but they only seemed to multiply with every passing minute. Each time she glanced at the king, he sneered at her with unabashed hatred. The queen was more resigned, but Taryn sensed her apprehension. Whether for her or the king, she couldn't be certain. At least the king didn't have the awful shadow behind him tonight. In fact, Taryn hadn't felt its presence since the throne room the day before.

Which didn't explain why there was a flicker of something just on the periphery of her vision the entire evening. Not malevolent, or at least she hoped not, it tracked her movements as stealthily as Kaida stalked rabbits. If there was one thing Taryn reviled most, it was being someone's prey. Yet this poacher was clever—who or whatever it was stayed well concealed and suppressed their ShantiMari—if they had any. But she suspected they were quite powerful. They had to be to keep up the deception the whole night. She knew from experience how exhausting it was to use shadows as a cloaking device.

When she mentioned the shadow to Rhoane, he scanned the

room, his jaw tense enough to crack a nut. With a slight shake of his head, he bent low and whispered, "I see nothing."

"Could it be Myrddin? I found something on the scrolls today that, I don't know, I think I'm being jumpy. Can we leave yet?"

He kissed her hand. "Of course."

They found Theo and Rainne on the dancefloor and said their goodbyes with a promise to see them the next day. They hadn't had a chance to speak to them privately at the feast, but Taryn hoped to discuss the worlds on Myrddin's list with the lad.

Once back in their rooms, Taryn showed Rhoane the marked page, and he bent over the sheet to study the smudge. He squinted and frowned and blinked his lovely eyes.

"I do not remember it being there, but I cannot make out what it is. Either I am getting too old, or it is illegible on purpose."

"What if…" Taryn bit her lower lip and frowned. "What if Myrddin has a tracking system? Once we touched the seal, he was alerted. I mean, I have alarms set on the seals in the Temple of Ardyn. It wouldn't surprise me if Myrddin set up something similar for the missing seals."

"It is possible." He scanned the other pages. "Earth does not have a smudge."

"Maybe it's because Brandt found that one before we returned to Aelinae. Or Myrddin already knew he had it. I don't know. But that presence at the feast—I hate coincidences. It might've been Myrddin spying on us." She stripped off the ugly robe and went to the balcony. "I hate that he's betrayed us like this. He was Brandt's best friend. I thought he was on our side."

"I am deeply troubled by Myrddin's betrayal as well. He was my friend, too." Sadness and simmering rage edged Rhoane's words.

"When we get back to Aelinae, I'm going to kick his ass."

"And I will join you."

If it wasn't too late. They'd only been gone a few days—was that enough time to wreak havoc? Probably not, but it would give him opportunity to set plans in motion.

Out of the corner of her eye, she caught the faintest flicker of movement. Kaida's ears perked up and her eyes trained on a spot directly in front of her. The shadow was in their room.

CHAPTER THIRTY

They thoroughly searched the suite of rooms, but to no avail. Whatever the shadow was, it disappeared the moment Taryn and Rhoane raced into the bedchamber and grabbed their swords. Even a blanket of ShantiMari from both of them produced nothing out of the ordinary. Not even a speck of power from anyone besides themselves. Which, to be honest, Taryn had half expected to find at least one thread of the queen's power floating in the rooms as a way to spy on them.

As it turned out, the queen was less suspicious of them than Taryn was of, well, everyone. They tumbled into the huge bed, exhausted from the day and the search, but also curious about the shadowy being. If it was Myrddin, his ShantiMari would've left a trail. Unless he'd become omnipotent and able to mask his power. If that were the case, then they were dealing with a demi-god and not just a mere mortal.

She sighed and rolled to cuddle Kaida. "Why does it always have to be so confusing?"

"If it was easy, anyone could do it." Rhoane cradled her against him.

"I thought you might say that. If we die before becoming

gods, I'm going to be more than a little pissed." She twisted so that she could kiss him. "There's a magnifying glass in the library. We can use it to better see the smudge."

"That is for tomorrow. Tonight is for us." He gently nudged Kaida off the bed and she leapt down with a snarl. "Do not swear at me, young lady. You are far too spoiled for a grierbas. What would your mam and sire say?"

That earned Rhoane a full-fledged growl and snap of her powerful jaws.

Taryn laughed at the both of them. "You can come back later."

Kaida skulked out of the room with her tail swishing back and forth with angry twitches. It reminded Taryn of the strange cat, Pora. Before she had a chance to ask Rhoane his opinion of the grey furball, she was swept beneath him and his lips claimed hers.

Warmth thickened her blood and she melted beneath his touch. Every fiber of her body, every nerve ending, every awareness attuned to him and his movements. His breath became hers; his heart beat in time to her heart. She clasped him to her and deepened their kiss.

The elven palace dissipated and they floated in a galaxy of stars. Not Earth's galaxy, or even Aelinae's, and she wasn't certain it was Cilachaem's, either. Yet she knew every glittering planet, each nebula. These were her stars—hers and Rhoane's.

He groaned against her throat and nipped her shoulder before sucking the skin with his hot mouth. His head traveled lower to caress and kiss her breasts before teasing her nipples with flicks of his tongue. She moaned and arched into his touch, her need building. It wasn't enough—she wanted it harder, faster, slower, more of this here, more of that there, more of it all, forever. If only the moment could last.

Rhoane hovered above her, a cheeky grin on his handsome

face. Time slowed and stretched all around them as he entered her.

"We have all the time in all the worlds, mi carae."

She gazed at him in wonder, grateful as hell for whatever luck had brought them together. They made love in a galaxy of their own making, coming again and again in their eternal bliss. With each rising climax, Taryn held Rhoane a little bit tighter, knowing he'd have to release his hold of time at some point and they'd return to the real world. For as long as she could delay the inevitable, she would.

They came undone together and she panted into his chest, too happy to speak, too fulfilled to think.

"Mind-blowing."

"What is?"

"You. Us. This." She waved her hands around them. "Especially you and that magical love sword of yours."

He laughed and it echoed across the ages with a gaiety that filled her heart. "Always at your service, Your Highness."

She took advantage of his offer, surprising them both. Space sex was much better than gravity sex, and with Rhoane stretching seconds into infinity, their stamina increased with each orgasm. She straddled him and bucked her hips, coaxing them both to another staggering climax. Instead of holding tighter, she flung her arms out to embrace the emptiness around them. Her cries rose until she was saying his name over and over again, interspersed with declarations of love for Rhoane. Only Rhoane. Always Rhoane.

Now she understood why the French called it *la petite mort* —the little death. He shattered her senses and destroyed her doubts with his love. Each orgasm was a step closer to a rebirth of sorts. He killed her—figuratively—with his faith until she believed anything was possible.

In the distance, where there had only been emptiness before, she saw a tiny flicker of light and she cocked her head, studying its fragile beating.

When next she blinked, they were again in the elven palace on the too-soft mattress, their limbs tangled.

"It was too much to hold it for so long. I am sorry, my love." Rhoane's eyes reflected the disappointment she felt, but how could she blame him?

"One day when this is all behind us, we can live among the stars forever." She meant it as a joke, but his face brightened and a wide smile broke the seriousness of his features. "Why are we always in the stars when we make love? I mean, you're the Son of the Terrarae—you'd think both would get equal time."

He kissed her nose and chuckled. "Always so considerate of others. Although we can see the stars, I do not believe we are in them, per se. For me, I see the terrarae first, the sky second. Perhaps we see what we are made of, but I think it is most likely we are between worlds."

"In the void?"

"Not the void exactly, but something different."

"You've given this a lot of thought." She kissed his lips and flipped them over until she straddled him. "I've also been thinking and feel it's high time I teach you how to manipulate shadows. I've used ShantiMari here several times now with no adverse consequences, so we should be safe to try. Besides, I couldn't possibly sleep now. I feel too alive."

It was true—her entire body vibrated with the aftereffects of their lovemaking. Her skin tingled and belly fluttered. The neurons in her brain snapped too fast for her to think clearly about anything except the two of them. It was if a part of her mind had been unlocked and information flooded into her, but she wasn't yet ready to process it.

"Shall we dress for our lesson, or stay naked?"

"I love when you say the word naked." She growled playfully and nibbled his ear. Between her legs, his cock pulsed and she giggled into his neck. "Once more on terra firma, then we'll start our lessons."

Gravity being the harsh mistress she was, they made love once more without the benefit of increased stamina or eternal time, but it didn't matter. In fact, it made the moment a little more real, more intimate, and a whole lot sweeter.

They discussed their plan of action while they dressed, and by the light in Rhoane's eyes, he was excited to finally learn how to cloak himself in shadows. She should've taught him the Dark trick much earlier, but there never seemed to be enough time or the right time.

They left Kaida to slumber peacefully in their huge bed and returned to the sitting room, where Taryn showed Rhoane how to use not just shadows, but the light to make himself all but disappear. He picked it up much faster than she had, and easily slid in and out of visibility. She wasn't too proud to admit she was a little jealous of his talent.

"Shall we practice outside our rooms?" He winked and cocked his head toward the door.

"What did you have in mind?"

"I would not mind a cup of grhom and we know where the kitchens are located."

Her stomach gave a rousing cheer as answer. "Let me just tell Kaida where we're going."

"Let her sleep. We will not be long."

Taryn hesitated, her pulse wild. "Is this what it's like to be a parent? Constantly worried? I don't know if I'm cut out to be a mum. I mean, she's a fully grown grierbas, capable of taking care of herself, but the entire time we were in Faerie, I was anxious about being away from her. And now, we're only going to the kitchens, but what if she wakes up and we're not here? It's like having a teenager who suddenly doesn't want to cuddle and my heart is breaking a little, but at the same time, I'm so damn lucky to have her in my life. This is making me insane. This much love," she put a hand over her heart and took several deep drags of air, "it's going to be the death of me."

Rhoane traced his thumb from her forehead down her cheek and finally to her lips. "You will make an amazing mother. Our children will be blessed with parents who love them and respect them enough to know when they are able to sleep alone in their own beds."

She laughed out loud at his seriousness, even though she knew he was being funny. She hoped. "I'm being foolish, aren't I?"

"A little, but it is sweet that you care so much. Why are you so concerned here, and were not on Aelinae?"

Taryn chewed her cheek, thinking. "I suppose it's because back home I trusted those around us. I knew if I left Kaida with them, they'd watch out for her, but here—I don't know anyone or trust them." She curled her arms around him and rested her cheek against his chest. The steady beat of his heart soothed her racing thoughts. "How the bloody hell are we supposed to create worlds full of autonomous people if I can't even handle being apart from Kaida for one day?"

"We have time before we have to worry about any of that." He wrapped them in shadow and shuffled them toward the door. "After a cup of grhom, you will feel better."

Carga used to say the same thing, and she always did feel better after a steaming mug of the chocolatey-spicy drink. But she wasn't convinced this time it would work.

CHAPTER THIRTY-ONE

Rhoane pressed his hands against his ass and arched back as far as he could go, wincing with each creak and crack of his joints. At nearly two hundred seasons, he was still considered a young man among the Eleri, but he was feeling his age this morning.

A steaming mug of grhom sat on the table beside the scrolls and a large magnifying glass hovered above it. They'd been in the library since breakfast—an awkward affair involving Rainne, Theo, the king and queen, and two empty seats for Therron and his missing brother Thaddeus. Rhoane had noted there wasn't a place set for Rori, nor were there provisions for Pora and Kaida.

They'd been summoned to the royal breakfast room just after daybreak by a servant who looked terrified to be bringing them the notice. Not wanting to upset their hosts, and with only a few hours of sleep, he and Taryn had stumbled through the halls to the intimate dining room. He'd half expected some sort of reprimand for leaving the feast early, but the queen hadn't spoken to them the entire meal. Nor had the king. They sat at their end of the table, eating their meal without looking at or speaking to anyone.

When Taryn had tried to engage the monarchs in conversation, she was met with stony silence. It was worse than a scolding, and incredibly childish. Their behavior had enraged him—how dare they disrespect their Darennsai. Instead of playing the stupid game, he and Taryn had left the room without being dismissed. They made their way to the kitchens where the same cook they encountered on their arrival was busy shouting orders to the scullery maids.

She'd been none too pleased to see them, even going so far as to order them out of her kitchen. That is, until he explained they were there to make grhom. Her eyes had lit up and a wistfulness softened her features. It had been too long since she'd heard the word, since her great-nan at least. They'd been forbidden from making the drink at the palace and as such, the tradition had gone out of practice. She herself had longed to learn the recipe, but it died with her great-nan. Rhoane had promised to write it down for her and that was that.

Taryn rubbed her eyes and yawned, which prompted a yawn from him as well. He returned to his study of the smudges, pulling the magnifying glass closer to the page. There was definitely something marked beside Cilachaem's name, but he couldn't make it out. Not a rune he knew, or a variation of one, but still rune-like enough he was frustrated he couldn't name it.

A shadow passed to his right and he stilled. He hadn't seen Taryn's shadow at the feast or in their rooms, but as a chill swept down his back, he knew it was with them in the forbidden section of the library. No guards stood sentry today, nor was there anyone else in the vast room. While the inhabitants of Elvenwood slept off the effects of the feast, he and Taryn had slipped into the library without incident.

And now there was a presence stalking them. He turned slowly in the direction of the shadow, but the air was empty.

"You feel it too, don't you?" Taryn studied the area, her brows furrowed.

"I saw something, yes. Is it the shadow from last night?"

"I think so." She rolled her bottom lip between her teeth and shook out her hands.

Those were her tells that she was preparing for a fight, but what was there to stab? His gaze went to the bookshelf behind him, where several tattered leather covers flopped open. Therron had said something about impaling a dark stain, which led to their librarian's death. The shadow might be the slain man's lingering spirit.

The papers Rhoane had been studying suddenly blew off the table and scattered on the floor. He and Taryn rushed to gather them and put them in a single pile beneath the heavy magnifying glass.

"What do you want?" He lifted his chin, ready to face the unknown. His hand hovered above his sword hilt and he opened a thread of ShantiMari.

"That's a loaded question, is it not?" A woman with long brown hair and matching eyes that bespoke of kindness appeared from nowhere, startling them both.

"Bloody hell!" Taryn grabbed her chest and glared at the woman. "You gave me a fucking heart attack."

Rhoane wasn't as boisterous, but his heart also rammed heavy in his chest. "Why are you stalking us?"

"Stalking? I wouldn't say I'm hunting so much as curious. Who are you? Why are you here? I feel a shift in the air with your presence, and I haven't decided if it's for good or ill, yet."

She wore a pale-lavender gown that covered little of her body, but that wasn't what caught Rhoane's attention. Behind her, fluttering gently, were the most exquisite wings he'd ever seen. They changed hue from iridescent to deep amethyst, mesmerizing him.

"You are a faerie?" He half reached for her wing before pulling his hand to his side.

"I am the Unseelie Queen Ishnara, although, I've been dead for over ten millennia." She shrugged and the ragged sort of edges of her wings curled in on themselves. "It's a terribly sad story that I'm sure will bore you. What I'm most interested in is the pair of you." Her gaze went to Kaida. "And your incredible beast. I've never seen the like. Even that creature you saved is not half as remarkable as your—what do you call her?"

"Her name is Kaida and she's a grierbas." Taryn took a protective step toward Kaida.

"And she is glorious. May I?" Ishnara stretched a hand toward the grierbas and Taryn nodded, but Rhoane sensed her apprehension.

It was for naught. Ishnara bent and scratched Kaida behind her ears and gave her ruff a full fluffing before rising to face them. Kaida whimpered when the ghost's hands stopped their petting.

"She is not the only remarkable creature here. I saw you two fly away. There haven't been dragons on Cilachaem since my time."

"What happened to them?" Rhoane released his grip on his sword and rolled his shoulders.

"Is this grhom? It's been ages since I've smelled these scents. Truly, you are a wonder." She lowered her face to Taryn's mug and breathed in, with a look of bliss covering her face. "You healed the Elvenwood tree, you can transform into dragons, and you know the old ways." She tapped her lips and scanned the books lining shelves from floor to ceiling. "Ah! Here we go." A book extricated itself from a high shelf and lowered to the table next to the papers. "Read this. I think you'll find it rather…illuminating."

A door opened far off in the distance and Ishnara glanced nervously toward the sound. A moment later, she popped out of sight. Rhoane felt the air where she'd been, but it was empty. Just a lingering coolness remained.

"What was that all about?" Taryn picked up the book and ran a hand over the front. "Gorgeous leather cover. Great condition. If we were on Earth, I'd say it predates medieval times, but here? I have no idea how old it is." She flipped through a few pages, her eyes growing larger the more she skimmed. "It's about the First God and the First Goddess. It documents the creation of Cilachaem and all the creatures that called this world home." She turned to the front of the book and then to the last page. "There isn't an author or date it was written."

"Because no one truly knows who wrote the book. The authors are generally attributed to the gods themselves," Theo said by way of greeting, his shoulders raised in a shrug. "Maybe you'd know more about that than us."

Taryn set the book down as if it might bite her. "We don't and we shouldn't read anything about the First Gods. If—and this is a huge if—we are them, then reading about ourselves might create a wrinkle in the time-space shenanigans and," she snapped her fingers, "poof! You no longer exist. Right now, the only thing I know is that we have to find the seals and save Aelinae. All of that can come later." She pointed at the book and shuddered.

Rhoane gave Theo and Rainne a conciliatory look. "As you might imagine, we are not yet prepared to accept our fates."

"But it is rather exciting, don't you think?" Rainne held her clasped hands in front of her chest with a rapturous expression on her pretty face. "You can't deny who you are, no matter how hard you try."

A loving glance passed between Rainne and Theo, one that was steeped in their history and unknown to Rhoane. If only they had more time to get to know the young royals, perhaps then he could impress upon them the need to reclaim their Eleri heritage.

"We are trying to decipher a symbol on this page. Maybe you can help?" Taryn beckoned them to the magnifying glass that was the size of a grown man's head and pointed to the smudge on Myrddin's page.

First Theo studied it, then Rainne, but neither had any idea what it meant. He would've been more surprised if they had known the symbols' meanings. With a frustrated sigh, he rolled the pages tightly and secured them with a leather thong. They hadn't found any mention of Merlin or Myrddin in Elvenwood's books, but the man had to have been there at some point to plant the seal inside the tree.

How? Why? He might've gone by another name or presented himself as something he wasn't. Whatever the case, Elvenwood no longer served their purpose. It was time to move to the next world, but neither he nor Taryn were eager to do so. If the next seal presented even half the misery this one had, it didn't give them much to look forward to.

"Why is the ghost of an Unseelie queen lingering in the elven palace?" Even though he couldn't see her shadow, Rhoane felt Ishnara's presence as a tickle on the back of his neck. Why had she shown herself to them? He doubted it was simple curiosity on her part.

"Why don't you tell them?" Theo looked lovingly at his betrothed. "She loves to tell this story."

"I confess, I do. It's the whole reason Elvenwood is as messed up as it is today." Rainne's face brightened and she directed them to comfortable chairs before she launched into a rather involved tale of love, betrayal, and a curse that had withstood thousands of seasons—or years, as they called them.

Rhoane and Taryn sat rapt as they listened to what could've been fiction, but Rainne presented as fact. When she came to a dark moment in the story where the then-Princess Ishnara faced a fire-eyed snake demon in the in-between, his breathing slowed and heart rammed against his ribs.

"Do you think this is the same snake-dragon-demon that attacked Rori?" Taryn's breathless question was the same Rhoane nearly asked.

"We believe so. But that means the thing has been around for millennia."

"The void, or in-between as you call it, is infinite. Time in there works differently than time out here." Taryn's eyes darkened and she stared at Rhoane. Her thought echoed his.

A buzz went through his body. "That is how he does it. Taryn, mi carae, you are brilliant."

Myrddin manipulated time within the portals to jump from world to world, but also to jump forward and backward in time. That had to be how he had hidden the seals on a world not yet created.

In the corner of the forbidden section, he saw Ishnara's ghostly form clapping close to her chest. She'd wanted them to learn this story.

"Ishnara wrote about it. Here." Rainne handed Taryn a small volume with a red leather cover. "I've read it so many times I think I've memorized it." Her sheepish smile revealed two little dimples in her cheeks, which made her look youthful and innocent.

Taryn took the book and tapped it against her lips. "Kaldaar roamed the void for thousands of seasons, but Myrddin's been bopping to and fro as well. Who controls the beast? Kaldaar, or Myrddin? And why?"

An awful realization blossomed in his belly—one that he wasn't quite ready to accept, but one that he would have to confront sooner rather than later.

What if Myrddin had hidden one of the seals in the void? Right in front of Kaldaar? But did that mean he was rebelling against his god, or working with him? Was the demon protecting the seal, or was it part of the demon? Either way, if he was right and the seal was in the void, they'd have to fight the creature to reclaim it. First, they'd have to find the demon in the infinite nothingness of the in-between. How was that even possible? Clever Myrddin set them an impossible task. He knew they'd search for the seals and constructed the most elaborate trap he could.

They might succeed, and then they would have all of the seals to keep Rykoto imprisoned, or they would die trying. If what they experienced in the elvenwood tree was any indication, the odds were not in their favor of prevailing.

As Taryn would say, they were fucked.

CHAPTER THIRTY-TWO

Duke Anje left the privy council in a huff. Those idiots didn't know a good idea if it jumped up and bit them on the nose. Eliahnna was more than capable of holding her own against the twits, but he'd been attending the meetings as a show of support to his niece. Also, to keep Lliandra's unintelligible ramblings at a minimum.

The councilors believed it was her fade, but Anje knew it was something far more terrifying and she was getting worse. Kaldaar had to be stopped. His manipulation of Lliandra wasn't good for the kingdom. But then, that was probably exactly what Kaldaar hoped to achieve—chaos on a grand scale.

He scrubbed a hand over his face and smoothed back his hair. When they only had Rykoto to contend with, that was bad enough, but now, Kaldaar was out of control. Why weren't the other gods involved? Why were they letting their brethren run rampant? He was going to destroy all of Aelinae if they allowed his misrule to continue.

His frustration wasn't just for the gods, but—he was ashamed to admit—Taryn and Rhoane. How could they leave Aelinae at the very moment Kaldaar returned?

A courtier approached and Anje placed his hand over his heart. The rampant thumping echoed in the confines of his skull. Once the courtier passed, he quickened his steps and practically ran to his rooms. Once inside he stripped off the cape he wore and paced in front of the windows, not seeing the lovely gardens beyond and the rose bushes his Gwyn had planted as a lasting reminder of their love.

His thoughts were firmly set on the direness of the situation at hand. Could Kaldaar be responsible for Taryn and Rhoane leaving? Was it their choice? Ebus insisted Nadra sent them offworld, but what if—he poured himself a tumbler of dreem and downed it—what if Nadra sent them on a quest, but hadn't counted on Kaldaar returning? Or—he chugged a second tumbler full of the strong alcohol—what if Nadra sent them away precisely because Kaldaar had returned?

"Gah!" He slammed the glass on the sideboard's wooden top and swore a string of curses that would make Taryn proud.

He needed a plan. They needed answers. The alcohol warmed his blood and made his brain loosen, opening possibilities he would've discounted without the drink. Who would have answers? Zakael, most likely. Lliandra, if she could string two sentences together and make sense. Myrddin, absolutely. But they'd agreed to pretend ignorance where the mage was concerned.

Ebus and Gian were following him and reporting their findings, but thus far, Myrddin hadn't left the palace or done anything inappropriate. If the mage knew they were onto him, he did a good job of pretending otherwise.

They were all playing a game of deception. Who would win?

Anje went to the south-facing windows and stared out at the calm sea. Brilliant white clouds floated on a field of cornflower blue that reminded him of Tessa's eyes. Such a sweet girl, and far too young to be pulled into the horrors that greeted them each day.

All three of his nieces were too young to have the mantle of responsibility thrust upon them. Taryn, the Eirielle; Eliahnna, the next Lady of Light; and Tessa, dear young Tessa—what was her role in Aelinae's future? Taryn often said she would make a great Captain of the Guard, and Eliahnna agreed, but she was not yet thirteen summers. Surely, they didn't expect her to lead an army at such a young age? He sighed and shook his head at the reality of their situation.

Soon, Aelinae would be at war. Another Great War to rectify the errors of the last Great War. But this time, would they be victorious? Or would Kaldaar and Rykoto have their revenge?

Thank the gods Hayden was safe in the Summerlands with his wife. He'd written to his son, begging him to stay there until their child was born. All he could do was hope Hayden had the prudence to listen.

To be fair, these were unprecedented times and even people he'd thought he could trust and who he believed had good sense had proved him wrong. Loyalties were breaking and battle lines being drawn. If something wasn't done to stop the despotic god, Aelinae was lost.

Anje's hands trembled as he poured yet another tumbler of dreem. This time, he allowed the liquid to burn down the back of his throat. A wild plan was forming in his mind and he needed all the courage he could muster to pull it off.

What better way to combat a power-hungry, attention-seeking whore of a god than with an even more insane deity? If he lived to tell the tale, he hoped one day he'd be remembered for his bravery and not stupidity.

Before he could change his mind, he went to the small cupboard in his dressing room and shut the door. The last time he'd used his special portal in Paderau, it was to take him to Caer Idris, a place he knew from childhood and had a deep connection to. But now, he was risking more than his life by attempting to create a portal in the Crystal Palace, a place of Light, to take him to the Temple of Ardyn, if not the, then one of the Darkest places on all of Aelinae.

He was a fool who'd lost his damn mind.

He pressed his hand on the wood and spoke the words aloud that would make a doorway from his room to the temple. Dark sparks lit from his fingertips and he redoubled his efforts. The dreem slurred his words and he spoke slowly, enunciating them as best he could. It was no use. He couldn't access the temple from here, but no worries. He knew a workaround.

This time, it took very little persuasion before his ShantiMari whipped him from the Crystal Palace to his private chambers in Paderau. The jump was brief, but left his stomach spinning. Damn dreem. Damn himself for drinking three tumblers full! *Liquid courage, my ass. More like liquid stupidity.*

He chuckled to himself and stumbled through his bedchamber, avoiding looking at the bed. Coming home was always bittersweet. This was where he'd built a family—and watched it be destroyed by his cousin. Anje swallowed a lump of melancholy, followed by a chaser of rage. Valterys had been responsible for the death of Anje's first born, his daughter, and his wife. Although he'd never admitted to the deeds, Anje knew the truth.

The only reason he'd spared Hayden was because of Taryn's birth and the turmoil that followed. By the time Hayden was born three days later, Valterys had been told his son died in childbirth and that there wasn't a surviving child. He'd been too devastated to care about Hayden, something Anje had always feared would result in future reprisal. Once Valterys saw that Hayden wasn't the Eirielle, nor did he have both Light and Dark Shanti-Mari, he left the lad alone, but instead took his revenge on Gwyneira and their unborn daughter.

Anje wiped his cheeks dry of the tears that wet them and snuffled a breath. It did no good remembering the past. Gwyn was gone, as were their children. He had Hayden and Taryn, as well as Tessa and Eliahnna to look after now.

A servant entered and yelped at the sight of him. He dropped the linens he carried and instantly dropped into a low bow. "Your Grace. I'm sorry, no one told me you had returned."

"It's all right, Jasper. No one knows I've returned and I'd like to keep it that way. I wasn't planning on staying."

"Your Grace, there's a, erm, an Eleri showed up not more than a bell hence. He says Carga sent him."

"Did he now? And where might I find this errant Eleri?"

Jasper directed him to the large sitting room where a season earlier Taryn had once first met her siblings. Those were heady days of uncertainty, but she'd proved to all of them that she was much more than the Eirielle. Pride swelled his heart and he blinked back a few tears. After speaking with the Eleri, he'd continue his mission. Yes, Eleri first, then the mad god.

When he entered the lovely, open space, his gaze was immediately drawn to the tall lad and a wide smile broke across his features. "Eoghan! My boy, what an honor it is to see you. But what brings you so far from home?"

As far as he knew, Eoghan had never left the Narthvier. Despite his warm smile, a chill snaked its way through his heart. If the Eleri thought it important enough to leave home, something horrendous must've happened.

"Your Grace." Eoghan bent at the waist and extended his right arm in the traditional Eleri bow. "I was told you are not in residence."

"And I'm not. I stopped by for a moment, but was told you were here and had to say hello." He greeted Aomori and Tinsley, secretly happy to see them still together. They'd survived the machinations of Marissa and Lliandra; they could survive anything.

The four of them sat and through their excited chatter, Anje learned that King Stephan had closed the borders, but also that Eliahnna had warned the Eleri of Myrddin's treachery. Smart lass. He hadn't thought of contacting the Eleri, but then, he'd had his hands full with Lliandra. He listened to Eoghan's harrowing tale of his trip to Paderau, made all the worse by the fact he had no idea what a city looked like and was terrified at the sheer number of people in Paderau.

Anje comforted him as much as he could, but he had no spare time to give the lad. After instructing Tinsley and Aomori to accompany Eoghan to Talaith—if Paderau frightened him, he would be horrified at the size of the capital city—Anje left them to speak with his Captain of the Guard.

If Stephan was closing the Narthvier, it meant he suspected war, as they all did. Paderau would not be left defenseless. Fortunately, his captain had already heard the rumors of what was happening in Talaith as well as the west, and was preparing his soldiers. Anje breathed a sigh of relief that at least this part of the kingdom wouldn't fall to Kaldaar's minions. He'd need to return as soon as possible, but how was he supposed to weigh the importance of Talaith over Paderau? For the moment, the best he could do was put people in charge whom he trusted and have hope.

With Eoghan settled and the soldiers taken care of, it was time to continue his mission. He'd lost a few bells, but considering Rykoto didn't know he was coming, he still had the element of surprise. He stood in his little room and breathed deeply. The activity of the past few bells had smoothed some of the rough edges the dreem had brought and he was able to concentrate on the words much easier. Within a few moments, his ShantiMari swirled in the tight space and he was whisked to the temple.

Instead of a cold, dark place like he remembered, the temple glowed golden from several braziers spaced around the center of the room. Torches burned from where they hung on the walls, with their flames dancing along the marble walls. He scanned the area, not seeing anyone else, but knowing it was easy to hide in the shadows.

The huge sacrificial stone sat heavy toward the back of the round temple, its gleaming white edifice a sharp contrast to the blood-stained marble he remembered. How he'd hated those trips with his father to see Rykoto. The god would consume the offering with loud smacks of his lips and grunts of approval. If only they'd known then what was to come.

Perhaps he had known and that was why he was so quick to accept Valterys's demand that he marry Gwyneira. Anje shoved all thoughts of his beloved wife from his mind. Her innocence had no business here in this temple of revulsion. He strolled around the columns, counting the seals embedded in each. Five were missing. He knew what that meant and yet his mind refused to accept that Rykoto's freedom lay in a few pieces of silver.

He reached for one of the seals and flinched at a shock of power. There was something familiar in the ShantiMari and he returned his hand to the marble, placing it lightly over the seal in a relaxed, unthreatening manner. Yes, there. Taryn had placed wards on the seals. Clever girl. He moved to the empty spaces and gently felt along the gaping hole where a seal should've been. More wards. He could only imagine what they were for, but knowing Taryn, she'd most likely placed alarms into the columns to warn her if someone tried to take a seal, and also if someone filled the empty slots.

If true, he surmised she was worried someone might try to free Rykoto, and for good reason. He'd been mentally terrorizing her ever since she arrived on Aelinae. Anje hoped the wards kept Rykoto from her mind and for half a heartbeat thought about adding his wards to hers, but decided it might do more harm than good. After all, he had a history with the god that could be exploited.

Even if that history was more than seventy-five seasons in the past, the god never forgot a slight.

It was time to face his fears.

He strode to the center of the room and looked up to the domed ceiling. "Rykoto, I have need of your wisdom."

A wall of flame burst from the floor and the face of his one-time god scowled at him. "You dare come here without a sacrifice to ask me for help?"

To be honest, he was surprised Rykoto made an appearance at all. He'd been fully prepared to beg and plead with the god.

"I don't have time to quibble. What does Kaldaar want?"

"Why should I care? He roams the terrarae while I'm stuck here in the prison you made for me."

"Petulance isn't a good look on you. I didn't make that prison for you—your own family did. The other gods that you betrayed, or have you forgotten?" Oh, he really shouldn't have said that. Even imprisoned, Rykoto wielded power in this temple.

The god's red flame eyes bore into Anje, and he braced himself for a lash of heat, but it never came.

"I have forgotten nothing. When I'm released, you shall all pay for your betrayal. I have forgotten nothing."

"You said that. Twice." Anje cursed himself for getting angry and softened his tone. "Kaldaar is using you, Rykoto. He doesn't wish for you to be free. Whatever he's promised, I guarantee you that you won't benefit from his rule." Bold lies, all of them, but he hoped there was enough truth in his words to worry Rykoto. He might be a petulant god, but he was still quite mad, and using his brother against him might be the tipping point Anje needed. "What is Kaldaar's weakness?"

Rykoto's laughter echoed off the marble, a limp wheezing sort of chuckle that made him think of death.

"He was exiled to the edge of nothingness for four millennia and has returned stronger than ever. What makes you think he has a weakness?"

"Because everyone has one, even gods." He hoped it was true.

"Then you best find it, and quick. Kaldaar grows stronger every day, as do I under my brother's care." The flames lowered and Rykoto fixed Anje with one last stare. "Now that your precious Eirielle is no more, you cannot hope to defeat us."

The room grew cold with Rykoto's disappearance and he shivered involuntarily. A slow clapping came from behind him and he whirled to see Zakael strolling into the temple.

"Well done, old man. You've managed to anger the very god I've been working to keep calm." Zakael traced his fingertips along the altar and grinned. "It was little more than a season past that I fought my sister in this very temple. Did she tell you what happened that night? Did she tell you *everything* that took place?"

Anje opened a thread of his ShantiMari, ready for any attack his nephew might throw at him. "You seem to want to tell me. I'm listening."

Zakael's face glowed in the light of the brazier and for a moment he resembled Rykoto: black hair, eyes of flame, lips twisted in a sneer.

"We were so close. The blood of both Light and Dark flowed on this very floor. Taryn cleansed the temple before it reached Rykoto, but now I know what he needs to grow stronger." Zakael's face took on the look of a fanatic, his eyes glassy and unfocused. "It was here." He tapped a spot of the floor where a small round disk was embedded into the tiles. "The blood of Light and Dark. My father's, and Marissa's. Just think how powerful that combination would've been. Rykoto would've feasted on it for days. But Taryn prevented it. Just after she helped deliver Marissa's child and then killed her. Killed her own sister. But not just Marissa—Taryn also murdered her own father."

Anje staggered against the brutality of Zakael's words. He knew the man was taunting him, but it was difficult not to react. They'd been told Marissa had died saving her sister Eliahnna from Valterys's sacrificial blade, but nothing about a baby.

"What happened to the child?" His mind whirled with horrible images of a child tossed into the frigid sea. But Taryn wouldn't do that. Not to a baby. Would she?

"That powerless brat? Given to his father. But not before

Marissa swore the child was mine, and then tried to tell Rhoane the same lie. The bitch deserved to die, and in truth, I probably would've killed her myself, but Taryn saw to it first."

A male child. A prince. Who? Where? He pulled his thoughts from the baby. Zakael was baiting him, but why? What was he trying to hide? Or, why was he telling Anje all of this now? Marissa's death had been several moonturns earlier, before the incident with Cashiel. What did it mean?

"People die, Zakael. You and I know this more than most. Those you love are taken from you for no other reason than petty vengeance." He affected a shrug as if he didn't care. "What do you get out of helping Kaldaar?"

Zakael glared at him and immediately changed his features to a look of indifference. "I never said I was in league with Kaldaar."

"No, but if you're fattening up Rykoto, there's a reason for it. Either you're working against Kaldaar, or with him, and since you're not a stupid man, I'm going to guess you're an agent of the one you believe will be the victor."

It was a guess. Just as his taunting Rykoto had all been guesses, but it made the most sense. Zakael was Overlord of the West now; he didn't need to align himself with either of the gods, but he had. Why?

"When all is said and done, dear uncle, I alone will be sitting on my throne in Caer Idris. I alone will rule Aelinae." His confident tone didn't reach his eyes. They darted to and fro, as if looking for someone.

"Do you really believe that? Do you honestly think Kaldaar will let you live? You're a threat to him. If there's anything left of Aelinae when he's finished, you won't have a throne to sit upon. That is, if you have any life left in you. Once you align with the gods, you're their puppet forever. You, more than anyone, should know this. Just look at what happened to your father."

"Taryn killed my father."

"Because he was going to sacrifice Eliahnna to Rykoto. I

thought you were smarter than this, Zakael." He turned to leave and paused. "Taryn killed your father and sister that night, but let you live. Have you ever asked yourself why?"

He didn't wait for an answer, instead he transformed into a levon and flew through the open door of the temple as fast as he could. The stench of the place made him gag. It was only in his mind, he knew, but Zakael had known just how to manipulate his emotions and that brought up a whole host of memories he'd tried to forget.

Perhaps the only way to help Taryn was for him to do the one thing he feared most—remember.

CHAPTER THIRTY-THREE

Taryn glared at the stupid book—the one she and Rhoane had supposedly written—and paced a circle around the sitting room where the three of them had been all afternoon. It was past time for them to leave, but the damn book kept her anchored to the palace. She didn't want to know what it said about them—or rather, the First Gods—yet at the same time she felt compelled to find out. What if it said they died? Could gods die? How? How the bloody bollocks were they supposed to become gods? What did it take? Would one day they sprout wings like Ishnara's and ascend to Dal Tara? How did this god thing work and why wouldn't anyone tell her what to expect?

Ignoring their alleged novel, she picked up Ishnara's little red book and flipped to the first page. The dead Unseelie queen's elaborate handwriting filled the space with her name and the book's title. Such a lovely and intimate account of a woman who'd not only overcome tragedy, but went on to thrive. Taryn rubbed a thumb over the words, feeling a kindred spirit with the faerie queen. The story of Ishnara's curse was intriguing, but not important to their quest. What she'd written about the demon in the void, however, was fascinating. She'd battled the thing and survived, which gave Taryn hope. Rhoane's suspicion that Myrddin had hidden a seal in the void and used the creature to protect it rang too true to be ignored.

It was something she'd do if she were an evil back-stabbing betraying twatwaffle like Myrddin.

Her hand hovered over their book, too afraid to pick it up. Rhoane had read it while she paced, but he hadn't said anything about the contents and it was driving her mad.

She snatched the offending thing and waved it at Rhoane. "Well? What did you learn?" She tried and failed to keep her tone level.

"I do not understand why you refuse to read it."

"Because, what if it tells us something we aren't supposed to know yet and that alters the course of not just our history, but Cilachaem's as well? You saw how I fucked up the timeline in London. What if that happens again?" Tears pricked the backs of her eyes and she blinked hard to rid herself of them. What was with all the crying lately? She thought she'd trained herself to withhold her emotions, but every other moment water works threatened.

"Everything we do alters the course of our history. Coming here, reading Ishnara's book, eating breakfast with the king and queen, healing the lycan, not to mention ridding the elvenwood of Myrddin's taint: we have already made an impact on this world we cannot erase. Whether it is for good or ill, we may never know, nor is it up to us to decide. We must live our lives, mi carae, without fear of how it affects others."

She slapped the book onto the table. "Is that what you told yourself when you murdered Zakael's mother?" Horrified at what she'd said, she gasped and covered her mouth with her hand. Where the hell had that come from? From the dark place in her heart she pretended didn't exist, but where all of her rage and pain lingered. "I'm sorry, that was unfair."

He wiped the tears that slipped over her cheeks with his

thumb and cupped her face with his palm. "I have been running from that truth for too long. I am relieved you know, but I am not glad for it." He breathed out and smoothed the braids in her hair. "I did what I had to do to ensure you were born. Would I do it again? Yes. Am I proud of myself for what I did? No."

His simple honesty hurt almost as much as knowing he'd murdered someone for her. Yet, she had zero authority to fling morals at him.

"I understand. Truly, I do. I feel the same about Marissa. I just wish we didn't have to do those things. We both had a choice, but not really." Her belly buzzed with guilt. "It would be easy to blame others like Kaldaar or Myrddin for manipulating us, but the truth is, we both killed for selfish reasons. How can we become gods when we're kind of despicable?"

"It is because we have done reprehensible things that we will be benevolent gods."

She tilted her head and scrunched her features. "I'm not following your logic. Because we murdered, we'll be kind? Sounds wrong."

"Because we know suffering, we will be kind. Because we know the darkness that lurks in the hearts of men, we will be forgiving."

"Hearts of men and women," she corrected with a grin. "We're evil bastards, too."

"You are anything but evil. Your sister, however…" He left the statement open, but they both knew what he meant.

Marissa was the worst of the worst, only bested by Zakael. Her family had some serious issues. Father: evil. Mother: borderline psychotic, narcissistic. Two half-brothers, one half-sister: all evil. Thank the gods for her sisters Eliahnna and Tessa. And for Hayden. Without them, and her Uncle Anje, Taryn might've lost hope that she would prevail against such over-whelming odds. Nadra had been right to send her away with Brandt. Being raised far from their influence with love and compassion was exactly what Taryn needed—what Aelinae needed, too.

Kaida nudged herself between them and whimpered until they both placed a hand on her head.

You must learn to forgive yourselves. Look at the good you have done. Balance is not achieved by having too much of one over the other.

She was right. Together and separately, they had done a lot of good, and not just for Aelinae.

A knock on the door startled them and Rhoane reluctantly went to answer. The queen might have given them splendid rooms, but she'd not allowed any servants to attend them. Which was fine by Taryn. It meant she didn't have to worry about spies in their midst. It also gave her great pleasure knowing the queen was probably upset that Taryn hadn't thrown a fit about being disrespected.

Rhoane returned a few minutes later with Theo in tow. The elven prince kept his eyes downcast and wrung his hands. She waited until one of them spoke before saying anything for fear she'd interrupt something important. Rhoane retrieved the book about the First Gods and handed it to Theo with a stern grimace.

"Read this, young prince, and remember. Reclaim who you are. Your brothers as well. In here is the truth of our people—a truth that has been buried for centuries and must be brought back into the light. Your ShantiMari is fading, as is the elven-wood tree." Rhoane motioned to Taryn, but she had no idea what he was talking about. "We have cleansed the tree of Myrddin's contamination, but it is not wholly healed. Only you and your people can fully restore the tree to its intended magnificence."

Theo bowed his head. "I have suspected as much for quite some time. What Mother and Father have done—" He shook his head and looked Rhoane in the eye. "What we cumulatively have done will be the downfall of us all. Possibly including Faerie and the rest of Cilachaem."

"The Eleri race will not survive if you do not heed my warning." Rhoane placed his hand atop the book Theo held. "You are not elves—you are Eleri. The difference is vast and yet miniscule. It is a thinking, a way of life that you have forgotten."

Pride swelled in her heart as she watched the interplay of emotions cross the features of the man she loved. Sorrow, despair, hope, determination, resignation: all the feelings she'd been battling the last few days danced in the depths of his eyes and curled in the wrinkles etched across his forehead. She'd never seen him as passionate about a cause as he was now.

"I promise you, my Surtentse, I will see that your wish is fulfilled. When Therron returns, I will impart the importance of this mission so that when he is king, he will rule our people as an Eleri sovereign."

A lighter knock sounded and Taryn left the men to answer, wiping her eyes with the hem of her robe as she walked. Rainne waited anxiously on the other side of the door and a flood of relief washed over her face when she saw Taryn.

"You're still here. I thought I had missed you." Rainne's cat Pora slunk between their legs to enter the room.

"Theo's here, too. He and Rhoane are discussing Eleri business."

When Theo saw Rainne with Taryn, his entire face softened and lit up with a dewy kind of love she hoped never diminished. Rainne's features mirrored her betrothed and it made her heart giddy to see two people battling the odds and winning.

"I never said congratulations on your betrothal." Taryn took both of their hands in hers and squeezed. "May your love always be as blessed as it is today, may your days know more sweetness than sorrow, may your nights be filled with stars and wishes that come true."

As blessings went, it wasn't half bad, but she regretted not giving it more consideration. She'd been too absorbed in her own problems to think of them.

"Thank you, my Darennsai. We are honored by your words." Theo raised their hands to his lips and kissed first Taryn's fingertips, and then Rainne's.

Rainne didn't speak, but stared at Taryn with huge, wonder-filled eyes. The woman's emotions slammed into her with brutal force, not in any way malicious, but as if Rainne couldn't contain them any longer. It hit her suddenly that to Rainne, she was like a rock star—someone admired, yet unattainable, and not altogether real. Taryn saw the woman's cursed childhood and how she'd prayed to the First Goddess for a cure, only to believe she'd been forsaken by the deity. For Taryn to bless her now was a rebirth of sorts in her faith.

She enfolded the woman in her arms and together they sobbed quietly. She'd never asked to be the Eirielle, or the Darennsai, or for godhood, but seeing what a few kind words could do, she understood that it wasn't about whether she sought divinity, but what she would do with the responsibility. From the corner of her eye, she saw tears shimmering in Rhoane's eyes, a wide smile on his face. Theo's cheeks glistened with fresh tears.

"I'd offer to get a handkerchief, but I think the lot of you might need a towel. Each," a distinctly male voice growled, but it wasn't Rhoane or Theo.

It took Taryn a moment to realize it was the cat speaking. She pulled away from Rainne with a question in her eyes. Rainne's smile was at once beguiling and mischievous.

"Your cat talks? Not just in your mind, but says actual words?"

Rainne nodded with a nervous giggle. "He does. I won't let him speak in front of others for fear they'll turn him into a science experiment."

"I knew something was off with that cat." Taryn chuckled and wiped her cheeks. "This palace is the strangest, most remarkable place I've ever been." Ghosts, talking cats, possessed monarchs—what next? She shuddered to even consider what might pop out of the woodwork.

"What a remarkable creature." Rhoane bent down to pet Pora. "Are there more like you on Cilachaem?"

"One and only." Pora stood on his back legs and puffed out his chest.

Kaida nuzzled him with her nose and he swatted her away.

"I think she's got a crush on me. Well, and the lycan, but mostly me."

"How is the lycan healing?" A pinch of guilt bit against her heart. She'd meant to check on him, but other events distracted her from visiting the healer's rooms.

"Eiodian expects a full recovery of his entire self." Rainne shoved a thumb between her teeth and gnawed on a cuticle. "How were you able to heal him?"

"It was mostly Rori." Taryn didn't wish to say more in case they didn't know about her unicorn blood. She made a mental note to ask Rhoane about unicorns being mentioned in the book. And dragons. And, dammit, she should've read the book herself. Now it was too late. He'd given the blasted thing to Theo, and her opportunity was gone.

"The queen has asked that you join us for dinner tonight. It will be an intimate meal to discuss the wedding, but we would be honored if you'd come. I think she feels bad about her appalling behavior at breakfast and would like to make it up to you. She was…well, she'd had too much to drink last night, and Mother rarely drinks."

"Tell them about the king," Rainne urged.

"Mother made a tea from the petals of the rose you created and it seems to be restoring Father's mind. He's a little confused at the moment, but like the lycan, we expect a full recovery." Theo's eyes widened. "We should feed the lycan tea as well."

"It couldn't hurt. As for your offer, I'm afraid we have to

decline. We have two more seals to find and then we'll return to Aelinae. Perhaps you can help us." She retrieved the sheet with the other worlds listed and showed it to Theo. "Do you recognize any of these names?"

He scanned the list, his eyes darting across the page, his brows furrowed. "Nasus sounds familiar, as does Esiurc. But the others, I've never heard of. Are they worlds you've created?"

"Maybe? Probably not? We have no idea, really, but they're written on this sheet and that means they're possible locations for the seals. I was hoping we wouldn't have to explore all the worlds to find them. That's a lot of open space to cover."

"Speaking of space, last night I saw the most remarkable thing." Theo drummed his fingers on the book he held and squinted at something only he could see. "It was after the feast and we went up to my tower, where I keep a larger telescope than the one you saw in my rooms. Anyway, as we were looking at the stars, there was a moment of…not silence, but stillness." He looked at Rainne and she nodded. "Stillness, yes. Then a new star blinked into existence. It hadn't been there a moment before, but we both saw it."

Taryn shared a glance with Rhoane, her cheeks warming. Their star, made from their lovemaking.

"It was as if we witnessed the birth of a world. It was utterly enchanting." Rainne held Theo's arm and gazed at him with adoration. "We saw it as a sign the gods had blessed us on the very night we celebrated our betrothal."

"Did you, erm, see anything else?" Rhoane asked cautiously.

"No, nothing. Just the darkness of space and the stars. Why? Was there something else up there?"

Yeah, two naked-assed people sexing it up between the galaxies. Taryn almost burst out laughing. If only Theo and Rainne knew how their blessing star had come to be. But she wasn't going to spoil their moment.

Did we create a world last night?

She took Rhoane's hand in hers and grinned. *I'm pretty sure we did.*

She pinched him and he yelped. "What was that for?"

"Just checking that we're still mortal."

Rainne and Theo watched them as if they'd lost their minds. Maybe they had. How could they create a world *before* they were gods? If they could create worlds, did that also mean they could destroy them?

CHAPTER THIRTY-FOUR

Taryn stood in the middle of Theo's study, with books making a clockwork circle around her. Each book represented a world listed in Myrddin's pages. Rhoane and Theo studied the prince's charts, trying to match Myrddin's descriptions with the planets marked on Theo's charts, but it was impossible to tell flora and fauna from space. If they were on Earth, with all of NASA's equipment, maybe, but with a single telescope cobbled together with the limited technology Cilachaem had, Taryn was surprised Theo was able to chart as many stars as he had.

So, she'd decided to let her sword pick the next world she and Rhoane would search. She closed her eyes and held Ynyd Eirathnacht with both hands.

"What should I ask?" She peered through half-open lids at Rainne. "Show me the seal? Where's the seal? Take me to the seal? Should I focus on the world or the seal?"

Rainne set down the sandwich she munched and frowned. "Where did you get this?" She held up a page from their cache of Myrddin's scrolls. "Theo, come look at this."

Taryn took the paper from her and read the first paragraph.

Her heart quickened and a quiet thrill ran the length of her. "It's truly possible? You can create portals out of thin air?" When she saw the man in the Shoogly Dragon do it, she hadn't quite believed what she saw.

"What?" Theo stood on her left and read the paper over her shoulder while Rhoane did the same on her right. "That's Therron's handwriting. What a sneaky, cheeky bastard." He flicked the paper and chuckled. "Did you steal this from his room?"

"I swear, I have no idea how it got mixed in with our papers." And she didn't. "This is the first time I've seen it."

Rhoane removed it from her fingertips and muttered to himself as he paced around her circle of books. He stroked his upper lip and glanced out the window before going back to the paper.

"Care to share with the rest of us whatever conversation you're having with yourself?"

He looked up, startled. "I know how we can find the seals."

"Just like that? Are you sure?" She didn't want to get her hopes up, but it would be amazing if he was right.

"Let me practice first." Rhoane glanced at the page and then spun his hand in a wide circle in front of him.

Pale-green light shimmered and the air undulated the quicker his hands moved. He spoke Eleri words that tickled her memory. Yes, just there—she knew what he was doing. It was a lost art of the Eleri, but the ancients remembered. How did Therron have the knowledge when he refused his Eleri heritage?

Rhoane stepped into the light and blinked out of existence. He and the circle simply vanished. Rainne gasped, her eyes darting from left to right. Kaida whimpered and scratched at the spot where Rhoane disappeared. Taryn buzzed with excitement and a healthy pinch of anxiety.

Theo chuckled and ran a hand through his silky golden hair. "I'll be an ogre's left nut."

"Theo!" Rainne playfully slapped his arm and the prince mumbled an apology.

Taryn stood with Kaida and waited, her heart in her throat and ears pounding.

Rhoane popped back into the room, and she exhaled the breath she'd been holding.

"That shall be extremely convenient." His grin was that of a young boy possessing a great secret. "Now you try, Taryn. Although, I would suggest you go no farther than our rooms on your first attempt. It can be…disorienting."

She read Therron's words and held her hand out to make a circle, but she couldn't do it. The words stalled on her lips. Waiting in the eternal nothingness of the void was the demon that had attacked Rori. She'd sensed it when they traveled from Earth to Cilachaem, and now, she felt its pull as if it were in the room with them.

It was waiting.

She could almost see the creature slithering toward her, orange eyes glowing in the darkness. She lowered her hand and turned from the empty spot where the snake-dragon-demon existed only in her mind.

"Taryn?" Rhoane rubbed her biceps and tucked a strand of hair behind her ear. "What is it, mi carae?"

"I can't." She swallowed her failure and looked at Theo and Rainne with an unspoken apology in her eyes. "It's too real now."

She turned away from them and strode to the balcony, where she leaned on the marble banister and gulped in the fresh air. Rhoane followed and stood beside her.

"Before, when we were on Aelinae, it was no big deal if I failed. I mean, it was a big deal, but Aelinae had been there before me, and I guess I always assumed it would be there after me. If I died, Aelinae still lived. But then, in London when I messed up the timelines—I know I wasn't responsible for the destruction we saw in London's future, but it felt like it was my fault. And now…" She glanced over her shoulder to Theo and Rainne in the sitting room, anxiously watching her. "If we die here, they cease to exist. There are people, families, a whole motherfucking planet that exists solely because of us. That demon in the void, he wants to kill us, Rhoane. I feel it," she pounded her fists against her abdomen, "in here. As sure as we're standing on this balcony, that demon is waiting for our slaughter. I can't do it. I can't go in there knowing I risk the future of these innocent people."

He lifted her chin until she was looking at him, and her heart nearly broke to see the sadness pulling at his features. "We cannot stay here indefinitely. To do so amounts to the same future you are trying to avoid." His strong hands cradled her face and he brushed his lips across her forehead in a featherlight kiss. "We were never meant to live in this form. I am sorry to be the bearer of this news, but we, at some point, will die. If that should be in the void with the demon, who is to say that will not be the impetus to our godhood?"

Damn him for being sensible and making it sound not horrible.

"Maybe you're right. I think I'm just freaking out because all of our friends back home are having babies and we just met these new friends and, well, I'm going to miss them." Tears welled in her eyes and she swiped at them with the back of her hand. "Why the fuck am I crying so much? This is ridiculous."

"You are in mourning, Darennsai. It is inevitable, but it does not have to be so painful. I am here. As is Kaida. We are by your side, always."

Kaida nudged her hand, and she buried her fingers in the soft fur. When she was on the boat suffering Cashiel's beatings, it was easy to take the abuse if it meant keeping her loved ones safe. A lump of guilt wedged into her heart. She didn't fear death—hell, hadn't she already died once in Ulla? What she feared most was screwing something up so spectacularly that those she cared about suffered instead of her. What a foolish, selfish thought. She'd do anything to avoid that—and Myrddin knew it. Kaldaar, too.

Well played, old man; well played indeed. He knew her weakness and exploited it perfectly, which meant he'd had to wait for her return. But how did that work? Her head throbbed with the familiar puzzle of time-space shenanigans. The only way she would defeat him was to confront her fears. In her own darkness lie strength. She just had to be brave enough to find it.

"I think I'm ready. Kaida, stay here in case it goes sideways."

She whispered the words and made a circle of shimmering frost in front of her. A dark void opened with glittering stars in the distance. Perspiration dotted her upper lip and she hesitated.

"Can you come with me?" Rhoane didn't have the same tenuous relationship with the void that she did and though she knew she had to overcome her issues, the thought of being in the darkness alone absolutely terrified her.

He took her hand and together they stepped through the undulating opening. A moment later, they were in their bedchamber as if nothing had happened. No demon attacked them. In fact, there wasn't time for anything menacing. Instead of being disoriented as Rhoane had warned, she positively buzzed. She made another portal and they popped back into Theo's rooms with ease.

Kaida nudged her hand and she pulled the grierbas close. "I'm fine, my love."

And she was. Her blood sped through her veins with increased vigor and her mind was clearer than it had been in days. She and Rhoane made two more jumps before she tried one on her own, each attempt fueling her in both body and spirit. After popping into Theo's study for a second time on her own, she felt confident she could make larger leaps.

She looked at the little group. "Who's up for a quick trip?"

"Leave me out of this. I am not a fan of the in-between." Pora crossed his arms, and Taryn had to remind herself he was a cat, not a furry human.

"What about you?" She looked from Theo to Rainne, delighted when they both nodded.

She made a wider circle and gripped Kaida with her right hand, Rhoane with her left. He held Rainne and she held Theo. Together, they stepped through the vibrating air and onto the soft grass by the pond at the Seelie Palace. It had been as easy as when she was alone.

"Where are we?" Rainne squinted in the bright sunlight.

"Near the Seelie Palace. I thought it best to stay far enough away that the queen couldn't sense my ShantiMari. Shall we have a look around, or would you like to go back?" She was like a kid eager to share her talent with everyone.

"Mi carae, we must go back. We have lost too much of the day as it is." Rhoane looked just as disappointed as she felt.

She could whine and beg, but he was right. As much fun as it was to hop from place to place, she couldn't run from her responsibilities forever.

"Fine. Everyone back in the portal." She pretended to sulk and made another circle for them to step through. "As long as you promise I get to play later."

Rhoane chuckled and shook his head. "You always surprise me, mi carae."

They returned safely to Theo's rooms, and she bounced with energy. Instead of draining her ShantiMari, each hop seemed to refill her, much like Ynyd Eirathnacht did. She gripped the hilt of her sword and cocked her head. What was the connection between the two?

"If you're done playing peek-a-boo, what say we pay the lycan a final visit before these kids leave us forever?" Pora wove in and out of Kaida's front legs as he spoke, his tail trailing along her chin.

His words were a gut punch to Taryn's senses. She hadn't

thought their leaving would be final, but Pora was right. Or was he? "We'll come back, won't we, Rhoane?"

"Of course."

"Do you mind if I keep this?" Theo held up the page with Therron's portal instructions. "He was always poking his nose in the forbidden section of the library and now I know why. It would be nice to know something he knows, for once."

"It belongs here, Prince Theo." Rhoane glanced at Rainne. "As do you, despite what you tell yourself. You will make fine rulers for Elvenwood."

"Oh, no. Therron and Rori will become king and queen once my parents have crossed the veils. If not them, then Thaddeus, once he returns."

Rhoane grinned and patted Theo on the back. "Do not be too sure of that, my friend. I had hoped to speak with Therron when he returned, but it appears your brother's path has diverged from ours."

"Is there a way to contact you when he comes home?" Theo looked up to the sky. "A message in the stars, perhaps?"

"We shall see. When our business is concluded on Aelinae, we will return. There is much we need to discuss. Including what happened to your darathi vorsi. I know what it is to suffer the loss of darathi, but I have hope that one day both of our worlds will know what it is to see the noble creatures flying through the skies once more."

"That would be remarkable." Rainne was watching Taryn with rapt attention. "Are they all like you? The dragons?"

"Not all of them, no. Those with dragon souls are rare." She didn't elaborate, nor did she tell them of their suspicion that Therron had a dragon soul. When they returned, all would be revealed, unless Therron discovered his fate before then.

They found the lycan enjoying a good scratching by one of the elven healers. His long black fur glistened with a healthy sheen and his eyes sparkled when he saw them approach. This wasn't the same raggedy creature that she'd first encountered. She knelt at his side and stroked his silky fur, marveling at the muscles that flexed beneath her touch.

Your healing is going well. Do you expect a full recovery? she asked in his mind, hoping he understood her meaning.

With your healing and your grace, I believe I will be back to my former self in no time.

It was Rori who was the catalyst to your recovery, not my ShantiMari.

True, but I feel you all inside me. You, Kaida, the Surtentse, *and the one with the mark on his cheek.*

Therron.

Yes, the prince. You are all part of me now. Your strength is knitting my body back together and weaving new threads of magic where mine were severed. Thank you.

Are you from Cilachaem?

His tsk sounded in her mind like a stab. *Absolutely not. London born and bred. I have a wife and child there. I'm sure they're worried sick about me.* He turned his caramel-brown eyes on her. *Can you get a message to them?*

We aren't going back to London, but Rori could. When she returns. Taryn pressed her forehead to his. *We'll be leaving soon. Is there anything I can give you before we go?*

You have given so much already. He licked her face and she giggled. *Sorry, sometimes my lycan urges overwhelm my human side. I wish I'd let my lycan loose when I was attacked, but I held back for fear of hurting others.*

Kaida nuzzled him and yipped against his throat, and he responded in kind. Taryn withdrew to let the two beasts have a moment to say their farewells.

Eiodian approached and she stood to face him. "He's from London and wishes to be reunited with his family. Can you see to it that he's escorted there safely?"

"I promise you I will. He has made a remarkable recovery."

The healer indicated they follow him and stopped at a cupboard. "I made something that I believe will help you on your journey." He hesitated a moment before opening the cupboard doors.

Inside, lying innocently on the dark wood shelf, was a curved bone about the size of her thigh. She reached for it, but stopped before touching the thing.

"What is that?" Rhoane asked the question she dared not speak.

"That is what young Rori pulled from her shoulder after battling the snake-dragon-demon from the in-between. This is only part of his fang." Eiodian lifted the wretched thing and bounced it on his palms. "I made a paste and also a tea from powder I harvested from inside the fang. I was hoping it might give you some of Rori's healing powers or at the very least, make you impervious to the demon's poison."

"Poison? That's just great. Now the thing is poisonous."

"Did you expect otherwise?" Eiodian said, completely serious. "Why put a demon in the in-between unless you want to make certain no one survives?"

"Way to sell it." She was going to be sick. Right there, all over his stupid handsome face and his stupid elven robes.

"Thank you." Rhoane grasped the healer's forearm and bent his head until their foreheads met. "When next we meet, may it be in sweetness and not sorrow."

"When next we meet." Eiodian finished the Eleri saying.

It should've filled her with joy that at least one of the blasted elves remembered the Eleri ways, but she was too focused on the fang and what the rest of the creature would look like. Eiodian gave them each a packet of paste he made from the horrid thing and a steaming mug of something that smelled like ass.

She pinched her nose and downed the bitter liquid. Faelara would've been proud of her. No complaining, just a one-and-done gulp that made her want to hurl. But she didn't. Barely.

"Do you have your crown? I think we're going to need all the help we can get, and if there's any power in that thing, wear it." She gripped her sword hilt and nodded. "I'm ready."

Of all the lies she'd ever told, that was the biggest. No one, ever, was ready to fight a snake-dragon-demon that lived between worlds. The gods knew she wasn't.

CHAPTER THIRTY-FIVE

The air undulated in front of them, and Taryn held her sword with a death grip. Please, she begged the swirling portal, don't be the demon.

"Take us to a seal." Her words were commanding, but respectful. There was no need to piss off the void, now was there? Especially when it held sway over their lives.

Rhoane held her free hand and Kaida was on his other side. They'd said their goodbyes to those in the palace and procrastinated as long as possible. It was time to face their fate. As one, they stepped into the darkness.

Her breath caught and she forced herself to ignore the trembling of her legs. She focused on an image of the seal. Any seal—it didn't matter which one; just please don't let it be near a demon. Adrenaline pumped through her blood, igniting her nerves and heightening her senses. If there was a demon in this portal, she didn't sense it. But then, that might be exactly what it was hoping to accomplish—a sense of safety before an attack. Well, she'd not be fooled so easily.

Faint light shone in the distance and they hurried toward it. Waves of apprehension from both Kaida and Rhoane washed over her, and she redoubled her efforts to pull them through the inky darkness quickly.

As they approached the light, a wide oval opened to reveal a world of lush green and sunshine. With a huge sigh of relief, she stepped through onto marshy land and allowed herself a moment to gather her wits. She almost couldn't believe they passed through safely. A part of her rejoiced at the ease with which they'd traversed the void, and another part of her questioned whether or not it was real.

She'd psyched herself into believing they were going to die in the void. The very fact that they hadn't was reassuring, yet confusing.

"We're here, right? We made it through?" She patted herself for confirmation.

"Where here is, I cannot be certain, but we did pass through the void unscathed." Rhoane pulled his sword from its scabbard and took a step forward. "I sense suffering here. I do not like this, Darennsai."

She sensed it, too. Recent suffering. "As always, be wary." She spun Ynyd Eirathnacht in her hand and gripped the hilt. "Let's see what's over there."

They stood on marshland that stretched to a ridge of trees that appeared innocent on first glance. But she remembered the Hben Firn near Menurra and how it had tried to kill them. They approached slowly, their boots making sucking sounds in the soggy soil. So much for approaching with stealth.

Not that it mattered. No movement came from the swampy forest. The closer they came to the trees, she saw vines hanging in close proximity to one another, as if they were used for traveling through the trees. In the branches above, shutters and doors peeked through thick leaves.

She remembered this place, but not from her own memories.

"Rhoane, I think this is Enghor's world."

"The creature you fought in Amdi's arena? This is where he lived?"

"I believe so. I promised him I'd tell his wife he died an honorable death and this was the vision he showed me." As well as the image of Zakael stepping through a portal.

She scanned the trees, looking for others, but they were still. Birds cawed high in the treetops, but no sound came from below. They stepped from the marshy ground into the forest proper and the stink of death slammed into her senses.

Kaida growled while she and Rhoane recoiled, their hands over their noses. Through the ferns and underbrush, she saw a foot here, a furred arm there. Even though she knew what was coming, she forced herself to step forward into a clearing.

Carnage. Absolute carnage met her. Bodies were strewn across the ground willy-nilly, as if someone had sprayed a blast of ShantiMari powerful enough to level a building. Congealed blood covered their shredded bodies. Bugs the size of her head feasted on the corpses, and she turned away to keep from being sick.

In the center of the clearing lay a woman, or at least Taryn thought she was a woman, but with all the injuries and blood it was hard to tell. It wasn't the woman who snared her attention, but a little boy who lay atop her mutilated body. He hadn't suffered the injuries of the others and that pristineness amid the horror was almost too much to bear.

There is a scent here that is familiar to me. Kaida sniffed the air, her nose twitching and lips raised in a snarl. *It is mixed with the others and hard to extricate into a single scent, but I know it.*

Rhoane went to the little boy and gently turned his horned head to the side. Above his left breast was a single puncture wound. His little hand grasped the woman's, and Taryn choked on tears.

"Who would do this?" But she knew.

"Zakael." Rhoane glared all around them. "I can sense his

ShantiMari. I am surprised you cannot." He pointed to a pit dug into the ground. "There—do you see his thread?"

She stepped closer to the pit and looked inside. Vicious spikes protruded from the bottom and there, above the spikes, she saw remnants of Zakael's ShantiMari. Her gaze went up the sides to a section of ground where the grasses and leaves were smashed. What had happened here? She studied the trees, looking for a reason, but came up empty. Why would Zakael murder these people?

A spear whizzed through the air and landed with a thunk into the tree she stood beside. She whirled around and saw several dozen warriors approaching, their arms raised with more of the deadly weapons.

"We have company. Kaida, be still." She sheathed her sword and held her hands up to show she meant them no harm.

Rhoane did the same, and Kaida sat on her haunches, her golden eyes alert.

The warriors—mostly men, but a few women among their ranks—spoke quickly in a language Taryn didn't understand. Flashes of Enghor speaking in her mind came to her, but not enough to make sense of what they were saying. One of the men pointed to the bodies and then to them. She didn't need to speak their language to know his angry words were accusatory.

Rhoane shook his head. "We did not harm them. We are here to help." He motioned from himself to the warriors.

The horns on their ram-like heads glowed a deep emerald and she hoped that meant something good. One of the women beat her ape chest and growled. She pointed to Taryn and the others nodded. A moment later, they surged forward, their shrieks enough to give her nightmares.

"Run!" Rhoane swung wide and snatched her hand, jerking her toward him.

She stumbled forward, hands outstretched, but he pulled her along and she found her footing on the uneven surface.

"Watch for traps in the ground. That's how they caught Zakael."

They ran full-out over logs and shrubs, dodging vines and low branches. Behind them, the war cries of their pursuers remained close and Taryn swore at the stupid trees that blocked their escape. Kaida loped at her side, easily missing a shoddily covered trap and leaping over a fallen trunk. What she wouldn't give for the grierbas's grace and agility. Even Rhoane looked like he was easily running through the rain forest. It was only her who was struggling.

A vine slashed against her cheek and she cried out. Another snagged her foot and she tripped, banging her head on a moss-covered rock. Rhoane grabbed her elbow and dragged her up.

"I can't breathe. It's too hot. You go on." She was heaving now, barely able to speak, let alone take in air.

"Darennsai, it is the forest playing mind tricks on you. Remember the Hben Firn?"

She did. Didn't she think that earlier? There were similarities…why were they the same?

"Rhoane, look out!"

Slim darts shot from one side of the forest to the other, narrowly missing their heads. They ducked and ran, her chest burning with the effort. It sure didn't feel like mind tricks. Her clothing stuck to her skin and her boots sunk in the muddy ground up to her ankle. Kaida's gorgeous white fur hung in brown straggles. No, this definitely wasn't her imagination.

Or was it? Was the rain forest messing with her and making her believe it was real, only to have her question the realness of it? Was a forest that smart?

She ran beside Rhoane, pushing herself to keep moving. Kaida's panting came from her right and she reached for the grierbas. Just as her fingers touched Kaida's fur, she heard the snap of a twig and winced.

A heartbeat later, they were scooped up into a large net, their arms and legs tangled in the vines.

"Fuck. Am I imagining this?"

Rhoane shifted and the net swung precariously. "I wish you were." His fingers stretched to touch hers.

The warriors made a circle and held their spears at the ready. The woman who'd pounded her chest spoke quickly to two males and they brandished machete-like knives.

"Where were they hiding those?" None of the beasts wore clothing, but upon closer inspection, she saw a leather belt slung low on their hips. Fur covered their human-like legs in varying shades of cream to black. Although, it was hard to tell considering they were as mud-splattered as Taryn's group.

A *thunk* sounded behind her and the net fell to the ground with a resounding *plop*. They groaned and rolled to free their limbs of the barbed vines, only to find themselves at the pointy end of several spears. They put their hands up and rose, being careful not to move too fast.

One of the men sneered and prodded them forward, away from Zakael's carnage and deeper into the forest. No more vines tried to attack her, nor did she stumble over fallen branches. Birds sang happily and critters buzzed nearby. It was an entirely different rain forest, and yet it was the same one she'd run through. Maybe it *was* all in her mind. She touched her fingertips to her cheek and stared at the blood on them. Her injuries, at least, were very real.

The sun was low in the sky by the time they reached a village of sorts. Cone-shaped structures made of dried palm fronds nestled beside a large river and in the trees, platforms stretched from branch to branch.

More of the creatures came out to stare at the newcomers, with many of them covering their children's eyes. In the center of the buildings, they stopped. Taryn took in the dense forest surrounding them, the fast-moving river, and the number of spears leaning against the closest hut. There was no way they could outrun these people. Not that she wanted to—tried it, wanted to die.

The archaeologist in her was interested in their culture, their way of life. Who were these man/ape/ram creatures? How did they come to be?

The sound of beads swishing drew her attention to the largest hut, where a dusky-furred male emerged. He alone wore coverings, but even then it wasn't much. A brightly colored caftan hung across his shoulders to drape over his torso and down to his feet. Around his neck, and encased in a leather thong, swung a palm-sized silver disk.

Rhoane, do you see it?

Aye. We should thank him for bringing the seal to us. At least this one was not so difficult to find.

You're joking, right?

His chuckle brushed her mind.

"You slaughtered our people." His heavily accented Elennish sounded like one long guttural slur and she winced against the accusation. "Now you die."

CHAPTER THIRTY-SIX

One of the beast-men approached Rhoane, babbling in their confusing language. He shook his head to indicate he didn't understand, but the male continued his ramble, hands gesticulating wildly, which didn't help at all. When he reached for Rhoane's sword, he put a hand over the pommel to stop him, but not soon enough. The wily bastard was too quick and grabbed the grip. He jumped back with a cry, his fists clenched and punching the air.

More spears joined the dozen that were already pointed at him, and he held his empty hands aloft. The old one with the seal parted the others to stand in front of Rhoane. His watery eyes were now dull, but Rhoane imagined once they were as verdant as the surrounding forest. He poked Rhoane in the chest and pinched his arms before grunting to the others with a nod.

Rhoane glanced at Taryn as if she might understand, but her expression was just as baffled as his emotions. These people were the same as the beast Taryn fought in Amdi's arena, but far less sophisticated. Had Enghor learned Elennish from Amdi, and if so, then how did the old one know the language?

"We eat you last." The male grunted again and waved over his shoulder as if to signal the conversation was finished; there would be no argument.

"Did you say eat?" Taryn glared at his retreating back. "That's disgusting."

The old one spun around, his hand whipping out so fast Rhoane barely saw it. The sound of his palm making contact with Taryn's cheek, however, rattled down to his bones.

His ShantiMari flared and spread out around them, trapping those in the village where they stood.

"You will not touch her again." His voice vibrated with his rage.

One of the men stabbed at Kaida, and she snarled in his direction.

"You have defiled our forest. We will sacrifice you to our gods and consume your remains to purify our lands." The old one didn't look so old as he stood before them, his body shaking from head to toe. "Put away your magic or you will anger our gods."

"Any god that demands a sacrifice is not worthy of your devotion." Rhoane took a step forward until his face was less than a hand's width from the leader's face. "We did not kill those people in the forest, but we know who did. We came here searching for that seal and will not leave without it. If you give us the seal, we will see to it that the one who slaughtered those innocents is punished."

"You will eat him?"

"No, because that's disgusting." Taryn snorted. "I mean seriously, did you see him? He's so rotten, I wouldn't even feed him to a dog."

Kaida snapped at her with her strong jaws, showing her teeth.

"No offense, girl." Taryn stroked the grierbas's head. "But would you eat him?"

Kaida shook her head and snorted.

"That's what I thought."

Rhoane stepped back from his intimidating posture in case

the others reacted to Taryn and Kaida aversely. He could feel the tension cracking against him from those around the tight circle. Their presence made the others nervous and frightened, and he knew from experience what happened when a mob turned to frenzied paranoia.

Taryn held out her hands and said softly, "We didn't come here to fight. Nor did we wish anyone harmed. Is there a female called Shailana among you?"

The group twittered and flinched, their worried glances going from the old one to Taryn and back. A spear tip edged its way closer to Rhoane's ribs, and he glared at the male who held the weapon. He backed off, but not by much. They were running out of time.

"I am Shailana," a female said from the back of the group.

At least, she sounded female, but when she stepped forward, he wasn't sure. The differences between male and female of the strange beasts was difficult to tell. The curve of their legs, the longer length of fur on their torso, and the smaller size of their horns were the only variances he saw.

"How do you know this name?" Her Elennish was slightly less guttural than the old one's, but still difficult to understand.

"I am called Taryn. I knew your mate, Enghor. I made him a promise to avenge him and his family. We are too late for the others, but we can offer you protection from any further attacks."

Shailana stepped forward and put a hand on the old one's arm. "Let them speak, mi carae."

Taryn glanced at him, her eyes narrowed, head cocked.

"How is it you know both Elennish and Eleri?"

The old one looked to the sky and blinked. "It is not for us to question the gifts we receive."

The gods, but which ones? Were they Aelinae's gods? Kaldaar? Rykoto? How did Zakael know to come here? Had Myrddin sent him through the portals to other worlds? Those and a dozen other questions zipped through Rhoane's mind.

"Have you seen a dark-haired man dressed like us here before? Eyes like storm clouds?"

The female called Shailana nodded, her eyes downcast. "Many moon cycles ago, he took our men. He took my Enghor. Is he dead?"

"I'm sorry." Taryn gripped Shailana's hand and a gasp went around the circle. "He died honorably."

Rhoane prayed Shailana didn't ask for details. If Taryn admitted that she'd been the one to kill him, they were dinner.

"You will avenge him? You will kill the one responsible?"

"He is called Zakael, and I will see to it personally that Enghor is avenged."

Taryn hadn't exactly agreed to kill Zakael, a fact that didn't go unnoticed by him.

"We will cleanse this forest of his taint and guarantee he cannot take any more of your men." Rhoane turned a slow circle to meet the wary gazes of those present. There were perhaps four dozen of the creatures, along with a smattering of children clutching their parents' hands. "I wish we could stay to keep you safe, but our path takes us to another world. If we are successful there, your brethren will return home with our blessing. But we need that seal if we are to succeed."

Rhoane pointed at the old one's chest, and he clasped a hand around the silver disk.

"The gods saw fit to give me this talisman. It is not mine to give away. You must prove yourself worthy to earn the reward."

Whatever it was, they would do it. He nodded to the old one and the group spread out. Spear tips pointed to the sky instead of to his gut, and he breathed deeply for the first time since arriving on this hostile world.

"How can we earn your trust?"

The old one looked to the river and Rhoane's gut tightened. "The river is sick. You must heal it."

"Where did you find the seal?" Taryn eyed the rapidly moving water, her jaw tight.

"On the shore, just there." He pointed and a small boy ran to a spot several paces away and drew a circle in the sand with his toe.

He and Taryn inspected the ground inside the circle, but there wasn't anything to give them a clue as to how the seal had gotten there, or where it originated from. Although, if he had to guess, he'd say it was from whatever was making the river sick.

"What is wrong with the river?" He picked up a handful of sand and let the grains fall from his fingers.

"We cannot fish. It is too fast. Our bellies are unhappy, being empty for so long."

Taryn paced the edge of the river while Rhoane knelt beside the boy who drew the circle. Kaida sat next to him, her ears forward, eyes bright.

I sense something in the water.

I do too. I don't like this, Rhoane.

It is a test, like the tree at Elvenwood. He should've expected it, but with the warriors threatening to eat them, he'd forgotten Myrddin's deviousness.

She sighed and rolled her bottom lip between her teeth. "It's probably a snake or something horrible like that."

"We do have large snakes, yes," Shailana offered.

"Thanks for that. Can't wait. Yay." Despite Taryn's sarcastic tone, Shailana beamed.

They came up with a plan—a shoddy one that would most likely see them both killed—and sat down to take off their boots. As Taryn reached for her laces, a spear appeared, preventing her from untying the complicated lacing.

"Only your male enters the water. Females do not fish."

"Oh, now that's just stupid."

Darennsai, now is not the time to argue. I will go. It will be fine.

You hate swimming and barely tolerate open water. They have to let me go with you.

Stay here with Kaida. I will let you know if I need assistance.

She glared at him, her lips so thin they almost disappeared completely. Finally, she leaned forward and pressed her mouth to his in a kiss that sustained him for the moment. He would be physically alone, but she would be with him. As she always was.

To the old one, he asked, "Give me your oath they will not be harmed."

"I promise, I will not harm them."

Rhoane noticed the phrasing of his words and squinted at the male. "You will protect them?"

"They have my protection, yes."

It would have to do. They could argue semantics all day, or he could do what he promised and see what ailed the river. With an annoyed grunt, he pivoted away from the beast-people and stormed toward the water. As he passed, Taryn stroked his arm and her ShantiMari wrapped around him in a protective embrace. It was her way of telling him they would be fine.

Sweat rolled down his back from the thick heat of the forest and from his own trepidation. It was true, open water made him uncomfortable, but he'd bested that fear long ago. Since Xianqin gave him the gift of swimming without needing fresh air, that didn't worry him, either. It was the unknown—what *something* was in the water that was making the river sick?

His mind spun with imagined horrors. A snake, or perhaps one of the reviled beasts from The Shallows near the Summer Seas, who were reported to be ten times the size of man with hardened darathi-like skin—strong as armor—and long snouts with hundreds of razor-sharp teeth. A crogall, they called it. He desperately hoped it wasn't one of those.

Warm water lapped at his thighs as he trudged deeper in the river. His power anchored him to keep from being swept downstream, but he had to fight the pull of the current just to take a step. Three more lunges forward and he was submerged in the murky water. Even with his heightened Eleri vision, it was difficult to see much beyond his outstretched hand.

Fish swam past, their colorful tails flicking as they turned to dash away. It was a riot of color beneath the surface. Greens of every shade, but bright blues and yellows, oranges and pinks—they flashed in and out of his sight, making watery rainbows.

One more step and he lost his footing on the sandy bottom. The current buffeted against him, but he kept ploughing onward in search of something terrible. If the old one knew what ailed the river, he should've said, but Rhoane didn't think he knew. At least, he hoped he didn't and it wasn't the other way around—the old one knew and feared whatever it was.

Most likely that was the truth of it, but he was committed. He'd made a promise and would keep it.

Mi carae, can you see anything from the shore? He sent the thought to Taryn and waited for a reply. *Taryn?* Still nothing.

His heart raced and he swallowed the panic that rushed up his throat. They weren't blocked from their ShantiMari; perhaps it was the water causing interference? Yes, that's what it had to be.

A shadow loomed in the distance, the shape similar to a large, fat horse. He gripped Claidholm Solais and approached with caution, ready for anything. The shadow grew larger the closer he came to the beast.

When he was three paces away, it turned its bulbous head toward him and opened its mouth. Rows upon rows of sharp teeth lined its jaws, with several the size of his forearm jutting out. A ferocious wave pushed against him with its roar. He held his sword in front of him and advanced to strike. Little ears flicked on the top of its rounded head and frog-like bulging eyes watched his every move. Five times the size of a horse, the beast floated in the water as if it were made of buoyant marshmallow. This was no crogall, but whatever it was, Rhoane didn't have a name for the beast.

The thing blinked and flicked its ears before swimming off, its thick legs paddling like a dog. Adrenaline rushed through his blood and confusion bumped through his skull. Wasn't this the beast making the river sick?

A flick of palest jade crossed his vision and he turned toward the movement. Another flick, but to his right. He turned, only to be teased to his left. He spun in that direction and startled at the face of a gorgeous woman. Her long tresses floated around her like a jeweled backdrop.

"What are you doing in my river?" Her childlike voice bubbled across the current to him.

"I seek whatever is making the river sick."

"And if I tell you it is I who am ill, will you heal me?" She cocked her head and grinned, revealing moss-covered teeth that came to sharp ends.

Her features shifted and she resembled his sister Carga; a moment later, Eliahnna, then Tessa, and finally settled on Marissa.

"What are you doing?"

"Making myself more attractive to you. Ahhh, yes." Her face morphed into Taryn's. Her scaled arms reached for him, and he flinched away from them. "Do you not like my appearance? Am I not your love?"

"No and no. You are nothing like my love."

She hissed and swam away, her tail a shade of obsidian, her hair equally as black.

"If you wish to heal the river, you must first heal me." Her voice drifted from the murky depths and Rhoane chased after it.

He swam past the huge beast with the awful teeth and then two more of the creatures, dodging their roars. More fish came into view, and more creatures he couldn't name, but he kept his focus on the swishing black tail. She kept just far enough ahead he could see her, but not close enough to catch up to her far superior swimming skills.

Twice, the current tumbled him into an outcropping of rocks. The last tumble brought a sharp stinging to his forehead followed by a stream of blood floating along the current. Disoriented, head raging in pain, he pressed on in search of the woman. Her laughter taunted him.

"Where are you, witch?"

Her face appeared inches from his own, her sneer dark and deadly. "I am no witch. I am the River Queen, and you'd do well to remember." Tiny shells made up her eyebrows and faint scales dotted her cheeks.

He gripped his sword and struggled to keep hold of his rising anger. Diplomacy was needed first, then possibly his blade.

"Forgive me, Your Majesty. You said you were sick. How can I heal you?"

"A kiss." Her smile was innocent and full of charm. "One kiss from you, and my ailment will vanish. The river will be tranquil, as it should be." Her visage took on Taryn's appearance again. "Will it make it easier if I have the face of your love?"

Sickness roiled in his gut. Marissa had raped him by pretending to be Taryn. He would not betray her again.

"I cannot kiss you."

"Cannot or will not?"

"Will not."

She hissed and flicked her ochre tail in his face as she swam away. Rhoane watched her leave and didn't follow. Xianqin had told him he would betray Taryn twice and then kill her. He refused to let that happen. He wouldn't betray Taryn. Not now, not ever.

He'd made a promise to the old one, yes, but his vow to Taryn superseded everything else. The river would have to remain sick. He turned back toward where they came and the awful realization that he didn't know where he was froze his movement. Beneath the water, everything looked the same. The same grasses waved in the current, the same fish darted past, the same sandy bottom; he couldn't retrace his steps or track his movements down here the same as he would on the terrarae.

He'd been a fool to blindly follow the queen. His best hope would be to get to the surface and find Taryn that way. The water darkened and closed in around him. When he took a step, he was pushed back. In every direction, it was the same. Step, push back.

Mocking laughter came from the darkness, followed by the golden glow of the queen. Her hair and tail fluctuated in shades from creamy white to mahogany.

"One kiss and the river is healed. Only then may you return to your love." She swam close to him, the little fins on her forearms vibrating with her movements. "Or stay here with me for eternity."

"I cannot."

A wicked grin twisted her face and she tilted her head to indicate something was behind her. His insides burned hot and then cold. His breath came in short gasps. Floating in the depths, her silvery hair fanning around them, were Taryn and Kaida. Their eyes were closed and they drifted as if asleep. Or dead.

"Their fate is in your lips, handsome." Her voice matched Taryn's, and Rhoane's stomach churned. "Just one kiss. It isn't that hard, now is it?"

He couldn't do it. He couldn't betray Taryn. Not even for one kiss.

He nodded and leaned forward. She squealed a strange sound similar to Kaida's yips and puckered her lips in preparation for their kiss. Beyond the façade of Taryn's face, he saw the stringy brown of her mud-streaked hair. She was no queen. At least, she was not his queen.

Slowly, he lowered his face to hers. A low moan bubbled from her, and she trembled from head to tail. When he was a breath from giving her what she craved, he slammed his sword into her chest and pushed his ShantiMari through the blade.

Her scream pulsed out from her mouth, creating wave upon

wave that fought against the current. Greenish blood oozed from the wound and he jerked his sword free.

"You have betrayed me!" She clasped a hand to her chest and shrieked.

Her wild thrashing buttressed against his power, but he pushed against it, gaining ground toward Taryn and Kaida.

Dozens of fish swarmed in to feast upon the would-be river queen, their tiny mouths full of sharp teeth, and he turned away from the carnage of their feast. Her screams followed him as he kicked and swam as hard and fast as he could. At last, he reached Taryn and grabbed her hand. To hold them both, he'd have to sheath his sword, which left him vulnerable, but he wouldn't leave either of them to drown.

He gripped Kaida's ruff with his free hand and swam until his lungs burned. His legs became sticks of fire, but he didn't stop. His head broke the surface and he pulled his two loves above the water for air. When neither of them responded, he shoved his despair deep and headed for the nearest shore.

Figures moved at the edge of the river and he hesitated. Then he saw the old one and rage fueled his movement. He dragged himself and his loves out of the water, his anger fully developed now.

"You promised to protect them! You lied to me." He lay his loves on the sand and grabbed the old one by the neck, lifting him off the ground.

"Rhoane! Mi carae, we are unharmed. We're here." Taryn's voice echoed through his brain and he turned to her as if in a dream. She wasn't real. Was she? If so, then who had been in the river?

Before him was the face he knew better than his own. Not the false face of the river witch, but his beloved's and she spoke true—they weren't hurt. His gaze went to the ground where two clumps of long grass lay at his feet.

"I did not betray you." He held Taryn's face between his

hands and kissed her sweet lips. "I would not. Could not. I would never betray you." His entire body shook with exhaustion and shame and relief.

"I know, mi carae. I know." Tears shimmered in her lovely eyes, making them look like a night sky of stars twinkling across a blanket of deepest blue.

"Look." Shailana pointed to the river, her eyes wide.

Where once the water roiled and foamed, it was now tranquil. He'd healed the river, but at what cost?

CHAPTER THIRTY-SEVEN

The little group stood at the edge of the forest, apprehensive. Taryn and Rhoane did their best to place wards around the village and the forest, but their world was vast and she couldn't be certain Zakael wouldn't find another way through. The chief handed her the seal and blessed them in his broken Elennish. He hadn't told them how he knew the languages, only saying they came from the sky, which could've meant anything and nothing, but she feared meant at least Kaldaar had been to the world. How many other places had he infected during his exile?

Enghor's mate Shailana gave them a banana bread-like substance wrapped in thick leaves and bid them well on their journey. Another villager gave them stones wrapped in leather while yet another gifted them shells from the riverbed. They accepted them all with gratitude, happy the situation had turned out in their favor.

Rhoane hadn't wanted to discuss what happened while in the village, but promised a full report once they were far from the river and whatever haunted him. Reluctantly, she'd agreed, even though she suspected it had something to do with her. She'd plastered a smile on her face and pretended not to be bothered by his secretiveness.

The air undulated in front of them and the villagers gasped, several backing away while making shooing motions with their hands. If she never set foot on this wild world again, it would be too soon. Even after their cleansing and protective wards, she couldn't shake the sense that something vile existed here—and it was very interested in what they were doing.

"Take us to the next seal," Taryn told her sword and pointed it at the swirling portal.

They stepped into the darkness and she pushed aside her mounting panic. *I am Taryn ap Galendrin,* she reminded herself, *walker between worlds. I do not fear the void.*

WE ARE HERE, *mi carae. We are with you.* Rhoane's words caressed her mind and she reached for his hand.

Let us hope the next seal does not try to kill us. Kaida's snarl echoed in the emptiness.

I think that's sort of the plan—kill us or make us stronger. Myrddin's no idiot, but I never thought he'd have such a vicious side.

Myrddin. Damn him and his double-crossing ass. Her list of punishments for the mage was as long as her arm. She cracked her neck and planted an image of the seal in her mind. They had two, which left two more to find.

A light shimmered in the distance and they sped up to reach it. As it elongated, she saw shelves of books and a cabinet filled with weapons. She stepped through the portal into a dimly lit library. Her gaze flicked over the surrounding area, but the rest of the library was in complete shadow. If someone were there, she couldn't see them or sense them, but that didn't mean they were alone. That sense of being watched lingered.

"Let's find the seal and leave before anyone discovers us."

"Darennsai, look." Rhoane stood in front of the cabinet, his face turned upward.

Nestled among weapons of every size and shape, the seal looked oddly out of place. Thin strands of ShantiMari criss-crossed the glass panels that separated them from the object they desired.

"It's warded. Be careful."

Kaida padded to a little area to their right and sat with a whimper. Her eyes focused on something Taryn couldn't see, and her ears pricked forward.

"Who's there?" She reached for her sword and withdrew it slowly. "Show yourself."

Five faces emerged from the shadows. Three with pale skin, two darker. It was the one in front who intrigued Taryn. Her skin was creamy at first glance, but the closer she came to them, Taryn saw beneath the mask she wore to a face of deep-brown hues and eyebrows like white down. Why would she hide her true beauty?

"I am Princess Cassia, and you are trespassing."

Beneath her disguise, her sharply tipped ears stuck up from between locks of snowy hair.

"You're Eleri."

Cassia muttered beneath her breath and the women with her stopped their approach. "Who are you to know of the Eleri?"

"I am Prince Rhoane al Glennwoods ap Narthvier." Rhoane placed his fist over his heart. "First Son and Surtentse to the Darennsai."

"If I'm supposed to know what that means, I'm afraid I don't." Cassia squinted at the seal. "Why are you so interested in this?" She sashayed to the cabinet and pressed her fingers against the glass. "They say it's guarded by powerful magic, but you see there, where it is empty? Eidyn's most infamous thief stole a dagger and disappeared from the city forever. Or so they say. Have you come to steal something?"

"We aren't stealing it so much as returning it to where it

belongs." Taryn tapped the glass above the seal. "This was taken from our world and we need to return it."

Cassia wasn't looking at the seal, but at Taryn's sword. "Is that —no, it's not possible." Her gaze went to Rhoane's weapon. "You carry the swords of legend. Who are you? And don't tell me all those titles again. Who are you really?"

Her disguise vanished and Kaida trotted to the princess. She rubbed her head along Cassia's thigh until the woman pet her. Without the mask, she was even more beautiful, but equally as lethal. Two daggers hugged her hips and tucked into a leather belt were several throwing stars.

"Your beast is rather unusual." One of Cassia's companions joined them and knelt to scratch Kaida's ruff.

"She is a grierbas. We hail from a world called Aelinae. I do not know where it is in relation to this world, but long ago, someone from our world hid this seal here. Where, exactly, are we?" Rhoane glanced first at Cassia, then to her companions.

"You are on Nasus, in the city of Eidyn." Cassia ducked her chin toward their swords. "You might want to hide those. Since the Purge, dragon iconography and artifacts are strictly forbidden, as are aerlghots."

"Air whats?" Taryn's heart thudded with Cassia's words. The woman's grief washed over her in thick waves.

"Folks with dragon souls, like you two." Cassia motioned to Taryn's sword. "May I? Ynyd Eirathnacht is more than a legend. She is the symbol of hope to our people. Her and Claidholm Solais. Together, they protect the dragons of Aerithilyn." Her eyes clouded and she glanced at the doorway. "We aren't safe here, and I've already said too much. But our dragons—they are dying. The few we could save from the Purge are in mourning for those we lost. If you could see them, perhaps that would help?" Tears shimmered in her ice-blue eyes and she blinked them away. "If I'm so much as heard whispering what I've shared with you, it'll be my death warrant."

Ynyd Eirathnacht glowed softly in her hands and a song rose from the blade. Not one Taryn recognized, but the words were full of hope. Of rebirth.

Someone on this world had slaughtered almost all of the dragons. Why? Did it have anything to do with Kaldaar and Aelinae's missing dragons? Her heart stuttered to even contemplate that they might've suffered the same fate. Three worlds in chaos, three worlds where dragons were either exiled or withering. It had to mean something.

And somehow Cassia knew about their swords. It might've been from Aelinae's elder gods—both Ynyd Eirathnacht and Claidholm Solais were forged long before either Taryn or Rhoane possessed them, so it stood to reason that perhaps Daknys or even Ohlin had been to Cassia's kingdom, but a little ping in the back of her skull warned her that wasn't the case. As with Cilachaem, she and Rhoane had a history with Nasus. Exactly what that was, she had no clue.

"When we've stabilized our world, I promise, we'll return to your kingdom and do what we can for your dragons."

One of the companions sniffled and Taryn's heart twisted with regret. If they had time, she would love nothing more than to see the dragons of Aerithilyn.

"Perhaps I can help you." Cassia gripped the sword hilt and tapped the tip to the glass. The door sprang open and she reached inside to snatch the seal from its resting place. "Now I can say I, too, stole something from the palace."

Taryn braced for a monster to attack them, but nothing happened. Cassia grinned with her wicked accomplishment, Kaida snurfed and whimpered while one of the companions pet her, and the world continued to exist.

Absolutely nothing happened. She should've been relieved, but it set her on edge. Why?

Cassia handed her the seal, and she took it with trembling fingers. It didn't bite her, or burn, or do anything to cause harm. She placed it in the leather pouch with the other two seals and tied it closed, still waiting for something horrible to happen.

"Thank you. Where were you for the other seals?" she joked, and Rhoane chuckled.

Cassia looked at her askance. "I don't understand."

"It's just—the first two seals were harrowing, as in, we nearly died trying to get them. But you…you just reached in and took it."

"Maybe you broke the spell that prevented you from getting the others with ease."

A commotion outside the library's closed door startled all of them and the companions disappeared into the shadows. Kaida growled toward the sound.

Taryn took her sword from Cassia and held it aloft. "We should be going."

"You can't make a portal. Not here. Magic is forbidden in Eidyn. They were probably alerted to your first portal. I know a way out of the palace where you won't be seen." Cassia's disguise slid back into place and she motioned to her ladies. They silently took up defensive positions near the door. "My Fianna Bel'en. Swordmaidens sworn to protect me and the best friends a princess could ever have."

Taryn tipped her head to the women. "I hope we meet again under friendlier circumstances." To Cassia, she said, "Lead the way."

They ran through cramped hallways and hidden passages until they reached a side door that opened onto the kitchen gardens. Cassia gave them directions to a pub where they would find a doorway that wouldn't set off any magical alarms.

"Is this pub called the Shoogly Dragon by chance?" Rhoane scanned the garden as he asked, his hand hovering above the pommel of his sword.

"It is. Do you know of this pub?"

"It appears many worlds have a Shoogly Dragon that acts as a roadway between the worlds. Does Aerithilyn have this pub?"

"Our kingdom is hidden from Eidyn and does not have any such pub or roadway, but you can find us if you search your heart. Blessings on your journey. I hope to see you soon." With that, she closed the door and left them alone in the garden.

A shadow loomed from their left and they ran in the direction Cassia had pointed. The same sense of evil she felt on Enghor's world had followed them here. If they could reach the Shoogly Dragon in time, they might be able to keep it from harming Eidyn. There was no escaping the shadow for her and Rhoane.

They ran harder, ignoring the shouts of servants and palace guards. This was ridiculous. They didn't know this city and even if they did, it would be difficult to outrun the shadow and the guards. She planted the name of the pub in her mind and made a portal in front of them to jump through. If they were going to be chased for using ShantiMari, she might as well actually use some.

They leapt into the swirling black circle and landed on a cobblestoned street that could've been in London or some other world. Sandstone brick buildings rose on either side of the street, with no pub in sight. The tangy scent of the sea stung her nostrils and she turned them in that direction.

Somewhere behind them, a cry went up and she heard shouts pinpointing their direction. Trying once again, she put Shoogly Dragon firmly in her thoughts and blocked out as much sound as she could. A fresh portal opened and they jumped through to yet another cobblestoned street. Several dozen people walked beside the squat buildings, oblivious to the fact that the three of them just appeared from nowhere.

The salty tang was gone, and Taryn swayed with the effort of making portals on the run.

"There." Rhoane pointed to a hanging sign with a dragon painted on it.

Up the road, Taryn sensed the shadow creeping closer and they sped toward the pub. A woman with long crimson hair watched them, her eyes wide, mouth gaping. Taryn slowed her step and held out a hand to stop Rhoane and Kaida's forward momentum. Something about the pretty lass spoke to her. She flicked a glance at the amulet she wore around her neck and sucked in a breath. Another trapped Faerie. Had she taken them back to Cilachaem by accident?

"What world is this?" she demanded as way of greeting.

"Excuse me?"

"Is this Faerie? On the world Cilachaem?" How the hell had she taken them back to Faerie? Why else would the woman be wearing one of the amulets? The world spun and she steadied herself with a couple of deep breaths.

"This is Nasus. You're in the city of Eidyn." The woman didn't seem concerned that Taryn asked if this was another world.

"You're wearing an amulet from Faerie that doesn't belong here."

Rhoane touched her arm and urged her to move on. "Taryn, we do not have time to spare."

"You're right. It's just…I can feel his anguish."

The woman wrapped a protective hand over the amulet. "Who?"

"May I?" Taryn reached out to touch the pendant and the woman flinched. She promised not to harm the faerie inside, but had to know how this amulet came to be on another world. After a moment's hesitation, the woman took the pendant off and handed it to Taryn.

"Why are you interested in a trinket?"

"It's much more than that. I promise I won't harm him."

"Who? I can feel magic surrounding the vial, but it's twisted. Do you know what it is?"

Taryn's fingers curled around the pretty bauble. "There's a faerie trapped inside. Alive, but unconscious." She met the woman's startled stare with a look of grave concern. "I recently met a woman from Faerie who had a similar amulet. Where did you get this? Here?"

How far did the treachery go? Amulets on Earth, on Cilachaem, and now on Nasus. The same worlds with missing dragons. How were they related?

"Definitely not. Magic is forbidden in Eidyn." Her voice lowered to a hush and she cast anxious glances around them.

The woman's words confirmed what Cassia had told them, and Taryn clearly felt her struggling to hide her ShantiMari. She was scared. Of Taryn and Rhoane, yes, but of something else. Being discovered, perhaps. Or of the shadow that chased them.

The woman stared at Taryn as if she recognized her and even lifted a hand as if to touch her, but then dropped it. "I bought the pendant from a woman in my village on Cilachaem. South of the Faerie kingdoms."

"We must hurry," Rhoane urged, and Taryn nodded reluctantly.

"Who are you? What's chasing you?"

Taryn tucked the pendant into a pocket and checked that the shadow hadn't reached them yet. "Nothing for you to worry about. It will leave with us." She reached out and stroked the woman's cheek with her fingertips, as reassurance she was safe, but also to connect with her. Something about her tugged at Taryn's heartstrings, calling to her, almost. In that brief connection, she learned the woman's name was Amaleigh and she was hiding much more than her ShantiMari. "Our meeting was not coincidence. I hope to see you another time." She patted her hip. "I will return him to his home."

"Thank you." The woman nodded and tears filled her eyes. Kindness lurked there, just beyond her fear.

They turned to leave, and Taryn spoke low, "Rhoane, she has a dragon soul." It was hidden, but it was there and it called to her own dragon.

"I sensed it as well. *Dearth lach nothrin de las vendrigas, der darathi vorsi.*" He whispered the warding wrapped in a blessing, and then touched his thumb to his forehead and lips before placing his fist at his heart.

The shadow slithered down the street toward them, and they sprinted the final few meters to the pub. Inside the musty room, she spied a doorway and rushed them through to a back room. If the pub had a cellar, she couldn't see it, but she felt the pull of the void in this room.

"Take us to the final seal." She held the tip of her sword against the door and said the words that would open a portal.

Just as the shadow filled the room, they stepped through the door into the absolute blackness of the void. No light shimmered in the distance and her heart rammed against her chest. Where was it? Where was the seal?

Mi carae. Rhoane's thought brushed hers and she peered into the inky darkness surrounding them. *It is here.*

She felt it, too. But what exactly *it* was, she didn't know. Or rather, she did know, but wished she didn't. Their final test. Cassia hadn't been hurt nor did she have any difficulty retrieving the seal. Why? What game was Myrddin playing? Maybe it was to give them a sense of false comfort. Perhaps even let down their guard. Well, that wasn't happening.

The seal was somewhere in the void, and she would find it or die trying.

I *am Taryn ap Galendrin*, she reminded herself when the darkness threatened to suffocate her. *I remember who I am.* Walker between worlds, the one who is and who is not—she was more than her carbon life-form.

She gripped the hilt of her sword and continued forward. Two drossfire globes bobbed in front of them, and two more at their rear, but the amount of light they cast was negligible in the absolute vacuum of the void. They'd been searching for hours, it seemed, but who could say how long it had actually been. She was beginning to think the damn demon was toying with them, which didn't bode well for her already shaky sanity. A sentient snake-dragon-demon was even more dangerous than one that was pure beast.

Kaida's fur brushed against Taryn's fingertips and an angry growl sounded in the darkness.

Do you sense it, Kaida? Where?

Close. Be wary.

Rhoane's body heat came from her left and she leaned into it for a last bit of comfort. A sound pinged to her right and she stiffened. Another came from behind and a third just in front of their drossfire globes. Yup, the thing was messing with them. Bollocks.

Drossfire glinted off Rhoane's sword and the Eleri words carved into the blade flared red like flames. If only she could read them, maybe they'd help. Or maybe if their swords broke into song, it would scare the demon into giving them the seal. Wishful thinking, and not as clever as she'd hoped.

I am Taryn ap Galendrin. I remember who I am. I am not afraid of man, nor beast, of gods, nor demons.

Liar. Seriously, her pants should be on fire with the amount of lying she was doing just to make herself take another step.

Without warning, a tail whipped out and smacked her and Rhoane in the chest. The air whooshed from her lungs as they flew backward and slammed into something hard. That shouldn't have been possible in the void. Taryn's nerves crackled. She felt behind her for the wall, and traced a scale the size of her head with her fingertips. The demon had them pinned against its body.

Breathe. Remember your training. This is our path, Darennsai, Rhoane cooed.

Righto. Because life wasn't difficult enough without having to fight a scaly—she twisted to see the thing fully—ten-meters-tall demon. And that was just an estimate based on her position. The bloody thing could've been twice that.

They scrambled away from the body and leapt over the undulating tail to face the creature. A snake-like head with frills on either side bobbed, its orange eyes glowing as if it were lit with an inner fire.

Kaida rushed the thing, barking and snapping her powerful jaws. Taryn followed, her sword lifted, ready to strike. She and Rhoane made contact at the same time, their blades slicing the scales with ease. Scars from previous battles, some still fresh, oozed a greenish goo that stank worse than the London sewers in summer.

She gagged and backed away, keeping an eye on the wicked-fast tail while also trying to keep the head with its deadly fangs in her periphery. One fang, she noticed, was broken close to the gum line. It was probably the one that had impaled Rori's shoulder. Taryn reminded herself that Ishnara and Rori had survived the demon, and so would they.

"We need a coordinated attack. Kaida, you go for the tail. Taryn, you aim for the heart—if you can guess where it is—and I will attack the head. On my mark."

They got into position and Rhoane whispered in their minds, *Now.*

She ran full-out at the thing and leapt as high as she could to impale the demon with her sword. A moment before she struck, it swerved to the side and she sailed through the air, missing it entirely. She landed with a grunt and ran back toward the creature, only to be knocked sideways by its tail.

Rhoane cried out and Kaida howled. Her side ached and she was pretty sure she'd cracked a rib, but that didn't stop her from rushing the thing for a third time. Her ShantiMari flared out from her, creating a barrier against another surprise swipe of the tail, and acting as a pre-attack for her sword. She made steps with her power and propelled herself to the top of its head.

Rhoane's sword stuck out from one of the frills and she glanced frantically at the floor, or what should've been a floor, but it was devoid of Eleri or grierbas. Where were they?

Rhoane? Kaida?

I am here. Continue on. We have a plan.

The demon shook its head, and she grabbed the hilt of Rhoane's sword to keep from falling off. It bobbed and wobbled from side to side, but she held firm. Out of the corner of her eye, she saw Rhoane charge the creature, his ShantiMari glowing iridescent in the darkness. He meant to blind the demon.

Kaida created a distraction by diving in to snap at the tail and then darting away. With those two engaged, she shoved her ShantiMari into the demon to search its memories to find where it hid the seal. Almost immediately, she gagged and nearly lost her balance. It wasn't the stench that knocked her sideways, but a force from the seal. Myrddin's ShantiMari.

Rhoane, I found it. The seal's inside the demon, she managed through her gagging.

Dammit. I had hoped that would not be the case. New plan.

She leaned over the side of the demon and gasped for breath while gripping Rhoane's sword as if her life depended on it. Between heaves, she pushed her power farther into the demon until she found the source of her sickness. Oh, he was one tricky bastard. The seal was inside the demon's heart. The only way to get it was to kill it. She channeled her Light ShantiMari into the seal, hoping it would make the damn thing glow like the North Star in a cloudless sky.

Can you see the seal?

Bit busy at the moment.

I can see it, Darennsai. Shall I retrieve it?

If you can, but be careful. Those fangs are coated with venom, and I'm not sure how effective Eiodian's potion is.

The demon's constant movement made her light-headed and her footing slipped. She fumbled her grip on Rhoane's sword and fell down the creature's face. It spewed a stream of green goo straight at Kaida, but Taryn took the brunt of the liquid. She screamed and writhed in agony, but clung to a scale with only her fingertips. Her skin sizzled and popped as it burned, but she held fast.

Her legs dangled precariously close to the venom-coated fangs and the demon shook its head to rid itself of her grip. A forked tongue lashed out, pushing against her. Her legs flew upward and her hold slipped. She swiped her sword at the filthy tongue, slicing it nearly in two. The thing shrieked and jerked its head backward, shaking violently. Her grip gave way and she tumbled arse first into the nothingness.

She landed on a soft cushion of Rhoane's ShantiMari. It lowered her to the nebulous floor and she lay on her back, gasping for air.

"Taryn?" Rhoane hovered above her, his brows pinched.

"I'm fine. Just need a minute."

He nodded and glared at the demon before racing back in to reclaim his sword that was still impaled in its head. His power soothed her enough she could stand, but her skin continued to blister and hurt like hell. She might've been scared before, and angry, but she was beyond pissed now. Kaida chomped on the demon's tail and refused to let go, even when the thing flung its tail back and forth with terrifying force.

Her grip loosened and Kaida's body thumped beside Taryn with an awful crack. Kaida staggered to stand, shaking her head.

"Easy, girl." She funneled a thread of her power into the grierbas to restore her energy and heal what she could, but her healing was fractured—she was too distracted with the demon.

If they didn't finish this soon, they had more to worry about than their flagging energy.

Taryn ran balls out to the creature's underbelly and slid her sword between the scales. She jerked upward, using her Shanti-Mari to propel her higher while keeping her sword embedded in the scales. It screamed and shook, doing its damnedest to rid itself of her and Rhoane. He stood atop the demon and she looked up in time to see him plunge his sword into the frilled head.

"Rhoane, use Claidholm Solais's light!" Why hadn't she thought of it before? His sword was literally named Sword of Light.

A heartbeat later, the demon shone from the inside out. Rays as bright as the sun streaked into the darkness and the thing shrieked a sound that would terrify gods.

Kaida snarled and raced forward, her gorgeous white fur covered in blood. Taryn could only hope it wasn't hers, but the demon's. She gave one final shove of her sword and flipped off the creature to land on her feet beside the shuddering tail. Kaida was a blur of white and red as she leapt to the torso and bit between the scales. Another cry from the demon was followed by hard thrashes. Rhoane was thrown one way, and Kaida another.

Taryn watched impotently as her two greatest loves vanished into the eternal darkness of the void. She screamed as the demon's mouth enlarged as if to swallow her whole. Huge fangs trembled toward her as its body quaked in a death spiral.

There was no time for thought. No time for indecision. No time. Fuck. No time.

Except…there was nothing *but* time.

Rhoane had taught her how to manipulate time and although her first few tries were tremendous disasters, she had to try again. Her brain hurt and heart ached and fear overwhelmed her senses, but it was the only way. If she didn't, then Rhoane and Kaida were lost to her for all time. Hell, they might be already. Every second of hesitation was their infinite doom.

Don't fuck it up. Find your loves. You can do this. I am Taryn ap Galendrin, Keeper of Stars, Eirielle, Darennsai, walker between worlds, the one who is and who is not. I will bring balance to Aelinae. I can control time and space. She repeated the words and shoved all of her insecurities to the side. There wasn't any room in her belief for doubt of any kind. To falter was to lose.

She whispered the words Rhoane had taught her and stretched her hands in front of her. The demon slithered in super slow motion, its cries extended and distorted. Blood splatter hung in mid-air beside shattered black scales.

She was Taryn ap Galendrin. Walker between worlds.

Parallel dimensions spread around her like a mirrored room in a fun house. She saw herself reflected back hundreds of times. Each reflection held something different and she searched them all until she found Kaida in one, and Rhoane in another.

The demon's fang came perilously close to impaling her head in one of the mirrors and she stepped to the side. That upset the mirrors and she swore at the stupid creature as she began her search again. They'd moved from one reflection to another, farther away until they were little more than specks. Panic gathered in the base of her neck, but she refused to let it take over her senses. Not now. Not with Rhoane and Kaida's lives tenuously attached to the void and the demon's whims.

Her ShantiMari swirled and expanded, acting as hands that grasped her two greatest loves and dragged them to her. She gripped them with all her might and released her hold over time.

The parallel dimensions contracted and sputtered, flinging Taryn, Rhoane, and Kaida out of the void into eternal nothingness.

CHAPTER THIRTY-NINE

Of all the ludicrous errands Kaldaar had sent him on, this was the worst. Zakael could only hope he'd appeased the god and wouldn't be punished. It was a complete waste of time, or at least a waste of Zakael's time, but he'd learned not to question Kaldaar's motives. The god had been pleased with the number of bodies he'd procured from other worlds and had said this was an honor, but Zakael didn't see it that way. What did a god need with a flower from another world, anyway? It was just a stupid rose, nothing more.

The question thrumming through his mind with persistent immediacy was whether or not he should tell the insane god what he saw in the dark void of the portal. Or rather, what he thought he saw. Zakael scratched his temple, trying to recall all of the details. They were ephemeral, just like the void.

But he had seen her—his sister Taryn. Brilliant silver hair flying, she'd battled a vicious-looking demon that was sure to give him night terrors for the rest of his life. Not her, though. Determination etched her features as she fought the creature, with Rhoane by her side. That blasted white beast that always traveled with them was there, too. He was sure of it.

Or was he? Was it all a dream? A terrible vision he'd hallucinated? It had felt so real, but nothing in the void was real. Hadn't Kaldaar told him that more than once? It was all fantasy created by the god to appease his loneliness during his exile.

Then why did he sense that Taryn was in danger? Why did he feel her suffering as if it was his own? She'd fought the demon to save Aelinae just as passionately as he'd watched her fight Valterys to save Eliahnna that terrible night at the Temple of Ardyn when Marissa gave birth to a child not of his blood and then had died at the hands of his sister.

Taryn was willing to not only kill, but to die for those she loved. Who was he willing to die for? He was willing to slaughter entire races if he thought it would elevate his position, but was he willing to forfeit his life for anyone?

Taryn. His beautiful sister. How wrong he'd been about her. About himself, too. But melancholy would only get him beaten if Kaldaar caught him moping in the halls. Yet something in him had shifted since seeing that little boy with his mother in the filthy swamps of that foreign world. He'd left them there, their bloody corpses littered on the forest floor, as a warning to Taryn that Kaldaar was gathering an army. As he'd turned from them to enter the portal, he'd had a moment of regret that blackened his heart. Or had it lightened it?

In that brief moment, he'd thought of how Taryn would see the carnage and felt remorse that he'd bring pain to his sister. Anje's words were poisoning him. What did he care if he hurt Taryn? Hadn't he reveled in the thought of possessing her? Yes, he had. And that's what made his heart ache until he longed to rip it from his chest. He'd always wanted to own Taryn—never love her, never know her, never be anything to her other than a master. Now that he understood—intimately—what that meant, the idea didn't look as appealing.

The one thing he never thought to be for Taryn was a brother. He was just one in a long line of family members who sought to control her and her powers. It had started with his father and ended with him. Lliandra and Marissa were no better. One feared Taryn; the other hated her. Despite it all, or perhaps in spite of everything, Rhoane loved Taryn more deeply than Zakael believed was possible. Her younger sisters and Hayden, Anje, Brandt's daughter, and that beast of a protector Baehlon—they loved Taryn, too. Who loved him? Who besides his mother had ever truly loved him?

And who had he ever loved?

No one.

Zakael pressed his fist to his chest and forced the traitorous thoughts to the back of his mind. If Kaldaar plucked them from his memory, he was as good as dead. Sentimentality made him useless to the god.

He hurried to his rooms—or rather, the rooms that should've been his but that Kaldaar commandeered as if Zakael were nothing more than a servant. It was his own damn fault. He'd been selfish and cruel his whole life and as Kaldaar oft reminded him, the god's base treatment was what he deserved. After all, Kaldaar didn't do anything to Zakael that he hadn't done to dozens of others.

It was poetic justice in the most fucked-up way possible. All of the little tortures and taunts that he'd invented to amuse himself and to abuse his victims, Kaldaar had mastered and used them against Zakael with such rapturous glee that Zakael had wished for death more than once. Just as his victims had, but he'd ignored their pleas and laughed in their faces, just as Kaldaar ignored him. Yes, he deserved everything Kaldaar gave him and more.

Voices drifted to him from the private sanctuary Kaldaar had claimed as his alone—no one was allowed in there, not servants or Cashiel, or even Zakael. It was where Kaldaar could think, he'd told them. And the door was never left ajar like it was now.

Zakael paused to clear his mind of everything that could be

mined for later abuse by his god. If Kaldaar left the door open, there was a reason for it. His god did not make mistakes, as he was often reminded.

"I don't care what you *think*. What do you *know?*" Kaldaar's voice rose to a screechy pitch and Zakael half-turned to leave.

"They fought the demon, but didn't kill him," Myrddin said, but he sounded tinny, as if he spoke through a conduit.

Zakael chanced a step closer to peer through the tiny opening in the door. Kaldaar sat in front of an exquisite, ornately framed black mirror that reminded Zakael of the runyon tree. Vines wrapped around the edges and thorns dug into the glass. In the reflection was not his god, but Myrddin's image.

"Do they live?" Kaldaar leaned forward, his fingers stroking his chin in much the same way Myrddin's fingers stroked his beard.

The similarities between the two were unsettling. Their mannerisms mirrored each other, but their voices were distinct.

"I can't say. If they are alive, they are not on any world I know."

Kaldaar's eyes were mean little glints of obsidian. "If you are lying to me, I will know. Or have you forgotten what happened in Lliandra's rooms?"

Myrddin looked suitably chastised, but something in the set of his jaw reminded Zakael of his own obstinance. Had Myrddin lied to the god and been punished for it? Zakael shuddered at the all-too-recent memories of his own punishments.

"I am, as ever, your servant. I tell you true, I don't know where they are."

Zakael swallowed the bile that rose in the back of his throat. Myrddin had betrayed them all.

Kaldaar rubbed a bony finger above the thin white line of his lips. "Tell the others they are dead. I will bask in their mournful cries and fuel my soul with their weeping. You have served me well, my son, but your work is not yet finished."

"What is your wish, Master?"

Of all the people he'd suspected of betraying Taryn, Myrddin was so far down the list he wasn't ever considered a threat. The great mage had played the best game of them all. He'd manipulated his position so expertly they all believed him an agent of the Light, when this whole time he was the Telraicht-Noir's most essential weapon. If Zakael wasn't so angry at himself for not recognizing the mage's deception, he might've been impressed.

Taryn… Ferran's balls, Taryn didn't know it was Myrddin who sent that creature to fight her in the void. She trusted Myrddin—they all had.

"Find Taryn ap Galendrin and kill her. Bring me the sword and her still-beating heart." Kaldaar spoke as if he were ordering a servant to run his bath.

The blood and the blade of the one who is and who is not. This was how Kaldaar would finally defeat Rykoto.

"What about that one?" Myrddin's gaze flicked to where Zakael spied on them. "Shall I kill him as well? He is powerful in both Dark ShantiMari and Telraicht-Noir. Feed him to Rykoto; then your brother will be strong enough to rise from his prison. With Taryn's blade, you'll have no problem cutting him down before he regains all of his strength."

Kaldaar turned toward the door. "Come in, my pet."

Zakael clenched to keep from pissing himself. Oh, how low he'd fallen. Once the most feared man in all of Aelinae, now he trembled at the slightest provocation.

"Yes, my Master?" Zakael strolled into the room as if he were invited to tea. He acknowledged Myrddin as if he'd always known the mage was a traitorous bastard. "Your Eminence."

That last part was a nice touch he hoped the god and mage appreciated.

"Do you have any objections to Myrddin murdering your sister?"

"None at all. Although"—he fought to keep his voice steady;

hells yes, he objected, but he had to play their game—"I would like to fuck her once before he does."

"You can fuck her corpse."

"As long as it's warm." Gods, but he made himself sick. Was this really who he was? How he used to behave?

"You'll stay here with me until it's done." To Myrddin, Kaldaar said, "Take Cashiel with you. He's ready."

This was news to Zakael. It hadn't been that long since Cashiel had died. He still longed for food and drink, even though his body didn't need it.

"I'll leave first thing in the morning. I have a few loose ends to tie up here." Myrddin bowed his head and vanished from the mirror.

Kaldaar rose and adjusted a velvet cloak over his bony shoulders. "What have I told you about eavesdropping, my son?"

"The door was open, and these are technically still my rooms." It was impertinent, but Kaldaar would've expected no less from him.

"Open?" Kaldaar's gaze whipped from one end of the room to the other, settling on a shadow in the corner.

An itch made its way down Zakael's back, and he shifted beneath his silk doublet. The scabs from his last beating rubbed against the soft fabric, tormenting him almost as much as the dread that continued to creep down his spine.

"What are you doing here?" Kaldaar took a step toward the shadow and spun back to face Zakael. "Get out. Leave this castle now. I don't care where you go. Just leave. You may return in the morning."

He waved his hand, and Zakael was flung outside the castle to hover over the sea like a cloud set adrift. Too stunned to think, he flailed a moment before regaining his senses and transforming into a levon. If Kaldaar wanted him gone, then he'd obey his god. For once.

He beat his wings and soared above the water until he was

well out of sight of the castle. Just as the sun disappeared to the east, he crested the highest peaks of the Spine of Ohlin, and flew as fast as he could toward Talaith.

What he was doing was reckless and would get him killed, but he knew in his cold, dead heart, it was the right thing to do. It was what Taryn would've done. And the last thing Kaldaar would expect.

CHAPTER FORTY

Hayden stood at his balcony and stared without seeing the sky turn from pinks to purples to oranges. His mind was scattered, with all thoughts centered around his cousin. He and Sabina had arrived in Talaith earlier that day on one of King Faisal's fastest ships, but it didn't matter—Taryn was dead. Myrddin had given them the news not more than a bell earlier. He'd said she died honorably fighting against a creature from another world. Protecting Aelinae, he'd told them. As was her burden as the Eirielle.

Rhoane and Kaida had died with her. At least she hadn't been alone in the end.

Hayden put his hand over his heart, where its steady rhythm gave him cold comfort. He didn't sense her death. He'd always thought they were close enough that if she died, he would know. But now? He wasn't sure of anything anymore. Was she on Dal Tara? His gaze went to the sky, where stars twinkled in the deepening night.

Taryn. He sent the thought out, but only silence answered him. *I miss you.*

A tiny speck on the horizon careened closer and he squinted

to see a bird flying straight toward him. At the last moment, he flung up a net of his ShantiMari to prevent the thing from barreling into his rooms.

The levon shrieked and tangled in his power, flailing its wings and clawing at the net with its talons. A moment later, the bird transformed into the form of Zakael, and he dropped to the tiles with a swarm of swear words that would make even Taryn blush.

"What the devil do you think you're doing?" Zakael stood and glanced around, his eyes wild. "Get inside, you daft cunt."

Hayden held out his hand and a stream of his power blocked Zakael's movements. "You're not coming anywhere near me or my wife. You have no business here."

Zakael didn't struggle or fight his hold, which surprised and irritated Hayden. He was hoping to at least make him suffer a little.

"That's where you're wrong. But if I'm seen here, we're all in danger. You have no reason to believe me, I know, but please trust me for one moment and we might save Taryn's life."

Hayden held his power and shook his head. "When have you ever cared about her life?"

"Let him in." Sabina stood at the balcony doors, her dressing gown of pale lilac matching the dusky sky. Red rimmed her eyes and tears glistened in the candlelight. "We should at least hear what he has to say."

"If you try anything, it will be the last thing you do." He didn't release his ShantiMari, but let Zakael step into the finely furnished sitting room. "Are you here to gloat? At last you can destroy Aelinae now that your half-sister is dead."

"I am here for none of those reasons and all of them. These past few weeks, I have been the slave of Kaldaar. He's far more vicious than I could ever hope to be, and it's been enlightening to be on the receiving end of such malice."

"Good. You deserve every ounce of abuse."

Zakael inclined his head. "True. I'm not here for sympathy,

but to warn you of his plans." He looked from Hayden to Sabina. "Kaldaar is going to raise Rykoto so that he can feast on his brother's remains to gain his strength. Then he'll unleash a war upon Aelinae unlike any we've seen before."

Hayden sucked in a breath. *Prepare Eliahnna to rule. Prepare for war.* Taryn's words vibrated against his skull and his gaze went to Sabina's abdomen. His child would be born during wartime. If they survived.

"I myself have procured him beasts from other worlds that are ten times the strength of your soldiers. You cannot defeat him on a battlefield. Especially without Taryn."

Sabina put a hand on Hayden's arm. "Then she is truly dead?"

"Not yet." Zakael took a long drag of air, and Hayden tightened his hold of power. "But he's sent Myrddin to kill her."

"Liar. You dare come into these rooms and accuse our friend of betraying Taryn?" Sabina moved quick as a carlix and held a dagger at Zakael's throat. "What deception is this that you'd cloud our mourning with veils made of lies and mistruths? Is Taryn dead or not? Answer true or you will swim with King Baldev tonight."

"I tell you true. Taryn is as yet alive. She did battle a creature in the void. I saw her from a distance, but the void works in mysterious ways. I could not call out to her or hear her, but I would swear I saw her and Rhoane with that horrendous beast of theirs."

"Kaida. The beast has a name."

"Fine. Kaida. I don't know what happened to them, but Kaldaar insisted Myrddin bring him Taryn's beating heart and her sword." Zakael held up both hands. "This I swear, or may Ohlin strike me down. Myrddin has been an agent of Kaldaar's from the beginning. He betrayed us all."

Sabina pushed the blade against Zakael's neck until a red line dripped down his throat.

"Watch him," she ordered and spun toward her dressing

room. A minute later, she returned with a copper bowl filled with ashes.

Hayden and Zakael stood silently while Sabina mashed the ashes with Zakael's blood and chanted. Smoke rose from the bowl, curling around Sabina's face like a lover's caress. It rose up and took the shape of a creature with frills framing its snake-like head. Wings fluttered behind it and Zakael gagged as it swiveled toward him.

"That's the creature."

"If you're lying, we'll know."

Hayden watched his wife with mounting pride. She showed no fear, even though he knew her legs trembled beneath her gown. He pressed his leg against hers as a sign he was there; he would keep her and the baby safe.

The smoke continued up until it reached Zakael's eyes. A forked tongue whipped out as if tasting him and the smoke dissolved.

"He is telling the truth," Sabina said.

Zakael's body slumped against Hayden's ShantiMari.

"We must tell no one. If Kaldaar knows we know, Taryn is as good as dead." Hayden gripped Zakael by the throat and lifted him off the ground. "Who else knows Taryn is alive?"

"Only Kaldaar, Myrddin, and myself. Although, I suspect Cashiel knows as well."

"Her half-brother?"

Zakael nodded morosely. "He is Kaldaar's newest Shadow Assassin."

Sabina set the bowl down and pointed to a chair. "Might as well have a seat. You're not leaving until you tell us everything."

Myrddin watched Zakael fly from Hayden's rooms and breathed a sigh of relief. He'd hoped the rash young man would defy Kaldaar and alert Taryn's friends that she wasn't dead. It hadn't been easy to tell the lie. Despite himself, despite everything, he'd grown fond of her, even respected not just her power, but her resilience. She and Rhoane had found all the missing seals and would soon return to lock Rykoto away forever—or possibly destroy him. Either way, he'd bought himself until morning to search for her—he hoped it would be long enough.

CHAPTER FORTY-ONE

Bright sunlight blinded Rhoane as he gazed up at the sky, too stunned to move. Everything hurt. Which was good—that meant he wasn't dead. He stretched a hand and touched Kaida's fur. Thank the gods. His other hand bumped Taryn's leg and tears pricked his eyes. When he last saw her, she was screaming into the void. Or perhaps that had been him. The raw fear he saw etched into her features had echoed his feelings as the darkness closed around him and blocked all sight and sound.

Somehow, they'd come together. There would be time later to discover how, but his first concern was Taryn. Always Taryn.

She lay on her back, gasping and choking against the dusty ground that rose in tiny fluffs around them. Her silken silver hair fanned around her like a halo and he hovered above her to block out the harsh sunlight.

"Are you well, mi carae?"

"Fucking shitbangers, it feels like something's broken. No, like everything is broken."

The relief he felt was indescribable, yet coated in a thick film of guilt.

"I will never betray you. Never. I do not care what Xianqin

said, or the gods say—I will never betray you. And I will not kill you. In fact, it is my objective to keep you alive. Forever and always. By my side. You are my life, mi carae. My love."

She blinked up at him, her eyes starry fields of midnight. "I don't know where that came from, but I'll take it. We decide our own paths from now on—how does that sound?"

"Enchanting." He grinned and kissed her before rolling to his side and grunting with the effort.

He needed to check on Kaida, but he had to catch his breath first. Taryn was right. It did feel as if everything was broken, including his lungs. Breathing was difficult and not just from the dust. The air was thin and arid and scratched as it went down his throat.

"Hello, darlings." A male voice came from just above him, and he blinked into the snout of something large and scaly.

No. No, no, no. They killed the demon, didn't they?

Taryn gripped his hand and squeezed until it hurt. "Are we dead and trapped in hell with the demon? An apparently gentle demon that calls us darling. Yup, we're dead."

"You are not dead, darlings. Although, I do worry about that one." The snout moved to the side, and both he and Taryn rolled toward Kaida.

"Mi carae denithlia," a female voice Rhoane knew from his childhood and never thought to hear again said to his left. Cherished love of my heart. Only one person ever said that to him, and he strained to see her against the blinding sunlight. "We have been waiting for you. All of you."

How was this possible? How was any of this happening? Rhoane's heart thumped triple time in his bruised chest and he wheezed against a wave of pain. "Mother?"

"I know you." Taryn peered at the woman. "You're Queen Aislinn."

His body trembled with the effort to sit up. "Are we dead?"

"No, my loves. You are exactly where you are supposed to

be." She stood and put a hand on the scaled jaw of the rather large and formidable-looking darathi vorsi. "I told you, Gilchrist. Have patience and they will come. And here they are. Finally, your exile is at an end."

"No, my queen. Our exile is at an end." Gilchrist nudged Kaida with his snout and she rolled toward Taryn.

Kaida. Dear gods, the nonsense the other two were saying could wait. He wasn't ready yet to comprehend their meaning. It was too vast, too important, too terrifying.

Head spinning, heart racing, thoughts whipping too quickly through his brain to form a coherent sentence, Rhoane reached for Kaida, intent only on making sure she wasn't dead. Blood stained her muzzle and chest, but when he ran his hands along Kaida's body, he didn't find any broken bones or obvious wounds.

"What is it, girl? What's wrong? Let me help you." Taryn eased her ShantiMari into Kaida, and Rhoane joined his power with hers.

The rush of ShantiMari softened the bruising on his body, but the sheer amount of pain that vibrated through his veins was staggering. He and Taryn directed their power into Kaida's mind, the both of them being gentler than they'd ever been in their life. Kaida was precious to them both. She was family. It wasn't just Taryn who'd missed her while they were at the Seelie Palace. Rhoane had suffered the pangs of separation from the grierbas as well.

He knelt beside Taryn, struggling to focus, his gaze wandering from Kaida to his mother. Was this another ghost? Or was she truly there? The darathi at her side had said their exile was at an end. Could it be true? Taryn's ShantiMari snapped against his, and he forced his attention back to Kaida. Together, they worked through Kaida's body, healing even the tiniest tear. At her internal organs, Rhoane sucked in a breath.

"She swallowed the seal."

"It's in her?" Taryn's voice vibrated with concern. "We have to get it out."

"Wait." Aislinn knelt beside him and he smelled her familiar fragrance of lilies. "Try this."

The until-that-moment-supposedly-dead Eleri queen picked several shoots of grass and rubbed them between her fingertips. Being far less gentle than he and Taryn had been, his mother jammed the mess into Kaida's mouth and sat back.

"You are really here?" Rhoane stared at his mother through unshed tears.

"Yes, darling. It is a long story that I will tell you later, but right now, your friend is about to be sick."

As if on cue, Kaida vomited the grass and coughed against the sandy ground. A moment later, she heaved and expanded her jaws to expel the seal.

"Well, that was totally gross." Taryn picked up the seal and wiped it on her tunic. "Feeling better?"

Kaida stretched and yawned as if she'd woken from a long nap. A lovely golden dragon nuzzled the grierbas with her long snout. Kaida licked her scales and yipped into her muzzle just as she'd done with the lycan. The dragon snorted and flicked a long tongue at Kaida's fur, cleaning it of the demon's blood.

"My queen." The golden dragon swiveled her head toward Rhoane. "He wears the crown you told us about."

"That is because he is the Darathi Vorsi Prince, Ahmbra." Aislinn rose and held her hand out to Rhoane. "Come. They are waiting."

"Who?" His brain snapped inside his skull and a powerful ache started in his heart. It wasn't from his injuries, but something else. Something he'd hoped for his entire life.

Taryn's dazed expression was clouded by sorrow. "You're hurt."

He swept his fingertips over his temple, unsurprised when they came away crimson.

"We need to heal him." Taryn scooted to Rhoane and held his face between her hands. "Your crown's a bit dented." Her lopsided smile melted his heart. "Probably your head, too."

He tried to chuckle, but it hurt too much. His crown burned against his scalp, but he didn't think it meant to harm him. Rather, it was trying to heal him, just as Taryn's sword had healed her when she was poisoned.

"Perhaps later, mi carae." He leaned forward to kiss her lips and sucked in the ShantiMari she opened for him. Her power rushed through his blood—warming, strengthening, healing.

"Can you stand?" Taryn and his mother helped him to his feet, and he swayed to steady himself.

The raging pain in his head subsided enough he could stand without assistance. He glanced at his surroundings and gaped, open-mouthed and unbelieving. The Crown of Awakening vibrated and soothing relief flowed from the intricately made silver piece, healing as it traveled the length of him. He'd only ever heard of this type of ShantiMari in stories, but as it seeped into his blood, it woke something primal that had been dormant for far too long.

"Taryn, look." He took her hand and kissed her fingertips.

Tears streamed over her cheeks to drip from her chin to the dusty ground. Where each drop landed, a pearl of white sprouted. He stared at the tiny buds, and then at Taryn. She wasn't looking at the ground, but at what surrounded them.

"Rhoane, we did it." She gripped his hand in hers and laughed with the gaiety of a child. "We found them."

In every direction, all they saw were snouts and scales, wings and tails in every shade and shape. At last, they'd found Aelinae's missing darathi vorsi.

CAST OF CHARACTERS

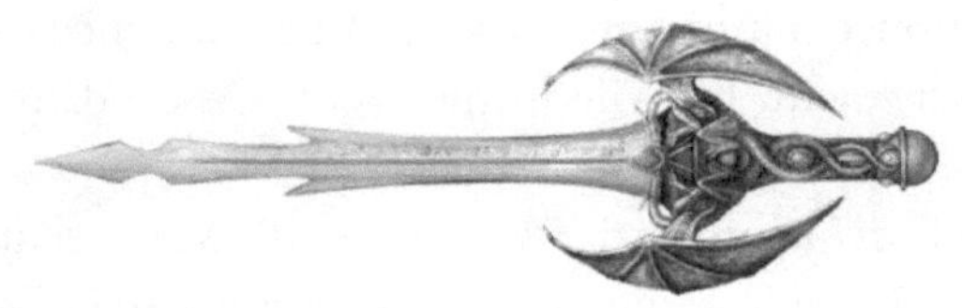

Acelyne (Ace-lynn) ~ Faerie. Witch believed responsible for kidnapping and imprisoning creatures into glass prisons. Deceased.

Adesh ~ Summerlander. A spice merchant in Talaith. Tabul's brother.

Ahmbra (Amm-brah) ~ A golden darathi vorsi living in exile. Conceived on Aelinae, she was born in exile and is the last of her kind.

Aislinn al Glennwoods ap Narthvier (Ay-s-lynn) ~ Queen of the Eleri. Aislinn perished in a ShantiMari accident when Rhoane was a young man.

Alasdair (Alice-dare) ~ A faerie servant in the service of Rhoane. Brother to Illanr and Carld.

Alswyth Myrddin (Alls-with Mere-din) ~ Mage with exceedingly long life. Myrddin is the advisor to Empress Lliandra and is often far from court on assignments from the crown. No known children or spouses. No known House.

Amanda ~ Aelan. A young woman living in Talaith with dubious ties to Adesh the spice merchant.

Amdi Agnar ~ Laird of the Ullan tribes. He claimed Kaleigh as his consort and has two sons with her. Descendent of House Agnar.

Anje ap Paderau (Ann-jee ap Pah-der-oo) ~ Duke of Paderau, father to Hayden, husband to Gwyneira (now deceased). Anje is cousin to the Lord of Darkness, and third in line for the Obsidian Throne. His father was brother to Valterys's father. A prince in his own right, Anje renounced his Dark heritage to live with his wife in the Light. Descendant of House Djeba.

Aomori di Monsenti (A-more-ee di Mon-scent-ee) ~ A young Danuri lord fostering with Tinsley in Paderau. Descendant of House Monsenti.

Arianna (Arr-ee-ana) ~ Faerie. Daughter to Queen Eirlys. Was one of the imprisoned fae with Rori. When Rori broke free, Arianna did not wake up.

Armando ~ Summerlander. Lover of Tarro. Whore in Nena's house. Marissa's favorite.

Baehlon de Monteferron (Bay-lohn de Mont-fair-on) ~ Danuri and Geigan knight employed by Empress Lliandra, sworn to protect Taryn and her House. Descendant of House Monteferron.

Baldev de Deistra (Ball-dev de Des-tra) ~ King of the Seas. Baldev lives within a vast complex at the bottom of the ocean. Merfolk are believed to be legends as they are not often seen. Once a year, on their naming day, merfolk have the option to walk among the other races on Aelinae. It is unknown if Baldev has ever honored the tradition. Married to Salaria. Father to several daughters and sons. Descendent of House Deistra.

Brandt Kaj Endion (Brant) ~ Aelan. High Priest of Talaith and advisor to Empress Lliandra, Brandt was commissioned with Taryn's safety when she was born. After his death, Nadra took Brandt to Dal Tara, (home of the gods), which allows Brandt to communicate with Taryn. House Arran.

Bressal ap Narthvier (Bress-all) ~ Eleri. Second Son to King Stephan and Queen Aislinn (now passed beyond the veils).

Carga ap Narthvier ~ Eleri. Daughter to King Stephan and Queen Aislinn (now passed beyond the veils).

Carina (Ka-reen-a) ~ Aelan. A member of Taryn's personal guard. Currently living in the Summerlands and training with Flik.

Cashiel (Cash-eel) ~ Second son to Lliandra, fathered by Esna fei Garrith. Given name is Kane, but now goes by Cashiel. Killed by Rhoane at the Ruins of Mallaqai. Is now Kaldaar's latest Shadow Assassin.

Cassie ~ Elf. Princess on Nasus who helped Taryn and Rhoane escape. Asked for help with dragons.

Cian MacNair ~ Faerie. Brother to Rori. Also a known assassin and spy.

Daknys (Dak-niss) ~ Elder Goddess. Daughter of Nadra and Ohlin, she is worshipped by the Light and Dark in the central area of Aelinae.

Darius (Dare-ee-us) ~ Artagh, Eleri and Aelan. One of Taryn's guard. They met in Celyn Eryri, but currently Darius is living in the Summerlands and training with Flik.

Darrew (Dare-oo) ~ Danuri lord, Chief Councilor to the Steward of Danuri.

Delarainne/Rainne (Rain) ~ Elf. Lady living at Elvenwood as the betrothed to Prince Theo. She hints at a past secret. Knows the entire history of Cilachaem, including Taryn and Rhoane's role in the world.

Donyatella/Dony ~ Until recently, believed to be Taryn and Brandt's landlord in London. It was discovered that Dony is part of an elite group of immortals knowns as Stone Guardians. She's been tasked with guarding over Taryn since her arrival in London as a baby.

Ebus (Ee-bus) ~ Race unknown. Spy employed by Taryn and Rhoane. Can see the Shadow Assassin.

Eiodian (Eee-dahn) ~ Elf. Healer at Elvenwood. Bears a remarkable resemblance to Baehlon.

Eirlys (Air-liss) ~ Faerie. One of two faeries queens living on Cilachaem, Eirlys is queen of the Seelie court.

Eliahnna Tjaru (Ee-lahn-ah Shar-U) ~ Aelan. Daughter of Lliandra. Her heritage is much debated since Lliandra has never publicly named her father. She is the heir to the Light Throne. Descendant of House Nadrene.

Ellie ~ Aelan. A maid in the service of Taryn. Currently living in the Summerlands and training with Flik.

Enghor (Ain-gore) ~ Beast forced to fight Taryn in the Ullan arena. With the legs of a man, chest of an ape, and head of a goat, he is not a creature from Aelinae.

Eoghan ap Narthvier (Eee-gan) ~ Eleri. Third Son to King Stephan and Queen Aislinn (now passed beyond the veils).

Esme Daj Valen ~ Faerie. Lady living at the Seelie Palace. Is remarkably familiar to Taryn and Rhoane.

Faelara Dal Arran (Fay-lara) ~ Aelan. Daughter of Brandt, Faelara is currently a lady-in-waiting to Empress Lliandra. Her Healing skills are legendary, as were her father's. House Arran.

Faisal dei Tarnovo (Fay-sal) ~ Summerlander. Sabina's father and the king of the Summerlands. House Tarnov.

Flik ~ Summerlander. Master swordsman who works for King Faisal training guards, spies, and assassins. Doesn't suffer fools.

Gagoiru/Gage ~ One of the fabled Stone Guardians of lore. Protects Taryn and Rhoane while they are in London. Has a special affinity for Kaida.

Gayvn ~ Taryn's twin. See 'Shadow Assassin'. Deceased.

Gian ap Brenbold (Jawn) ~ A faerie found in Valterys's dungeon.

Gilchrist (Gill-krisst) ~ Elder darathi vorsi living in exile. Mate to Jinnipher.

Guillermo (Ghee-er-moe) ~ Human. Head chef at the pub below Taryn's flat in London.

Gwainne Agnar (Gw-ayn) ~ First son to Amdi Agnar and his Eleri wife Kaleigh. Heir to the Ullan Laird.

Gwyneira Tjaru ap Paderau (Gwin-eera ap Shar-U) ~ Aelan. Sister to Empress Lliandra, wife of Duke Anje, mother to Hayden. Gwyneira died after childbirth when Hayden was a young man. Houses Nadrene and Djeba. Deceased.

Hayden ap Valen ~ Aelan. Lord Valen, Marquis of the province Valen, son of Anje and Gwyneira. Hayden is cousin to the heirs of the Light Throne and the Obsidian Throne. Descendant of House Djeba. Newly married to Sabina dei Tarnovo.

Helena ~ Elf. Queen of Elvenwood kingdom on Cilachaem. Wife to Thane, mother to Therron, Thaddeus, and Theo.

Hensen ~ Elf. Librarian at Elvenwood who met a grisly end.

Illanr (Ill-an-or) ~ A faerie maid in the service of King Stephan. Sister to Carld and Alasdair.

Iselt (Ee-selt) ~ A blacksmith at Celyn Eryri with secrets and a past he's trying to hide. He is half Artagh and half Eleri. Currently living at the palace in the Summerlands at Taryn's request.

Ishnara ~ Faerie. Unseelie queen whose ghost is lingering at Elvenwood due to a curse. Deceased.

Janeira (Juh-nair-a) ~ An Eleri warrior of great standing, excellent skill, and deadly capabilities.

Jayved dei Tarnovo (Jay-ved) ~ Summerlands prince. Heir to Faisal and Prateeni. Brother to Sabina.

Jinnipher (Gin-i-fur) ~ A darathi vorsi living in exile. Mate to Gilchrist.

Julieta ~ Younger Goddess. Daughter of Rykoto and Daknys.

Kaida (Kay-da) ~ A grierbas Taryn rescued in the Narthvier. Companion to Taryn ~ they have the ability to speak with each other in their minds. Kaida can track the Shadow Assassin.

Kaldaar (Cal-dar) ~ Elder God. Son of Nadra and Ohlin, worshipped by inhabitants of the Southeast until his banishment after the Great War. Kaldaar hasn't been seen in Aelinae in over five thousand seasons.

Kaleigh al Fyrnwood ap Agnar (Kay-lee) ~ Eleri. Sheanna living among the Ullans. The sworn concubine to Laird Amdi. Kaleigh has two sons with the laird.

Lliandra Tjaru (Lee-on-dra Shar-U) ~ Aelan. Empress of Talaith, Lady of Light. Mother to Marissa, Taryn, Eliahnna, and Tessa. Lliandra is directly descended from the goddess Nadra. She is thought to be a just ruler who thinks of her subjects in all matters. House Nadrene.

Loghan Agnar (Logan) ~ Ullan prince. Second son to Amdi Agnar and his Eleri wife Kaleigh. Acclaimed healer. His entire body is covered in tattoos that are meant to aid in his healing.

Lois Tranton ~ Human. Works at the museum in London. Was an associate of Taryn and Brandt's.

Lorilee ~ Aelan. A maid in the service of Taryn. Sister to Mayla. Currently in the Summerlands training with Flik.

Mallaqai (Mal-ah-kai) ~ Aelan. A witch who once lived on the plains of the East. She is responsible for the disappearance of Aelinae's darathi vorsi. Deceased.

Marissa Tjaru (Shar-U) ~ Aelan. Crown Princess of Talaith, heir to the Light Throne, daughter of Lliandra and Esna (not named in books one or two). Descendant of House Nadrene.

Mayla ~ Aelan. A maid in the service of Duke Anje. Sister to Lorilee.

Meg ~ Faerie. Witch living on Cilachaem. Helps Taryn and Rhoane get into the Seelie Palace.

Micha Askell (Mike-uh Ask-elle) ~ Aelan. Baehlon's intended wife. Daughter of Lord Askell. House Askell.

Nadra ~ Mother of Aelinae, Great Mother of all Creation. Along with Ohlin, Nadra created Aelinae. Mother to Daknys, Rykoto, Kaldaar, and Verdaine.

Nikala St. James ~ Businesswoman Taryn and Rhoane meet in London. She's part of a larger conspiracy that tangentially involves Aelinae. Appears to be an ally.

Ohlin (O-lynn) ~ Father of Aelinae, Great Father of all Creation. Along with Nadra, Ohlin created Aelinae. Father to to Daknys, Rykoto, Kaldaar, and Verdaine.

Oliver ~ Aelan. A servant in the service of Hayden, Lord Valen.

Percival ~ Marissa and Armando's child. He was born in secret and only a few know of his existence. Since male heirs are unwelcome at the Crystal Court, Taryn gave him to Armando to raise.

Phantom ~ An unknown entity manipulating Celia, Herbret, and Marissa. The phantom is thought to be an agent of Kaldaar.

Pora (Pour-ah) ~ Cat. Companion to Rainne, Pora is keeping a secret.

Prateeni dei Tarnovo (Pruh-teen-ee) ~ Summerlander. Sabina's mother and the Queen of the Summerlands. House Tarnov.

Rhoane al Glennwoods ap Narthvier (Rone) ~ Eleri. First Son of Stephan, King of the Eleri, and Aislinn, Queen of the Eleri (now passed beyond the veils). At birth Rhoane was prophesied to be the Eirielle's protector. When he was old enough, he took an oath forsaking all others and devoting his life to upholding Verdaine's prophecy.

Rori MacNair ~ Faerie. A faeries spy and assassin Taryn once met in a vision. They meet again in London, and then on the world of Cilachaem. Rori's ties to Taryn are unknown, but their paths continue to cross.

Rykoto (Ree-ko-toe) ~ Elder God. Son of Nadra and Ohlin, worshipped by inhabitants of the Northwest and of the Dark. Rykoto was imprisoned in the Temple of Ardyn after the Great War.

Sabina dei Tarnovo ~ Summerlander. Daughter of King

Faisal and Queen Prateeni. Currently fostering with Empress Lliandra in Talaith. Sabina's ShantiMari was unlocked after the ordeal at the Stones of Kaldaar. Descendant of House Tarnov. Recently married to Hayden ap Valen.

Saeko (Say-koh) ~ A maid in the service of Taryn. Currently living in the Summerlands and training with Flik.

Samantha Taylor ~ Human. Taryn met her at the museum. She has ShantiMari, but it is latent.

Shadow Assassin ~ Was once Taryn's twin brother Gavyn. Stillborn, he was stolen from the Crystal Palace the night Taryn was born. His master raised him to hunt Taryn. He is used as an anchor to the god Kaldaar. Since Gavyn's demise, Kaldaar has raised a new Shadow Assassin—Cashiel.

Shailana (Shay-lana) ~ Unknown species. Mate to Enghor.

Silar (Sy-lar) ~ One of the fabled Stone Guardians of lore. Protects Taryn and Rhoane while they are in London.

Stephan ap Narthvier ~ King of the Eleri. Direct descendant from Verdaine. Married to Aislinn. Father to Rhoane, Bressal, Carga, and Eoghan. Stephan firmly believes the Eleri are stronger on their own, away from the other races of Aelinae. He opposes the Verdaine's prophecy regarding his son, Rhoane.

Tarro (Tare-O) ~ Danuri. Assistant to Margaret Tan. Lover of Armando.

Taryn Rose Galendrin (Tare-in) ~ Daughter of Lliandra, Empress of Talaith, Lady of Light and Valterys, Overlord of the West, Lord of the Dark. Raised on Earth, Taryn grew up unaware of Aelinae, believing Brandt was her grandfather and only family. House Galendrin.

Tessa Tjaru (Shar-U) ~ Aelan. Daughter of Lliandra and Razlog (not named in books one or two). She is fourth in line to the Light Throne. Descendant of House Nadrene.

Thaddeus/Thad Mistwalker ~ Elf. Son of King Thane and Queen Helena. Status: Missing. He is believed to be trapped in a glass prison.

Thane Mistwalker ~ Elf. King of Elvenwood. Currently believed to be possessed by an evil presence. Husband to Helena, father to Therron, Thaddeus, and Theo.

Therronysus/Therron Mistwalker (Ther-ahn) ~ Elf. Elf living on Cilachaem in the kingdom of Elvenwood. Heir to the throne, but Rhoane sees another path for Therron. Has a dragon soul, but is unaware of this fact. Son of King Thane and Queen Helena, brother to Thaddeus and Theonysus/Theo.

Theonysus/Theo Mistwalker ~ Elf. Youngest brother to Therron, son of King Thane and Queen Helena. Interested in astrology.

Timor (Tim-or) ~ Aelan. A member of Taryn's personal guard. Currently living in the Summerlands and training with Flik.

Tinsley Alcath (Tins-lee All-koth) ~ Aelan. A young lord with business ties to Duke Anje and is often at Paderau Palace. Descendant of House Alcath.

Troyanna Djeba ~ Aelan Wife to Valterys Djeba, mother to Zakael. House Djeba.

Tug ~ Giant. Lives on Cilachaem. Helps Taryn search for seals. Gentle being and one of Tameri's favorite characters.

Valterys Djeba (Val-terr-iss D-jj-ay-ba) ~ Aelan. Overlord of the West, Lord of the Dark. Father to Taryn and Zakael. Valterys is directly descended from the god Ohlin. When living, he ruled his kingdom with a tight grasp on its economy and trade. His subjects thought of him favorably. House Djeba. Deceased.

Verdaine (Vare-dane) ~ Elder Goddess. Daughter of Nadra and Ohlin, she is worshipped by the Eleri in the Narthvier.

Xianqin (Shhawn-kin) ~ Darathi Eneari. Thought to be the last of her kind, most on Aelinae believe her to be a mythical beast and not real.

Zakael Djeba (Zah-K-ay-el D-jj-ay-ba) ~ Aelan. King of the West. Son of Valterys and Troyanna. Descendant of House Djeba. Currently serving as Kaldaar's minion.

GLOSSARY OF TERMS

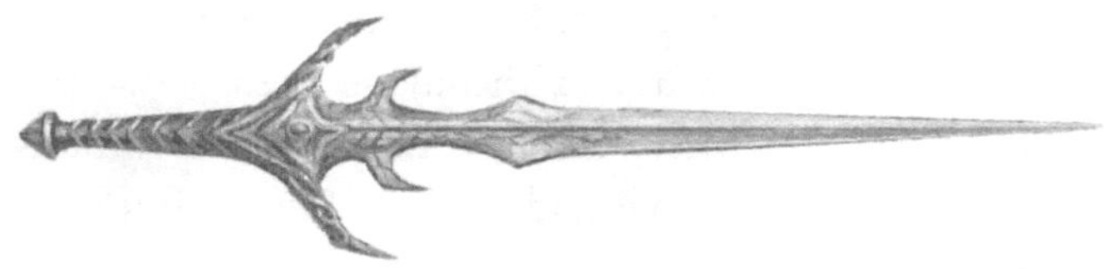

Aelan (Ay-lan) Any person born of Aelinaen descent. These are usually men and women descended from the Elder Gods: Nadra, Ohlin, Daknys, Rykoto, and Kaldaar. In modern times, Aelan refers to those not of another race.

Aelinae (Ay-lynn-ay) A world created by Nadra and Ohlin. It is disk-shaped with waterfalls at the edge of the world, and volcanoes beneath it.

Aelinaen(s) (Ay-lynn-ee-an) Of or having to do with Aelan culture.

Air Faerie Winged Faeries who call on the elements of air for power.

Artagh (R-tah-g) Related to the Eleri, Artaghs lack the Eleri Glamour, as well as the sophistication of the ancient race. They are rumored to be the best at making weapons and working with metals, especially the fabled Godsteel found only in the Haversham Mountains. Outsiders are often distrusted and it's rare to find Artaghs far from their caves.

Atharrach (Ath-ah-rock) A term Taryn found written in Myrddin's papers. Meaning uncertain, but she believes it is a name given to one who wishes to usurp Rhoane's position as Surtentse.

Bells Aelinae's term for hours or time telling.

Caer Idris (Care Ee-dris) The ancestral home of The Overlord of the West. Currently, Zakael, Lord of the Dark, name calling himself King of the West sits on the Obsidian Throne.

Carlix A sleek, winged feline who makes her home in the mountains known as the Spine of Ohlin. One of the first creatures to inhabit the planet of Aelinae. Often referred to for their flexibility and quick responses, the number of people who have actually seen a carlix is few.

Celyn Eryri (See-lynn Air-ee) The mountain home of the Empress of Talaith. It is here the Light Celebrations take place every Wintertide.

Cere City in Faerie with a Shoogly Dragon. Located close to the Seelie Palace.

Cilachaem World Taryn and Rhoane are believed to have created. A peaceful world where elves and faeries rule their kingdoms, but tensions are rising between the races.

Claidholm Solais (Kleeve Solish) Sword of Light. Ohlin had this sword made for his daughter Verdaine during the Great War, but she refused to use it.

Cllynellren (Clen-elle-aren) Ancient name of the great tree where the Weirren resides.

Crogall An alligator or crocodile like creature living on Enghor's world.

Crystal Court The accepted nickname for the court of the Empress of Talaith.

Crystal Palace The accepted nickname for the palace in Talaith where the Empress rules. It's fabled walls are made from a thin layer of rock clear enough to see through, yet unable to be penetrated by weapons or ShantiMari. No one knows who built the great palace, or where the stone came from.

Cynfar (Sin-far) The Eleri name for a talisman given to someone. Usually a pendant, it can also be a bracelet, earrings, or even a small stone. It must be kept close to the recipient for maximum benefit, hence the use of jewelry.

Dal Ferran (Dahl Fair-en) The fiery pits of hell beneath Aelinae's surface.

Dal Tara (Dahl Tar-a) A celestial resting place for the Gods and those they deem worthy. It is located in the second quadrant of the Meirdia Nebula.

Danuri A Province located in the West. The second largest city to Caer Idris, Danuri is widely known for their wine and ale making skills.

Danurian Anyone of Danuri descent.

Darennsai (Dar-en-sigh) An ancient title given to Taryn by the Eleri. Most don't know the true meaning of the word, thinking of it as nothing more than an honorific bestowed upon her by the Goddess Verdaine. Only a few know the word means, Daughter of the Sky. Less an oath than a promise that one day Taryn will sit at the side of Verdaine, as a goddess in her own right. The Eleri reject this idea.

Dark The part of ShantiMari that is derived from the sun. Only men are skilled in the ways of the Dark, except for the anomaly. To have Dark powers does not automatically make one bad, or evil. There are many men who use their Dark Shanti for good.

Dark Master A highly skilled practitioner of Dark ShantiMari.

Dark Shanti The male side of ShantiMari.

Darathi Eneari (Dah-rahth-ee Ehn-eer-ee) Fables water dragons of Aelinae. Found mostly in the Summer Seas, their kind have not been seen for many millennia. Only a few on Aelinae have seen the sole surviving darathi eneari in person: Faelara, Rhoane, and Taryn.

Darathi Ostgur Shoogly Dragon. The name given to pubs located on worlds across the universe. Inside each pub is a doorway, or portal that can be used to access any other Shoogly Dragon. A network of pathways between worlds.

Darathi Vorsi (Dah-rahth-ee Vor-see) Aside from the carlix, *darathi vorsi* are the oldest creatures on Aelinae. Several thousand seasons ago they disappeared from the planet, but the Eleri hold the belief that one day they will return.

Delante (Day-lan-t) A dance performed with a group of people.

Dreem A whisky-like drink that ladies don't usually partake of.

Drossfire Light or flaming balls made from ShantiMari.

The East A geographical location on the map indicating all lands, properties, kingdoms, etc east of the Spine of Ohlin. Includes the Narthvier, Ulla, Talaith, and the marshes near Kaldaar's Stones.

Eirielle (Air-ee-elle) The one of prophecy. Said to be the destroyer or the savior of Aelinae, depending on which prophecy you read. Only one Eirielle is ever said to be created, but that doesn't stop those of the Light and Dark from trying to make one. The Eirielle is rumored to possess all the strands of Shanti-Mari: Light, Dark, Eleri, and Telraicht-Noir. Although, the last is only known to the Brotherhood.

Eiriellean Prophecy A collection of prophecies that record various oracles' visions and ramblings about the Eirielle. Throughout history, there have been those that decried the prophecies, and those that touted them as truth. Nearly everyone fears either version coming to pass.

Elennish (Elle-enn-ish) The oldest language on Aelinae still spoken in the East and West.

Eleri (Ee-ler-ee) A mysterious clan of elf-like men and women who live in the Narthvier. They stay within the borders of their forest and don't like outsiders coming on their land. The Eleri share a collective conscious, in that they can call on the wisdom of past and future Eleri in times of duress. The oldest race on Aelinae, they and the *darathi vorsi* share a common bond. Thought to be caretakers of the beasts, when the *darathi vorsi* disappeared, it was a time of great mourning for the Eleri.

Fadair (Fah-d-air) The name Eleri have given to anyone not Eleri. It is meant to be used as a way to signify someone not of Eleri descent, but often it is used as a disparaging slur against non-Eleri.

Fade The natural progression of those with ShantiMari. A fade can last anywhere from a few moonturns to several seasons. With the fade comes a weakening of power.

Faerie Cakes Small cakes light in texture, but filling. Made with sponge cake and jam, these are Taryn's favorite. Don't ever leave a plate sitting around or she'll eat them all.

Feiche (Fee-ch) A large black bird similar to a raven, but faster and a bit bigger. They hunt in packs and are capable of taking down a small horse if so inclined.

Frost End The time between Wintertide and Summer. On Earth, it would occur around April.

Gaarendahl (Gare-en-doll) An older castle located between the Spine of Ohlin and the Summer Sea. It belongs to Valterys's family, but Zakael uses it most often.

Gargoyles Mythical immortals known as Stone Guardians. They take on the appearance of humans. Powerful, not believed to have ShantiMari of their own, they are endowed with other gifts.

Geigan (Guy-gan) A warrior race of people. Dark in coloring, they are rumored to be the source of mating with the Sitari.

Glamour A slight shimmering beneath the skin. Found only on Eleri.

Godsteel A metal forged by the Artagh of Haversham. Stronger than any other metal, godsteel is unbreakable. Long ago, only the gods could wield weapons made of godsteel (hence, the name), but at least two swords have made their way into mortal's hands. Rhoane's and Taryn's. But there are rumors that a few other swords have been tainted by Telraicht-Noir ShantiMari. Their owners are unknown at this time.

Grhom (Gr-om) A spiced drink made by the Eleri. It has healing properties and gives strength through the many ingredients used to make it. Taryn likens the taste to a thick chocolate mixed with chai. Occasionally, the Eleri will add alcohol to the drink.

Grierbas (Greer-bah) A large, wolf-like animal that makes its home in the Narthvier. Wild and territorial, grierbas keep away from civilizations, even avoiding the Eleri.

Gyota (Gee-o-tah) In Eleri, *gyota* means 'destroyer'.

Harvest The months during the season between Summer and Wintertide. On Earth, this time is referred to as Fall.

Haversham A mountainous region where Artagh mine for gems, minerals, and the necessary metals to make weapons. Highly guarded, outsiders are not welcome in Haversham.

Helben A city north of Caer Idris. That far north, the city is covered with snow for most of the season.

Hben Firn Jungle forest on the outskirts of Menurra in the Summerlands. Usually a peaceful place full of blooming flowers and luscious plants.

Hildgelt (Hill-d-gel-t) A Danurian ornamentation made from thin layers of blown glass.

House The family name by which most Aelans associate themselves. Every House has their own color and insignia. It is by these outward displays members of nobility and the court can recognize another's importance.

House Galendrin Ohlin created this House for Taryn on her crowning day. This is the highest honor anyone could hope to achieve and has only been granted once.

Horiscus Tree Tree found on the beach near the Crystal Palace. Legend tells of a princess who was nourished by the tree for seven days and seven nights.

Kitka An animal from Faerie. A cross between a fox and a carlix, the kitka lacks the ability to fly, but is commonly regarded as one of Faerie's fastest animals. Nocturnal. Not often seen by others.

Lan Gyllarelle (Lahn Gill-a-rell) A vast lake located in the Narthvier. Its waters are rumored to hold healing properties. The Eleri often hold ceremonies on the banks of the lake.

Lake Oster Located between Talaith and Paderau, Lake Oster is often used as a stopping point for travelers. Fresh water and an abundance of fish refresh stores between the two great cities.

Larell A flower found on the banks of Lan Gyllarelle. Is rumored to have healing properties.

Levon (Le-von) A sleek black bird. Faster than any other birds, the levon is a favorite form of transportation for those competent in transformation.

Light A strain of ShantiMari found in females born on Aelinae. Not all women exhibit traits of the power, but are able to pass on Light ShantiMari to their daughters. Eleri females have Light ShantiMari, but their powers will differ from the Fadair's in that they use nature as a catalyst and Fadair use the air and sky. The Lady of Light is able to manipulate weather and has slight control over the sea.

Light Celebrations A week long event featuring competitions of physical prowess. The celebrations began as a way to offset the dreariness of Wintertide.

Light Throne The ancestral court of The Lady of Light, otherwise known as the Empress of Talaith. Also referred to as the Crystal Court. The actual throne is made of ancient oak from the Narthvier. Woven into the planks of wood is a thin layer of crystal.

Looking Glass A clear orb used for scrying. Can also be used to spy on someone. Ranges in size from a small marble to a large boulder. One of the lost arts, but still used by some with powerful ShantiMari.

Lycan A wolf/man hybrid creature Taryn and Rhoane encountered at Elvenwood. His ShantiMari had been brutally stolen from him and he was close to death.

Mari (Mar-ee) The female side of ShantiMari. Also referred to as Light.

Mallaqai's Ruins An ancient castle now in ruins. Mallaqai is believed to have made a vortex during the Great War and forced all of Aelinae's darathi vorsi into exile.

Menurra Capital city of the Summerlands.

Mi Carae An Eleri saying that means 'My heart, my truest love'. It is not spoken lightly, and acts as a bond between two people. When *denilithia* is added, it translates to 'Cherished love of my heart'. Usually spoken between a parent and their child.

Mind-Speak A form of communication used between two people within their minds.

Mount Nadrene (Mount Nay-dreen) The holiest place on Aelinae, Mount Nadrene is where Nadra sent Taryn through a portal to Earth. It is also a cavern filled with glittering crystals and a large lake. Some believe the cavern is the birthplace of all the gods and goddesses of Aelinae.

Nadra (Nah-d-rah) The Mother Goddess, she and Ohlin created Aelinae.

Narthvier (Narth-veer) A vast forest covering the northeast portion of Aelinae. The Eleri make their home in the Narthvier, or vier as some call it. The Eleri are protective of the forest and use veils to dissuade unwelcome visitors. Only the Eleri know how to raise the fabled veils.

Obsidian Throne The ancestral home of the Lord of the Dark. The actual throne is made of the same oak planks as the Light Throne. Within the wood fibers is woven obsidian granite.

Ohlin (Oh-lynn) The Great Father, he and Nadra created Aelinae.

Paderau (Pah-der-oo) A vast city ruled by Duke Anje.

Paderau sits between the Narthvier and Talaith, which makes it a busy port city for trading goods.

Paderau Palace The home of Duke Anje and his family.

Privy Council A body of advisers to the Empress of Talaith. The council is made up of senior members of the highest Houses. On occasion, as with Hayden and Duke Anje, a junior member can represent their House in council. Also included in the privy council are the High Priest, and captains of the guard or military.

Ravenwood The less formal home of the Duke of Anje. When in residence, he oversees the local businesses.

Runyon Tree A black, gnarled tree with sharp thorns embedded in its trunk and branches.

Sabinth Aarendhi Seventeenth Vessel – mentioned in papers found in Talaith's library, this vessel is needed to propagate Kaldaar's followers.

Scyver Magic Hunters found in London.

Seal of Ardyn Seals created by the Elder Gods to keep Rykoto imprisoned in the Temple of Ardyn.

Season Aelinae's term for the passing of one calendar year. The difference in time between a season on Aelinae and a year on Earth is approximately one season equals nine months on Earth.

Shanti (Shahn-tee) The male side of ShantiMari. Also referred to as Dark.

ShantiMari (Shahn-tee Mar-ee) Two halves of the same whole. ShantiMari is a power found in all things on Aelinae. Within men and women, it manifests itself in varying degrees from no visible signs, to extremely powerful. Those in positions of great power will have more ShantiMari than those born to the lesser clans or Houses. ShantiMari is often referred to as Light and Dark, or female and male. Within the confines of Shanti-Mari are rules, or etiquette. The power can be culled from the smallest pebble to the stars themselves. Wielding more power than one is capable of controlling often leads to a painful death.

Shadow Assassin Neither alive nor dead, Shadow Assassins were the elite force of Kaldaar's army. Only a powerful Master can create the demons.

Shadow Spawn, Shadow Soul Nicknames given to the Shadow Assassin.

Seelie Faerie term. On Cilachaem there is the Seelie and Unseelie courts. The exact differences between the kingdoms has been lost to history, but the current queens can be differentiated in the ways they rule their kingdom. The current Seelie queen believes she is more rational and dignified than the current Unseelie queen.

Sheanna (Shee-ahn-a) An exiled Eleri. When an Eleri is *sheanna*, they are required to cut their hair and live outside the borders of the Narthvier until a certain amount of time has passed. Once they return to the Narthvier, they must complete the purification ceremony before they are considered to be Eleri once more.

Sitari (Sit-ar-ee) Blue skinned warrior women who live in a community devoid of men. Their island sits at the southernmost edge of Aelinae. It is rumored their preferred mates are Geigan males. Sitari women can be found in other kingdoms of Aelinae, usually scouting for the strongest to procreate with. Once coupling has been achieved, the Sitari return to their island. Male offspring are said to be sacrificed to their goddess.

SIRE Business in London where Brandt purchased the Seal of Ardyn before he and Taryn returned to Aelinae.

Spine of Ohlin The range of mountains stretching from the Temple of Ardyn in the far north to the Summer Seas in the south.

Summerlands An island kingdom located south of Talaith in the Summer Seas.

Summer Seas The body of water covering the entire southern area of Aelinae.

Surtentse (Sir-tants) An ancient title meaning 'Son of the Terrarae'. Verdaine gives this honorific to Rhoane.

Sword of Ohlin Also known as Ynyd Eirathnacht. Ohlin had the sword made out of godsteel for his daughter, Daknys. The bearer of the sword must be pure of heart and worthy of the weapon.

Talaith (Tal - eth) The capital city of the East. Ruled by the empress, also known as The Lady of Light.

Telraicht Arts (Tell-rah-ckt) A twisted version of ShantiMari that binds one's soul forever to the banished god, Kaldaar. Practitioners can be either male or female, but females become barren once they invoke the Oath of Fealty. Because of this, they are viewed as Brothers alongside the men.

Telraicht Brotherhood (Tell-rah-ckt) The oldest, most secret religion in Aelinae's history. Much of the Brotherhood is unknown to any except those who are counted among the members. Once a practitioner is invited to join the Brotherhood, they are challenged to a series of tests, many of which require virginal sacrifices. See also Vessel. Membership is often passed from one family member to another, but the terms must be satisfied before being accepted. Those who do not satisfy the requirements, or are not deemed worthy are destroyed.

Telraicht-Noir Shanti and **Telraicht-Noir ShantiMari** (Tell-rah-ckt Nwaarh) Also called simply Noir. See also Telraicht Arts. This form of ShantiMari uses chaos to fuel its power. External and internal sources give practitioners their strength. They pull their power from the world around them, or the inner conflict people try to conceal. The use of Telraicht-Noir Shanti-Mari is shunned by the Light and Dark, but there are those who have found a way to manipulate the strands of light and shadow into a woven tapestry of devastation that cannot be traced. These are Masters that even the Telraicht Brotherhood fear.

Temple of Ardyn (Ar-din) Rykoto's temple and source of power. He was imprisoned here by Daknys and the Elder Gods after his defeat in the Great War.

Terrarae ~ Aelinean name for earth, or ground. The substance upon which life is built.

Treplar (Treh-p-lar) Round apple-like, spiky fruits from the Summerlands.

Trisp A thick alcoholic drink.

Ulla (Oo-la) A kingdom located in the far East of Aelinae. The Ullans are a tribal people, following their herds throughout the season. Ullan horses are of the finest stock.

Unseelie Faerie term. On Cilachaem there is the Seelie and Unseelie courts. The exact differences between the kingdoms has been lost to history, but the current queens can be differentiated in the ways they rule their kingdom. The current Unseelie queen follows the custom of providing a learning experience of sorts that involves pleasures of the flesh.

Verdaine (Vehr-d-ane) Daughter of Nadra and Ohlin, goddess of the Eleri.

Verdaine's Prophecy When Rhoane was born, Verdaine prophesied that he would be exiled from his people until the *gyota* returned. His fate would be tied to the one who is and who is not for all time.

Veil A mysterious barrier preventing outsiders from entering the Narthvier.

Vier ~ Nickname of the Narthvier.

Vorlock A huge, lizard-like creature with heavy scales and a wide frill around its head. Vorlocks contain a poison that can kill a man or woman instantly.

Weirren (Weer-en) The ancestral home of the Eleri King and Queen.

Weirren Court The gathered nobility of the Eleri live among the many buildings interwoven through the ancient tree that makes up the Weirren.

Weirren Throne Built into the oldest tree on Aelinae, the Weirren Throne is a living, breathing seat.

The Shallows Geographical area located to the west of Danuri. Swamplands and marshes.

The West Geographical area located to the west of Ohlin's Spine. Includes the kingdom of the Overlord of the West (now called King of the West), Danuri Province, and Haversham.

Western Seas The body of water located off the Western Coast of Aelinae.

Woodland Faerie Faerie folk who make their home in the forests Aelinae, most commonly found in the Narthvier. Woodland faeries grow to be around three feet in height, although some are taller. They are the exception. Woodland faeries share a special bond with nature and can cultivate new species of living plants or animals.

Ynyd Eirathnacht (Inid Air-ath-nack-t) The name of Ohlin's sword, currently in the possession of Taryn Rose Galendrin.

AUTHOR NOTES

It is always a pleasure to be able to thank those who have helped make this journey remarkable. First, last, and always, I have to thank my fabulous husband, David. He's my greatest cheerleader, harshest critic, and best life partner I could ever wish for. All my love, always.

This book saw many iterations and the wonderful Lynn Trahan helped me through one of them. I value her as a reader, and as a friend. Thank you, my darling.

She's also responsible for getting me to finally nail down a recipe for grhom! Thank you for trying out several options to make the best damn drink we could.

And finally, to my family for always believing in me. Anything is possible when you have love.

ABOUT THE AUTHOR

Tameri Etherton is a *USA Today* Bestselling and award-winning author of dangerous fantasy and paranormal romance with magical ever afters. She grew up inventing fictional worlds where the impossible was possible.

It's been said she leaves a trail of glitter in her wake as she creates new adventures for her kickass heroines, and the rogues who steal their hearts.

She lives an enchanted life traveling the world with her very own prince charming. When at home, she enjoys many cups of teas and cuddles from their two massive Maine Coons, Pora and Ember.

Read More from Tameri Etherton and explore the *Aetherverse* at www.TameriEtherton.com